PRAISE FOR *THE LAST GOOD GIRL*

"A timely look at a subject that's making headlines across the country . . . entertaining." —*Kirkus Reviews*

"Timely, tense, and well-researched." —*The Sacramento Bee*

PRAISE FOR *A GOOD KILLING*

A "Best of the Best Summer Books" pick by *O, the Oprah Magazine*

"[Leotta is] a writer exceptionally well-informed about crimes against women. . . . These are smart, tough-minded tales, well worth a look." —*The Washington Post*

"This highly entertaining thriller shouldn't be missed." —*Library Journal* (starred review)

PRAISE FOR *SPEAK OF THE DEVIL*

"If you relish hard-hitting, take-no-prisoners cops, and a sharp, committed prosecutor who doesn't hesitate to face down evil, *Speak of the Devil* is for you. . . . An excellent book." —Catherine Coulter

"The moment you start reading, you'll realize Allison Leotta doesn't just write about this world. She lives in it—and works in it. She's absorbed all its darkest parts. That's why *Speak of the Devil* comes to life in the most haunting and best way." —Brad Meltzer

PRAISE FOR *DISCRETION*

Named One of the Top Ten Best Books of the Year by *The Strand Magazine*

"Imagine one of the best episodes of the TV series *Law and Order: SVU*, but set in Washington, D.C., instead of New York City." —Associated Press

"A first-rate thriller. Leotta nails the trifecta of fiction: plot, pace, and character. Ranks right up there with the wonderful Linda Fairstein." —David Baldacci

PRAISE FOR *LAW OF ATTRACTION*

Named One of the Best Legal Thrillers of the Year by *Suspense Magazine*

"[A] racy legal thriller . . . tackling a still-taboo subject." —*The Washington Post*

"This is a major debut, and Leotta is a female John Grisham." —*Providence Journal*

THE LAST GOOD GIRL

ALLISON LEOTTA

TOUCHSTONE

New York   London   Toronto   Sydney   New Delhi

Touchstone
An Imprint of Simon & Schuster, Inc.
1230 Avenue of the Americas
New York, NY 10020

First Touchstone trade paperback edition May 2017

TOUCHSTONE and colophon are registered trademarks
of Simon & Schuster, Inc.

For information about special discounts for bulk purchases,
please contact Simon & Schuster Special Sales at 1-866-506-1949
or business@simonandschuster.com.

The Simon & Schuster Speakers Bureau can bring authors to your
live event. For more information or to book an event, contact the
Simon & Schuster Speakers Bureau at 1-866-248-3049 or visit
our website at www.simonspeakers.com.

Manufactured in the United States of America

10 9 8 7 6 5 4 3 2 1

The Library of Congress has cataloged the hardcover edition as follows:

Names: Leotta, Allison, author.
Title: The last good girl : a novel / Allison Leotta.
Description: New York : Touchstone, [2016] | Series: Anna Curtis series
Identifiers: LCCN 2015046724
Subjects: LCSH: Public prosecutors—Fiction. | Missing
  persons—Investigation—Fiction. | Women college students—Crimes
  against—Fiction. | BISAC: FICTION / Contemporary Women. | FICTION /
  Suspense. | FICTION / Family Life. | GSAFD: Suspense fiction. | Mystery
  fiction. | Legal stories.
Classification: LCC PS3612.E59 L37 2016 | DDC 813/.6—dc23 LC record available
at http://lccn.loc.gov/2015046724

ISBN 978-1-4767-6111-4
ISBN 978-1-4767-6112-1 (pbk)
ISBN 978-1-4767-6113-8 (ebook)

For my two sweet boys,
the best storytellers in the family

FRIDAY

1

The guy had beautiful white teeth and a dimple that appeared when she made him laugh, but all Emily could think was, *College is where romance goes to die.*

They stood on prime real estate, belly-up to the bar at Lucky's, pressed together by the swell of bodies around them. The air was thick with sweated perfume, cheap beer, and the recycled breath of hundreds of young adults in their sexual prime. The boy drained his Bud, set the bottle on the bar, and issued a mating call.

"Wanna do shots?"

Translation: *Wanna get wasted, get laid, get out of my bed, and never to talk to me again?* There were no boyfriends in college. There were only hookups.

Emily smiled at the boy, tilting her head cutely to the side. To the world, she probably looked like any other carefree girl basking in a Friday night. It made her wonder how many of these girls were just like her. Pretending. Maybe all of them, in one way or another.

"Sure," she said.

The dimple reappeared. The boy turned to wave over a bartender.

Over the hum of conversation and Pitbull, Emily heard the bells of the clock tower outside, striking midnight. Twelve solemn bongs marking the start of March 24, 2015. She'd heard those bells chiming on the hour, every hour, her entire life. As a girl, she'd lain in her pretty pink bedroom listening to their bass chimes, wondering what it'd be like when she was a college student herself, the adventures and grown-up secrets that would finally be revealed to her like beautiful presents to be unwrapped, one by one. That seemed like a very long time ago.

Tonight, the chimes meant Dylan and his friends would walk into the bar soon. She had to get out of here.

The bartender delivered two shot glasses filled with shimmery blue potion.

"I'm sorry," she told the boy. "You're totally nailing the horny-but-caring-frat-boy thing. Maybe put your hand gently on my shoulder when you look in my eyes? Try it on one of them." She gestured to all the shiny, uncomplicated girls who thought their prince was behind the next $1 pitcher of beer. Emily missed being one of them. "I gotta go."

She picked up the first shot glass and downed the blue drink, then shotgunned the second one too. She tossed a twenty on the bar, grabbed her white North Face jacket, and threaded her way through the crowd. Preya and the other girls were somewhere in here, but Emily couldn't see them.

Wrapping her silvery scarf around her neck, she pushed out the front door and into the quiet night. She coughed on the cold air. March was Michigan's ugliest month. Dirty snow huddled at the curb, trapped in the purgatory between white powder and the warm April sun. Across the street, the bell tower shone like a warning as its twelfth chime echoed over shivering trees. The night seeped through Emily's sweater, pulling goose bumps from her skin. She shuddered, zipped her jacket, and looked down the street—right at what she feared most.

A raucous bunch of Beta Psi boys rounded the corner. Dylan was in front, of course. He was the alpha dog in any pack of males. Tall and swaggering, dressed in clothes that were both effortlessly casual and painfully expensive, he could be a poster boy for fratty privilege. The other guys clustered around him, vying for position.

Emily froze a few feet from the entrance to Lucky's. Its cone of light still surrounded her.

Dylan's eyes locked on hers. He smiled, walked over, and stood in her space. Too close. The other boys formed a semicircle around her. She felt unsteady.

"I don't want any trouble," she said.

"Doesn't seem that way," Dylan drawled. "Seems like you're doing everything you can to stir the pot."

"Whore," said one of Dylan's minions. The kid snorted, cocked back his head, and spat. His phlegm arced through the air, reflecting the light from the bar's neon signs, glittering and ugly. Everyone watched the loogie as it hung suspended for a moment at the top of its arc. Then it headed back down and splatted on her boot. The boys' laughter was loud and vicious. Anger pulsed through her gut, more acidic than any shot at Lucky's.

"You're disgusting," she told Dylan. "And you can't even fight your own fights."

Dylan frowned at his friends, and they stilled. Their silence was more ominous than their laughter. Emily was keenly aware that she could not control this situation.

"Head in," Dylan told the other guys. "I'll be right there."

"You sure, dude?"

"Yeah."

The boys did what they were told. Music pulsed then quieted as the bar's door swung open and shut. Emily tried to move away, too, but Dylan's hand clamped onto her arm. They faced each other, a boy and a girl alone on an empty stretch of sidewalk, breathing fog into the night.

"Have you thought about what you're doing?" he said. "Like, really thought about it? Because, it's kinda crazy that this is how you want to play it."

"I'm not playing."

His fingers squeezed her arm through the puffy coat. "You know what this means for you? You are *done*."

"Oh, Dylan." She smiled. "I'm just beginning. I'm writing an editorial too. It'll be in next week's *Tower Times*."

"Bitch," he said slowly. "My family will end you."

"I know who your family is. And pretty soon they'll know who you are too."

Emily yanked away her arm away and strode off, warmed with the satisfaction that her words had cut him. For a moment, she heard nothing but the sound of her footsteps clacking triumphantly on the pavement. The whisper of wind through trees. A car passing, its tires slicing through salty slush.

Then footsteps, sharp and angry, behind her. She glanced back. Dylan was following her.

"Leave me alone!" she yelled.

He strode faster. His hands were fists.

On her left were shops, closed for the night—dark. On her right was North Campus Street, then campus itself—darker. Trees, dorms, the library. A little farther in was the president's house and the pretty pink bedroom of her childhood. None of these places offered safety.

Ahead, the lights from the shops ended in a yawning stretch of black. It was a block-long hole dug out for construction, surrounded by a chain-link fence. Students called it the Pit.

She hugged her purse and tried to walk faster, but her ankle-high boots had disastrously high heels. Dylan wore rubber-soled boat shoes. The slap of his footsteps grew louder, closer.

She broke into a run.

So did he.

She looked over her shoulder—he was right behind her. Wind whipped her long brown hair into her eyes. She shoved it back, stumbled, and pushed herself harder. She was running as fast as she could when she felt his breath on her neck.

SATURDAY

2

The fire crackled and sighed, saturating the room with golden light. Anna balanced a laptop on her knees as she edited an appellate brief. Jody sat next to her, flipping through TV channels while holding her infant to her breast. The baby finished feeding and unlatched, and Jody wiped her daughter's mouth with a cloth. The infant met Anna's eyes with a milk-drunk smile. Anna felt the surge of love she did every time she looked at her little niece. She set her laptop on the coffee table and reached over. "Let me burp her."

"Thanks." Jody handed Leigh to her sister and refastened her nursing bra. She stood and stretched, then padded to the kitchen. "God, I can't stop eating."

"You're burning like a thousand calories a day just producing milk. Go crazy." Anna spread the cloth on her shoulder and shifted the baby onto it. Three weeks ago, she had no idea how to hold an infant. Then Leigh was born. After helping with dozens, maybe hundreds, of feedings over the past three weeks, Anna was starting to feel like a pro. She stood and walked around the room, stroking Leigh's back and humming "Hush Little Baby."

She stopped as an image flashed on the TV: grainy surveillance video, the type that only became relevant when something terrible happened. It showed a pretty young woman in a white jacket talking to a handsome young man on a sidewalk. The young woman's long dark hair was elaborately curled, her mouth stained with lipstick. She'd clearly prepared for a big night out, maybe primping for some boy—maybe this boy. The young man held her arm and leaned into her space. Anna couldn't tell if they were sharing a secret or having a fight. The girl pulled her arm back, turned, and walked away from him. The boy strode offscreen after her. The news anchor, Carmen Harlan, looked grave as she said, "Emily Shapiro has not been seen since around midnight last night. Anyone who has information about her whereabouts is asked to call the police at the number below."

Anna murmured a few words of prayer then turned away from the screen. She felt an instinct to jump in, but this was not her jurisdiction. It was not her case.

"Poor baby," she murmured, her lips brushing Leigh's soft hair. "So much scariness in the world. You'll stay with me and your mama till you're thirty, right?"

Anna inhaled the sweet baby scent and wondered if there was anything more satisfying than the feel of a warm, contented baby on your shoulder. The thought surprised her. She'd never longed for a baby before.

Now wasn't the time to start.

She walked to the back window and looked out at the backyard. A few chickens pecked through the pale winter grass. Beyond them were rows of apple trees, bare for the winter, then an abandoned warehouse, its windows shattered and black. A mile farther, the Renaissance Center lit up the night sky. The linked skyscrapers were Detroit's iconic, ironic skyline, an attempt at renewal that had been a blip in the city's steady decline. But it did make a striking backdrop to the orchard. Not many farmers had a view of skyscrapers. Cooper's urban farm was the ugliest, most beautiful place Anna had ever lived.

She caught a glimpse of Cooper walking through a row of apple trees. He wore well-loved jeans, work boots, and a flannel shirt that stretched across his chest. His big white shepherd, Sparky, trotted at his heels. Cooper saw Anna in the window, smiled, and lifted a jug of cider in greeting. Anna waved back. The mere sight of him made her smile; it was an involuntary reaction, like her mouth watering for fresh-baked cookies.

It was too bad, really. Because, like a batch of cookies, Cooper was something to be savored briefly. His very deliciousness was his danger.

Anna had carefully built a life for herself in Washington, D.C. Everything she'd ever worked for—and she'd worked hard—was in D.C. Nine months ago, she'd come home to Michigan to defend Jody in a criminal case. Cooper had protected them when the whole world was against them. They'd been living in Cooper's house ever since Jody's home burned down. Cooper was a good friend and they shared a strong attraction, so Anna supposed it was natural that she'd ended up in his bed. But she'd been clear with him from the start. She was still reeling from her broken engagement. What she and Cooper had was a fling, just two friends having fun. They both knew she was going back to D.C.

And yet . . .

The back door opened and the click of the dog's paws preceded Cooper's asymmetrical footsteps. He walked up to Anna, bringing the scent of fresh air and pine trees with him. He kissed her lightly, then bent down to kiss the baby in her arms. She leaned her head up to meet his eyes.

"You look gorgeous," he said. She was dressed up for a night out with him.

"Thanks. You don't look so shabby yourself."

"I look like a man who needs a shower and a shave. But who am I kidding? With you on my arm, no one'll be looking at me."

In fact, Cooper got more than his share of double takes. He was tall, with a shock of black hair and cornflower blue eyes. His body was honed from farmwork rather than a gym. Anna had known him since he was a skinny, bookish boy in her elementary school. Back then, his lopsided grin looked too big for his face; now it fit him perfectly. She was still surprised every time she glanced at her old friend and saw how gracefully he'd grown into his skin.

Anna's phone buzzed in her pocket. Cooper took the baby so she could pull her phone from her jeans. The picture of the incoming caller showed a chiseled African American man with shining green eyes, holding a laughing six-year-old girl on his shoulders. Jack and his daughter, Olivia. Anna had taken the photo a year ago, back when she and Jack were still engaged to be married. Back when she thought she'd be Olivia's mother. Before everything fell apart.

She looked at Cooper apologetically as her thumb hovered over the send button. Cooper saw the picture and sighed.

"I'll be upstairs taking a shower," he said.

Anna watched him walk to the living room to give Leigh to Jody. His gait had a little hitch that strangers might interpret as a swagger but which was the result of an IED explosion. Cooper had served as an Army Ranger in Afghanistan, where he lost the lower part of his left leg. After coming home, he'd chosen urban farming because he loved Detroit and wanted to help rebuild it. And maybe he had to prove that he could do anything. He was optimistic, determined, and resilient. He'd be fine, Anna assured herself.

She pressed send. "Hello."

"Hi, sweetheart," Jack said.

She broke into a smile. "Hi, Jack. How are things in D.C.?"

"Actually, I'm in Michigan. Staying at a hotel in Ann Arbor. A few miles from you."

She pulled the phone away as if it had burned her ear. In her life, there were two worlds: D.C., home to her job, Jack, and her friends; and Michigan, home to her sister, Jody, and their rusting hometown, where Anna had nursed her broken heart and found comfort in Cooper's arms. These two worlds were separate and did not overlap. Hearing that Jack was in Michigan was like watching Han Solo walk into a *Hunger Games* movie.

"Wow. That's a surprise." Anna's mind and heart raced. "Why are you here?"

"You've heard that the Department of Justice assembled a task force to investigate sex assaults on college campuses?"

"Sure."

"The head of the task force was named Acting Deputy Attorney General last week. The AG asked me to fill her shoes. I said yes, of course. Now I'm visiting colleges, and I'm here on the midwestern leg of the tour."

Anna's emotions cycled through relief and disappointment. Jack wasn't in Michigan to see her. He was just here for work. Jack was the Homicide chief at the U.S. Attorney's Office in D.C., the country's largest USAO. His reputation for integrity, hard work, and effectiveness made him one of the most respected federal prosecutors in America. When the Justice Department had a high-profile investigation, it often called on Jack for leadership.

"That's an important task force," Anna said. "Good to know you're on it."

"I'm actually calling to ask for your help."

She paused. They'd broken up for complicated reasons last year. Three weeks ago, Jack had called, resolved every complication, and asked her to come back to him. She hadn't given him an answer yet. She still didn't know it herself.

She wondered if this phone call was his way of tipping the

scales—asking her to work with him because that was where they'd always bonded. As teammates, joined together to fight crime and keep communities safe. He knew the task force was exactly the sort of job she'd love.

"I appreciate you thinking of me," she said. "But I have to say no. It would be too messy for us to work on the task force together. "

"I agree," he said. "I'm not asking you to join the task force."

"Oh."

"I just need your help brainstorming. Have you seen the video of the missing girl from Tower U?"

"Yeah, on the news. Her poor parents."

"I need to figure out a way we can investigate."

"Mm, that's tough," Anna said. "Kidnapping, assault, homicide—it's all local crime. The DA's office has jurisdiction."

"I know. That's what makes it so frustrating. The boy in the video—his father, Robert Highsmith, is Michigan's lieutenant governor. Before that, Robert served as a DA himself. He has all kinds of ties to state law enforcement. A lot of people around here owe him favors. I'm not confident the locals will conduct a fair investigation."

"I see." Anna looked into the living room, at the baby sleeping in Jody's arms. One day, Leigh would grow up and, with any luck, go to college. Anna thought of Olivia, whom she loved like a daughter, and who would head to college in about ten years. Both girls would face all the wonderful and terrible things that could happen to young women on their own for the first time. "Did the kid call her any names?"

"He called her a bitch. It's clear on the video."

"We could investigate it as a federal hate crime."

"I like your aggressiveness," Jack said, "but you know what a high bar that is. Assaulting a woman isn't enough to make it federal. It has to have been *because* of her gender."

"'Bitch' is based on her gender."

"If that was the test, half the DV assaults in America would be hate crimes."

"Look," Anna said, "it's enough to open a grand jury and see if there's any *further* evidence of gender-based animus. The grand jury's powers are wide and broad. It gets us in. Now, today. When it's crucial. You know how important the first forty-eight hours are. Maybe this girl wandered, drunk, into a ditch and is freezing in the cold. Or maybe she was abducted. The best chance to find her alive is *now*—and getting smaller every minute."

"True. Okay. Is there a federal prosecutor around here you'd recommend? Someone who knows Michigan but doesn't have ties to the Highsmith family? Someone we can trust."

"Jack. I see what you're doing."

"Of course you do."

"I'm in."

"Thank you." He sounded genuinely relieved. "You'll run the investigation into her disappearance with a couple good FBI agents. You'll report to me and coordinate with the task force."

"Got it." Anna transitioned into full work mode. "Is there any criminal history on either the boy or the girl?"

"Nothing as adults. But they're both young—she's eighteen and he's twenty-one. Anything they did as juveniles, any campus disciplinary charges, wouldn't show up in NCIC."

"Has a grand jury been convened?"

"Here in Detroit. I introduced the case to them, and we have full subpoena power."

"To investigate a federal hate crime?"

He paused just a second before saying, "Yes."

Right. Jack didn't need her to advise him on the federal hook. Anna didn't care. If she could help this girl, she had to.

"What's the case number?" she asked.

She found a notebook and jotted down the information. Names, dates, DOBs, addresses. Still on the line with Jack, she jogged up the stairs to change into work clothes and apologize to Cooper for postponing their date.

"Anna, one more thing," Jack said. "This is a sensitive case. Emily's father is the president of Tower University. Dylan belongs to Beta Psi, a college fraternity in the Skull-and-Bones tradition. Four U.S. presidents were alumni, along with countless senators and CEOs. People are already making calls. These are the big boys. Handle them with care, and watch your back."

"Got it."

She'd prosecuted congressmen, street gangs, serial rapists. She could handle a bunch of frat boys.

3

By the time Anna changed into a black pantsuit, FBI Agent Samantha Randazzo had arrived at Cooper's house. As Anna jogged down the steps, Cooper was letting the agent into the foyer. Sam's eyes scanned the house in wonder. It was an old lumber baron's mansion, rehabbed by Cooper till it shone with its former glory.

"Sam!" Anna rushed down the steps and hugged her friend. "You're still in town."

"It's gonna take some time to wrap up the Upperthwaite investigation," Sam said, hugging her back. "Glad to get the old team back together. What *is* this place?"

"Detroit's best hope," Anna said. "FBI Agent Samantha Randazzo, meet Cooper Bolden, my . . . friend."

"Nice to meet you." Samantha sized up Cooper with the same sharp eye she'd focused on his house. Cooper gave the women two portable mugs filled with steaming coffee.

"You know the way to an agent's heart," Sam said.

Anna gave Cooper a chaste kiss, conscious that she was doing it in front of Sam, who had been invited, then uninvited, to her wedding with Jack.

"Good luck," Cooper said. He'd been calm and understanding when she told him that Jack asked her to work this case. *Of course you have to help,* he'd said. He hadn't questioned the wisdom of working with the man she'd tried so hard to get over.

A knock at the front door interrupted their good-bye. On the front stoop was a big man whose powerful arms were covered in tattoos. His nose had been broken, more than once, and a scar crossed his chin. He wore a leather motorcycle jacket and held up a tiny pink tutu. "Won't this look adorable on Leigh?"

"Hi, Grady," Anna said. "Jody's in the living room."

"Thanks."

Grady kissed Anna's cheek, shook Cooper's hand, and walked through the house. Anna was glad to see Leigh's father here. Jody deserved a good time on a Saturday night—and the baby deserved a chance to get to know her daddy. Grady was a bartender whose one-night stand with Jody had led to Leigh. He'd only recently learned that he was the father. When Jody was pregnant, facing years in jail, she desperately wanted her baby to go to Anna, and Anna only. Jody hadn't told Grady about her pregnancy. He learned when he saw her sitting in the courtroom cradling a huge belly. The new parents were still getting to know each other—at a much slower pace than they'd started.

Cooper took Anna's coat from the rack and held it up. She slipped her arms into it, thanked him again for understanding, then stepped out with Sam into the chill of the night.

A black Durango with federal government plates was parked on the driveway. Anna climbed into the passenger seat, while Sam got behind the wheel. Although Anna was sorry to bail on Cooper, she welcomed the sense of getting back in the saddle, the opportunity to make a difference. There was nothing she liked more than heading out with a good agent and trying to set the world right.

"What've we got so far?" she asked.

Sam steered the big truck onto the street and pointed to an iPad on the console. "Two surveillance videos. Why is your boyfriend farming in the middle of Detroit?"

Cooper's was the only house still standing on his street; the rest had fallen or been burned to the ground. A few blocks away towered an abandoned skyscraper, its dark windows like a thousand blind eyes.

"He's trying to save the city." Anna flipped open the iPad cover. "Finding a way to make it economically viable. All while providing fresh food for the locals."

"He's not a practical one. But he's cute."

"I know. He's not really my boyfriend either. He's . . . it's complicated."

Anna tapped the play button. The first video was the one she'd seen on the news, Emily breaking free of Dylan and walking away. The time stamp started at 12:02 A.M. The second, stamped 12:03, showed Emily walking about a block farther, still followed by Dylan, who was breaking into a run. Her shimmery scarf trailed behind her like a cape.

"The first was taken by a video camera mounted outside a bar called Lucky's," Sam said. "Multiple sources put her there immediately before this interaction with Dylan. The second is from the Bank of America about a block away."

"After that?"

"Nothing. After the bank, there's a construction site nicknamed 'the Pit,' and then the block becomes residential. There's no video on the street after the bank. We've pulled all the video in a ten-block radius, but there's nothing else. Neither Emily nor Dylan appear again."

Anna looked at the clock on the dashboard: it was 9:55 P.M. on Saturday; the girl had last been seen at midnight the night before. Twenty-two hours for her roommate to discover her missing, to report it, for local police to decide it was actually an issue, then to pull the video and see the interaction between her and Dylan. Twenty-two hours for DOJ to realize they should step in. Twenty-two hours in which anything could have happened. The young woman could be lying in a frozen ditch, succumbing to hypothermia. Maybe she had broken bones or a concussion. Maybe she was tied up in a closet—Anna had a case like that once. Maybe she was wrapped in trash bags in a dumpster—Anna had a case like that once too. She wasn't sure she could stand that again. Her stomach was tight with urgency.

"Has anyone spoken to the boy? Dylan?" Anna asked.

"Not yet. The press hasn't gotten word that it's him either. He may not even know that he's been named."

Sam pulled onto the Lodge freeway as Anna pulled up Facebook. More and more, social media allowed her an intimate glimpse at the lives of the people she was investigating: instant, free, and without a subpoena.

Anna swiped through Emily Shapiro's Facebook pictures. Emily was a pretty eighteen-year-old with gray eyes and long dark hair. She had a pointy chin that gave her an elflike charm. Her interests were listed as theater, music, friends, and cooking. There were pictures of her walking dozens of different dogs on campus, and posts where she urged people to adopt them. No pictures with her family.

Dylan's privacy settings only allowed her to see his profile picture. She'd have to subpoena the rest. Dylan was a good-looking young man with brown hair and an all-American grin. There was nothing about his photo that said he was dangerous. But you couldn't tell much from pictures. The nicest people might look like trolls on camera, while the most photogenic smiles could mask horrific secret lives.

"Let's go right to the boy's house," Anna said.

"Sure."

"What kind of search team is assembled so far?"

"Campus police are searching campus. Local police are searching off campus. I've got an FBI tech working on finding her phone and setting up an alert on her ATM and credit cards. We've asked farmers in the surrounding area to search their land."

"Good," Anna said, though the idea of finding the girl in a cornfield was chilling.

They passed out of Detroit and the asphalt got smoother. In the suburb of Southfield, golden skyscrapers dominated the skyline. Detroit was sometimes described as a doughnut; the city itself was an economic hole, while the surrounding suburbs were full of wealth and infrastructure.

They passed out of the suburbs, drove through a stretch of farmland, and then entered the town of Tower Hills. It was a self-contained college town and one of the most cosmopolitan places in Michigan. The campus was treed and grassy, dotted with historic stone buildings and jewels of modern architecture. The surrounding streets were lined with funky shops and coffeehouses. A five-story clock tower stood on the northern end of campus; it was on half the postcards of the college.

Sam pulled onto a wide U-shaped street across from the campus. The outer side of the street was lined with stately Georgian mansions, identically constructed of red brick, black shutters, and white columns. Only the Greek letters on their porticoes were different.

"Fraternity row," Anna said. She'd come here with friends a few times herself, for road trips in her college days. The fraternity facades were lit from below, which would've made them look important and formal, except that they were swarmed with college kids stumbling drunkenly around, whooping and laughing. Although the

Tower student body was less than 20 percent Greek, fraternity row was the place to party. It was Saturday night, almost eleven P.M. Things were just getting started.

Sam pulled up to the curb in front of a house with the words BETA PSI in black block letters across the white portico. Despite the cold weather, a long line of students snaked from the front door, down the steps, and onto the sidewalk. A doorman sat at a table on the front porch, screening the potential partiers before letting them in.

Anna and Sam got out of the car and strode up the walk, past the line of students, to the front door. A few kids yelled at them for cutting the line. Music pounded inside the house.

The doorman was a young man wearing a Beta Psi T-shirt. On his table was a list of names under the words HIGHLIGHTER PARTY.

"Hey," the kid said. "Do you have an invitation?"

"Not exactly," Sam said.

"Turn around," the doorman said. "So I can see your ass. If it qualifies, I'll let you in."

Anna looked at the line of girls waiting to get into the house. Were they all willing to turn around and see if they "qualified" to get into this party? She couldn't believe this was happening in 2015— and that the young women were going along with it.

"Or you could tell a joke," the kid said. "But it has to be a good one."

Sam flashed her FBI badge and a smile. "How's that? Pretty funny, right?" The doorman stared. "Thanks for the invite."

Sam pushed open the front door. A wave of indoor air—hot, human, and jungle humid—hit Anna's face. The interior was dark except for bright slashes of neon. The bulbs in the chandeliers were black lights, glowing purple. Everyone wore white T-shirts covered in neon writing. Many held highlighters and were drawing on one another's shirts and skin, leaving colorful neon designs that glowed under the black lights. It was like walking through the negative of a photograph. Everything white shone purple, everything neon fluoresced, and everything else was shrouded in black.

They pushed through the crowd in the foyer. Rooms sprawled darkly in every direction, each throbbing with music and packed with glowing young people. The scent of beer, sweat, and Axe body spray was everywhere.

"I'm looking for Dylan Highsmith," Sam shouted to a young man near the staircase. He eyed them appreciatively and flashed a drunken smile, which made his teeth glow purple. Sam was obviously not a student, but she was a beautiful woman in her midthirties, with a mass of dark, curly hair. She wore black pants and a black leather jacket, and she rocked them. Anna herself was twenty-nine, probably too old to be mistaken for a student, but she had long blond hair, and her long coat hid the fact that she was wearing a pantsuit.

"What's it worth to you?" the kid leered.

As a young woman in a profession where people expected a gray-haired man, Anna was used to being underestimated. She'd learned to use that. Being underestimated could be a power in itself.

"We'd be really grateful if you could point us in the right direction," Anna said, smiling at him.

"That way." The kid pointed and smiled back. "Dylan's wearing the crown. Want a drink?"

They followed his finger into a large back room. It was dominated by a Ping-Pong table, held up by four seminaked boys on their knees, acting as the legs of the table. Neon designs glowed on their exposed skin. On the surface of the table were four Solo cups filled with beer. Four boys were playing beer pong in the dark. The white ball glowed purple as it bounced back and forth. Neon-hieroglyphed girls watched and cheered. When the ball splashed into one of the plastic cups, the player in front of it lifted it and chugged. He almost got to the bottom, gagged, and stumbled to the corner. "Boot! Boot! Boot!" yelled the crowd, as the kid vomited into a garbage can.

The players on the other side of the table roared with victory and high-fived. One of the victors wore a shiny white plastic crown, glowing purple. He had dark hair, perfect teeth, and jeans that might've cost more than Anna's weekly salary. Sam and Anna made a beeline for him. "Dylan Highsmith?" Anna asked.

He looked her up and down, then grinned. His teeth glowed bright purple. "Hey, babe." He reached out and grabbed Anna's butt, a big fleshy handful, which he squeezed and used like a handle to haul her into his chest. He brought his leering mouth down, breathing beer fumes into her face. Anna was so surprised, she didn't think about how to react. She just reacted. She shot her knee up, hard, into his groin. He grunted, let go of her, and doubled over. The crown tumbled off his head.

Dammit, Anna thought, as she stepped back. That was not going to facilitate the kid's cooperation. Nor was it going to look good on Sam's 302, the FBI report that would summarize the witness interview.

Dylan straightened up, narrowed his eyes, and took a threatening step toward her. Sam drew back her leather jacket, revealing the badge and gun at her waist. "FBI Agent Samantha Randazzo. This is Anna Curtis, Assistant U.S. Attorney. I suggest you take a moment to collect yourself, sir."

A few kids hooted at the realization that Dylan had groped and then been kneed by a federal agent. A girl with honey-colored hair and Tory Burch flats picked up the plastic crown and held it like something precious.

Sam said, "Do you need medical attention?"

Dylan stared at the badge and shook his head. His beer-pong partner came over and stuck out a hand. "Peter York," he said. He carried himself with the self-assurance of a boy who grew up in a country club and had been trained from an early age on how to interact with servants and other lesser beings. "Can I help you?" The girl holding the crown fitted herself into Peter's side.

"We're investigating the disappearance of Emily Shapiro," Sam told Dylan. "Where can we talk privately?"

"Emily Shapiro is a crazy bitch," said the girl.

"And you are?"

"Whitney Branson, one of her roommates." She swiped a manicured finger quickly under her left nostril, then her right.

"Shut up, Branson. Don't say anything till I come back." Dylan pulled out his phone. "I need a minute," he told Sam. He walked to a corner and made a call.

"Can I offer you a beer?" asked Peter.

Sam took out her notebook and asked for their names and DOBs. Anna scanned the party. It had quieted considerably. The students stood in clusters, watching them and whispering. The space around Anna and Sam had grown, as if law and order were contagious.

Only the four miserable boys under the Ping-Pong table hadn't moved. They kneeled on the sticky floor, arms raised above them to hold up the tabletop. They looked like the statue from *Atlas Shrugged,* only far less dignified. They wore only underwear. Every inch of their exposed skin, head to heels, glowed in highlighter designs: slashes, doodles, Greek letters, and cruel words. PLEDGE. SLAVE. WHALESHIT. BEER BRINGER. PISSANT. One of the boys met her eyes, and Anna startled. She wasn't sure—the black lighting was weird and the kid was out of context—but something about his face looked familiar, like a shadow of Cooper's. The boy quickly looked away.

Dylan strode back into the group. "This conversation is over," he said.

"Why?" asked Anna.

"Because I don't feel like talking to you, and I don't have to."

"It's true, you don't have to talk to us," Anna said. "But you should. There's a girl missing. We might still be able to find her alive. But we really need your help. You were the last person to see her alive."

"Let me make this totally clear," Dylan said. "I'm invoking my right to remain silent and to have an attorney present when questioned by you. I'm also asking you to leave this house, which is private property. Leave. Now." He turned to Peter and Whitney. "Was there anything unclear about what I said, witnesses? My lawyer would love if there were. We pay him seven hundred fifty dollars an hour, and he can't wait to dig in." Dylan looked at Anna. "He's particularly interested in the fact that this prosecutor assaulted me in my own home. I may just bring charges."

"Here's some free legal advice," Sam said. "Grabbing someone's butt is a sex assault. Ms. Curtis could've put you in the hospital and it would've been legal self-defense. You're lucky you only got a quick knee."

It didn't change the fact that they didn't have a warrant—and they didn't have enough evidence to get one. They had to leave.

■ ■ ■

As soon as they were outside, Anna and Sam each pulled out their phones. Anna called Cooper.

"You okay?" Cooper answered on the first ring.

"Yeah." She spoke softly, cupping her hand around her mouth.

Her breath came out in clouds through her cupped fingers as she strode toward the Durango. "Is your brother Wyatt a member of the Beta Psi fraternity at Tower University?"

"Yeah. Why? Is he in trouble?"

"No. But he might be helpful. I'm investigating another kid in his frat, and I'd like to talk to someone on the inside. Can you get him to meet with me?"

"I'll try."

"Thanks."

When she hung up, she got in the car and turned to Sam, who sat in the driver's seat reading a text. The agent's lips were pressed in a grim line. "What?" Anna asked.

Sam looked up. "They located Emily's cell phone and purse."

"Where?"

"At the bottom of the Pit."

To: [Class List: Media in the Internet Age]
From: Professor Ginger Robinson
Date: August 25, 2014
Re: First Assignment

Welcome back to returning students, and welcome to incoming freshman! Thanks for choosing "Media in the Internet Age" for your elective. I'm so glad that you signed up for this yearlong interactive class. I hope you had a wonderful summer and are ready to jump back into exploring, learning, and growing.

This e-mail is to give you your first assignment, which begins before we even meet the first time, because now is such an interesting time for you, and it should be captured.

Please record at least one video per week, in which you describe your experience as a college student—your reaction to your roommates, teachers, the college itself. This is a video log of your time here, also known as a vlog. This assignment will continue throughout the year. It is my hope that you will not only grow comfortable talking on camera, but that this will be a project which will allow you to look back and track how much you've changed and grown, and to reflect on the forces that shape us.

Please start this week. Describe how you feel as you arrive at school and settle in. This is the only week where I'll ask for specific content, which is the following: (1) Describe yourself in three words. (2) Tell me your greatest strength and your greatest weakness. (You should get used to these questions, by the way, as you'll be asked them in job interviews for the rest of your life!)

In future sessions, your vlog can be as simple or elaborate as you'd like. Some students find this to be quite cathartic. The only minimum is that you record yourself for at least five minutes every month.

Get creative. Sing, if the spirit moves you! Dance! Dress up as your teachers and impersonate them. Film three minutes of yourself being President Shapiro. Eat your least favorite food from the cafeteria on camera. Time-lapse how fast a Domino's pizza is devoured by you and your friends. Or just talk, share what you're feeling and thinking. Viewers respond to authenticity. This is your experience.

Create your own channel on BlueTube, with the settings on "private" so no one else can view them. Upload all your videos for storage, but do not publish them to the public. Do not view them yourself until the end of the year. You may be amazed to look back and see the changes in yourself. In May, you will review your videos and choose your top five, which most encapsulate your student experience. Submit those to me.

Our first class meets on September 3, 2014, in Vamvas Auditorium. Please arrive at two P.M. in loose and comfortable clothes, and with a willingness to open your hearts and minds to other students.

VLOG
RECORDED 9.1.14

Okay.

Um.

Hi.

I'm Emily Shapiro. Nice to meet you.

This is . . . weird, talking to my phone. I hope somebody doesn't walk in and think I'm a freak. I guess I could say I'm FaceTiming. Or just explain that this is an assignment. It's just, everyone here is so academic. The place is full of National Merit Scholars and assorted whiz kids. Everyone's elective is, like, macroeconomics. I don't want to be the one intellectual lightweight. Sorry, I don't mean to offend you, Professor Robinson.

Jeez. That was stupid. I should start over or edit that out. Or . . . not? Maybe that's the point. Maybe a vlog is extra honest 'cause there's no going back and erasing. You can see me realizing I'm an idiot in real time.

So, okay, it's September 1, 2014, and this is my first day as a freshman. The leaves are gold, the sky is blue, and I have to admit, I'm pretty psyched. I've lived on this campus my whole life—but I've never really been in it. It feels kind of surreal that this is finally my time.

Okay, so you know my little secret: my dad is the president of the university. I don't tell most people, but you recognized me at the meet and greet. A lot of professors don't; the campus is big enough that I can get lost in the crowd. So, anyway, you know why I won't be doing any imitations of President Shapiro for class, ha ha. Or maybe I will! I'll be the best at it.

So, you might ask: Why Tower U? Why not UCLA or Columbia, some coast, where I didn't have my dad looking over my shoulder? In a word: money. It's free for me to go to school here.

And you know what? It's okay. I've wanted to be a student here for so long, it just feels natural. And my dad won't harass me much. He's too busy politicking, being president.

So it's, like, here we go.

I moved in today, finally have a dorm room of my own. I guess I can just hold up the phone and show you. Here, check it out. It's a three-person suite. This is the study-slash-living room. See that big stone fireplace? It's historic. They say Henry Ford used to whack off into it. Yikes, sorry. But that's what they say.

Anyway . . .

Here's our couch. Three desks. Through here is the bathroom. Tiny, right? I don't know how three of us are gonna fit all our Sephora. Should be interesting.

And here's the bedroom. The top bunk is mine. Not my first choice.

But before we get into that, I should check off the assignment. I'm supposed to tell you three words to describe myself. Okay, so, let's see. I'm . . . smart, cheerful, and creative. My dad says I'm "spunky," which I think makes me sound like an '80s sitcom character. My mom, if she were still around, would say I'm a good girl. I think she meant that as a compliment.

My greatest strength: my parents had mostly finished raising me before everything fell apart. My greatest weakness: how much I miss my mom.

Sorry. Give me a sec.

Where are the stupid tissues when you need them?

Okay.

Okay.

Better.

Let's talk about normal stuff. The first day of school, the big moment, right? Today's the day.

I got here today before either of my roommates did—I just had a five-minute commute from Dad's house. He drove me over, although his mind was somewhere else, distracted by the phone that's permanently attached to his right hand. The dorm room was empty. I put my bags on the best bed, the single by the window. But Dad looked up from his call long enough to say that wouldn't be fair to the other girls, that we should wait and talk about how to split things up. Then he went back to his very important call, phone pressed to one ear, finger pressed to the other. That finger to his ear really bugged me because I was, like, the only other person in the room.

But, anyway, I didn't take the single bed, because he was right. I should wait for the other girls to come and talk about it with them. I'd never met them before, though we'd e-mailed after we got assigned. I wanted to get off on the right foot. I set my bags down and started unpacking my toiletries into the bathroom.

Whitney Branson came next, towed by both parents and two grandmothers. All the Branson women wore Tory Burch shoes. I wondered if they got a bulk discount. Whitney's from Bloomfield Hills; she has long dark-blond hair and a full set of Louis Vuitton luggage. She walked right past me, over to the single by the window, set her suitcase down on it, and said, "I'll take this bed."

I glared at my dad, but he'd put his phone away and was busy meeting Whitney's parents, giving them the full charm offensive. I realized Whitney's family must have money, lots of it. You know what they say: the most dangerous place on campus is anywhere between Barney Shapiro and a donor. He can sniff out trust funds like a French pig can sniff out truffles. Or, as the Wall Street Journal put it, he is "a world-class fund-raiser."

Here, look, you can see Whitney's stuff. She's been here four hours and already there's like twenty thousand dollars' worth of Nordstrom hanging in her closet. She's got the perfect Calvin Klein comforter set; the perfect Urban Outfitters fluffy decorative pillows; the perfect Pottery Barn rug, which is actually cute but which she didn't bother to ask whether I minded if she put down. Oh, and a stash of coke in the one drawer of her desk that locks. She offered me some. It's not my scene, but at least she shares—that's something, right?

Preya Parikh came in next. Dad greeted her parents like old friends. Turns out, Preya's mother is the dean of English at U of M, and Dad's known her forever. So I'm guessing my new roomies were not assigned at random. Dad chose them for me. But that's okay, I guess. At least he cared.

Preya asked which bed I wanted, and we divvied up the bunk bed. Our parents talked and helped us put on the sheets, and then there were hugs and tears and—finally—they were gone.

Okay, I have to admit—I'm trying to be cool, but—I'm excited. I'm in! I've been waiting for this moment my whole life.

When I was really small, my mom used to dress me up in a little Tower University cheerleader outfit, red and white, with red ribbons in my pigtails. They'd take me to football games, and we'd sit in the president's box. Dad would hold me up in the front row of the box, and people in the seats in front of us would look back and say how cute I was. Then at halftime, Mom and Dad would take me down to the field, and the cheerleaders would let me come out with them as they did their routine. Once the *Tower Times* ran a front-page picture of me like that, holding pom-poms as the cheerleaders smiled at me. I got to play on the field during halftime so much I thought it was just a normal thing to do.

Then, one time when I was about nine, I saw some kids in the stands pointing at me and laughing. I realized in that moment—I can't believe I'd never noticed it before—that I was the only person out there who wasn't an official cheerleader. I was, seriously, so embarrassed. The kids weren't laughing in a friendly way. I suddenly noticed all the people in the bleachers looking at me. A sea of strangers, judging. I stopped wearing the cheerleader outfit after that. All I wanted was to dissolve into the crowd.

That's kind of how I feel now. Not that I want to dissolve into a crowd, you know? I want to stand out—but for who I am, not for who my dad is. I don't want to be anybody's mascot.

Does that make sense?

Well, anyway, after our parents left, Preya, and Whitney, and I went to the cafeteria and got some lunch. Whitney is funny and aggressively pretty, like she cares about her looks so much you have to wonder what she's trying to make up for. Preya's pretty too, but in a less showy way. She seems really smart, like scary smart, but not obnoxious about it. We met some of the other kids in our hall. I didn't tell anyone that my dad is the president. They might find out at some point—it might be inevitable—but I'll be a regular student as long as I can.

Then I went to the Theater Department, where you guys were holding an open house. It was nice to meet you, Professor Robinson! Or Ginger, like you said I should call you. I loved the open house. Dad is pushing poli-sci or economics, but I really don't want his life. I want something . . . else. Now is my time to figure out who I am, not just the president's daughter, but as my own person.

So that was today. Now I'm back in my dorm room, and tonight I'll go to my first college party. I'm so excited! I've been seeing kids go to frat parties all my life, but I was never allowed to go.

My dad was a Beta Psi—it was his frat back in the '80s, and he says it changed his life, like it set him on the course to success. But he never let me go there for parties, at least not when I was in high school.

But, hee hee, he can't stop me now! As of today, I'm officially a college freshman, and I can go to any party that any other college freshman can go to.

Preya and Whitney will be back here any minute to get ready, and we'll go together. It's the Beta Psi Welcome Back Party.

So, um, I guess I should say good-bye and start getting ready. Shower, makeup, hair. Whitney said she'll bring a bottle of vodka to preparty.

Now for the big important question of the night: Do I wear the dark jeans or the shirtdress?

Sorry if I seem ridiculous. It's just that . . . I feel like I'm standing on the brink of something big. Something real. The world is full of possibilities. Who knows, maybe I'll fall in love tonight.

4

From under the Ping-Pong table, Wyatt watched the two older women walk out of the frat house. He groaned with relief. He recognized the blonde; his parents had a picture of her and Cooper on their fridge. She'd just started dating his brother. What was her name? Ella? Etta? Anna. Wyatt hoped she hadn't recognized him. He didn't want his big brother to hear about this. He flexed his arms, which were exhausted from holding up the tabletop, and shifted his knees, which throbbed painfully against the hard, sludgy floor.

Wyatt knew he was lucky to be in this position. Beta Psi was his way off the farm, his road to the American dream. He'd seen Cooper's road—through the army and Afghanistan—and knew its cost was too high. Wyatt planned to keep both his legs.

But the path through Beta Psi had its own price—and it wasn't cheap. Wyatt had learned that early and often in the pledging process. But he was almost to the end of that. In just five days, Hell Week would be over, and—if he played things right—he'd be in. Into a life of privilege and power. Wealth and respect. It all flowed from the brotherhood and his place in it.

There were thirty-eight pledges, and only twenty spots. Wyatt wanted one more than he'd ever wanted anything in his life.

Dylan Highsmith strode over to the Ping-Pong table, his face twisted with fury. He grabbed the tabletop and threw it off them. The rectangle of painted plywood flew up and away from Wyatt's head. Some kids screamed and ran to escape its trajectory. It landed with a thud against a wall. Suddenly, Wyatt's arms were free. The relief didn't last long.

"Get up, whaleshit," said Dylan.

Wyatt's legs were cramped from squatting under the table. He stumbled as he stood. The other three pledges were the same. They met one another's eyes nervously.

"Down to the Crypt," Dylan said. "Now!"

Wyatt's stomach clenched. But he and the other pledges shuffled toward the basement door. Dylan was their pledge master. The rest of the kids at the party watched them with amusement. "In formation," Dylan growled. They quickly fell into a straight line; at this point, they were great at lining up. Most hazing seemed to start with baby-faced boys getting themselves into a straight line, like overgrown kindergartners.

Dylan went first; the pledges counted to ten and shuffled down the steps and through a hallway to the Crypt door. The first pledge knocked three times short, two times long, and three times short. The metal door swung open with a groan. The room was lit only by candles, which threw a dim, disconcerting glow after the neon and black of the party upstairs. The highlighter marks barely showed up on their skin in the candlelight. It was quiet down here, with just the ghost sounds of the party upstairs. The walls of the old house were thick. The door shut with a metallic thud.

"On your knees," Dylan said.

The four pledges in underwear lined up kneeling. Wyatt's knees protested at being pressed to the floor again. Ahead of them was a mahogany coffin, elevated on a marble pedestal. The coffin was covered in a Beta Psi banner and three pillar candles. Behind the coffin was a wall of large stones, the foundation of the house.

The three other walls were regular drywall, painted black and hung with pieces of history from the fraternity: a framed bar tab signed by President Taft, who'd been a member; a Lucite box holding a gold medal from the 1920 Olympics, when another member had won the decathlon before becoming secretary of state; a mast from a yacht owned by the CEO of one of the largest retail companies in the world. These were the brothers who'd come before, symbols of the life he would lead if he made it.

Wyatt grew up on a farm in a rural corner of Holly Grove. He hated it. The backbreaking work. His lungs full of hay and dust. The kids at school mocking him because his clothes had manure stains. He was getting off the farm. He'd get a job in a hedge fund. An ergonomic chair, Zagat-rated restaurants, clean fingernails.

In contrast to the priceless mementos on the walls, the floor of the Crypt was plain concrete, sloping toward a large drain in the middle. During certain rituals, the drain was key.

Dylan and Peter stood before them, pulling on black robes. Wyatt closed his eyes and tried to prepare himself. When Dylan wore the white plastic crown, he was a cool, kind of mean, but pretty funny guy. When he put on the black cloak, another side of him came out. Dylan raised the hood, so his face was barely visible. Peter did the same. They looked like twin emperors from the dark side.

"Take your underwear off," Dylan said.

The pledges looked nervously at one another. Was he serious?

"Take 'em off!"

Wyatt took his boxers off and threw them in a corner. So did the other three. The four pledges were naked, kneeling. The kid next to him, Alex, was shaking and trying not to.

"Get on your hands and knees."

They did. Dylan took a paddle off the wall.

Wyatt was relieved. They'd done this before, though never naked. Dylan brought the paddle down on Wyatt's exposed ass, harder than anyone had ever hit him. Wyatt flew forward and crashed into the coffin's marble stand. Its corner scraped his hands.

"Get back on your knees, boy!"

Wyatt did. Dylan hit him again. Again. Again. Dylan was furious; Wyatt could feel his fury coming through the paddle. Was Dylan hitting him because the feds had humiliated him tonight? Was this his way of getting his power back? Or was this because of what Wyatt had seen? He'd never told anyone. Maybe this beating was a warning not to. The paddle came down again. The impacts echoed off the stone wall. Pain shot through his spine.

"Okay," Wyatt said. "Okay. Please, stop."

Dylan paused, the paddle midair. "Who said you could talk to me, whaleshit?"

Beta Psi had three rules: (1) trust the brotherhood, (2) what happens in the house stays in the house, and (3) trust the brotherhood. Dylan *was* the brotherhood. This, Wyatt reminded himself, or something like it, had happened to every brother who'd passed through the house. It happened to boys who became presidents and CEOs. If everyone else could take it, so could he. It brought them together. It bonded them. And in a way, the hazing made the brotherhood seem more precious. For every indignity Wyatt endured, one more cost was sunk into his commitment to the frat house. By now, the tally was precious.

"Seems we've got to find something to shut his big mouth." Dylan's voice was full of laughter. Maybe he wasn't hitting him for any reason. Maybe he just enjoyed it.

Dylan made the pledges turn ninety degrees, so that they were lined up face to ass, like elephants in the circus. Dylan's face was a few inches from Tom's butt.

Dylan pulled out a bottle of vodka and poured it down Tom's back. The liquid spilled off the sides of Tom's torso and onto the concrete floor, snaking its way down to the drain.

"What the fuck?" Dylan roared. "You're wasting vodka, whale-shit." He made Tom straighten back up to kneeling, so the vodka would run down through his butt crack. Then he grabbed Wyatt by the scruff of his neck and forced him closer, until Wyatt's nose was literally in Tom's ass. He poured again. "Drink it!"

Wyatt opened his lips and let the vodka running through Alex's butt crack flow into his mouth. He swallowed a mouthful, and more came down. Tears stung his eyes. He told himself it was from the 80-proof alcohol, nothing more. But he knew, somewhere deep down, that this humiliation would linger long after the bruises from the paddling faded. He swallowed more vodka. His head spun with the insanity of the situation and the alcohol swelling his stomach. Still, Wyatt drank. Dylan poured, Tom let it trickle down his ass crack, and Wyatt sucked it down. The whole time, Wyatt stared at the presidential signature on the wall, keeping himself focused on his goal, knowing it would all be worth it in the end. Until his balance teetered, his vision blurred to black, and he passed out, naked, in a puddle of vodka on the floor of the Crypt.

5

Anna looked back at the frat house, where the line of hopeful young revelers had only grown. She walked to the side, so she could see into the backyard. It was a parking lot. Unlike the front of the house, the back was dark and empty.

"Sam," Anna said, pointing to a lot. Sam retrieved a duffel bag from her truck. They walked to the edge of the lot and read the signs. It was a public parking lot; they didn't need a warrant. The cars inside were an impressive collection: among Jeeps and Grand Prix, there were three BMWs, two Audis, and a shiny red Dodge Viper. Sam began running the plates on each car. Anna walked from car to car, glancing in the windows. She saw the usual college detritus: empty pop bottles, backpacks, lacrosse gear, packets of condoms.

"Bingo." Sam pointed to the red Viper. "Registered to one Robert Highsmith."

Anna pulled two flashlights from the duffel bag. The women shone the lights on the car. The black leather seats were shiny and clean. The floor was spotless. The interior was as empty as a car in a showroom. "That's the cleanest car I've ever seen a college kid drive," Anna said. Sam took out a camera and snapped a couple photos. They walked around the shiny red sports car, looking for scratches or dings. There were none.

But as Anna shone the light on the trunk, she saw a long red-brown smudge by the keyhole. She pointed it out to Sam, who took several pictures, then pulled on a pair of rubber gloves and took out a small white box. Inside were two long Q-tips and a small vial of purified water. She dipped a Q-tip in the water, then rubbed it on the smudge. It came off, reddish brown on the wet swab. She placed the swab into the box.

"Possible blood on the trunk. That's enough to get a search warrant for the car," Anna said. "Can we get officers to guard it while we apply?"

"Yep." Sam said. She made the call, and five minutes later, two officers stood near the car. They would stand guard until the FBI came to tow it.

"Does Michigan have a traffic camera system like D.C.?" Anna asked. Around D.C., speeding cameras also took photos of nonviolating cars. They didn't send tickets to those cars. But police officers could use the pictures to see what cars had passed near a crime scene. "We can see if Dylan took any drives last night."

"I'll look into it," Sam said.

The two women got back in the SUV. "Let's see the purse and the Pit," Anna said. "Then we can put those in the warrant too."

They drove on North Campus Street, the line between campus and off campus. They passed Lucky's bar, then the Urban Outfitters and Bank of America on their left—the route Emily had walked with Dylan following her. The cute college setting ended at the construction sight. Floodlights ringed the block-long stretch surrounded by chain-link fence. Inside was a massive square-shaped dirt hole going down two stories below street level. The walls of dirt looked like a canyon. The bottom of the site was covered with construction equipment and piles of metal and lumber. Down there, six police officers and two K-9 dogs searched for signs of Emily.

Sam and Anna got out of the car and walked into the night. Anna pulled her coat tighter around her. The chill in the air instantly turned her cheeks and nose cold. A girl who was hurt and lying outside in this weather did not have a good chance of lasting long.

They walked up to a cluster of officers and agents on the sidewalk. "Hey, Joe," Sam said. "Let me see the purse."

A stocky officer wearing blue latex gloves nodded gravely and pulled the purse out of a box.

"Already processed for prints and DNA?" Sam asked.

"Yup. No usable prints. We'll process the swabs for DNA."

Fingerprints often didn't stay on soft items like leather.

Anna and Sam each put on gloves, and Joe handed the purse to Sam. She pulled out a wallet; inside was $57 in cash, a student ID card, a driver's license, an ATM card, a gym membership card, and a MasterCard. Tucked in a pocket were three tampons, a tube of lipgloss, a keychain with a fuzzy giraffe and four keys, a travel-sized bottle of Jim Beam, breath mints, and an iPhone. Anna felt dizzy looking at this—the hopeful possessions of a college girl going for a night out. She felt the same sense of wonder she did when she was at a museum and saw an ancient artifact, thinking *Real people really touched this, a thousand years ago*. It was always hard to try to convince herself, to make her mind feel that as real. *Just twenty-four hours ago,* she thought, *this purse was Emily Shapiro's most important possession.* And yet here it was, covered in grime from being fingerprinted, being held by police officers wearing blue rubber gloves, while its owner was out in the world, somewhere, with no way to call home. It was terrifying how quickly the universe could take a simple thing like a purse and turn it into a piece of evidence in a criminal case.

Sam tried to unlock the iPhone, but it was password protected. "Send it to the FBI field office, and get a tech on it," Sam told Joe. "Meanwhile, we'll see if a parent will sign off on letting us in."

Sam walked down the long dirt ramp into the Pit. Anna went back into the SUV and took out her laptop. In the forty minutes that Sam was checking out the Pit, Anna drafted an application for a warrant to seize and search Dylan's car, and another one asking to search the Beta Psi fraternity house. She located the local duty magistrate for the Eastern District of Michigan—he lived just down the street in Tower Hills. She called him, waking him up. She apologized for the midnight call, introduced herself, and told him she needed an emergency search warrant. He said she could email him the warrants and then go to his house. Anna went to the top of the ramp and called for Sam. "We've got a judge!"

A moment later, Sam emerged from the Pit, carrying a single brown suede boot in her gloved hand. "This was Emily's shoe," she said. "We'll confirm with DNA. But it's the one that appeared on the video."

Anna's stomach clenched as she looked at the shoe. Emily was like a reverse Cinderella—fleeing at midnight, losing a shoe, but ending up somewhere much more sinister than a castle. Sam bagged the shoe and gave it to the officer in charge of chain of custody. Anna and Sam got back into her Durango in grim silence.

Ten minutes later, they pulled up to a house in an upscale neighborhood. Magistrate Judge James Schwalbe met them at the door in a bathrobe over pajamas. His thick brown hair was mussed from sleep, but he greeted them with a fatherly smile. His wife, in her own matching bathrobe, had them sit at the kitchen table and offered them coffee, which they gratefully accepted. "I heard about that poor girl," the wife said, handing Anna a mug. "I hope you find her." Anna thanked her. "Me too." Judge Schwalbe had already printed out the documents Anna had e-mailed. He sat next to Anna, put on his reading glasses and read carefully through them. When he looked up, he shook his head.

"You don't have enough evidence to search the fraternity house," he said.

Anna agreed—there wasn't much, so far, indicating that evidence of a crime would be found inside the frat house—but she'd tried anyhow, hoping that sentiments like the judge's wife's would help.

"Can we call you again to reapply if we find more evidence tonight?" Anna asked, worried about waking him again at three A.M.

"Of course. That's what the duty judge is for. Good luck."

He signed the warrant allowing them to seize Dylan's Viper. They thanked the judge and left the house. As soon as they were outside, Sam called her agents and ordered them to tow the car and start processing its interior.

Meanwhile, she and Anna headed to the university president's house. Anna took a deep breath and tried to brace herself. She always hated this part. In a job full of difficult moments, there was nothing quite like talking to parents about losing a child.

SUNDAY

6

Sam pulled up to the president's home, a beautiful Georgian standing on a circular drive in the middle of campus. Behind the house sprawled trees and then acres of campus, crisscrossed with tidy footpaths. The clock tower shone from its crown-jewel position just north of the house. The lights in the house were blazing although it was close to one A.M. Anna didn't worry about waking anyone.

Anna had looked at the Tower University website on the way over. It showcased the huge breadth of the campus, from scientists holding test tubes to the Division I football team. The university was home to ten thousand undergraduate students, with activities ranging from the skydiving club to atom splitting at the nuclear lab. Many of the students had been top students or athletes at their high schools, which the university highlighted in links to *U.S. News & World Report* rankings. There were pictures of the Jewish Students Group at Hillel, the LGBT Students Group, the Hiking Club, the College Republicans.

Pictures of the president were easy to find, though his wife was more elusive. Anna had finally found a picture of Emily's parents together: a handsome white couple in their fifties. He wore a tux; she was in a sequined ball gown. The caption read: "President Barney Shapiro and his wife, Beatrice, Attend the Black-and-White Ball, Which Raised $1.5 Million for the University's Cancer Research Center."

Anna and Sam walked up to the house. The front yard was beautifully landscaped with native plants, Anna learned from a sign on the edge of the lawn. The doorbell chimed with the first stanza of the Tower University fight song. This was a house made for entertaining, for impressing visitors and welcoming donors. The woman who answered the door, however, didn't match either the decor or the picture of Emily's mother. This woman was in her midthirties, with spiky platinum blond hair and five piercings in her left eyebrow. She wore a crimson leather sheath dress, high-heeled black boots, and a massive statement necklace made out of what appeared to be old engine parts.

She looked them up and down. "You're the police?" she asked skeptically.

"Yes, I'm Anna Curtis, a federal prosecutor. This is Samantha Randazzo, FBI. May we come in?"

The woman nodded and opened the door wider. They stepped into a long marble foyer. Long-stemmed lilies blossomed in a crystal vase on a pedestal table in the center.

"I'm Professor Kristen LaRose," the woman said, leading them through the foyer. They passed a high-ceilinged ballroom on the right, then a dining room with a banquet-length table on the left. "A friend of the family."

Anna glanced at Sam. Sam shrugged in a way that said, *Hey, you never know what you'll find behind people's front doors*. Kristen led them to the back of the house, where an open-concept kitchen-living-room area seemed the only place meant for a family rather than visiting dignitaries. A man in a suit was pacing the length of the room, a cell phone to his ear. Anna recognized him from the pictures: Emily's father, Barney Shapiro. He walked to the kitchen, turned, and paced over to the end of the living room, turned, paced to the kitchen, turned. He didn't seem to notice the two additional women in his home. At first, Anna thought he was distraught, trying to figure out where his daughter was. But a snippet of conversation proved otherwise.

"I don't care if the Chinese give us a *billion* dollars," he told his phone. "We can't put Mandarin characters up on a hall. Can you imagine the Big Three's reaction? We can call it Hu Hall, but we can't look like Chinatown."

They stood waiting for him to get off the phone. Kristen went up to Barney as he pivoted by the stove. She put her hands on his chest to stop his pacing and whispered into the ear that didn't have a phone clamped to it. As Kristen whispered, her hands stayed on his chest. Anna wondered where *Mrs.* Shapiro was. Barney looked over and saw Anna and Sam standing in the doorway. He held up a finger as he continued talking on the phone. "Yeah. Maybe we could put the characters up in a classroom. See if they'd go for that."

He hung up and turned to them. He smiled a big warm smile, the type that charmed donors and alumni. But it was wrong here.

"Hello," he boomed. "Sorry to keep you waiting. Always a fire to put out. I'm Barney Shapiro." He offered a hearty handshake as Anna and Sam introduced themselves. "Please have a seat."

He gestured to a white L-shaped couch, arranged around a coffee table with another crystal vase of fresh-cut flowers. Anna and Sam sat on one side of the L, Barney and Kristen sat on the other. Kristen sat so close to Barney that their thighs were touching.

"So how can I help you?" he asked.

"Sir, your daughter has been missing for twenty-four hours," Anna said. "Have you been made aware of this?"

"Of course. When I was a student, I definitely went 'missing' twenty-four hours at a time. Those were some of the best twenty-four hours of my life." He chuckled. "I'm certain that Emily is just out somewhere having a fun time and will show up soon and feel embarrassed that the authorities were called."

Anna tried to gauge whether he was putting on a good face because the possibility of his daughter being abducted was too terrifying to fathom. She saw only humor and politeness in his eyes. If he was worried, he was good at hiding it.

"I hope you're right," Anna said. "But there are indications that it could be far more serious than that. We're certainly taking it seriously." She glanced at Kristen. "Can we talk in private? I have some information to share that is for the family only."

"Kristen is my fiancée. Emily's mother and I have separated, and Kristen and I will be married next fall, after all the legal machinations are taken care of. Kristen is part of the family."

"Where is Emily's mother?" Anna asked.

"California. That's where she lives now."

"Okay. We're trying to compile a list of all the places Emily might have gone off to, her regular schedule, her friends," Anna said. "Can you tell us about that?"

"Well, sure." He pulled out his phone and starting swiping. "I can access the registrar's office right here. I'll pull up her schedule."

"Thank you, sir," Sam said. "But we already pulled all her information from the registrar. We know which classes she's taking. We know she lives in Springer Hall. We know she entered college with twenty credits from AP testing. What we're hoping for is more personal information about your daughter."

"I see." He lowered the phone.

"Who were her best friends on campus?" Anna asked.

"I'm . . . not sure. I'd guess her roommates."

"We met one of her roommates, Whitney Branson. We didn't get the impression that they were all that friendly. The opposite, in fact."

"I didn't realize there was any tension there." Barney frowned.

"When was the last time you spoke to your daughter, sir?"

He looked uncomfortable. "That would be about eight weeks ago. At my birthday dinner. We had a—a bit of a falling-out."

"About what?"

"I told her that Kristen and I are getting married. Suffice it to say, Emily didn't approve."

Kristen looked down demurely, but before she did, Anna saw triumph flash across her pierced brow.

"And you haven't spoken to your daughter since then?"

"Correct."

Angry footsteps clicked down the marble foyer. An elegant woman in her midfifties strode into the room. She wore tasteful beige pants, an ivory blouse, and a well-coiffed salt-and-pepper bob. Anna recognized her from the pictures: Beatrice Shapiro. Emily's mother. Barney's wife—or ex-wife, depending on what stage their lawyers were in.

Anna and Sam stood to greet her, but Beatrice ignored them. She stood directly in front of her husband, who also stood. They did not touch.

"Barney." Her voice was low and carefully controlled.

"Beatrice." His tone matched hers. "I told you, you didn't need to come."

Her eyes narrowed. "You have no idea what I need. Or what Emily needs."

"Look, you don't need to fly in here just because Emily took a little frolic and detour. Did you check around your Buddhist retreat? Maybe she's just off 'finding herself' too."

Beatrice shook her head. "You are the world's biggest asshole."

Kristen stood and whispered something in Barney's ear. He nodded and spoke to Beatrice. "How did you get into this house?"

"Aspiring Trophy Wife might've changed the locks," Beatrice said, "but she didn't check with the courts. This is still my house; my name is still on the papers. I had a locksmith make me an extra key last time I was in town."

He sighed and shook his head. "Beatrice, for the hundredth time, I'm sorry to have hurt you. But this is going to be Kristen's home soon. I bought you out of your half of the estate. You're going to have to give us some privacy so we can all move on with our lives."

"You think you can just throw money at me and make it all go away." Beatrice's voice rose. "It's not about money. It's about lies and broken promises. It's—"

Anna held up her hands, one palm pointed at each parent. "Excuse me. If you don't mind, could you please discuss your separation later? We need to focus on Emily now."

Beatrice blinked, then nodded. "Of course. That's why I came here despite my husband's suggestion that I was not needed." She introduced herself to Anna and Sam, then sat in an armchair across from the couch. "Please tell me what's going on."

Anna summarized what they knew.

"Her purse in the Pit!" Beatrice glared at her husband. "This is not some 'frolic and detour,' Barney. For an intelligent man, you can be such a moron."

Sam held her hands up. "Please, let's try to stay civil. For the sake of your daughter. Take ten deep breaths."

Beatrice did as she was told, closing her eyes and putting her hand on her chest as she breathed. It seemed to help. "Thank you," she said, opening her eyes.

"You don't happen to know the password on her phone, do you?" Anna asked. Both parents shook their heads.

"If you give us permission to unlock the phone, we'll have a much easier time convincing Apple to let us in."

"Of course," Barney said.

Anna handed him a consent form. He skimmed it then signed, as calmly as signing a credit card charge at the supermarket. Anna took the form and handed it to Beatrice, so the warring spouses wouldn't have to touch each other.

Beatrice signed it then asked, "Do you know who the boy in the videos is?"

"His name is Dylan Highsmith."

Finally, Barney reacted. He flinched. "As in Robert Highsmith's son?"

"Yes."

His Adam's apple pulsed up and down the length of his throat. Interesting that this was the first time Barney had shown any fear involving his daughter's disappearance.

"I should have known," Beatrice said.

"What do you mean?" Anna asked.

"That boy is a menace." Beatrice pulled her own phone out of her purse. She moved to sit next to Anna on the couch. She went to her videos, then swiped until she found the one she was looking for. The date on the video was September 2, 2014, at 6:48 A.M. About six months ago. The frame was frozen on Emily's face, blurry and obscured with the triangular play button. "After we separated," Beatrice said, "I went to California. I had to get away from Barney and his midlife crisis. But Emily and I would Skype at least once a week. She called me god-awful early on her second day as a freshman. Apparently, she'd gone to some party the night before and had just stumbled home. She was so distraught, I recorded the Skype call."

Beatrice pressed play. On-screen, Emily's face became animated, red, and sobbing. She was sitting at a desk in a dorm room. Behind her was a stone fireplace. The windows were pale gray, suffused with early morning light.

"Emily, my poor baby," said Beatrice's voice on the video. "Try to calm down enough to talk. I can't understand what you're saying. First wipe your nose."

Emily snuffled and reached for something offscreen. Her hand came back with a tissue. She blew her nose into it.

"There you go," said Beatrice. "Now tell me what's going on."

Emily took a deep breath. "I went to a party last night."

"Okay."

"I think—I think—something terrible happened."

"Honey, what?"

"Oh God." She started crying again. "I don't want to be that girl."

"What girl?"

"The girl who got raped!"

"Emily! Oh my goodness. What happened?"

On-screen, Emily lowered her face to the desk and cried even harder. Only the top of her head was visible, brown hair shaking in tempo with her sobs. Beatrice let her daughter cry for several minutes, until her sobbing quieted and she raised her head. Her eyes were so puffy, they were just slits.

"I danced with him," Emily whispered. "I thought he was cute. I thought he liked me. Shit, I'm so stupid."

"Em, I need you to back up. Where were you?"

"A party. My first college party! What a joke."

"Okay, so you're dancing, at a party. And then what?"

"He gives me a drink. The Killer Heart Throb, he calls it. Red and fruity, really sweet. He asks if I want to see his fish tank. I say sure. I'm going up the stairs one minute—and the next thing—I wake up. I'm in his bed. And he's there on top of me—inside me."

"Wait, honey. Are you saying he was having sex with you?"

"Yes!"

"Did you—well, did you want to?"

"No! I didn't want to have sex with anyone! It was my first night out! I opened my eyes and this kid is on top of me, his face is a few inches from mine and he's pumping away. I said no. No! I pushed his chest. He shoved his tongue in my mouth. I blacked out again."

"Oh, my poor baby. How much had you had to drink?"

"Some. But the way I just suddenly blacked out—I'm thinking—he drugged me? Bill Cosby style."

"Oh my God."

Emily started to cry again. Anna glanced up at the girl's father, who was listening to his daughter describe being raped. His face was contorted. Anna wondered if this was the first time he'd seen this video. Kristen massaged his arm and whispered something in his ear. He shook his head.

On-screen, Beatrice asked, "How did you get out of there?"

"I woke up, trapped," Emily said between sobs. "He was sleeping with his arm draped over me, like we were some happy couple. Right next to the bed there was a big fish tank full of these little sharks. They swam around in circles, looking at me like I was something to eat. I climbed out from under his arm, threw on my clothes, and ran out of there."

"Good," Beatrice said. "Do you know the boy's name?"

"Dylan."

"Dylan what?"

Emily looked away from the camera, bit her lip, then looked back again. "Highsmith."

"Oh," Beatrice said. "I see."

"What does that mean?" Emily's voice was louder.

"Nothing, honey."

"I know who he is, Mom."

"Okay. Where did it happen?"

"At a fraternity house." Emily paused. She whispered, "Beta Psi."

Beatrice gasped. "Your father's house."

"It's not about him," Emily said wearily.

"You have to report this."

"I'm not sure I want to."

"Why in the world not?"

"Isn't it obvious? I just started here. Beta Psi is, like, the best frat on campus. They can make or break me. If I report this, everyone will know me as 'the girl who cried rape.' People will point and whisper and I'll spend the next four years eating alone."

"Your father's fraternity can't get away with this."

"This is not about my father."

"It is about him. It's about his college's failed policies."

"Mom—"

"It's about his administration's medieval view of women."

"Mom—"

"It's about his—"

"Mom! Stop! This is not about Dad. Can you please put your hate on hold for just a minute and try to listen to what I'm saying?"

"Honey, I totally hear what you're saying. You're saying your father's college failed you. And I'm saying he needs to be held accountable."

"I'm not reporting this just to hurt Dad."

"Why should we shield him? He deserves to be punished for every bit of misery he's caused."

"I don't know why I even told you this. I just wish I hadn't. Good-bye."

Emily's hand reached toward the screen, and the recording went black. Anna's heart went out to the girl, who had probably cried offscreen for quite some time after the recording ended.

"Can we get a copy of that?" Sam asked Beatrice.

"Of course. I'm glad to help." Beatrice looked at her husband furiously. "Someone around here needs to do something."

"How did you record the Skype call?" Anna asked. "I didn't know that was possible."

"There's an app," Beatrice said. "With everything going on with my divorce, I thought I should be prepared."

This woman was organized, tech-savvy, and consumed with fury. Anna thought her own family was messed up—but whatever her own mother's limitations, she'd always known that her mother had her best interests at heart. There were perfectly good reasons to report the rape—Anna would have encouraged Emily to do it. But Emily clearly thought her mother was motivated by revenge.

Anna said, "This happened six months ago, last September. Did Emily end up filing a complaint against Dylan with the university?"

"I think so," said Beatrice, "but she stopped talking to me about it. Her father would know, it's his university. Barney?"

"I'm so sorry." Barney shook his head. "But I can't talk about that. Any complaints made through the Disciplinary Committee are strictly confidential. I'm not at liberty to disclose them."

"I understand that would normally be the case," Anna said. "But . . . a girl is missing. Your daughter."

"In some sense, that makes it even more important for me to follow standard procedure. I can't give a case special treatment just because my family member is involved."

A shriek rang out as a streak of tasteful beige flew across the room. Beatrice Shapiro grabbed the crystal vase from the coffee table, raised it above her head, and brought it down on her husband's skull.

VLOG
RECORDED 9.4.14

I can't believe I'm the statistic.

One in five.

It's like—we all knew it. It's in half the videos they make you watch online before school starts. They say it over and over in orientation. One in five girls will be raped in college.

We joked about it as we were getting ready, putting on lipstick, trying on outfits, giggling. Which one of us will it be? Ha ha ha! Hilarious.

And here I am. A few days ago, I was raped. Oh my God, did I just say that? It's insane. I can't get used to the words.

I was raped?

I'm a rape victim?

This is not who I want to be.

And I kind of wonder if I can not be it by just . . . not being it. If a tree falls in the woods and no one hears it, does it make a sound? If a girl is raped but no one knows, is she really a victim?

I could just pretend it never happened.

I'm sorry, wait, did I just say that? Ugh. I rolled my eyes at those girls in the video, the ones who didn't report for months after being assaulted. Because they were "torn" or "ashamed" or thought it was their fault. Get it together. If you're mugged, you don't worry about whether you were "asking for" a mugging. Report it, be strong, move on.

But here I am.

Not sure I can bring charges.

Not sure I can pretend it didn't happen either.

Because I keep thinking about it. Flashing back to that moment. Waking up, with Dylan on top of me. Freaking out—and not being able to do anything about it. Trying to get up—and slipping back down into darkness. It's like that nightmare where you're running and running from some monster, but your feet don't move. I knew I needed to get out of there, and I just passed out again. Thinking about it makes my heart pound, makes my stomach clench. But I can't stop thinking about it.

In class, I'm supposed to be taking notes, but I'm feeling Dylan's weight on my hips. I'm choking on his tongue. I'm seeing those sharks, circling. I'm smelling his beer breath.

I can't even imagine going to a party. I can't imagine taking a drink from a boy, ever again. The idea of it makes me sick. This is supposed to be the best time of my life, and all I'm doing is trying not to throw up.

Mom wants me to go to the police. Not because it'll help me. Because it'll hurt Dad. His college is so messed up, CNN will say, the president can't even protect his own daughter. She'd watch all the cable news shows, cackling.

I can't trust Mom's advice at all. It's so sad. She didn't used to be this way. She used to be a good mom. But last year changed her. All she cares about now is getting even, getting back at Dad for ruining her life. Everything is about that now. Every piece of advice she gives me is really a strategy either to get information about Dad or hurt him. I see Preya talking to her mom, getting feedback without a hidden agenda, and I'm so jealous. I so wish I had a mom like that.

I feel so alone.

And Dad. What a cliché—falling for a woman almost young enough to be his daughter, a woman who works for him. Lying about it for months before Mom caught him. No question, he was a terrible husband. But he's not a terrible dad. I still love him, and I don't want to hurt him. I definitely don't want to tell him about my sex life.

What am I even doing, talking about my family on the vlog? This is supposed to be an assignment, not therapy. Whatever. I'm obviously not posting this anywhere. But it helps, actually, to talk about it. Even just to myself. Because I'm the only one who can figure this thing out.

So.

What the hell am I gonna do?

7

Water, flowers, and shards of crystal exploded across the living room. Blood spurted from a gash in Barney's hairline, spattering the ivory walls with crimson. The president slumped sideways on the couch. A red stain spread on the white cushions under his head. Beatrice cradled her hand as blood poured from her palm, where the broken vase had sliced. Her expression was one of shocked uncertainty, as if wondering whether to apologize or hit him again. Samantha grabbed Beatrice, pulled her arms behind her back, and pushed her chest first against a wall.

"Oh my God! Barney!" Kristen clambered to kneel over her fiancé. She cradled his head in her hands, which were instantly soaked crimson. "He's dead. You killed him! You crazy bitch!"

"My daughter is missing and he won't help the police!" Beatrice tried to lunge at Kristen. Sam held her tight against the wall.

Anna herded Kristen to the opposite side of the room, near the kitchen, so that she and Beatrice wouldn't tangle. "Stay right here," Anna said. "Call 911." Kristen didn't answer. "Can you do that, Kristen?" Anna raised her voice. "I need your help. Kristen, can you stand right here and call 911?" Kristen blinked, then nodded and took out her phone. Anna strode back to the couch, carefully wending her way through the broken crystal, scattered flowers, and water. She knelt next to Barney. His face was slack and pale, almost as white as the sofa had been a few moments before. Blood continued to spread across the cushions, the only movement on the couch. The president himself was still as stone.

Anna cursed under her breath. She'd handled hundreds of domestic violence cases. She knew that every tense domestic situation presented danger. She just hadn't expected to find it here in this beautifully appointed academic home. But it was a lesson she often repeated: domestic violence wasn't just a problem for the poor and uneducated. It could happen to anyone, anywhere. All the Arhaus furniture and philosophy textbooks in the world couldn't guarantee against primeval rage.

Anna held her breath as she picked up Barney's arm and put a finger on his clammy wrist. She felt nothing. Oh God, was he dead? Could a man be killed with a single blow from a crystal vase? Anna once had a case where a man had been killed with a hamster cage. She supposed anything was possible. Still holding her breath, she moved her fingers a centimeter over on his wrist. There was his pulse: strong, even, and fast as a bird's. She finally exhaled. "He's not dead," Anna called to Sam. Her relief was mirrored on the agent's face.

Kristen was giving the address to the 911 operator. Anna said, "Tell them to send an ambulance."

Anna plucked several tissues from a box and held the wad firmly to Barney's head wound to stanch the flow of blood. Crimson quickly soaked through the Kleenex to her fingers. She kept the pressure firm and steady. Her hands were already covered with his blood. At some point tonight, she'd have to find time to go to a hospital and get hepatitis meds.

Barney blinked and looked at Anna. He brought his hand to his head and found her wrist and the tissues there. He pulled away his red-stained fingers with a look of confusion, tried to stand, and collapsed back onto the pillows. "Stay still, Mr. Shapiro," Anna said. "An ambulance is coming. We're going to get you to a hospital."

He nodded and closed his eyes. Several pink flower petals clung to his hair.

Sam took out her handcuffs with a sigh. This was not what they wanted or needed to be doing now, but it had to be done. Sam fastened the metal bracelets to Beatrice's wrists, behind her back. "Ms. Shapiro, you are under arrest. You have the right to remain silent. Anything you say can and will be used against you . . . "

"Are you joking?" Beatrice interrupted. "My daughter is missing and you're arresting me?"

"If I witness an assault, I'm obliged to make an arrest. Even if I wanted to hit him myself. You have the right to an attorney. If you cannot afford an attorney, one will be provided for you."

Three minutes later, two marked police cruisers and an ambulance screamed up to the president's house. The EMTs bundled Barney onto a stretcher and hustled him off to the hospital. The police officers took Beatrice into their patrol car and drove her off to the central cell block.

Anna stood with Sam on the president's columned porch, watching the parents of their missing girl being carted off by the local authorities, red and blue lights flashing away into the night. She glanced at her watch. Thirty-seven minutes had passed in this house, and they were no closer to finding Emily.

VLOG
RECORDED 9.18.14

I can't sleep, but I can't really wake up. At night, I lie in bed, staring at the ceiling, trying not to think about what happened. For hours. In the morning, I sleepwalk my way to class. I can't focus on the lecture. I can't focus on anything really.

I can't eat, either. My stomach's tied in knots. The idea of getting food in there is ridiculous. All the other girls worry about the freshman fifteen, but my jeans are getting looser. The one perk to all this, I guess.

Preya keeps asking me if I'm okay. I keep telling her I'm fine—but I know she doesn't believe it. She's got this worried look every time she sees me. I get it, I'm a mess. I don't put on makeup anymore. All my cute back-to-school clothes are hanging in the closet with their tags still on. I have one pair of sweatpants I love, and I'm wearing them over and over. They're soft and warm and I'll take comfort anywhere I can get it right now. They . . . um . . . yeah, they might be smelling a little funky. I can't bring myself to care.

Preya wants me to go out with her. To parties, to the bar, to the honors retreat. I just don't want to. I want to sit in my room, watching Netflix. In the last three days, I've watched every episode of *Downton Abbey*. I was never into *Downton* before. But there's something soothing about watching the Dowager Countess fight for her family.

And I like to walk the dogs. You know the dogs they use to practice surgery at the vet school? They always need walks and stuff. When I was a kid, I loved to volunteer; it was like my favorite thing to do, but I hadn't done it in a long time. Years, I guess. I never thought it would be my only extracurricular activity in college. But you know what? Dogs don't ask you a bunch of questions you don't want to answer.

So, anyway, today I was walking this dog, Fenwick. He's one of my favorites, a big yellow mutt who smiles when you scratch behind his ears. So I'm walking Fenwick, and he's sniffing around, and I'm not really paying attention to where I'm going. He's sniffing these bushes for a while, and finally I look up and see we're right in front of the campus police station. I must've been walking him for a long time, because that's more than a mile from the vet clinic. I didn't mean to go to the police station. But there I was. I tied Fenwick to a bike rack and wandered in.

I don't know what I thought I was doing. I'd been in the campus police station a few times before, when I was a little girl, always with my dad. He'd go for a tour of the new equipment, or to pay an official visit. The police would all coo over me, let me play with their handcuffs. The president's daughter is everyone's favorite kid, at least when the president is around. The last time I was in the station I was maybe nine years old. They gave me a toy police badge and a lollipop.

This time, no one seemed to recognize me. I was just a regular girl to them, not the First Daughter. Which was kind of a relief and also, actually—I'm, like, ashamed to admit this after all my big talk about wanting to be a normal girl—kind of disappointing.

I asked the officer at the front desk if I could talk about something that happened to "a friend." There was a lot of waiting, and then a policeman who couldn't be much older than me took me to a small room. His name was Officer Quentin. I told him what happened to me . . . but not really. I said maybe it happened to a friend, like hypothetically, and that my friend wasn't sure if she wanted to press charges or anything. She just wanted to know what her options were. I didn't tell the officer that Dad is president; I didn't tell him my last name is Shapiro.

Officer Quentin said it was really smart of my friend not to press charges. He said a lot of times it's harder on the victim than the rapist. The process would be long. My friend would have to tell her story over and over, to strangers. The most intimate and embarrassing details. And even then, there's no guarantee the guy'll be punished. He said a lot of times the victim's better off just letting it go and moving on with her life.

When I went back outside, Fenwick's whole body seemed to wag. I squatted down and scratched behind his ears and got his big toothy smile. Seriously, that smile was the best part of my day. I looked around at all the kids going back and forth to class. It was a clear, sunny day, a postcard view of what a university should look like. Diverse students.

Perfect grass. Shiny, happy people holding hands. And all I wanted was to bury my face in this dog's neck then go home and watch reruns on Hulu.

Across from the campus police station is the admin building. It reminded me of all the red-tape crap my dad complains about—and Title IX. You know, the law that's supposed to, like, make sure college girls get equal sports teams as boys. The last few years, Dad's been pissed because it's also been used to mean colleges have to protect girls against being raped. He's all, like, how am I supposed to know what happens in every dorm room and off-campus party? He obviously doesn't say that sort of stuff officially. He mumbles it under his breath in the house, to me and Mom—I mean, back when Mom was around. In public, he's all like, "The safety of all our students is of utmost importance, and we'll make sure the requirements of Title Nine are strictly enforced," blah blah blah.

So I walked across the street, tied Fenwick up again, and went to see the Title IX coordinator, a grandma named Yolanda Skanadowski. I never met her before, but I've heard her name. She's been around forever. She's old-school Title IX, like, more prepared to demand a girls' volleyball team than to sort out rapes. Her office was bright and pretty and smelled nice, and maybe that's why this time I didn't say it was "a friend." I said it was me. Not President Shapiro's daughter, me. I didn't tell her my name. I just said, "This happened to me." First person. A girl who's sitting in front of you. I told her the full story. She listened and nodded and offered me a box of tissues and a bowl of Jolly Ranchers when I cried.

But you know what? In the end, Yolanda was even worse than the police. She asked if I played any sports, and I told her, yeah, I was on the soccer team in high school. And she smiled and said that rape was sort of like a sports game, that I should look back on the night and try to figure out if there was anything I could have done differently. You know, did I drink too much? I'm eighteen, underage drinking is illegal, so I have to admit I kind of contributed to what happened, don't I? Maybe I drank so much I was in a blackout, not drugged? Perhaps I could have chosen not to go upstairs with Dylan? All in this vaguely British voice, and a tight, prim smile. Yolanda said I should simply think about how I could've done things differently, and "use that knowledge going forward."

In her mind, this was my fault. If I'd only behaved like the proper young lady Yolanda Skanadowski was in 1952, or whatever, I wouldn't have been raped. She seemed more worried about what I did than what he did.

I knew it would be hard to face Dylan. His frat brothers. My classmates. Kids can be mean, you know? I'm afraid of being judged, blackballed, laughed at. But being slapped down by the school, which is supposed to protect me? That was a surprise.

I guess that's what stings most—getting punched by someone I thought was supposed to be on my side. If a bully hits you, your body hurts. If a friend hits you, your soul hurts.

When I went back outside, Fenwick jumped up, put his paws on my chest, and kept licking my face. Maybe he was just happy to see me. Or maybe he liked the salty taste of my tears.

8

By the time Mrs. and Mr. Shapiro were carted off to the jail and hospital, respectively, it was two A.M. Anna was exhausted, but there was no time to stop and sleep. Every minute that passed was a barrier separating her from the likelihood of finding Emily alive. So she and Sam got back in the Durango and drove to Emily's dormitory.

As they drove, Anna called Jack. "Things have gotten messy." She described her night so far.

"So," Jack said slowly. "The suspect assaulted you, you assaulted him back, and the victim's mother assaulted her father. It *has* been a busy night."

"I'm sorry." Anna's chest was tight with the urgency of finding this girl, and the feeling that things were only getting worse.

"You're not the one who needs to be sorry," he said. "I want to punch him myself."

"I didn't want drama. I just want to find the girl." Anna was relieved that she wasn't in trouble. Sometimes, with Jack, she felt like she was a kid and he was her parent. A benevolent, logical, loving parent, but still. She wondered if many young women felt that way about their lovers. Ex-lovers. Whatever.

"I'm not surprised by the drama," Jack said. "Case like this, emotions are running high. But I'd put money on President Shapiro asking not to press charges."

"He's gonna need stitches. A lot of stitches. There was so much blood."

"Head wounds tend to bleed a lot. But this is a man who doesn't like bad publicity. He'll want to keep this as quiet as possible, believe me. Plus, their daughter is missing. If anything makes people distraught, it's a missing kid. I can't imagine how I'd feel if Olivia was missing. I'd cut Nina some slack in that situation, even if she went a little crazy."

The idea of Olivia being missing, possibly abducted, sent cold shivers down Anna's spine. She got a glimpse of what it must be like to be Beatrice Shapiro.

When Anna and Jack had been engaged, Anna devoted herself to earning Olivia's trust and becoming a substitute mother. She'd read parenting books, learned how to roast a chicken, gone to parent-teacher conferences. One of the things Anna loved about marrying Jack was becoming Olivia's mom. Then Nina returned to town, a move no one expected. She'd been gone for years as part of an undercover operation. Nina wanted to be a mother to Olivia again, and a wife to Jack. In the process, Anna saw that Jack still cared deeply about his ex. When an emergency rocked the courthouse, he had gone to protect Nina, not Anna.

It was almost a year ago, but Anna recalled with perfect clarity composing the e-mail telling friends and family their wedding was canceled. She had still been deeply in love with Jack. Soon after that, Anna had been called to Michigan to defend Jody in a murder trial, and she'd stayed there for almost a year to see it through.

"I'm not so surprised the father stonewalled you," Jack said. "Tower University has been slow to cooperate in the task force investigation, and their Clery Act compliance is a joke. The good news is, our investigations dovetail. We can both get different information and share it with each other."

They hammered out a plan. Eighty percent of practicing criminal law is logistics, though there's no class for that in law school. Jack would contact the local prosecutor to try to get Beatrice released as soon as possible; they needed her active in the investigation, holding press conferences, giving information, available for calls. Anna would try to interview Emily's friends. They'd meet when they were done. Anna's stomach clenched at the idea of seeing Jack in person. She hadn't seen him in six months, and seeing him was always a visceral experience for her.

Sam pulled the Durango in front of a massive stone building with ivy creeping up the sides. Springer Hall had arched windows, carved pillars, and a recessed stone front porch. Its foundation stone said 1872. The dormitory had been standing on this corner for almost a hundred and fifty years. For the last six months, it had also been the home to Emily Shapiro.

A few kids were stumbling back into the dorm, making their way home after the bars' two A.M. closing time. Several rooms had lights on, but most of the windows were dark.

Inside, modern amenities supplemented the historic architecture. A stately marble floor held a whirring robotic vending machine, offering items from energy bars, earbuds, and disposable razors to condoms and lube. Anna did a double take on the condoms. She'd started college only eleven years earlier, but condoms hadn't been displayed in her dorm lobby then. Sex was an obvious part of college life but hadn't been so frankly and openly on offer. She supposed it wasn't a bad idea to have protection easily available. Still, she wasn't sure about the wisdom of packaging sex as an option as casual as a snack.

Anna and Sam walked up two floors, then down a long, quiet hallway. They knocked on the door to room 217. It was opened by a petite young woman whom Anna recognized as Emily's roommate, Preya Parikh. Anna had been worried about waking the girl, but she clearly was wide-awake. Anna and Sam introduced themselves. Preya said, "Everyone will be so glad to see you. They're all here for Emily."

Preya invited them into the living room, which was bright, crowded, and buzzing with conversation. All the available seats, and even the tops of the desks, were covered with students. Anna counted ten besides Preya: seven women and three men, all in their late teens or early twenties. They were talking to one another, peering at one anther's phones, tapping on laptops. A few glanced up at Anna and Sam, but many were engrossed in what they were doing. Preya clapped and said loudly, "Guys! Hey! It's the feds. Give them your attention." The room quieted as the students looked up.

"Hi, I'm Anna Curtis, a prosecutor." Anna met their eyes one by one, trying to make a connection. These students, she knew, saw her as The Man, even though she was closer in age and perspective to them than to many of her colleagues at the Department of Justice. The students simultaneously wanted her to fix things and were skeptical that she would. "Agent Randazzo and I are looking into Emily Shapiro's disappearance. I understand you're all here for the same reason?" The kids nodded. "So first off, I'd like to ask, has anyone seen or heard from Emily since midnight Friday night?"

Crickets.

"We've been comparing notes," said a woman with plastic cat's-eye glasses. "No one's seen Emily. She hasn't texted or Snapchatted. All her social media's quiet. She hasn't posted to Facebook, Twitter, Yik Yak, Vine, Instagram, Words with Friends, anything, since Friday night."

Of course she hadn't; her phone had been in the bottom of the Pit. Anna glanced over to make sure Sam was listing all the apps in her notebook. They would subpoena the tech companies to get access to everything Emily had posted and anyone she'd interacted with.

"We'd like to talk to you one by one," Sam said. "And hear anything you've learned. Plus any information you have about Emily—her friends, her interests, and whether you've heard anything about what happened to her last night."

The kids nodded; they would cooperate. Anna thought of the kids partying at the frat house, how different they were from this crowd. A college as big and diverse as Tower had a place for everyone. Environmental activists and young Republicans. Jocks and nerds. Boozy good old boys and millennial feminists.

Anna asked Preya, "Can we talk somewhere alone?"

Preya led them through a bathroom and into the bedroom. There was a bunk bed and one single bed by a window. Preya pointed to the top bunk. "That's Emily's."

On the nightstand was a picture of Emily as a girl, maybe ten years old, standing with her mother and father in front of the clock tower on a sunny spring afternoon. The good old days. Anna looked at the picture and sensed the longing of a girl whose family had exploded. Anna's own family had exploded, in a different way. She'd felt a similar urge to remember the good times.

"I haven't seen Emily smile like that in a long time," Preya said.

"Why do you think that is?" Anna asked.

"It's been a hard year for her. You probably heard what happened with Dylan."

"Tell us about it."

"She didn't like to talk about it," Preya said. "So I only know bits and pieces. I know he assaulted her at a frat party, like our first night here. And she took her case to the campus Disciplinary Committee. When Whitney found out—Whitney's our third roommate—

she was pissed. Whitney's dating a guy at Beta Psi, and she thought Emily was taking everything too far, bringing down the house. They haven't really spoken to each other since."

"Sounds like a tough living situation."

"Yeah, it wasn't good. But Whitney spends most of her time at the frat. So that helped keep them away from each other. But after Emily saw her reaction, she didn't like talking about it, not even to me. So I don't know much about what happened to her case within the university. What I do know is that Beta Psi has a reputation. They call it the 'rape factory.'"

"Who calls it that?" Anna said.

"Everyone."

"Do you know anyone else who was sexually assaulted there?"

"No. Just lots of talk, rumors. Older girls tell you never to go upstairs with a boy there. But Emily probably hadn't heard that the night Dylan attacked her. It was her first week as a freshman."

Anna nodded. The first week was a notoriously dangerous time for freshman girls, who came in bright-eyed and naive. A disproportionate number of rapes happened in that first week; experts called it the Red Zone.

"You're the one who called in the missing persons report this morning—or I should say Saturday morning," Anna said, glancing at her watch. "What made you do that? A lot of college students might spend a night and a morning out, and their roommate might not think anything of it."

"Mm, yeah. Emily wasn't that way. After that first party, she didn't go out much. We've been roommates for six months, and she hasn't really partied at all. If she did go out, it'd be with a bunch of girls, like to see a movie. She didn't like being around guys. But last night I asked her to come with us to Lucky's. And she finally agreed."

"So, what happened last night?"

"I've been trying to get her to go out more. I thought it would be good for her. And when we got to the bar, I thought she was having fun. She was talking to some cute boy. Next thing I knew, I saw her walking out the front door, alone. I just assumed she was going to get some fresh air. When she didn't come back after, like, five minutes, I went out after her. But she was gone. Just, like, vanished. She wouldn't have gone anywhere without telling me, not without a good reason." Preya's big dark eyes filled up with tears. "It was her first night out in forever. Because of me. And now this has happened."

"It's not your fault," Anna said, handing her a tissue. She always kept Kleenex in her purse; they were as necessary to her job as a mop was to a janitor. Preya blew her nose.

"Had she been drinking?" Anna asked.

"Not really, I don't think." Preya wiped a tear. "We didn't pre-party in the dorm. I saw her get a beer at the bar, but I don't know if she had any more than that. We'd been there, like, an hour before she left."

"What was Emily's relationship with Dylan?"

"There was no 'relationship.' They didn't talk. Once or twice, she saw him on campus, and it scared the crap out of her, but she just walked away. It's a big campus. You don't necessarily run into somebody unless you're trying to. She was the butt of some jokes, mostly from other kids, not Dylan. I think Emily and Dylan just ignored each other, except within the Disciplinary Committee case. Until . . ." Preya trailed off.

"Until what?" Anna asked.

"Two days ago." Preya looked at Anna with big, scared eyes. "I think she did something big. And it changed everything."

VLOG
RECORDED 9.23.14

Holy crap. I'm, like, reeling.

Dylan's done it before. And he'll do it again. Unless I stop him.

Ugh.

Why does it have to be me? I'm not any kind of superwoman. I don't even raise my hand in class.

But, I'm—wait. Lemme start over, tell this in a straight line.

Okay, so I went to the student health center today. I haven't gotten a good night's sleep in like three weeks. I thought they could give me Ambien or something. But I got a lot more than that.

They led me to an office with a nameplate that said DR. SUSAN BLUM, MS ED. Dr. Blum is a pretty psychologist with brown hair and a warm smile. I told her what happened, and, unlike everyone else, she didn't blame me or tell me to go away. She said what happened to me happened to a lot of smart, nice girls. She rolled out the notorious "one in five" statistic—but she added something I haven't heard before. She said six percent of the boys commit ninety percent of the rapes on campus. Can you believe that? It's crazy. The guys who do it, they do it over and over. They're predators.

Dr. Blum said that "given the statistics" Dylan had probably done it before—and would do it again if no one stops him. She said he's probably been perfecting his routine. I asked if she knew anyone who'd been raped by Dylan. She kind of looked at me for a second, like she wanted to tell me something—but then she said she's bound by confidentiality rules and stuff. But, she said, some survivors talk to this Title IX activist named Heide, and I could call and see if Heide could help.

So, I call this girl, Heide, and guess what? She knew other girls who've been assaulted by Dylan. Like, what are the chances? I actually asked her that. And Heide said a lot of girls come to her, and she starts to hear the same names over and over. She said nothing would change if girls like us didn't take a stand. I told her I wasn't sure. She said she understood—and then she asked if I wanted to talk to one of those other girls. I'm not sure why, but I said yes.

So a little while later, this girl calls me. Tells me what happened to her two years ago—which was exactly what happened to me three weeks ago. Like, insane. She didn't do anything back then. Didn't report it, didn't bring charges. Thought she could make it go away by just not thinking about it. Sound familiar? But, she said, it was worse, trying not to think about it. Like in elementary school when you do that thing where you try not to think about a pink elephant and of course all you can think about is a pink elephant. She said it's been eating her up inside, all these years.

And she kept apologizing to me. Like what happened to me was her fault, for not doing something before. It was so sad. It was like she almost felt worse about how she reacted than about the assault.

And that got me thinking. What if I'm in her position one day? Like, another girl calls me up and tells me Dylan raped her—two years from now? How will I feel then, if I hadn't done something today?

Shitty, is how.

Fuck.

Dylan's family is gonna flip out—and they have the money and power to seriously flip. His fraternity, with their secret-handshake-boys-club-running-the-world thing, is gonna blackball me from every party on this campus.

But this'll never change if I don't report it.

I really don't want to go to the police and make this whole thing googleable. But if I just file a complaint through the university, it'll be confidential. Sealed and private. No public record. I won't be tagged forever as a "rape victim."

Oh man. I didn't come here to be an activist. But I can't just, like, walk away from this.

I'm filing a case against Dylan.

For better or for worse. We'll see, huh?

9

"What did Emily do two days ago?" Anna asked.

Preya chewed her thumbnail as she spoke. "I'm not sure, because I didn't see it myself. But from what I hear, she was keeping, like, a video log of her college life. And she published it on BlueTube."

"What's BlueTube?"

"Like YouTube but just for Tower University stuff. Go red and silver."

"Why were the videos a big deal?"

"Because she announced that Dylan raped her. Before the vlogs came out, it was whispered about, but I'd say that like twenty kids, max, knew about it. Because Disciplinary Committee stuff is secret. When she posted her vlogs, she called him out as a rapist. It was a big public throw down."

"Can we see the vlogs?"

Preya shook her head. "No. They're not up anymore."

"Did Emily take them down?"

"I don't know. I never got a chance to ask her about them. I didn't even hear about it till today. Some other kids watched the vlogs, and word got out. But the videos were taken down before I could see them."

"Do you know anyone who actually watched the videos?"

"No. It's all like a game of Operator—I tried to trace it back—I heard it from Donna Hebel, who heard it from Jill Miner, who heard about it from Karin Beyer, who heard about it from a friend's cousin. Everyone out there"—Preya gestured to the other room in her suite—"is the same. Everyone's talking about the vlogs, but no one saw them."

"Got it." Anna made a note to look for the vlogs and subpoena BlueTube if she couldn't find them online. "Do you know how Dylan reacted to the vlogs?"

"I hear he was pissed. But I don't know. I'm not his BFF."

"Did Dylan ever call here? Or come by?"

"No. Not when I was here."

"Are you aware of whether he ever threatened Emily?"

"Uh-uh." Preya shook her head. "I think I would know if he did."

"Is there anyone else Emily had any tension with? Fights, jealousies, any reason anyone had to dislike her?"

"Actually, if I were you, there is one other person I'd talk to."

"Who is that?"

"Professor Kristen LaRose—and her crazy ex-husband."

There was more crazy? Anna thought they'd reached their limits at President Shapiro's house.

"Why them?"

"Well, first, can you tell me, will people know what I say to you? I don't want anyone to know this is coming from me."

"For now, the investigation is confidential. But if this goes to trial at some point, we might need to disclose who told us what."

"If this goes to trial? That means Emily would be hurt or dead, right?"

Anna nodded.

Preya looked like she was going to cry again. "I'll tell you everything I know. My mom's a professor, and academics talk. Everyone says they're into ideas and logic, but you come down to it, it's one of the gossipiest professions on the planet. And the Shapiros' split has been, like, huge. If there was a *National Enquirer* for college scandals, they'd have been on the front page for the last couple years. They're the Kardashians of academia."

"Why is that?"

"Beatrice and Barney were a golden couple. He's the president, but she did a lot to get him there. Like, dedicated herself to his career. She was the ultimate hostess and networker. And she was good at it, elegant, charming, warm. She could work a room. She could work *you*—but she was so good, you didn't really notice she was working you."

"So what happened?"

"Beatrice caught them having sex on Kristen's desk."

"Oh."

"She must've suspected for a while—she had keys made to Kristen's office and was able to bust in. She brought a professional investigator with. He took photos, and Beatrice cleaned Barney out. He got the house, but just because he's the president. If there was any possible way Beatrice could've gotten that, she would've."

"Sounds like an ugly situation," Anna said. "But how do you think it's related to Emily's disappearance?"

"Okay, so Kristen's husband, Landon, was so massively pissed off about the affair, he makes Beatrice look like a model of anger management. When Kristen left him, Landon got kind of . . . unhinged. Stalked her. Called her hundreds of times a day, started showing up at her classes and office. Banging on doors, yelling, scaring students. He posted a sex tape they'd made to one of those revenge porn sites. Obviously, her students all checked it out. Kristen was livid. She was ready to sue him; she wanted him arrested. But Barney convinced her not to do it—not even to get a restraining order. Barney just quietly got the videos taken down; he can really manage situations. But I'm not sure he could manage Landon. The man is distraught and, like, seriously mentally ill."

Anna made a note to check in with the scorned husband. She asked Preya some more questions, and Sam wrote everything down. The conversation would be memorialized in Sam's 302, her write-up of the witness interview.

"Thank you for telling me all this," Anna said. "You never know in these situations what's important and what's a footnote."

"Please let me know if there's anything else I can do to help," Preya said. "Emily is one of the sweetest people I know."

After Preya was done, Anna and Sam spoke to the other students one by one. They learned that Emily was quiet and kept to herself. Preya appeared to be her best friend on campus. Emily's other friends were kids from her one elective class and an honors retreat she'd gone on that summer, before school started. She hadn't joined any clubs or sports teams. Anna guessed that much of her free time had been spent on the disciplinary case. Pursuing a rape case could be a substantial extracurricular activity in and of itself.

The last person they spoke to was a woman named Heide Herrmann. She was a tall brunette who looked a little more mature than the other students. Heide had graduated from Tower University two years earlier and was twenty-four, half a decade older than the other students assembled in the suite.

"So how did you know Emily?" Anna asked.

"After she was assaulted," Heide said, "she came and spoke to me. I encouraged her to press charges."

"Why did she come to you?"

"It's what I do. I'm a Title Nine activist." Heide pulled up the hem of her jeans and showed a "IX" tattooed on her ankle. "I was assaulted at Tower when I was a student. They swept it under the rug. That's what the college has always done. They don't want to believe that rape is a problem on campus. They don't want parents to be worried, or for applications to drop. Did you know that Dartmouth's applications dropped fourteen percent after a rape allegation?"

Anna nodded.

"No parent wants their kid going to Rape U. So the colleges pretend it doesn't happen," Heide said. "For a long time, they discouraged girls from coming forward. If the girls did come forward anyhow, disciplinary boards often find the boys 'not responsible.' Because they can get sued for kicking a boy out—but not for letting him off. I've been trying to change things. My organization is called Survivors."

Heide handed Anna a card. Anna hadn't heard of this particular organization. There were small outfits like Heide's across the country, grassroots efforts trying to shine a light on the issue.

"Where's your office?" Anna asked.

"I run it out of my apartment. You can do a lot with a laptop and Twitter."

"Do you know what happened with Emily's Disciplinary Committee charges against Dylan?"

"She never told me. I tried to follow up with her, but I never heard back. That happens a lot. Some survivors just want to forget." A note of anger tinged Heide's voice. "And they don't want to go through the circus that is our criminal justice system."

Anna didn't have time to debate now. "How'd you end up here in Emily's dorm tonight? If you didn't keep in touch with her?"

"I heard it on Twitter, like everyone else. And unlike the authorities, I actually care about what happens to women on this campus."

"The authorities care," Anna said.

"Not in my experience."

"Here I am."

"You sure weren't here before."

"I'm sorry you've felt neglected," Anna said. "I'm sorry about what happened to you when you were a student. But right now, I need to find Emily. And so I need to know any information you have about where Emily might be or what happened to her."

"Try the rape factory."

"The Beta Psi frat?"

"Yep."

"We already have."

Heide smiled angrily. "You haven't even scratched the surface."

"What do you mean?"

"Have you seen the Underground?"

"The underground what?"

"See, this is exactly what I'm talking about. If anyone cared about the women on campus before this, you guys would already know."

Anna fought back her frustration. "*I* care, Heide. And if you care about Emily, you'll tell me what you know, as quickly as possible."

Heide pursed her lips, but met Anna's eyes. "They say nothing important goes down in the Beta Psi house aboveground. All their secrets, all their crimes, all their skeletons—it's all below the Crypt, in what they call the Underground."

VLOG
RECORDED 9.25.14

My dad doesn't mean to be a dick. It's like—he just can't help himself.

I thought I was doing him a favor, actually, going to tell him myself so he wouldn't hear through the university grapevine. I still think that was the right thing to do. But, holy crap, it did not go well. I guess I started off wrong by going to see him in his office. I thought I could avoid his girlfriend there. She's, like, totally moved into Dad's house. But the thing is, there in his office, sitting at his big old desk, he's the president—not the dad.

His door was closed, and Zelda said he was in with donors, so I sat in the waiting area. Zelda asked all about my first semester—more questions than my dad has, actually. Hell, maybe I should've told Zelda. She's been his secretary forever, used to let me play on her copying machine and stuff. When I was little, I loved to make copies of my hands and face while Dad worked. He worked a lot.

Anyway, he finally came out, laughing with a bunch of Chinese guys who must've come with big checkbooks. I said hi, and Dad said they were all going to lunch. I told him I really needed to talk to him. That was my second mistake, I see that now. He was distracted and busy. But Zelda stood up and said she'd take the Chinese group to the restaurant and Dad could meet them there. Dad kind of hesitated, but then let me come into his office and sit in a guest chair. He sat behind his desk. That's kind of messed up, when I think about it, actually. Why didn't he just sit next to me? There's another guest chair. But he never did, the whole time I was growing up. If I saw him in the office, he was behind that big desk, like a wall between us.

So, anyway, this was the first time we'd been in the same room since he dropped me off for school. He'd called me once or twice to check in, but I hadn't picked up. It was so weird to look at him across the desk. To him the world probably looks pretty much the same. But my whole universe had, like, totally changed.

I said something polite like, "How are you?"

He said something polite back like, "I'm well. How are you?"

And then he went like this, looking at his watch. Like could I hurry up, please? I should've left. But at that point I felt like I just had to get through it.

I said, "Dad, I have to tell you something. I went to a frat party. I was drugged and raped. And I'm going to bring charges against the boy."

He rocked back in his chair and studied me like he was wondering if this was a practical joke. Here, this is my best President Shapiro impression.

"Oh my God, Emily. Are you serious?"

And I'm, like, "Do you think I'd interrupt your meeting for a prank?"

And he's all like, "No, of course not, honey. My poor girl."

He actually got up and sat in the guest chair next to me. He reached forward and put an arm on my shoulder, almost a hug. He's a famous hand shaker, but he's never been great in the hugs department. I let my head rest on his shoulder. It felt so good, for just a moment, to be supported by someone. He asked me to tell him what happened, but I really didn't want to get into the details. It's, like, so embarrassing to talk about that stuff with your dad. So I said I just wanted to tell him who it was and what I was doing. And then I said it was Dylan Highsmith, and that I'm filing charges through the college.

Dad sat back in his chair. Hug time was done.

Okay, so this vlog is for theater class. I'll act out our conversation. Imagine I have on a power tie and a stick up my ass for the President Shapiro parts.

"Honey, that's a big step. Maybe we should talk about this some more before you decide to pursue such a major decision."

"I've thought about it, and talked about it, and I know what I need to do."

"It's not an easy process, for anyone. I would imagine especially for the president's daughter. And even more so if the accused is a Highsmith."

"Are you worried for me?" I asked, "Or for your college?"

And he said: "I have to consider both."

I couldn't believe he came right out and said it. I mean, I know it's true. But couldn't he at least pretend, while he's talking to me, that he cares about me more than his school? At least in the moment when I'm telling him I was raped? Like I said: he can be a dick. I guess he saw the look on my face.

So then he was all like, "Of course you take precedence, Emily. But sometimes what's good for the college might also be good for you. If you report this, it becomes a rape statistic for the campus, and then applications go down, the reputation goes down, the value of your own degree goes down."

I was like, wow. I didn't know I could single-handedly destroy the school. Just by telling the truth.

"It's not an easy process."

"It's a process your school runs."

"That doesn't mean it's the right course for you, my daughter, to take on one of our highest-donor families."

I hated him a little bit in that moment. He's such a politician, it's almost like a mental illness.

I stood up and left. And here I am, back in my dorm. Fuming. Because fuming is better than crying.

Dr. Blum says that when I'm talking about the rape, it's a hard subject for people to discuss; they don't know what to say, you know, so I should try to interpret their words in the best light possible. I've always been Daddy's little girl. The cute little university mascot. Maybe he has a hard time separating those two things, the girl and the mascot. Maybe Dad really was just worried about me. About how hard it'll be. About my overall happiness. Maybe if I hadn't stormed out, he would've said that.

But the impression I got was that he was worried about me second and the university first. Because that's how it's always been.

10

W e have to get under the Crypt," Anna said.

"Yeah." Sam drove down Detroit's deserted Michigan Avenue. "But we don't have enough to get a warrant."

"Not yet, anyway." Anna thought about the young man in his underwear below the Ping-Pong table. "I might know someone who could just *invite* us in. Show us around."

"Get on that."

"I am. I have to massage it."

"Interesting strategy for a sex-crimes prosecutor."

"You're sick, Randazzo."

"That's why you love me."

The FBI's Michigan field office was a tall concrete building with a view of the Detroit People Mover. At three A.M. it wasn't moving many people. Sam pulled into the underground garage.

An impromptu command center had been assembled inside the FBI field office. A conference room was filled with agents in dark suits and computer technicians in khakis. They were talking softly, tapping on computers, picking through a bag of desiccated bagels. As Anna walked into the bustle, her eyes were caught by one person in particular: a handsome caramel-skinned man sitting at the head of the table. She stopped in the doorway and stared at her former fiancé.

Jack was pointing to something on his computer, talking to two police officers. He wore a dark suit and blue tie; his hair was completely shaved, which gave him a tough-guy aura despite his buttoned-up clothes. Heading up the command center, he radiated authority and control. He looked like the man you'd want looking for your daughter.

Sam cleared her throat, and Anna realized she was blocking the doorway. "Sorry," she murmured, stepping out of Sam's way. She was exhausted. She wasn't prepared to see Jack for the first time in six months.

He looked up from the computer, and their eyes met over the heads of the officers. For a moment, everyone else faded into the background. She only saw the man she loved—the one she'd planned to spend her life with—gazing at her with a tender smile. He got up and walked over to her. She looked up at his green eyes and remembered what it was like to wake with them as the first thing she saw in the morning.

She stuck out her hand, projecting professional politeness as well as she could given her emotional state and sleep deprivation. "Nice to see you, Jack."

He smiled back, as if they were sharing an inside joke, which in a way, they were. He shook her hand with gentle formality. "Nice to see you too, Anna. Thanks for agreeing to join the team."

His hands felt warm after the cold outdoors. She saw that he was still wearing the watch she'd given him. On the back, she'd had inscribed: *I want to spend all my time with you.* Her left thumb touched her ring finger, the empty space the diamond engagement ring used to encircle. For a while, it had been like a phantom limb—her thumb would go to tap it, to connect with the security and safety it represented, and for a moment, she'd be panicked to find that it was gone. Had she lost it? Was it stolen? Then she'd remember handing it back to Jack when they broke up, and she'd feel a greater sense of loss than any jewelry theft could cause. She wondered where the ring was now.

Sam was watching as she poured coffee. Anna realized the handshake had gone on too long. She drew her hand away from Jack's.

"Glad to help," she said. "First things first. Has anyone eaten anything besides bagels all day?"

Jack shrugged and looked at the crumpled Bruegger's bag like it was the first time he'd noticed it. "We're mostly running on coffee and adrenaline."

"No one can do their best work on an empty stomach. I'm ordering pizza."

She pulled out her phone, turned away, and called for Domino's to deliver ten extra-larges. She used the time to take a deep breath and refocus herself. When she hung up and turned back to Jack, she pointed at his computer.

"What leads have you got?" she asked.

He led her to the laptop and gestured for her to sit next to him.

"Unfortunately, not much." His voice was so deep it resonated inside her chest. "The purse and shoe are the last best signs of her. There's no video of her anywhere after the ones you saw. No activity on her e-mail, social media, and so on. Based on what you and Sam found tonight, we've upgraded the case from 'missing person' to 'missing under suspicious circumstances,' and a possible abduction. We sent a BOLO to every police station in the state, sent out a Missing Endangered Person alert, got more personnel on the search teams."

"Okay," Anna said. "I'm subpoenaing the university for every document related to Dylan Highsmith—including every sexual assault charge brought against him. I don't have anything solid yet, but it looks like he might've targeted other girls on campus during the four years he's been here. We're also trying to get enough probable cause to get a warrant to search the frat. Hope to have it soon."

"Good."

She told him about Emily's vlogs. "So obviously, I'm going to subpoena BlueTube and try to get the videos. Do we know anyone in their subpoena compliance department?"

"Never even heard of BlueTube."

"I looked it up. Apparently, it's like YouTube for Tower students and alum. It's not a university site, it's a private company started by a Tower alum a few years ago. Seems pretty successful—they have lots of hits. I don't know anyone there either."

Too bad. Paperwork moved so much faster if you had someone inside. She set up her laptop and started typing up subpoenas. Usually, she would lose herself in the work, but not tonight. The whole time she was typing, she was aware that Jack was working right next to her. Less than an arm's length away. Their nearness, their shared goal—it felt both foreign and heartbreakingly familiar.

They worked until there was nothing else that could be done. A little before five A.M., Jack said, "Go home. Get some shut-eye."

"I could help the search team."

"Out in the cornfields? You're a lawyer. Your talents are better employed in a court than in a ditch. Get at least four hours of sleep. That's an order. It will do you good when you start back later this morning. The university has been reluctant to turn over any information. I hope it won't continue on that course—I hope the president will come through to help his daughter. But up till now, every one of his actions has been to protect his university. Your subpoenas are likely to spark a legal fight. I need you at your best. Sleep."

"Okay." Anna appreciated his concern, even as she felt a bit like a kid listening to her dad say it was bedtime.

Sam drove her back to Detroit. "You want to sleep in a spare room?" Anna asked. Sam shook her head. She had a hotel room. The FBI agent waited until Anna was in the dark house before driving away. Anna tiptoed up the staircase, stripped off her suit, and climbed into bed with Cooper.

"Everything okay?" he asked, turning to her sleepily.

"Not really. We didn't find her. Yet."

He stretched out his arm, and she curled into his chest.

"I spoke to Wyatt," Cooper said. "He'll meet with you."

"Oh, good! Thank you. When?"

"Tomorrow." Cooper glanced at the clock. "Today, actually. Breakfast at my parent's house. He's not happy about it. You'll just have to charm him."

"I'll do my best."

"In my experience, you're gifted at charming Bolden men."

She laughed. They fitted themselves into each other and he kissed her forehead. She heard Cooper's breath return to the deep, steady rhythm of sleep. She didn't follow him there quickly. Her thoughts kept circling around the missing girl, and all the places she might be: ditch, dumpster, cornfield, frat house. She looked around at the details of the bedroom, as if she'd never seen them before. She and Cooper had been comfortably sharing a bed for a few months. But right now, as she lay with her hand on his chest, she was very aware that she was in the arms of a man who wasn't Jack.

11

A nna had first visited Cooper's family farm for his eighth birthday party. She remembered her mother driving her down the Bolden driveway in their Ford minivan, looking at the sprawling acres of soybeans and corn, the big red barn and white clapboard farmhouse. It looked so different from the grid of ramblers where her family lived. Anna didn't remember much about that long-ago birthday party, except that they'd all gone to the barn and jumped from the hayloft into a pile of hay beneath. There was some fabulous cake made from scratch, not bought at the A&P. And a feeling of warmth from his mother.

Eight-year-old Anna hadn't realized what a golden era that was for her family. Her father still had his job at the auto factory and only drank a few beers a night. He'd only hurt their mother two or three times, few enough that they could write the incidents off as anomalies rather than a pattern. After the bank foreclosed on their house—after their father lost his job, his sobriety, and the last shreds of his self-control—Anna would look back on the time she was eight as a sort of magical "before."

Riding up the long driveway on Cooper's big black motorcycle, Anna felt the full stretch of the twenty years that had passed. In the interim, her father had inflicted his final, cataclysmic beating; her mother finally left him; he moved out of state. Anna had gone to law school and then to her dream job in D.C., prosecuting sex crimes and domestic violence. Cooper had gone to fight in Afghanistan and come home minus a leg. Jody had stayed in Michigan to work on the GM assembly line and had just become a mother herself. They were the adults now, running the world, making the choices that would eventually shape their own children's lives.

Anna sat behind Cooper and held tight to his waist as he steered his motorcycle up the dirt drive. The bitter March wind whipped past her helmet, snaking down onto her neck. It was too cold to ride a motorcycle, but that didn't stop Cooper. Since the blast in Afghanistan, he hated confined spaces, especially cars. His big white dog, Sparky, was a service animal, specially trained to help Cooper manage his PTSD. Cooper was one of the most cheerful people Anna had ever met—except when he was having a PTSD reaction, in which case she never knew what to expect. Once, he threw her to the floor at the sound of a car backfiring. He was constantly on high alert, looking for danger, ready to jump into code red at any moment. That might not be a bad way to live in Detroit—but Anna hoped he'd feel more relaxed on his family farm.

Most things from your childhood look smaller when you visit as an adult, but the Bolden family farmhouse actually looked bigger. Anna supposed it was because she'd lived in D.C. for years, getting used to the confined spaces and shrunken square footage of apartments there. The Boldens' farmhouse looked positively palatial. It was surrounded by a white picket fence, acres of sleeping fields, and a white winter sky.

As Cooper shut off the motorcycle, Anna took a deep breath. She hadn't visited since they started their relationship. Seeing parents was such a big step, signified so much, she hadn't wanted to imbue their "fling" with such magnitude. Now she felt sorry that she was coming here for the first time as part of an investigation.

"Don't worry," Cooper said, sensing her unease. "They already love you."

Anna doubted that was true—they hadn't even met her as an adult—but she smiled at Cooper and took a deep breath.

Inside, the house was warm and bright, filled with the scent of bacon and cinnamon. Cooper helped Anna peel off her layers of outer gear and hang them in the front closet. He held her hand and led her through the house to the sound of laughter. The kitchen had yellow gingham curtains, a farmhouse sink, and copper Jell-O molds on the walls. Cooper's mom stood by the stove, using a spatula to conduct a symphony of bacon, eggs, and French toast. Two of his brothers were vying for space at the sink to wash their hands. They all looked up.

"Cooper!" His mom set down her spatula and bustled over with a smile. She had silver hair tied in a thick ponytail, a white apron over a blue skirt, and impressively muscular calves. She took him into her arms and held him tight, as if he were still a boy and not a grown man a foot taller than her.

"Hey, Ma." Cooper handed his mother a bouquet of flowers he'd gotten at the farmers' market the day before. Anna watched approvingly. Her great-aunt used to say: *If you want to see how a man will treat you, look at how he treats his mother and sisters.*

"Thanks, dear." Cooper's mom turned to her. "And you must be Anna. I know not just because Cooper talks about you all the time. You look just like you did when you were eight—only taller."

"Hi, Mrs. Bolden." Anna reached out for a handshake, but Cooper's mom laughed and pulled her into a hug.

"Please, call me Susie. I'm so happy you're here."

Anna gave her a box of Krispy Kremes.

"Oh, my favorite. Come sit, sit, have some coffee." Susie bundled them to the table. "Have one of these delicious doughnuts."

"We can't stay for breakfast, Ma. I'm just hoping to say hi to Wyatt, then we have to run. We'll come back another day for the full Sunday-breakfast-and-church routine."

"Now, now, there's always time for breakfast. Plus, Wyatt's not even here yet." Susie reached to smooth a cowlick in Cooper's hair; Cooper grinned and ducked, the instinctual move of every boy who's ever had a cowlick. Anna understood his mother's need to fuss over Cooper. She understood his need to refuse to be fussed over.

His dad and two younger brothers came over to say hello. Anna remembered Bryce and Zane as dark-haired munchkins a few grades younger than her in elementary school; now they were as tall and broad as Cooper, with the same lean, muscular frame draped in denim and flannel. They still worked on the family farm. Cooper's dad was a big, quiet man with wind-browned skin and lines radiating from his eyes like sunbeams.

Anna helped set the table and chatted with the family about the farm. The whole time, Susie kept cooking and glancing at her watch. When the eggs were done, Susie called everyone to sit. "Wyatt knows when breakfast is served," she said. "We're not going to let the food get cold waiting for him."

Anna realized why Susie had been glancing at her watch. She wondered if Wyatt was going to blow her off. Meanwhile, she ate one of the best breakfasts of her life. The men were mostly quiet, scarfing down their food, but Susie was animated and talkative. "This is my favorite part of the week," she told Anna. "Surrounded by all my boys. And now you! It's wonderful."

"These eggs are great," Anna said.

"Laid this morning," Susie said.

She asked Anna about her life and plans.

"Well, I live in D.C. and my job is there too," Anna explained. "I was just here in Michigan to help my sister. And now, I guess, I should be gearing up to go back. But my office hasn't insisted yet, and I've been doing my work remotely, keeping my head down and hoping no one will notice for a while. Until yesterday, it was working."

"I hope you make it work as long as possible. I haven't seen Cooper this happy since he left for the army."

"Mom." Zane elbowed Susie. "You're embarrassing him."

"Well, so what." Susie swatted in Cooper's general direction. "She should know."

Cooper refilled Anna's coffee and said, "She does."

Anna smiled at him. "I did know. But it's nice to hear from his mom. Thanks, Susie."

"Thank *you*." His mother beamed. "Nothing makes a mother happier than seeing her child happy."

Anna blushed and looked down at her plate. She appreciated the vote of confidence, but felt the pressure of not just Cooper's happiness but his mom's too. She wasn't supposed to be his happily ever after. She was just supposed to be a friend with benefits. That was not something she wanted to mention to his mom.

In the pause, she heard the sound of the front door opening, and footsteps coming into the house. Susie exclaimed, "Wyatt!" She got up and met her youngest son in the kitchen doorway with a hug. "Look at you! So handsome."

Anna glanced over at the young man, whom she'd last seen kneeling under a Ping-Pong table. Wyatt was ten years younger than Cooper, but he was obviously a Bolden, with the family's signature dark hair, tall height, and crooked smile. What separated Cooper and Wyatt now were wardrobe and attitude. Wyatt wore khakis, boat shoes, and a polo shirt that looked like a foreign costume in the farm kitchen. But the biggest difference was in their eyes. While Cooper's were clear and honest, Wyatt's were guarded and wary, shifting away from Anna's gaze to look anywhere else.

Wyatt shook her hand while looking at something over her shoulder. He slipped past her and took his seat at the table. "Hey, guys," he murmured as he piled his plate with cold eggs and bacon.

"You're late," his father said.

"Sorry." Wyatt took a bite of bacon.

"It's disrespectful to your mother."

"Oh, Craig, it's fine," Susie said. "Just be glad Wyatt comes home some Sundays at all. He's busy studying, pledging. How is that going, honey?"

Wyatt shrugged. "Okay."

"When does it end?"

"This is Hell Week. I shouldn't even be here. I'm supposed to be at the house. But everyone is even more hungover than I am, so I'm hoping they won't notice. At the end of Hell Week, they'll decide if I'm in."

"I'm so glad this will end soon. It's been hard on you."

Bryce and Zane stood and cleared their plates. "You wanna give us a hand with the bales when you finish?" Bryce asked Wyatt.

Wyatt shook his head and took a slice of French toast. "Not dressed for it."

"Okay, Princess." Zane gave his brother a cupped-hand Miss America wave.

Wyatt smiled. "Fuck off."

"Language!" said Susie.

After Wyatt was finished, Anna and Cooper helped clear the table. Then Cooper said, "Can I have a sec with you, Wyatt?"

Wyatt shrugged, which seemed to be his default gesture, and followed Cooper into a sunroom with a long view of snowy fields. Anna came in and closed the door. Wyatt leaned against a sideboard and waited.

Cooper said, "I need your help. Actually, Anna does. She's a prosecutor, and she's looking into the disappearance of Emily Shapiro. She thinks Beta Psi might be involved in some way. She's hoping you can show her around."

Wyatt nodded and glanced Anna's way. "I saw Anna last night.

She can talk to the leadership if she wants to stop by the house again."

"The leadership won't let me in," Anna said. "And I don't have enough evidence for a warrant. But if I were an invited guest, I could take a look around without one. Any member can invite me in."

Wyatt shook his head. "There's no way. I'm just a pledge. I can't do that."

"You have full authority under the law," Anna said.

"This has got nothing to do with the law," Wyatt said. "The brothers would not approve."

"You realize," Cooper said slowly, "they're not really your 'brothers.'"

"Not yet," Wyatt said. "But after Hell Week they will be."

"You just met them."

"They'll be on my side rest of my life. They'll be my business partners, my network, the guys who'll stand up for me at my wedding."

"You have three brothers. Me, Zane, and Bryce," Cooper said. "You need to rethink your priorities."

"I have," Wyatt said. "I don't want your life, tilling through biohazard in the middle of Detroit. I don't want Dad's life, toiling away in the dirt. I want out, and Beta Psi is the way."

"There's a missing girl," Cooper said, his voice rising. "You're going to have to live with what you do now for the rest of your life. Every morning you wake up. Every night you try to go to sleep."

"I'm not a bad guy. But I'm no superhero, either." Wyatt shrugged. "I didn't sign up to be the breaker of cases. I'm not willing to lose my leg for my country. Or for anything, frankly. There's a federal investigator on it." He pointed to Anna. "Let her do her job. I've got nothing to do with this. Don't try to make me the middleman."

"I'm asking you to be a human being."

Anna saw the fury in Cooper's eyes. She put her hand on his arm and spoke quietly to Wyatt.

"You don't need to be a hero," she said. "Maybe you could just slip me into the house and show me around for a few minutes? Quietly. What I'd like to see are the rooms below the Crypt. The Underground?"

"Ha." He laughed in her face. "You think you can just slip in without anyone noticing? There's like forty guys living there. Plus, there's no way you can get into the Underground."

"Why not?"

"I haven't even been there. Pledges aren't allowed."

"How come?"

"That's where all the secret stuff is, I guess."

"Do you know what kind of secret stuff?"

"It wouldn't be much of a secret then, would it?"

"Look, Wyatt," she said. "I don't want to hurt your chances with the house. I can see it means a lot to you. But a girl's life might be at stake. Is there any way you can take me around? I can come any time of day, whatever will work for you."

"No. Not happening. Sorry."

Cooper stepped forward. "When did you get to be so selfish?"

Anna gently pulled him back.

"Tell you what?" she said. "Maybe we can just talk. Here, off the record. I won't include your name in any paper I file with the court if I can help it, and usually I can help it. Just a little off-the-record information for me could make a big difference in getting a break in this case. You could help without risking your position at your frat."

Wyatt crossed his arms over his chest and looked at her for a long moment. Then he nodded. "What do you want to know?"

"Most important, did you see Emily Shapiro at the house two nights ago, the night she disappeared?"

"No. I was there for a party, in charge of the bar. I didn't see her."

"You're in charge of the bar? Aren't you, like, nineteen?"

"Yeah." He grinned. "It's kind of the fox in charge of the hen-house. I'm supposed to tag everyone's alcohol and give it to them one by one, at least that's what's in the national's alcohol policy. In reality, I'm just doing whatever the older brothers say. And they say fill 'er up."

"What about Dylan? Was he there?"

"I saw him early, leaving the house, maybe a little before midnight. I didn't see him after that."

She couldn't get a warrant based on that. To search the frat she needed to show that there was reason to believe evidence of a crime could be found there. According to Wyatt, Emily hadn't even been at the frat, much less hurt or abducted from it.

"What's Dylan like?" Anna asked.

"He's my pledge master. He's a good guy."

Anna saw discomfort flash on Wyatt's face and knew he was lying to her. After being a prosecutor for three years, she had a decent internal lie detector. Unfortunately, that didn't mean she could detect what the truth was.

"Do you know if anyone else saw Dylan that night?"

"No idea. I wasn't in charge of watching him."

"Have you heard anything about what happened to Emily?"

"Only what's on the news."

"I was told something about Beta Psi's reputation," Anna said carefully. "I don't want to insult you. But maybe you can help me understand. One student told me that it was called the 'rape factory.' Do you know what that's all about?"

Wyatt looked out the side window, at the acres of rolling farmland. He bit his lip, then turned back to her.

"That's bullshit. Some urban legend claims the brotherhood has the recipe for a roofie."

"A date-rape drug?"

"Yeah. I've never seen anything like that."

"Do you know any other girls who have accused Dylan of assaulting them?"

"You'll have to ask Dylan."

They spent another half an hour talking. Anna got more evasions, half-truths, and flat-out lies from Wyatt. Finally, she and Cooper said good-bye to Wyatt and his parents.

"Come back anytime, hon," said Susie, pulling her into a warm hug. Anna said she would.

Anna and Cooper walked outside to his motorbike. Cooper said, "I can't believe what a little turd my brother's turned out to be."

"He's young," Anna said. "He's a pledge during Hell Week. He doesn't want to invite in a prosecutor his pledge master kicked out; it's understandable. Besides, he actually told us some stuff. Just the confirmation that there's something under the Crypt is helpful. Believe me, people lie to me a lot more than Wyatt just did. Sometimes I feel like that's my primary job as a prosecutor: to be lied to all day."

"How do you deal with that?"

"You hope, in the middle of all those lies, to find a nugget of truth. That can make the difference."

They reached Cooper's Harley. He unfastened the helmets and handed one to her.

"I hope this made a difference. I wish I could help you more." He leaned down and kissed her lightly on the lips.

"This was helpful. Thanks for setting it up, Coop. Your family is great. Well, most of them anyway."

Law Offices of Kaiser, LeGrand & Dillon
1001 K Street, NW
Washington, DC 20001

October 15, 2014

Yolanda Skanadowski
Title IX Coordinator
Tower University
Tower, MI 48021

Re: *Shapiro v. Highsmith, Disciplinary Case No. 14-073*

Dear Ms. Skanadowski,

I have been retained to assist Dylan Highsmith in the above matter. I have reviewed the documents you sent him, including the summary of Emily Shapiro's charges and the proposed panel for the Disciplinary Committee. Mr. Highsmith is anxious to put forth his case at the hearing, and for an opportunity to clear up this entire matter. However, as his lawyer, I must insist on due process during this proceeding. I write to note several objections to the manner in which you are handling this case.

First, in your letter you note there will be evidence that Dylan has "sexually assaulted several women before Ms. Shapiro." I ask that this sentence, and all like it, be stricken from the record and never shown to the individuals who will make up the disciplinary panel. Such a statement is highly prejudicial. Moreover, it has never been corroborated. Your letter indicates that this charge is supposition from Ms. Shapiro. As such, it is pure hearsay and should not be admitted at the hearing. Your own University Handbook states that in disciplinary hearings, "Hearsay is not permitted; evidence must be given by the parties themselves." To be in accord with your own rules and regulations, you must exclude this evidence. Moreover, in order to protect my client's due process rights, he must be afforded the chance to confront any witnesses against him. If there is a witness to the charge that he sexually assaulted someone besides Ms.

Shapiro, please inform me within the next two weeks. If I do not hear from you, we will assume that no such evidence will be offered and will prepare our defense accordingly.

Second, we object to the proposed panel. In your memo, you note that the three panel members consist of: (1) a food service manager named Barbara Bini Martin, (2) an English professor named Darlene Marks Hicks, and (3) a student named ReBecca Lannoo-Christensen. We object to the last two proposed panel members.

Professor Hicks is a well-known critical feminist scholar who has published several articles about, in her words, "how the history of patriarchy in America has harmed women's economic opportunities." Her most recent article, published last year, was entitled "Want Equality? Don't Hire Men." Before that, she wrote an article for the Huffington Post, entitled "Why Man-Bashing Is Necessary." While Professor Hicks may be well qualified as a professor, she is obviously not a "fair and open-minded" person on the topic of gender relations and sexual assault, as required by your student handbook for any panelist who sits on a sexual-assault case. For this reason, we ask that Professor Hicks be taken off the panel and replaced with someone who does not have a history of "man-bashing."

For similar reasons, we ask that the student named ReBecca Lannoo-Christensen be removed from the panel. A quick look at Ms. Lannoo-Christensen's Facebook page reveals that she volunteered at a local rape-crisis center last year. As such, she is not a "fair and impartial" arbiter of a rape charge. We ask that she be removed from the panel and replaced with someone impartial.

Of course, while I am a stickler about procedure, I am committed to ensuring that the substance of this matter comes out as fully and robustly as possible. To that end, Mr. Highsmith will be submitting a statement of his own to the committee. I hope that we will be able to find an appropriate resolution to this matter.

Very truly yours,
Justin Dillon, Esq.

12

Cooper drove Anna from his family's farm to Tower University, where she had a nine A.M. appointment with the general counsel. They pulled up to the modern glass building that was the university's administrative headquarters. She took her helmet off, shook out her hair, and stared at the words over the entrance. Two-foot-tall letters proclaimed this to be HIGHSMITH HALL. She forced herself to breathe.

"Want me to come in with you?" Cooper asked.

"I do. But you can't."

"Got it. I'll pick you up later?"

"Thanks, but I have no idea when I'll be done." *And Jack might be there.* "Sam will drop me off whenever we finish up."

She handed him the helmet and kissed him lightly, then waved, trying to look nonchalant, as he drove off. But as she stood in front of Highsmith Hall, Anna had the disquieting feeling that she was up against something bigger than she'd anticipated. She squared her shoulders, walked inside, and took the elevator to the top floor.

Although it was a Sunday morning, a receptionist waited behind the wide desk that served the penthouse suite. The receptionist nodded when Anna said she had an appointment, telling her to sit in one of the leather chairs in the waiting area. Anna took a seat and looked around her. Big windows framed the beautiful campus. On the wall hung portraits of the university's past presidents. Although the medium had changed—going from oil paintings in the 1800s to black-and-white photos in the 1950s to color pictures in the modern era—the subjects all had something in common. They were all white men. The last was Emily's father.

Twenty minutes after their meeting was scheduled, the GC emerged from his office. "So sorry to keep you waiting." He greeted her with the requisite firm handshake. "I'm Bryan Frink. Come on in."

Anna followed the general counsel into his office. If Pottery Barn ever wanted to start an Ivy League Academic collection, they could copy Frink's place. It had the Persian rug, walls of books, antique desk, and deep leather couch. The room smelled of lemon furniture polish and exclusivity. Anna sat in the guest chair and he sat behind his desk. His chair was higher than hers, she noticed, forcing her to look up at him. She decided the twenty-minute wait had been deliberate. This guy was full of cheap parlor tricks to try to establish his dominance.

That actually made her feel more confident. He was worried—as he should be. The general counsel was the university's top lawyer, responsible for handling most day-to-day legal questions for the organization. Frink led an office of a dozen other lawyers. They might handle issues as diverse as employment discrimination lawsuits brought by janitors, slip-and-fall lawsuits brought by visitors, or the collection of student debt. In most of those cases, the university would have more power and resources than anyone else. Against the federal government, however, the university was equally matched. Hence Frink wanted the higher chair.

"So how long have you been an Assistant U.S. Attorney?" he asked.

"Four years," Anna said.

"You look awfully young."

Anna suppressed an eye roll. She supposed there was a chance older men meant it as a compliment when they told her how young she looked. "As you know, I'm investigating the disappearance and possible abduction of Emily Shapiro. I have a subpoena with three requests. One is for all campus records involving the disciplinary case that Ms. Shapiro brought against Dylan Highsmith. One is for the paperwork from any other campus disciplinary cases against Dylan Highsmith. The final one is for Dylan's campus disciplinary record, generally."

She slid the papers across the desk. Frink did not reach for them. He templed his fingers and smiled as if she'd just said something cute.

"Surely, you don't expect us to turn over confidential university records."

"They're not protected from a criminal investigation, Mr. Frink.

Those are grand jury subpoenas. Court orders. You've been ordered to come to the grand jury yourself and bring those papers. But to save you the inconvenience of having to come and testify, you may simply give the papers to me and I will deliver them to the grand jury." This was standard practice for grand jury document production. "Preferably today. The sooner we have the records, the sooner we can use them to help figure out what happened to Emily Shapiro. Which I'm sure you'd like to know too."

"I can see that you're very passionate about this, Ms. Curtis. Good for you. It's wonderful to find work that you care about, isn't it? But this is a simple matter. I'll explain it as concisely as possible so I don't waste any more of your time. Tower University is not turning any of those documents over to you. They are our confidential records, protected by the Family Educational Rights and Privacy Act. You have no indication that Dylan Highsmith was involved in Ms. Shapiro's disappearance or even that foul play was involved. And so your subpoena is improper, and we have no obligation to honor it."

"The grand jury's powers are broad. It may subpoena *anything* it thinks may be useful for a criminal investigation. We certainly think Dylan's records will be useful."

"And we respectfully disagree."

"If you do not appear in the grand jury on Monday—that is, tomorrow—you'll be in contempt of court."

"On Monday, I will be moving to quash this subpoena."

Anna cocked her head. "There's a girl missing. She's a student of yours—not only that, she's the daughter of your president. I'd think you'd do anything in your power to help us find her."

"We don't believe this will help find her. She hasn't even been missing for two days. She's probably just sleeping off a hangover at a friend's house. And you should know that President Shapiro has been recused from this matter because of his personal interest in the case. I have been charged with determining what's best for the university."

"I have to warn you, sir. If you decide to go this route, I will ask the court to hold you and the university in contempt for failure to comply with a grand jury investigation. There can be civil fines and even possible jail time."

He couldn't suppress a shift of discomfort as he said, "I doubt that." Anna looked at him for a long moment, trying to figure out his angle. As a matter of law, she was in the right. As a matter of public relations, he should cooperate. And yet something outweighed all that.

"Your legal analysis is missing something," said a deep familiar voice behind Anna. She twisted in her chair—and saw Jack walking into the office, as coolly and authoritatively as if he were the one who had called the meeting, rather than crashing it. He sat next to Anna, nodded at her, and turned to the GC. "You seem to have forgotten the Clery Act."

"Hello, Jack. Nice to see you," said Frink, although he did not seem happy to see Jack at all. "I didn't realize you were leading this investigation."

"I'm not. But Ms. Curtis's subject matter and my task force share a lot of ground, as you know."

"These issues aren't related at all." Frink's voice was softer, Anna noticed, and he looked away now as he spoke. He was far more cowed by Jack than by Anna, although they shared the same power under the law.

"What an interesting perspective," Jack said. "I'm not sure anyone else would agree. A missing woman was last seen being followed by a man against whom she brought rape charges. Charges that were, incidentally, not reported to the Department of Education as required by federal law under the Clery Act. Seems like it could be a big hot mess for your organization, Bryan."

Even in the lower seat, Jack's eyes were level with the GC's. Jack pulled a paper from his briefcase and pretended to study it. "According to my records, your university reported to the Department of Education that zero rape charges were filed on campus last year. Or the year before that. Or the year before that. In fact, going back two decades, Tower University has a perfect record for zero rapes on campus. Incredible statistics."

Frink pushed a pencil around his desk.

"I mean 'incredible' in the literal sense of the word," Jack continued. "They are not credible. They are outright lies. We know of at least one rape that was reported to you and which was not then reported to us—the one involving Emily Shapiro. And we all know the one-in-five statistic. I'm adding Tower University to a list of colleges being investigated by the Department of Justice. I'll also be investigating whether anyone in the university or general counsel's office made a false statement, which as you know, is a felony."

Frink picked at the pencil's eraser.

"That's not negotiable," Jack said. "But what's still in your control is how this spins out. I could announce it today. Bad timing for you, press-wise, not that that's any of my concern. Or I could hold off for a few weeks, concentrate on other facets of our investigation. I could also ask the Department of Education to levy fines instead of imposing jail time. Cooperation has its benefits. But you have to decide to cooperate. Today. This is when it counts. Now."

Frink tore the entire eraser off. He looked at the pencil in one hand and the pink eraser in the other. He set them down and cleared his throat. "This is blackmail."

"Not at all," Jack said calmly. "A prosecutor has quite a bit of discretion in deciding how to proceed with a case. A cooperative university gets a lot more leniency than a reticent one. And you know what they say. The cover-up is always so much worse than the crime."

"I'll have to check with some of my colleagues, then get back to you," Frink said. He stood and gestured toward the door, indicating the meeting was over.

"Take your time," Jack said. He didn't move from his chair. "I'll wait right here."

Frink stared at him. Jack smiled back. Finally, Frink nodded and walked out of his office.

Anna turned and looked at Jack. Only a twitch at the corner of his lips revealed that he enjoyed bullying the GC into doing the right thing. Anna was torn between admiration at his effectiveness and annoyance at his taking over her meeting.

"Why are you here?" she whispered.

"You told me you had this meeting scheduled."

"I didn't ask you to come."

"I thought you might want some backup."

"If I wanted 'backup,' I would've asked for it."

"Come on, Anna. He wasn't taking you seriously. Now he is."

"No one's going to take me seriously if my boss barges into my meetings. I was about to get to the Clery Act."

"Do you want a gold star for independence or do you want to find Emily Shapiro?"

She closed her mouth, because arguing with Jack wouldn't help their cause. But she was annoyed. Back when they first started working together, she appreciated his leadership. But she had become a much more seasoned lawyer since then. Their relationship hadn't changed, although she had.

Soon, Frink came back into the room. He handed a file full of papers to Jack.

"This is all the paperwork from the disciplinary file in the *Emily Shapiro versus Dylan Highsmith* matter. Unfortunately, I can't give you the rest of Dylan's files at this time. I'd like to be able to turn them over. But we could get in trouble for violating confidentiality. Dylan has lawyers too, you know—even more threatening than you are. Watch out for them. I'm cooperating as much as I can with you, but I still have to move to quash your subpoena tomorrow. We'll argue about it in court. That way, if the judge does order us to turn the documents over to you, the university will have legal cover. If you're right, it'll just be one day's delay."

His tone was a thousand times more conciliatory than when he was talking to Anna. Then, he'd been a man in charge, condescending to a young whippersnapper. Now, he was a supplicant doing his best to please someone who could destroy him. Even as Jack handed the files to her, Anna felt a little bit smaller in her seat. She shook it off, consciously straightening her spine. She had what she'd come here for. At least part of it.

"Let's call the court now," Anna said. "I'd like to ask the judge to hear us this afternoon."

"I'll need more time to research the legal issue than that," Frink said.

"Sounds like you've done all the research you needed before you came in today," Jack said.

Frink sighed, then nodded his agreement. Anna called the duty magistrate she'd seen the night before. The judge agreed to hold an emergency hearing that afternoon at four P.M. in his chambers. "File any papers you wish for me to consider by two P.M.," Judge Schwalbe said. "It's Sunday, so it might be difficult to find the court personnel. But this is urgent, and I'll make sure we're ready to hear this today."

They bid Frink good-bye and headed out to get their briefs started. Things were finally going their way. As she and Jack walked out of Highsmith Hall, Anna clutched the file and, despite herself, grinned at Jack. He smiled back in that old way, the way that said they were a team, unstoppable. Her stomach dipped at the sight of that smile.

To: Tower University Disciplinary Committee
From: Dylan Highsmith, Class of 2015
Date: November 2, 2014
Re: Campus Disciplinary Case No. 14-073

I'm writing in response to the summons sent to me by the Disciplinary Committee. I have to say that I was shocked to get it. My mother taught me right from wrong, and I would never—let me repeat, never—treat a woman the way Emily Shapiro claims I treated her. With all due respect to Ms. Shapiro, I don't know why she would say what she said. I've spent the last week trying to figure it out, and all I can come up with is that she must have been very intoxicated and confused. I am sorry that she feels badly; it hurts me to think that she felt hurt as a result of our time together.

But I'm getting ahead of myself. I guess first I should tell you a little about myself. I'm a senior, the class of '15, majoring in business and economics. I'm twenty-one years old. I have a 3.6 GPA. I am copresident of the Greek Council and pledge leader of my fraternity, Beta Psi.

I grew up in Grosse Pointe and was lucky to have the support of wonderful parents. My father led by his example of how to work hard and strive for your goals. My mother was the president of my school's PTA. Her example as a mom is one I respect so much, and it has instilled me with a respect for all women.

I respected Emily Shapiro when I met her on September 1. She came to my fraternity house for our annual Welcome Back to School fraternity party. As you may know, this party is a campus tradition dating back to 1922. The party is open to the public, on a first-come-first-serve basis. I did not invite her there but was happy to meet her at around eleven P.M. in the lower-level basement party room. She was there with a group of freshmen from her dorm. She was smiling and friendly. We started a conversation about how she liked her first week of college life. What I remember most about her was that she had a big smile and she laughed a lot. She might have been tipsy, but she certainly was flirting with me.

Someone was serving an alcoholic red fruit punch, and Emily kept getting more of it. I regret that I did not take steps to stop her from drinking. I did not, however, encourage her to get refills.

I was drinking whiskey and Coke. When I met Emily, I had probably had about three drinks. As the night continued, I continued to drink and became very intoxicated.

One of my frat brothers was acting as DJ, and an impromptu dance floor formed around him. Emily and I danced for a while. It was house dance music, not slow songs, but she danced close to me anyway and kept putting her hands on me. I did the same to her. Our interaction was friendly, close, and increasingly romantic.

At some point, we went back to the living room, and Emily found someone who gave her another glass of punch. I think this was her fourth cup. I had my sixth or seventh Coke and whiskey of the night. We were both laughing, slurring our words a bit, and both tipsy, but not to the extent that either of us were unable to give knowing consent. Drunk as we both were, I'm sure that she was more sober than I was.

We talked for a while more, and I mentioned that I have a big fish tank with sharks in my bedroom. She asked if we could go see it.

We went upstairs to my room, a single bedroom on the second floor. It has a bed, a desk, a dresser, and a three-hundred-gallon fish tank with six miniature sharks. I've always loved sea life. I showed Emily the tank and told her how I got into it. My dad taught me to scuba dive when I was thirteen. We didn't have much in common before he taught me how to dive, and we really bonded with diving. Some of my best memories are being underwater. Emily said that was really sweet. She put her cup of punch down on my desk and kissed me. I kissed her back. Things got more physical, quickly.

Let me take a break and tell you: I am not normally the type to kiss and tell. I've been raised to be a gentleman, and I'm intensely uncomfortable going into the details of what happened between Emily and me that night. But I understand that, in this situation, I have to tell you what really happened. So forgive me if I get into details that seem inappropriate. In normal circumstances, this would be private information.

She pulled off my shirt, and then her own. She brought my hand to her breast and I caressed it. I unclasped her bra, and she pulled off her own pants. We engaged in some heavy petting, and then she pulled my pants and underwear down. After that, she got up from the bed and searched around the room until she found where her pants had dropped. She got a condom out of the pocket of her jeans. The fact that she had brought protection, and went to find it, reinforced my understanding that she was a willing participant.

She pushed me back on the bed, so I was lying on my back. She put the condom on me, then straddled me and put me inside of her. She rode me vigorously. She grabbed on to the headboard in order to move herself even more energetically on me. Throughout the encounter, she gave verbal indications that she was enjoying herself. She said, "Oh, Dylan, you feel so good," and "I love what you're doing to my clit, keep doing it," and "Your dick is amazing."

Again, I apologize for relating these details here. In any other circumstance, I would not reveal such intimate moments.

Emily never said "no," or "stop," or "I don't want to do this," or anything indicating she didn't want to do what we were doing. After we were finished, we went to sleep in my bed. I thought we had had a good time together. Everything we did was consensual; moreover, Emily initiated each step in our sexual relations and expressed throughout that she was enjoying herself.

I woke to the sound of laughing. It was morning, and the room was light. Several of my frat brothers were looking in my door. One of them, Alan Lee, took a picture of me and Emily together and said he was sending it on Snapchat. That's when Emily woke up. When she heard what Alan said, she freaked out. She yelled at him not to do it, and as far as I know, he didn't. Then she got dressed, really quickly, and left. I was so tired, still probably a little drunk, and starting to feel the beginnings of a hangover, so I didn't chase after her. I went back to sleep.

I didn't call or text her later that day either. I thought we had just had a good time together—one fun night—not that this was the beginning of a long-term relationship. Over the next few days, she texted me two or three times. I was in a busy period of my life and didn't get around to texting back, although I meant to. I heard later that she was interested in dating me, and when I didn't text back, she was upset.

I believe her anger over my failure to call or text was a big part of her decision to report our night as a sexual assault. Several mutual friends have suggested that this is a case of "a woman scorned."

Again, I'd like to offer my sympathy to Emily. Looking back, I shouldn't have allowed her to drink so much. I should have called her the next day, just to make sure she was doing okay, even if I wasn't going to pursue a long-term relationship. I'm sorry for these things. But I want to make this clear. I did not sexually assault Emily Shapiro.

I'll be happy to answer any questions that Emily or the Disciplinary Committee have at the hearing, and hope to be able to clear this matter up to everyone's satisfaction.

13

Anna read Dylan's statement with skepticism. She knew the words weren't his, not really. Several lawyers had pored over Dylan's official statement before it was sent over to the university's Disciplinary Committee. The attorneys would have listened to Dylan's story, then written the brief themselves, and charged a small fortune for the work. Dylan might have changed a word or two, then signed his name.

And these were good lawyers—she was familiar with the law firm whose letterhead was at the top of the documents making Dylan's case. Kaiser, LeGrand & Dillon was a prestigious D.C. white-collar boutique founded by a former prosecutor and a couple BigLaw veterans. They were acclaimed for their federal criminal defense, but they also had a niche representing men accused of sexual assaults on college campuses and were regarded as one of the best firms in the country on that topic.

Anna looked at the carefully crafted statement, each word painstakingly chosen for maximum effect. Emily Shapiro, going in by herself, had been up against a Goliath and probably hadn't even realized it.

Anna's phone rang, pulling her attention from the file and back into the world of the command center. Dozens of agents bustled about, each engaged in some aspect of trying to find Emily Shapiro. Sam was on the other side of the room, poring over a map with a Tower University officer, discussing which alleyways had been searched and where to dispatch K-9 units. Anna pulled her phone out of her purse. Jody was calling. She considered letting it go to voice mail; she wanted to keep working. But her sister was home alone with a baby—Anna needed to make sure she was all right.

"Hey, Jo," Anna answered. "Everything okay?"

"Yeah, I'm—actually—Grady's coming over again tonight. I'm

calling to see if . . . would you mind if I borrowed your white silk shirt?"

Anna almost laughed, but stopped herself. Jody was slow to warm to men, including Grady. Especially Grady. The fact that he was the father of her child sometimes seemed like something she held against him. His paternity held a power over her—the power to influence and possibly even take her baby. A little romance between the parents might be a good thing. Or it could be disastrous. In any case, Anna was happy to let her use the shirt.

"Sure," Anna said. "There's a silver belt that looks really cute with it too."

"Cool, thanks. Sorry to bother you. Everything okay there?"

"Okay. Not great."

"You find the girl?"

"I'm sure you'll hear about it on the news when we do. Listen, I'm heading to court with Jack in a few minutes, and I—"

"Wait—" Jody interrupted. "Jack?"

"Um."

"Jack *Bailey*?"

"Yeah."

"Annie!" Jody practically shouted in her ear. "You're working with Jack again? That is the worst idea ever."

Anna held the phone away from her face and glanced around the command center. No one else seemed to have noticed the explosion from her phone. Anna brought it back to her ear, covered her mouth with her hand, and spoke softly. She hoped anyone watching would just think she was trying to muffle the sounds of the room.

"I had to take this case, Jo," she said. "There's a missing girl. A college freshman. We've got search dogs sniffing to find her—or her body. She could be Olivia one day. She could be Leigh. Wouldn't you want someone who's good at what they do? Someone who cares?"

"Come on, Annie. There are like a thousand federal prosecutors. Why do you have to be the one to do this?"

"Because I was the one who was asked."

"Jack did the asking, I assume?"

"Well, yeah."

"What a coincidence."

"I happen to be a sex-crimes prosecutor. One of the few federal sex-crimes prosecutors in the country. And I have ties to Michigan without having ties to the kids' families. So I'm the right choice for this."

"Of course you are. Jack's too smart to do anything that couldn't be defended. I'm not talking about your legal qualifications. I'm talking about your heart. This puts you back a year. You were just getting over him."

"I know." Anna sighed. *Maybe*—the thought crept unbidden into her head—*I don't need to get over him. Maybe we can have that happily ever after we were planning a year ago.* "Look, I'm not asking for your dating advice. Wise as it is. I just need to find this girl. Hopefully before it's too late."

"Okay, sis." Jody's voice softened. "Are you holding up?"

"Yeah. No. I could use some sleep. But I'm not really going to be able to sleep till we find her. I'm going to be out late again tonight probably. So don't stay up or worry."

Anna glanced down at her watch. She had to be in court in forty minutes.

"Do you think the Highsmith kid hurt her?" Jody asked.

"Too soon to tell. I want to search his frat house, but I don't have enough evidence yet. There's a lot of power on his side. It's hard to get cooperation here."

"I know what that feels like." Jody had had her own harrowing fight against a powerful group of men. In her case, it was a local football team. So many of the cases Anna handled were sparked by the evil men did when they were in groups. Sports teams, street gangs, fraternities, Congress. There was something about powerful males hanging in packs that brought out the worst in them.

In Jody's case, she had fought back, hard, using her own rules. That was her personality. Anna was more likely to change the system from within, Jody from the outside. Either way, Jody understood why Anna had to fight.

"In fact, I was thinking about what I could do to help," Jody said.

"There's nothing you can do to help."

"Come on. Surely you could use a beautiful young woman to go to the fraternity and get the inside scoop."

"Absolutely not."

"I really want to help, Annie. Tell me what I can do."

"If I tell you to do something, you're considered a government agent—and you'll be breaking a hundred rules you don't even know about. You want to help? Pick up some coffee. We're out." Anna could hear Leigh's little muffled coos, and the sound of Jody kissing her sweet cheeks. She felt a lump in her throat. "And take good care of that baby."

"I do that anyway."

"I know. I wish I could kiss her right now. I keep thinking about her, Jo. How do parents cope with having their kids out there, when anything can happen to them?"

"They say having a baby is like having your heart outside your chest, walking around in the world."

Jack strode into the command center. He nodded at Anna, then walked over to Sam and conferred with her about the map.

"I've got to go," Anna said. "Kiss that baby for me."

"While you're out there, make sure you protect yourself too. You know I'm on your side no matter what. I just can't stand the thought of you getting hurt again. For what it's worth: I vote for Cooper."

"You just want me to stay in Michigan so you have a babysitter for Leigh."

"Well, yeah, of course."

Anna was smiling as she hung up. As she put her phone away, Sam dropped a police lab report in front of her. It was the preliminary report from Dylan's car.

"You're gonna want to read this," Sam said.

14

The report confirmed Anna's fears. The red-brown smudge on Dylan's car was human blood.

"Do we know whose blood?" she asked.

"Not yet," Sam said. "They just completed the serology. Still waiting on the DNA."

"Were there other biological materials on the car?"

"Yeah. A small patch of blood inside, on the driver's-side floor, and a patch of semen on the front passenger seat. Nothing in the trunk."

"How fast can the lab do the DNA?"

"Two to three days if I push them."

"Push," Anna said. There was always a long wait to get DNA testing done, even if a "rush" was requested. Having someone like Sam advocating made a big difference. "We can use Emily's hairbrush to get a DNA sample from her. Dylan will be harder—he's not cooperating, so we won't have a sample from him."

"But he's not so important at this point. If it's his blood, you might expect that in his own car. If it's Emily's, it's a different story. And then we'll be able to get a warrant to swab Dylan."

"Yep. For now, let's go get his disciplinary papers. The judge arranged a special hearing for us."

■ ■ ■

The Theodore Levin U.S. Courthouse for the Eastern District of Michigan was a massive concrete structure sitting on a full block of Lafayette Boulevard in downtown Detroit. Although the courthouse itself was in pretty good shape, the streets around it were simple urban blight. Next door stood the old Free Press Building, a historic twelve-story gothic structure that was abandoned. The paint on the lamp posts was filthy and peeling. Anna knew that only one in ten of Detroit's streetlights actually worked.

Despite the location, the federal court was an incredibly prestigious place to work—especially for judges. They said being appointed a federal judge was like going to heaven without having to die first. Federal judges had life tenure, a six-figure salary, and their pick of the best law students vying to be their law clerks. Magistrate judges were a step below in terms of rank—their term was eight years, not life, and their rulings could be immediately overruled by a district judge. Still, many magistrates had big egos. But Judge Schwalbe didn't seem to suffer from black-robe syndrome. He welcomed Anna and Jack warmly at the door to the courthouse, unlocking it from the inside to let them in. Since it was Sunday, the courthouse was closed. He waved them through the unmanned security post.

"I assume I'm safe from a couple of AUSAs?"

They laughed and walked in.

Only a few lights illuminated the courthouse. The wide marble hallways were so quiet and empty, they reminded Anna of the city of Detroit itself. But the courtroom was plush, warm, and brightly lit. The university's lawyer, Bryan Frink, already sat at a table and nodded as they walked in. A court reporter had her stenographic machine set up in front of the judge's bench, and a young woman who Anna guessed was his law clerk sat at the deputy's table. Judge Schwalbe stepped into a small robing chamber, where he slipped into his robe. It was always amazing to see the transformation that a black robe could effect on a person. One minute, he was just a regular guy with a nice smile and an impressive head of hair. The next he was a ruler.

Anna sat next to Jack at the other counsel table. Again, she had the feeling of traveling back in time, to a place where they were a united team. They'd co-chaired several cases. He was always lead counsel; she was always second chair. It made sense since he was ten years older and far more experienced. Even now, although she had called this hearing and would be the one speaking, he was clearly in charge.

The judge took the bench, and Anna focused on the task at hand.

The clerk said, "Now calling the case of *In re: Grand Jury Original Number 2015-US-1324*."

The lawyers stood.

"Bryan Frink on behalf of Tower University."

"Anna Curtis for the United States."

She felt a shot of pride every time she identified herself in court. She represented the entire country; her job was to fight for the interests of everyone. Her goal wasn't just to win—it was to do justice. To figure out the truth and then to do the right thing. Sometimes figuring out the right thing was the hardest part—but it was always the goal. Few lawyers had such a luxury.

"Please be seated," the judge said. "We're here today to hear the emergency motion by Tower University to quash the subpoena issued by the government to obtain documents from the university. Because this hearing deals with grand jury materials, the transcript will be sealed while the investigation is ongoing. It may be released to the public at a later time, depending on the outcome of the case. I want to thank my law clerk, Rachael Findlay, and the court reporter, Joan Koenig, for coming in on a Sunday afternoon for this important matter."

The ladies smiled up at him.

"Let's start with the government. Ms. Curtis?"

"Thank you, Your Honor." Anna stood. "Our case is very straightforward. We're investigating the disappearance of Emily Shapiro. In doing so, we have learned that Ms. Shapiro brought charges against another student, Dylan Highsmith . . ." She laid out the facts they'd uncovered so far. "As part of our investigation we've subpoenaed Tower University to obtain all paperwork related to Mr. Highsmith. Per DOJ policy, I've gotten permission to issue a forthwith subpoena, to get the documents now. Every hour of delay could be costing this girl her life. It is well within the grand jury's jurisdiction to ask for such documents. We are glad the university agreed to turn over the first set of documents, those involving both Ms. Shapiro and Mr. Highsmith. But we are frankly surprised that it's being so recalcitrant in turning over the rest of the papers, those involving Mr. Highsmith and other women. We need them, as soon as possible, in order to allow this investigation to go forward."

Judge Schwalbe said, "Is Dylan Highsmith a suspect in Emily Shapiro's disappearance?"

Anna hesitated. Saying yes would start a war. Not immediately— this was a closed hearing. But if news of the hearing leaked, the press would be all over it. Dylan would be named, publicly, as a suspect, and his Google results would forever reflect that. Every employer who ever looked him up, every girl who ever went on a first date with him would see that he had been suspected of kidnapping a young woman. Just by naming him, Anna would change the course of his life forever.

It would also get his lawyers riled up. Once he was named as a suspect, the best legal team money could buy would try to block the investigation in any way they could. It would also affect his father's political career. Could the lieutenant governor ever be elected to state office again, if his son were a suspect in a kidnapping case?

And yet, he was.

"Yes, sir," Anna said. "Mr. Highsmith is a suspect."

The judge looked sternly over his reading glasses. "Mr. Frink, you've moved to quash the government's subpoenas. What is your basis for this?"

Frink stood and straightened his tie. "Your Honor, these are confidential documents. Per university policy and under the Family Educational Rights and Privacy Act—"

The judge waved his hand. "Of course. But all kinds of confidential documents may be subpoenaed. Your confidentiality doesn't trump a grand jury subpoena."

"Well, Your Honor, we wanted to be sure we were crossing all our *t*'s and dotting our *i*'s before we just willy-nilly turned over such sensitive documents. As you know, we agreed to this expedited hearing—"

"You agreed to cover yourself." The judge pulled off his glasses and waved them at the GC. "And you know it. I have to tell you, Mr. Frink, I'm extremely disappointed at the university's handling of this case so far. My God, there's a missing girl! You're lucky that the prosecutors didn't ask me to hold you in contempt. In the future, I expect you to be fully cooperative with the government's investigation. If this matter comes before me again, I warn you, I will not be as lenient as I am today."

Anna kept her face neutral, although inside she sent up a cheer.

"Yes, sir," Frink said.

The judge said, "I'm ordering Tower University to turn over all the documents listed in the subpoena."

"It might take us some time to collect all the documents and make sure they're properly—"

"Today," the judge said. "Do whatever you have to do to make it happen. I'll give you three hours. If the government doesn't have its documents by eight P.M., I'll start levying fines. A thousand dollars per minute. Now your rear is covered."

Anna swallowed back a lump in her throat. So often in her job, she saw people at their worst. Hiding things. Lying. Cynically taking whatever path offered them the most advantages, then justifying that path as the right one. She'd recently had a case where the judge was not only biased but corrupt. This judge had no agenda. It made her choke up to see someone so squarely on the side of justice, just doing something for the right of it.

There was a hitch in her voice as she said, "Thank you, Your Honor."

She couldn't wait to see what was in those papers.

15

Jody carefully painted the lavender nail polish on her pinky finger. "Amazing." She held her left hand up and studied her manicure. "It looks like a simple coat of nail polish. But it can detect date-rape drugs."

Grady held Leigh and walked the infant around the living room. He was a natural with the baby—but Jody still wasn't sure she liked the sight of her tiny daughter in the man's tattooed arms. Just because Grady fathered the baby didn't mean he was trustworthy. She hardly knew him. But Cooper would be here too.

Jody had just fed, diapered, and burped Leigh and expected the infant would sleep for the next five or six hours. The men should be able to hold down the fort for that long. It gave her just enough time to do what she planned.

"How does the nail polish work?" Grady asked.

"No idea," Jody answered. "But the package says it turns dark purple if you stick it in a drink that has a date-rape drug in it."

"What if the kid doesn't talk to you?"

"Come on. Who's not gonna talk to this?" Jody twirled in a circle. Normally a ponytail kind of woman, she'd blown out her long blond hair. She'd squeezed herself triumphantly into her prebaby jeans. She wore high-heeled boots and a low-cut black shirt, which revealed the porn-star cleavage that was one of her favorite parts about breast-feeding.

"You look gorgeous. I'd rather you stay home and talk to me." Grady walked over and kissed Jody. The baby cooed, and Jody looked down.

"She smiled!" Jody said. "That was her first smile! Did you see it?"

"It was incredible. Let's see if we can get her to do it again." Grady kissed Jody once more, letting his lips linger this time.

Jody had to force herself to pull away. "If you don't stop, I'm not gonna get out of here."

"How about you don't?" Grady said softly. "Stay in with me."

"I have to do this."

"It's dangerous. I don't like it."

She stepped away from him. "It doesn't matter what you like. You don't get to tell me what to do. Do you want to babysit Leigh or not?"

He sighed. "Yes. I want to spend as much time with her—and you—as I can."

She glared at him. He'd been trying to get closer to her since he found out he was the baby's father. But his paternity made her uncomfortable. As the father, he had rights. What if he tried to get custody? What if he hurt Leigh, the way Jody's father had hurt her?

Cooper walked in from the kitchen. "Go easy on the poor guy, Jody. I do believe he means well."

"Sorry." Jody took a deep breath. She knew she wasn't fair to Grady. But she desperately needed to protect her daughter from having the childhood she and Anna had.

Cooper handed her a granola bar and a bottle of water. "Are you sure you don't want to tell Anna what you're doing?"

"Nope. If she knows, I'd be considered a government agent. But if I go on my own, I'm just a civilian—and I can do pretty much anything. Then she can use it afterward, untainted."

"Are you sure she *wants* you to do this?"

"I'm sure she *doesn't*. Which is exactly how it has to be."

Jody had a deep need to help her sister. Last year, Anna had come home and saved her after Jody was charged in a homicide case. Without her, Jody might have had her baby in jail, and almost certainly would be behind bars tonight and for years to come. She'd given Anna a hard time, but Anna had stuck by her.

Jody admired what Anna was fighting for tonight. Jody herself had been sexually assaulted as a teenager—and the people in charge hadn't helped her. She believed in taking matters into her own hands when the system failed. That's what she was going to do tonight.

"At least keep your cell phone on," Grady said, "so we can track where you are."

"Yeah," Cooper said. "Grady and I want a text from you every fifteen minutes. If we don't hear from you, we're coming."

"Okay." Jody appreciated that Cooper didn't try to stop her. "I hope Leigh behaves for you guys."

"Oh, she's great," Grady said. He kissed the baby's head. "Even when she's crying. She's the best."

Jody cocked her head. "You know, you do look pretty good holding Leigh."

Grady's smile was the biggest she'd ever seen on his face. Cooper reached over and stroked Leigh's cheek.

Jody said, "We'll have to get you one of your own, Coop."

A shadow crossed Cooper's face before he smiled. "I'll work on that."

Jody left knowing her daughter was in good hands.

■ ■ ■

Half an hour later, Jody parked by the Beta Psi fraternity house. The sky was dark, but the building glowed with strategically placed exterior lights. She swallowed back a wave of nervousness, walked up the steps, and knocked on the door.

A kid in a Beta Psi T-shirt opened it. "Yes?"

He looked so young to her. She was twenty-six, and he couldn't be more than eight years younger, but he seemed like a baby. Jody thought of college kids as being the same age as her. But, she realized, she'd passed them by. Seeing this baby boy made her pause, for just a moment, and think about where she'd be right now if she'd gone to college instead of straight to work on the GM assembly line. Some office job? Law school, like Anna? Would she even be in Michigan? But now wasn't the time for self-reflection. Now, she just had to hope this boy didn't think she looked as old as she felt.

"Hi," she said, smiling and cocking her hip to the side, in a way that said the world belonged to her. "I'm here to see Peter."

That was the thing about kids these days. They put everything up online. It was ridiculous. In less than ten minutes on a computer, Jody had discovered all she needed to know about Dylan Highsmith and his closest circle of friends. She knew Peter York was one of his best buddies. And Peter was out of town the next few days.

The boy opened the door and gestured toward the back of the house. "Check the living room."

Jody thanked him and walked toward what she hoped was the living room. She recognized Dylan immediately. She'd gotten to know his handsome face online. He was sprawled on a couch, watching TV while scrolling through his cell phone. A bunch of boys, and a few girls, sat around him. Everyone held either a beer or a cell phone. She was kind of disappointed. She thought of college as this amazing world, a universe apart, where you went to become a better person. But this could be any living room of any autoworker in Flint, except autoworkers kept their living rooms a lot cleaner than this.

Dylan looked up from his phone and let his gaze travel up and down her body. Jody met his eyes, liking the interest she saw there. He wanted her, and she could use that.

"Help you?" Dylan straightened a fraction on the couch, the frat equivalent of standing when a woman walked in the room.

"Yeah, hi. I'm looking for Peter," Jody said in her best helpless-little-girl voice.

"I'm sorry," Dylan said. He actually got up from the couch, stepping over a couple guys. "He's not here tonight. He went to visit his parents in Chicago."

"Oh no! I'm Jody. We're supposed to study together tonight. Guess he stood me up."

"I'm sure he'll be sorry to hear that he missed you." Dylan put an arm casually around her shoulders. "It must've slipped his mind. He had to leave town unexpectedly; his mom needed surgery. I'm sure he'd want me to offer you some hospitality. Come on over, have a seat."

He shooed some kids to make room for Jody on the couch. She sat next to him.

"Pledge!" Dylan addressed the kid who'd let her in. "Get this lovely lady a beer."

Jody watched the young man go to the mahogany bar in the corner. He opened a bottle of Bud Light; the top came off with a hiss. He brought the bottle to her. Since she'd seen it being opened, she wasn't worried about it being drugged. She took a sip. It tasted fine.

"So you're Peter's friend?" she asked innocently.

Dylan shifted so his thigh was brushing hers. "Guilty as charged."

She sat watching TV with him, occasionally talking, making light jokey comments. Dylan kept sending the pledge to get more beer. The pledge kept bringing her fresh bottles, which she carefully watched him open. Soon Jody felt herself getting drunk—but just the familiar intoxication of alcohol. After two episodes and five beers, she knew she would have to pump and dump her milk when she got home; no way could she feed Leigh with the blood alcohol content she was acquiring.

Just thinking about her baby made her breasts tingle. She looked down and saw that she had leaked milk right through her bra and onto her blouse.

He probably wouldn't notice the wetness on her shirt, she told herself. The only light in the room was from the TV. Plus, Dylan was a college kid. Even if he saw the wet spot he wouldn't assume it was from a leaky mama's boob. Just in case, she deliberately let her beer bottle tip, and some of it spattered down.

"Oops." She giggled.

Dylan smiled and put his hand on her thigh. Finally. She met his eyes and took his hand off her leg. "I just met you," she said.

He smiled and removed his hand, the picture of gentlemanly restraint. But one commercial break later, his hand was back on her leg. Her breasts ached and throbbed. She felt more milk leaking out onto her shirt. If Dylan didn't make a move soon, she was going to explode, or at least get mastitis.

"Oh my God, I'm so drunk" she said. "I should go."

"No, this is the best part," Dylan said, pointing to the TV. "You have to see this."

Her heartbeat accelerated as he got up and walked to the bar. He stood behind the counter and mixed a drink. His hands and the drink were out of her sight, hidden by the counter. He came back to the couch, holding two plastic Solo cups. Was it just her imagination or did one of the other boys give him a sly grin?

Dylan handed her the cup. It was full of ice and red liquid. "We're out of Bud. Do you like fruity drinks?"

"Love 'em," Jody said. In fact, she had some experience with date-rape drugs. They often tasted salty or bitter, but sweet or salty drinks could mask the taste. Smiling at Dylan, she dipped her index finger into the drink, in what she hoped was a subtle gesture. It was hard to tell. She was already pretty tipsy.

"Cheers," Dylan said.

He held up his plastic cup. She did the same. They clinked softly against each other.

"Cheers." She smiled at him. She brought the cup to her mouth and pretended to drink. She could feel the cold liquid on her lips and hoped that those drops weren't enough to do her in. She pretended to swallow and lowered the cup.

Dylan was looking deep into her eyes. If she didn't know better, if she were, say, an eighteen-year-old girl at a frat for the first time, she might think he was looking at her that way because he really liked her.

She took her index finger out of the drink and looked shyly down at her hand. The nail on the finger she'd dipped into the drink was now a dark purple—several shades darker than the lavender on the rest of her fingers.

He'd slipped a roofie into her drink.

Even though this was exactly what she'd come here for, her heart started to pound now that she saw the reality of it. If she drank this cocktail, she would black out. He would take her somewhere and do whatever he wanted to her. Maybe invite his friends to, also. The idea infuriated her as much as it terrified her. She became very aware of the fine line between safety and devastation.

Shakily, she set the cup down on a coffee table. She stood. "I've gotta head out," she said.

"Wait," Dylan said. "You didn't finish your drink."

She walked toward the door. "Thanks for your hospitality."

He followed her into the foyer and put his hand on her arm. "Where are you going?"

"I really need to go study."

"Come on up to my room." He smiled at her. "You can study there."

She tried to pull her arm away. His grip tightened; she couldn't break free. Her stomach dipped. She looked toward the living room. The people watching TV were blocked from view. She and Dylan were alone in the foyer.

"That's a nice offer," Jody said. "But I—I don't have my books."

"You said you came here to study with Peter."

"I, well—I was going to use his books."

"What class are you guys in together?"

"Um, social studies. You're hurting my arm."

"Who are you?" Dylan's smile turned into something ugly. His fingers bit into her flesh. "What are you doing here?"

VLOG
RECORDED 12.1.15

There's awful, and then there's the special brand of awful reserved for college sex-assault disciplinary hearings.

I had to sit there and listen to Dylan lie and lie and lie. All these gory details about the hot, wet, acrobatic sex we had. While a student, a Ph.D., and a food-services lady tried to keep straight faces.

Ugh.

Ugh, ugh, ugh.

I want to rip out someone's hair. Dylan's. Yolanda's. Mine.

It was in a seminar room in the English Department, like we were all there for a lecture on Nabokov. Which kinda made sense, since Dylan's story was total fiction.

Yolanda Skanadowski sat at the head of the table. She was supposed be like a judge or something, but mostly she sat there like a lump in oatmeal. The three "adjudicators" had been chosen by . . . God knows how. Not because they know how to handle rape cases. Seriously, it was a cafeteria worker from Holmes Hall, still wearing her name badge. A bald engineering Ph.D., who might know how machines work but has no idea about the mechanics of sex. And a pimply sophomore from Topeka.

It's like a trial, I guess, but there are no lawyers. No real judge either. Maybe it's supposed to make you feel more relaxed? But all I got was the feeling that no one knew what the hell they were doing.

The only person in the room who had any legal knowledge was—get this—Dylan. You could tell he'd been superprepared by some expensive lawyer. It wasn't just in his words. It was in his whole way of sitting there. He walked in like Mr. Humble, head down, nodding respectfully at the panel. What a crock. Dylan Highsmith has never walked into a room like that in his life. Someone coached him on how to act like a nice young man. If only they'd done that twenty years ago. We wouldn't've been there today.

I had to go first. The whole time I'm talking, Dylan was sitting right next to me, so close he could have touched me. It was horrible. And he's shaking his head sadly the whole time—when I said he drugged me, he raped me—not like it was so sad that he did it, but it's so sad that I'm a crazy nutjob. I had to avoid looking at him most of the time, or I couldn't have kept going. But I did look right at him when I said he took away my feeling of being in control of my own body. He rolled his eyes—let that nice-boy act slip for just one minute. I hope someone saw that. Then he was Mr. Humble again.

He sucks. But you know what? The panel sucked even worse.

The student from Topeka asked if I was into Dylan when I first met him. Okay, fair enough, I did like him. Topeka asked if I wanted to hook up with Dylan when we went upstairs. I guess I thought we might kiss or something. He asked if I started kissing Dylan. I did not. At least not when I was awake and conscious—who knows what he did to me when I was passed out. So then Topeka asked, was it possible that I was acting in a blackout? That I was just drunk, not drugged? No, not possible, I said. He asked if I remembered Dylan's hand on my breast? No. Did I remember my nipples getting hard? Definitely no. Did I remember him taking off my panties? No. Did I remember him fingering my vagina? Was I moaning? Was I wet? No, no, no. God, no.

That's when I saw that Topeka had his hand under the table, moving rhythmically. I think he was playing with himself! I stared at him, and he stopped, but later on he started again. I couldn't even process it.

Anyway, that's when the engineering Ph.D. jumped in, with all his brilliant questions. How do I know I wasn't aroused if I can't remember? How do I know I wasn't saying yes to everything Dylan did? Maybe I was wet? How wet do I normally get during arousal?

Oh my God. I'm like, shut up. I mean, I didn't actually say that. But I wanted to.

Meanwhile, Dylan's just sitting there, looking respectful and serious.

I started to tell them how Dylan's raped other girls. And that's the one time he interrupted. All polite and formal. "Excuse me," Dylan said. "But I think this was discussed before the hearing, and it was decided that no other relationships would be mentioned."

Yolanda flipped through some papers and nodded. "Yes, that's true," she said. "Emily, please stick to the events of September 1, 2014. That's all we're here to talk about today."

It's bullshit. Of course it matters that he's done this before. But whatever, it's like they don't even care. Or they don't want to hear it, because then they'd have to do something about it.

Then it was his turn to speak. It was all such an act. Totally scripted. Dylan turned to the panelists and meekly introduced himself. "Hello, I'm Dylan Highsmith. I'm nervous and scared about these proceedings, but respect the work of the panel and the effort you are going through to find the right solution for all the parties here." Christ. He sounded like a very polite young paralegal. Then he turned to me. "And I would like to start by apologizing to Emily. Emily, I'm sorry you left my room feeling the way you did. I thought we had a wonderful night together, one that we both enjoyed. I would never want you to feel used. Obviously, you did, because here we are. But I want you to know, I never intended for you to feel that way."

It was so obnoxious. Like this was about some strange way I ended up feeling instead of some terrible way he'd acted. I'm just oversensitive. And the engineering prof is nodding his head sagely, like, yeah, he totally gets this. I wanted to scream.

So then Dylan goes into his song and dance about what happened. It's all pretty much true until we get to his bedroom. Instead of me passing out, he has me hitting on him. I kissed him; I took off his pants; I stripped myself down. I told him how to touch me: harder, faster, a little to the left. I'm riding him like a cowboy.

The three panelists were looking at me, imagining me doing all these things. Two men and one woman, who I've never met before and hope never to meet again.

I have never felt so gross in my entire life.

It's not supposed to be this way. I read the University Handbook. We're supposed to get a fair hearing where everyone feels comfortable and heard. Easier said than done, I know. But still. This was horrible.

And now I just have to wait. They've taken the case "under consideration" and will render an opinion "in due course." What does that even mean?

So I go home and it's been, obviously, like one of the worst days of my life. I open the door to our suite, and Preya and Whitney are sprawled on the couch, eating pizza and watching *Say Yes to the Dress*. I shouldn't be surprised; life goes on, and I hadn't told anyone what was happening today. But still it was so weird to see regular life just meandering along.

I don't know why—I've kept it inside all this time—but I sat down and told them everything. What Dylan did three months ago. Why I've been so depressed all semester. The kangaroo court today. Preya turned off the TV and patted my back and was supportive in her quiet way.

Whitney was furious, though. Not at Dylan. At me. For bringing charges. She said it was going to ruin the frat, make them stop throwing parties, get them shut down. She said I wasn't raped—I just had morning-after regrets. I was angry Dylan hadn't called. I wanted attention and the "status" of being a rape victim. Yeah, because being a rape victim is so much fun!

I should've known. Whitney is obsessed with Beta Psi. She's been hanging out with this Peter guy, not dating, obviously, because those guys don't date, but answering all his booty calls and generally following him around like a puppy. "The guys are going to be at Lucky's at eleven o'clock!" she'll say, and be sure to be there at 11:15. She's so up in their business, she could be Beta Psi's official scheduler.

So she yelled at me for a while, then demanded I drop the charges. I laughed in her face. I haven't gotten this far in the process to call up Yolanda and tell her I was just kidding. Fuck Dylan. And fuck Whitney too. I said that.

Whitney's face got as red as her Marry Me lipstick, and she stood up and screamed so much, spit was flying out of her mouth. All these dire threats: I'll be blackballed, I'll be an outcast, I'll never be invited to another party again.

Like I want to go to parties. I told Whitney exactly how much she scared me. And then I told her what I've thought of her from day one. She's a spoiled, selfish, shallow, coked-out ditz who only got into Tower because her parents donated their way in. And her nose job sucks.

Oh man. I'm not proud of myself. I don't enjoy making people feel bad. I would've never said those things to Whitney—though they're true—except I was at the end of my rope. I was totally overwhelmed by everything that happened today.

Whitney sucked in a breath like I'd just kicked her in the stomach. Then she grabbed her bag and stormed out. The last thing she said was, "You'll be sorry."

The door slammed shut. Preya and I looked at each other and burst out laughing. It felt so good—and strange—to laugh. I haven't done that in such a long time. I don't know what made it funny, except the whole thing was so ridiculous. Preya was like, "I think she was trying to scare you." I was like, "Totally." Which was the funny part. As if that girl can do any worse than what's already been done.

16

Dylan's hand felt like a steel vise on her arm.

"Let go of me," Jody said.

Dylan narrowed his eyes. "Not till you tell me why you're here."

"To study with Peter, like I said."

"That's bullshit, and we both know it."

He hauled her toward the staircase. She tried to yank her arm away, but he was too strong. Her feet skidded along the wooden floor. Panic rose in her throat. She didn't want to yell and get everyone to come running. She'd wanted to slip in and out unnoticed. But she could not let him drag her upstairs.

"Okay, okay, okay," she said. "Wait. Just stop and I'll tell you."

He didn't stop; he dragged her even harder. They were at the staircase.

"I'm . . ." She tried to think through her panic. She looked at the large frame on the wall. Across the top, it said: BETA PSI, CLASS OF 2014. Below were pictures of several dozen boys wearing blue blazers and ties. "If you have to know, okay, I'm here as a prank. From my sorority. I was, like, supposed to steal your composite."

Dylan stopped pulling her. "What sorority?"

"Please don't be mad, okay?" She desperately tried to remember the names on the houses she'd passed on the way here. "Gamma Phi Delta. Please don't tell my sisters, okay? I'll get in so much trouble."

He loosened his grip. Then he smiled and let go. He took the picture off the wall and handed it to her. "Make sure it's back before our Playboy Mansion party."

"I totally will," Jody said. The picture was huge and unwieldy, hard to hold, but she moved as fast as she could. "Thank you *so* much!"

He opened the door for her. She fled from the fraternity house.

She walked quickly to her car, sure he was going to run after her and grab her. She made it to her Yukon, popped the trunk, and stuffed the picture in. She threw herself into the driver's seat, slammed the door, and pressed lock.

But even the solid *clunk* of the doors locking couldn't stop her shaking. Her heart must be going a hundred beats a minute. Her breath, coming in fast gulps, quickly steamed up the cold windows. She was too drunk to drive, but at least she felt some level of safety in the car.

She pulled out her phone and took a picture of her trembling hand, with its four lavender fingers and one dark purple nail. Then she texted the photo to Anna, along with a link to the website of the date-rape-drug-detecting nail polish.

Jody texted, Maybe now you can search the frat.

17

Anna looked at her sister's text. "Oh God, Jody," she murmured. "What have you done?"

She started to respond, then stopped. Texts could become evidence. Jack always said, "Don't put anything in a text or e-mail that you don't want published in the *Washington Post*." She would talk to her sister in person.

■ ■ ■

Anna parked in Cooper's driveway and looked around her new car with satisfaction. It was a gray Chevy Impala with government tags. Not exactly glamorous, but it was all hers, at least while she was investigating the case. Anna was a Detroit girl at heart; she thought there were few things as empowering as your own car.

The file from Tower University sat on the passenger seat. She picked it up with distaste. Bryan Frink had given it to her at 7:55 P.M.—five minutes before the court-imposed deadline. Three separate women had pursued sex-assault charges against Dylan through the university. Their cases all ended without an official finding against Dylan—two had stopped pursuing charges, and in the last, Dylan had been found "not responsible." Anna would reach out to the women in these three files.

Despite massive efforts, there was no further sign of Emily. No clothes in fields. No sightings in town. No activity online. It had been over forty-eight hours. If she were lying in a ditch, she was already dead. Now Anna had to turn to the bleak hope she was tied up in some closet.

Anna grabbed the file and walked up Cooper's driveway. Her exhausted mind thought, *It's good to be home.* She immediately brushed the thought away. Whatever instinct told her that this was home had to be suppressed. Anna had long ago learned to trust her head, not her heart, in romantic matters. Her relationship instincts were like a broken compass. Only her logic could be trusted. Logic said D.C. was home.

Inside, Sparky greeted her with a wag of his tail and a lick. Anna scratched under his chin, then walked to the living room. The embers of a cherrywood fire still glowed orange.

Cooper himself was sleeping on the coach, holding Leigh in his arms. The baby snuggled into his broad chest with a blissed-out smile on her face. Anna knew the feeling.

Anna stopped and watched them for a moment. There was something beautiful about the big Army Ranger holding the tiny infant. Leigh let out a little cooing sound and Anna went over. She sat on the couch and stroked the infant's soft hair.

She loved this baby. That love had sparked an understanding of how deeply she wanted to be a mother too. Despite how cruel the world could be—or because of it. There was nothing as pure and simple as the love of a child and the deep urge to protect her. She looked at Cooper, his thick eyelashes fanned out on his cheeks. He'd be a great father. She could tell by what she knew of him: his resilience and gentleness, his optimism and generosity. She could tell by how he'd fought for her and Jody when the world was against them. She could tell by the way he held the baby, with tender protectiveness, even in his sleep.

Jack, too, was a wonderful father. Anna didn't have to speculate. She'd seen him with Olivia. Her own idea of what a good father should be was based on Jack's relationship with his daughter. Anna missed that little girl so much, it sometimes felt like a hole in her chest. She wondered what Olivia was doing now. Did she still use the nightlight Anna got her? Did she still like to be patted to sleep? Anna found herself patting Cooper's leg.

She knew what her life with Jack would be like because she'd lived it. She would live in his beautiful yellow Victorian in Takoma Park, a fun and quirky suburb of D.C. They'd be a husband-and-wife prosecutor team. They'd commute in together, walking through the pretty neighborhood to the subway. Olivia would start calling her Mom, as Anna had long dreamed. She'd be half of a D.C. power couple, with all the attendant privileges and stress.

Life with Cooper was more uncertain. There were far fewer

options for a lawyer here than in D.C. Could she see herself living permanently on this farm? Would Cooper ever want to leave? He loved this city, what he'd built, the connections he'd made with other community leaders who were fighting to bring back Detroit. They'd made a big difference. Although a lot of the city was abandoned and blighted, there were some genuine bright spots: coffee shops, breweries, a vibrant art scene, farm-to-table restaurants that featured Cooper's kale. A sense of opportunity had come when the city hit rock bottom. Cooper and people like him were taking that opportunity and doing creative, wonderful things to bring it back. But this was no place to raise a child. And if there was one thing Anna had learned about herself, it was that she wanted to start a family.

The front door opened and the unfamiliar sound of high heels clacked on the foyer floor. Anna straightened and stood as Jody walked into the living room. She was dressed to kill, all flowy blond hair and tight jeans. Her low-cut blouse was wet across her breasts. She grinned excitedly at Anna and held up lavender fingernails.

"Hey, sis!" Jody said in an excited stage whisper that wouldn't wake the baby. "Have I got a story for you!"

"I'm a little scared to hear what could make you leave your baby for the first time."

"Grady babysat—he's actually better with her than I expected. And then he came and drove me home. It was the most exciting night I've had in a while. I mean, wow, a serious rush. I went to the Beta Psi house at Tower."

Anna stared at her. "Please tell me this is all a big joke."

"No. I got some great evidence for you." Jody held up her one purple fingernail and explained her night. "It means he slipped a drug in my drink!"

Anna was furious. "You could've been in serious danger!"

"I knew what I was doing."

"You absolutely did not know what you were doing. When I send someone into a place undercover, we have all sorts of protections. They're miked up so I can listen. There are police watching, making sure the undercover is safe. There are police stationed outside, ready to rush in if things get out of hand. What if you didn't notice he'd spiked your drink? You'd be in Dylan's bed right now, being . . ."

She was so upset, she couldn't even say the words.

"Annie, it's okay. I wasn't going to drink anything I didn't see opened right in front of me. And what else were they going to do? They're a fraternity, not the Mafia."

"You're an autoworker, not a police officer."

"No. I'm more effective than the police." Jody grinned.

"This Wild West spirit is what got you in trouble in the first place," Anna said. "I just got you out of it. We don't need any more."

"That's actually why I did it." Jody's face got serious. "You helped me. I wanted to help you."

"You might have asked!"

"If I asked, you wouldn't have let me. Plus, then I'd be a government agent. This way, you can use my evidence."

"I'm not sure I can use it. You're my sister. It's not like you're a neutral party. You totally have a bias."

"You'll sort it all out."

Anna closed her eyes. She felt the warmth from the dying fire on her eyelids. She took a deep breath and tried to remember that her sister was trying to help. And the fact that a date-rape drug had been served in the house might give her the evidence necessary to search the house for the drugs. Anything else she found during that search would be admissible in a case against Dylan.

"It was a good idea," she said at last. "I just wish I'd thought of it myself and had it done with an undercover agent."

"That wouldn't have been nearly as much fun," Jody said.

"My work isn't about fun."

"None of your life is, really."

Anna was too tired for this. Still, she asked, "What's that supposed to mean?"

"You're devoted to your job. That's great, I mean, it's commendable. But you need more than that, Annie. Even your fiancé, Jack, was someone who was sort of your boss. Everything in your life is about being a prosecutor."

"I'm proud of being a prosecutor, and I am trying to save a girl's life."

"I hope you do. But, Annie, at some point or another, you're going to have to think about your own life—and what you really want to be doing with it."

Jody stood and gently picked up her baby from Cooper's arms and took her upstairs.

Cooper opened his eyes, which crinkled when they saw Anna. "Hey, you."

"Hey, you."

"You doing okay?"

She shook her head. "I'm either going to get a big break in my case, or I'm going to get kicked off it."

"Come here," he said. "There's nothing like lying down next to someone who loves you. That's the best place on earth, for me at least."

She lay down next to him on the couch. He shifted so his arm went around her and she could snuggle into his chest. He was right. She felt instantly better. She fell asleep right there on the couch.

MONDAY

18

'm sorry," Anna told the judge. "It's not how I would normally conduct an investigation."

She stood in Judge Schwalbe's chambers, Sam at her side. The judge sat behind his desk, looking at the papers in front of him with distaste, as if she'd just served him a sandwich on moldy bread.

She didn't like drafting this warrant any more than he liked being asked to sign it. But she'd had a long discussion with Sam and Jack this morning, going over the pros and cons of using Jody's evidence. It wasn't good to use your sister as an undercover investigator. There was a taint of nepotism and bias. One's sister certainly had an incentive to shade the truth to help the other. So Jody's testimony was problematic, to say the least. In a perfect world, Anna would send in a neutral investigator to replicate what Jody had done. The problem was, they might never be able to repeat the results Jody had gotten. Frankly, Anna was amazed at what Jody had accomplished. A seasoned investigator might not do better with years of training and months of planning.

And they needed to go in and check out the fraternity house, now, while there was still a chance that evidence inside could help them find Emily alive. They couldn't wait to see if they could repeat Jody's success. So Sam had interviewed Jody and written up her visit in the affidavit supporting their application for a search warrant. Anna disclosed in the paperwork that she was Jody's sister. Of course, that's what the judge focused on.

"Ms. Curtis, as the prosecutor, you are entrusted with special duties: fairness, impartiality."

"Yes, sir."

"Making your sister an investigator does not confer your investigation with an air of impartiality."

"As noted in the affidavit, I didn't *make* my sister an investigator.

I never asked her to go to the fraternity house. She chose to do it, completely on her own. I learned of it afterward."

"That's slicing the baloney rather thin, don't you think? How did she even know to go there, unless you divulged secret grand jury information to her?"

"I told her no 6(e) information," Anna said.

He looked at her with disappointment. Anna felt a pang in her chest. She liked this judge and wanted him to like her too. The judge sighed and shook his head.

"I'm very disappointed with this. I'm going to sign it, because I do believe it establishes probable cause that you'll find evidence of a crime—the crime of drug-facilitated sexual assault—within the house. But you're asking me to put the reputation of this court at stake in doing so. I expect the government to uphold the highest standards, Ms. Curtis. I gave you the benefit of the doubt before. But I will have to examine anything you bring to me very closely from now on."

"Yes, sir."

"And Ms. Curtis. I received a motion from Dylan Highsmith's counsel." He handed a paper over his desk to her. "You'd get a copy tomorrow, but you might as well see it now. They're moving to have you disqualified from the case. They claim that you physically assaulted the young man when you went to talk to him at the fraternity house."

"I—"

Sam put a hand on her arm and cut Anna off. "I was there and that isn't what happened."

"You will respond to those allegations in due course. I'll demand that. My clerk set up a time for an evidentiary hearing on Monday. We'll take testimony on this, and I'll decide if you can keep the case. Ms. Curtis, you'd better make hay while the sun shines."

■ ■ ■

Driving to Tower University, Anna was quiet.

"Don't worry about it," Sam said. "Every defendant accuses the police or prosecutor of misconduct. The best defense is a good offense. If they didn't do it at one point or another, they wouldn't be worth their seven hundred and fifty an hour."

"I really did kick Dylan in the balls."

"He grabbed you. The police can't be recused from every case where a suspect starts a brawl. It'll be fine. It's just a bunch of chest thumping."

Anna nodded, leaned her head back on the headrest, and tried to believe Sam.

The FBI SWAT team was waiting for them in a church parking lot. At seven A.M., they were the only cars there. The March morning was cold and quiet, the sun rising into a low gray sky. Anna got out and hugged a tall, slim FBI agent named Steve Quisenberry. Steve and Sam were partners; they'd all worked several cases in D.C. Steve had a searing intellect and a gentle manner that made witnesses trust him. This morning, he also had muffins and coffee. Sam punched him in the arm and took a chocolate chip muffin. Anna gratefully poured a cup of coffee from the Panera box.

While Anna and Sam had been in court making the legal case for their search, Steve had planned its execution. He'd spoken to Jody and gotten the layout of the frat house. He'd pulled public records for the floor plan. He ran background checks of the inhabitants. Now Steve handed everyone an operations plan and briefed them. Twenty-three agents in FBI flak jackets stood in front of him, scarfing muffins and coffee while he spoke.

"We can expect to encounter around forty frat boys who live there," Steve said, "and whatever guests may be sleeping over. The newest members sleep in a single big room on the third level. More senior members sleep on the second floor, where there are ten bedrooms. The first floor holds a foyer, a kitchen, a large living room, and three smaller TV dens. And the basement has two rooms: a giant one for parties and then a smaller one that can be sealed off with a metal door. That's got to be the ritual room, called the Crypt. There are no records of any rooms below the Crypt, although we have rumors that such a room exists."

Steve handed out papers where he'd sketched out the layout of the house. "There are reportedly no dogs on the site, and no one living at the house has a gun registered. However, four of the men have prior arrests."

He listed their names and arrests: one drug offense and three petty assaults. Anna could sense the agents' hackles going up. Every raid could be dangerous, and a criminal history, however petty, made it more likely there would be problems.

After a few questions, the agents loaded back into their cars and drove to the fraternity house. They parked at the curb in front of Beta Psi. Anna and Sam both pulled on bulletproof vests. "Good luck," Anna said. She would go in for the search but was not allowed until the FBI agents had cleared the house of people.

"See you in a minute." Sam got out of the car and took a long rifle out of the trunk. Anna watched as the other agents filed out of their cars and lined up behind Sam and Steve. In the early morning, they were the only movement on the street. Gone were smiles and muffins. The agents were heavily armed and wore the grim looks of professionals about to do a job that required total focus. The agents moved with quiet, deadly grace as they formed a line and strode up the front yard of Beta Psi. Sam led her team up the front porch. Anna sent up a quick prayer for their safety. The entry was the most dangerous part.

19

This was the second time Sam would walk through the fraternity's front door, but now she'd do it on her terms. She rang the doorbell and knocked loudly. "FBI, police!" She started counting. "One-one-thousand. Two-one-thousand." If she got to thirty, she'd signal for the agent with the battering ram.

At twenty-one, the door opened. A skinny white guy wearing checkered pajama bottoms and an undershirt squinted into the morning light. Sam held up her badge. "FBI. We're here to execute a search warrant."

The kid blinked at the collection of federal agents on his porch. "What's your name?" Sam asked. He opened his mouth, but no sound came out.

Pop science said there are two reactions to fear: fight or flight. But in Sam's experience there were three: fight, flight, or freeze. She appreciated those who froze. It was better than a chase or a gunfight. She put a gentle hand on the back of the boy's T-shirt and, in the manner of a mama lion taking a cub by the scruff of his neck, guided him out of the house, onto the porch. The kid looked around with bugging eyes.

"Take a deep breath," Sam said. "Everything's going to be okay. Let's try this again. What's your name?"

"L-l-l . . . L-l-l-l—" He eventually managed to say, "Lou Griwatsch."

"Hi, Lou. We're going to go into your house now, and as long as you cooperate, you'll be fine. Can you tell me how many people are in there now?"

He stared at her.

"Are there any weapons in the house, Lou?"

He held his hands up. She almost felt sorry for him. Almost, because as a member of this fraternity, he had to be one of the most privileged boys in America.

"What about any animals? Dogs?"

"I d-d-d—" He took a breath and tried again. "I d-d-d—"

"Stay out here," Sam said. She handed the kid off to another officer.

She turned back to the house, raised her rifle, and pushed the door open. The foyer was empty. Her team followed her in. It was a grand wood-paneled space with ten-foot ceilings and scrolled woodwork she hadn't been able to see during the highlighter party. A chandelier hung from the ceiling. But she couldn't dwell on the interior design. Now she had to clear the place, make sure no one could jump out and kill an agent. She strode toward the grand sweep of the staircase.

A low, guttural growl stopped her. A big Doberman stood in the hallway to her right. Its lips curled back, baring pink gums and rows of gleaming white teeth. Saliva dripped from its snapping jaws.

"Crap." Sam pointed her gun at the dog.

"Wait," Steve said.

She kept her finger on the trigger but said, "You have thirty seconds."

Steve reached into his jacket and threw something at the Doberman. A little bone-shaped biscuit landed on the floor in front of the beast. The dog stopped barking and cocked its head at the biscuit. It looked at Steve, then back at the biscuit. "It's okay, girl," Steve said softly. The dog took one hesitant step forward, paused, then snapped up the biscuit. She looked back up at Steve. "Good girl." Steve threw another treat, and this time the dog ate it without hesitation. "Sit," Steve said. The dog sat. He put a biscuit in his hand and held it out. "Come." The dog trotted over and ate the biscuit daintily from Steve's palm. Steve scratched behind her ears and murmured what a good dog she was. As he did, he took a leash from inside his jacket and latched it to the dog's collar. He handed it to a younger agent. "Take her outside."

"Softie," Sam said. Steve shrugged, but a smile played on his lips. Over beers tonight, she would tease him without mercy, but secretly she admired that he always tried to work with the dogs in the homes they raided—and he was mostly successful. Dogs trusted him.

The agents split up as planned. Sam and Steve jogged up the front staircase to the second level. At the top, she took out a mirror on a retractable pole. She used it to look around a corner, saw no one, then swung around, gun first. Sure, these were just frat boys, but fifteen years at the Bureau had taught her: you never know.

The dark wood hallway was lined with multiple doors. It looked like a B and B but smelled like sweat socks and weed. She knocked on the first door then went through it.

The bedroom was dim and dank, with dirty clothes piled on the floor. A single young man slept in a bed. He cracked an eye. "FBI, police," Sam said. "Executing a search warrant. Get up."

The kid raised his head off the pillow. He looked at Sam and smiled. "Okay, this is worth getting up for." He sat up. He wore boxer shorts, which did little to hide that fact that he was excited. "Go ahead," he said. "I've been a bad boy. Do you want to put me in handcuffs? And spank me?"

Sam kept her gun pointed at the young man and kicked open the closet. No one was inside.

"I don't know who sent you," the kid said, as his eyes traveled from her curly dark hair, to her snug cargo pants, to her steel-toed boots. "But I will have to thank him. C'mere, baby."

Sam heard a muffled choke in the doorway. Steve was trying not to laugh. Sam kept her eyes on the kid but spoke to Steve. "Should I toss him a biscuit?"

"Nah. I didn't bring another leash."

"I'm not a stripper, sir," Sam said to the kid, using her deepest, scariest Voice of Authority. "This is a real gun with real bullets, this is a real badge, and you need to put on a real pair of pants."

The kid tripped on his clothes as he rushed to pull them on. Sam escorted him out to the hallway and handed him off to an agent who led him away.

She went to the next bedroom. A frat boy lay in bed with two blondes, who shrieked when Sam announced herself. Sam sighed as the blondes frantically pulled on lace Hanky Panky underpants. Didn't anyone go to college to *study* anymore?

The next suite was empty—the only movement was miniature sharks zigzagging in a huge aquarium. Sam strode through the bedroom and into the attached bathroom. There she found Dylan Highsmith in boxer shorts, standing by the toilet. Water swirled down, in the last throes of a flush. Dylan looked up triumphantly.

Sam cursed under her breath. Whatever he'd flushed was now gone. "Sir, we're conducting a search warrant. You have to leave the house now." She let him put on clothes, then steered him out to the hallway.

"This is a total violation," Dylan said, as Sam handed him off to another agent. "My father and his lawyers will get this all thrown out. And they'll get your badge too."

"You know what every guy whose house I search tells me?" Sam smiled. "They tell me they'll have my badge. And guess what? It's been fifteen years. I've still got it. Tell your father to give it his best shot."

■ ■ ■

Anna leaned on the unmarked Taurus, sipping coffee and stomping her feet to stay warm. Soon boys started to pour out of the frat. A few girls too. They were groggy, in pajamas or mismatched clothes. They came out quietly, with murmurs and shuffles. It looked like a fire drill, not Waco.

When Dylan Highsmith came out, the other boys clustered around him. He pulled out his cell phone and made a call.

Sam gave Anna a thumbs-up and Anna walked up the driveway. As she passed him, Dylan said loudly into his phone, "Yeah, let's get her disbarred."

Anna ignored him and walked into the house. She nodded to Sam. "Let's go see what they've got stashed in here."

MEMORANDUM

To: Dylan Highsmith, Emily Shapiro
From: Yolanda Skanadowski, Title IX Coordinator
Date: January 5, 2015
Re: Disciplinary Committee's Written Memorandum of Verdict, Case No. 14-073

Procedural Background:

On November 13, 2014, this committee convened to hear the case of Emily Shapiro versus Dylan Highsmith, wherein Mr. Highsmith was charged with sexually assaulting Ms. Shapiro. Testimony was taken from Ms. Shapiro and Mr. Highsmith. No physical evidence was presented.

Verdict: Responsible.

Reasoning:

Considering all the testimony, the committee concludes that Mr. Highsmith is responsible for sexually assaulting Ms. Shapiro. There was not enough evidence to support Ms. Shapiro's charge that Mr. Highsmith drugged her with an intoxicating agent in order to render her unconscious and sexually assault her. However, there is ample evidence that Ms. Shapiro was extremely intoxicated from the effect of alcohol, and that a reasonable man in Mr. Highsmith's position would know, or should have known, that she was incapable of giving informed consent. Therefore, when he had vaginal intercourse with her, it constituted a sexual assault.

Punishment:

Mr. Highsmith will be expelled from Tower University, effective today. He will not graduate from Tower University. His transcript will indicate that he was expelled for a violation of the student honor code. Mr. Highsmith is ordered to stay away from the Tower University campus. If he is found on the campus, he will be considered trespassing, and all appropriate legal action, including criminal and civil charges, will be pursued.

VLOG
RECORDED 1.6.15

Oh my God. I feel like I can breathe again. Like, I didn't even realize this huge heavy barbell was sitting on my chest, till finally something came and lifted it off.

Justice.

They found him "responsible." That's like the college equivalent of "guilty." And he's being kicked off campus. Expelled! He won't graduate. He'll have, like, a permanent mark on his record. Every employer that ever looks at his transcript will ask him why, and he'll have to answer. He'll come up with some cover story, obviously. But I hope he thinks of me every time.

Did they nail him because I'm the president's daughter? Maybe. Oh well. It's rough justice, I guess.

In the real world, he'd get jail time. He'd be, like, wearing an orange jumpsuit and trying not to drop the soap in the shower. It's totally what he deserves.

But at least this is something.

Someone heard me, believed me, tried to make it right. It's like—wow. That feels amazing.

20

et's go down to the Crypt," Anna said.

Sam shook her head. "The metal door is locked. We're trying to pick it."

"If you can't?"

"There's always dynamite."

They walked through the living room, where Anna recognized the flat-screen TV and antique bar from Jody's description. Behind the bar, an agent was packing bottles of liquor into boxes. She watched with interest as he pulled out a gallon milk jug filled with red liquid. By end of the day, every drop of alcohol would be taken out of the house and transported to an FBI lab to be tested for date-rape drugs.

But the warrant allowed for more than liquor bottles. The FBI could search any area where a date-rape drug might be stored. And if they found evidence of any crime—say, the crime of abducting Emily Shapiro—they could seize that evidence too. Unorthodox as her method had been, Jody had unlocked the house for them.

Anna and Sam headed up the stairs. Other than the Underground, the thing she most wanted to see was Dylan's room. Sam handed her a pair of latex gloves, which Anna snapped on.

Dylan's room was the best one in the house, with large windows overlooking the clock tower. It smelled of cologne and a more organic musky scent, the smell of a college boy learning to do his own laundry. It was neat, except for the unmade bed, which Dylan must've jumped out of when he heard the raid. His desk was lined with expensive men's colognes. In the aquarium, the sharks regarded Anna suspiciously as they circled.

Over his desk hung a framed sorority composite: a big frame filled with dozens of portraits of young women. Each woman wore a black V-neck, pearls, and a big smile. Each had her name inscribed below her portrait in lovely script. Someone had written in black Sharpie on the glass above their faces. "Slut," said the handwriting over Jennifer Welch's portrait. "Ball-buster," it said, over Joette Schisler. "Bitch," it announced above Susanne Sachsman. Each girl had her own description written above her face. Whore, cunt, heifer, dyke, dicktease, cow. Several of the girls' portraits had mustaches or horns drawn on them.

"Charming," Sam said.

"I love it," Anna said. "Hatred of women is an element we need for a hate crime. This is Exhibit A."

Sam placed a placard on the composite and took a picture to show where it had been found. They would seize it as evidence.

The FBI agent opened Dylan's desk drawers. They held pencils, condoms, Chapstick, and notebooks, each neatly lined up in its own plastic container. Dylan or his mom had made careful decisions at the Container Store. A prescription bottle made Anna's heart beat a little faster, until she saw it was Ritalin. A lot of college kids used it to study because they believed it helped them concentrate. It was prescribed to treat ADHD, and Dylan's name was on the bottle. It was not a date-rape drug.

A lower drawer held a bunch of student notebooks. Sam said, "Drugs come very small these days." She took out a notebook and flipped through it. "LSD comes on sheets of paper." Anna glanced at the pages as Sam flipped. Dylan's handwriting was so neat, it could be its own font. But in the end Sam shook her head. "Just notes from class."

Sam opened the closet and shone the flashlight in. Something shimmery glinted in the corner. She pulled aside a line of shirts, revealing the floor below. On the closet floor was a soft white pile shot through with silver threads. Sam picked up the fabric, which unspooled and revealed its shape. It was a silvery scarf.

Anna remembered the video of Emily striding away from Dylan. A shimmery scarf had flowed behind the girl like a cape.

It appeared clean; there was no obvious blood or stains. A tag read URBAN OUTFITTERS. They would test for DNA and see if Emily's skin cells were present.

A massive boom shook the house. Dust sifted down from the ceiling and landed on Anna's eyelashes. She brushed it away and looked to Sam, who gave her a satisfied smile. "Sounds like they got into the Crypt." Sam folded the scarf into an evidence bag, and they headed down the stairs.

■ ■ ■

The air in the basement smelled of smoke and burnt metal. The metal door to the Crypt was still attached to the wall by industrial hinges, but the doorknob side was now a bubble of twisted metal no longer latched to the frame. Steve pushed his safety goggles back on his head and grinned at Sam.

"You're even better with TNT than dog treats," Sam said.

"You just have to understand your opponent. Everything has its weakness."

"Don't tell Steve that my weakness is chocolate-covered strawberries," Sam said to Anna. "Or maybe do."

Sam and Steve unholstered their guns and flashlights and pointed them ahead. Sam pulled the mangled door and it swung open with a metallic groan. The Crypt was completely dark inside. Sam shone a flashlight around until the beam landed on a light switch. She flicked it on and the room was illuminated. After a moment, she said, "Clear."

It was a large basement room with a cement floor angling down to a single drain in the middle. Three walls were drywall painted black, hung with framed artifacts. One wall was stone, apparently part of the foundation. At the front, up on a large marble pedestal, was a mahogany coffin. Steve opened the top of the coffin; the interior was lined with black velvet. It was empty.

Anna walked around the room, taking in the artifacts: a bar tab signed by President Taft, a mast, an Olympic medal in a Lucite box. She recalled the rumor Heide Herrmann had repeated: all the secrets are *below* the Crypt. But how did you get below? There was no obvious break in the wall or floor. Anna knelt down by the drain. It was dank and black, with a faint gurgle coming from deep below. She tried to pry off the grate, but it was firmly bolted.

A room below the Crypt might be a myth, one of those college legends that held more intrigue than truth. Anna looked around the room more slowly. She let her gloved hands travel over the Lucite case, the wood of the mast, the stones in the wall. She knocked on the black drywall. She looked inside the coffin and touched the smooth, cool velvet. "Sam," she said. "Do you have a blade?"

Sam pulled a box cutter from her tool belt and cut the velvet lining in a line around the top. When she was done, she lifted the sheared velvet out of the coffin. There was no wood below. In the bottom of the coffin was a horizontal door cut in the marble pedestal. The door was painted glossy black with the fraternity's Greek letters stenciled in gold. A circular iron latch was bolted to one side. Sam grabbed the latch and pulled up. The door creaked open until it was resting against the back of the coffin. Through the opening was a series of gray stone steps descending into darkness.

VLOG
RECORDED 1.19.15

Dylan's gone, but in a way, his ghost is still, like, haunting the campus. Everywhere I go, there's a little bit of his horrible spirit.

Whitney's not talking to me, except to say I "ruined Dylan's life." I don't see her that often now—she pretty much just hangs out at Beta Psi—but when I do, it's totally painful.

Obviously, Dylan's friends are still here—and they hate me. Like, really, really, really hate me. And, wow, those Beta Psis know a thousand different ways to call you a slut. They could write their own entry on Urban Dictionary. It's like—I'm trying to be strong. I keep my eyes straight ahead. I pretend not to notice when they spit at my feet. But it's scary, and it's humiliating. I try to act like I don't even notice them, but my heart races every time. I see other kids watching. Their faces are sympathetic, but they don't want to sit with me.

Online is worse. There's a limit to what people will say to your face. On Twitter, it's a free-for-all. "You're a lying whore," one kid tweeted at me. Another wrote about the encrusted state of my genitals. One kid tweeted, "Someone should shut that bitch up."

Preya says not to worry. She says it'll pass. They don't have a long enough attention span for it to go through February.

God, I hope she's right. I hope they break before I do.

21

Anna boosted herself onto the marble pedestal and climbed into the coffin. Sam was already several steps ahead, descending the stone stairs into darkness. With each step Anna took, the air got colder—first on her ankles, then her arms, then finally a waft up the back of her neck. She shuddered and took one last look at the Crypt as her head was at coffin height. Then she was fully underneath it, with only blackness ahead. It would be ironic, she thought, if the last thing she ever saw was the inside of a coffin.

She chided herself for thinking that way. She had an armed FBI agent in front of her, and one following behind. This was perfectly safe.

Still, it was hard not to be chilled as the darkness swallowed her whole. The air was dank and musty. The only sound was the shuffle of their feet echoing off stone walls. Anna couldn't hear the search team in the house above; she doubted they could hear anything down here. The only light was Sam's flashlight in front and Steve's behind her. The stairs kept going, down and down, until the light from the door in the coffin was just a memory.

She reached out to steady herself. The stone wall was moist and cool, mossy in places, and she was just thinking it wasn't so creepy when something skittered across her wrist. She yanked her hand away. *It was a roach,* Anna told herself. *Maybe a millipede. Not a big deal.* There were roaches in Superior Court. She rubbed her wrist to try to erase the tickle of the creature's many legs. The stairs kept going down. She did not reach for the wall again.

Finally, they reached the bottom. Sam shone the flashlight around. It was a long hallway with a cement floor. On the walls were iron sconces holding charred torches. Anna could see as far as Sam's flashlight beam. Then it was black. They kept walking.

Fissures in the stone walls and leaching mineral stains indicated this passage had existed for a long time. A torch hung every twenty feet or so. Anna wished the torches were lit, both for light and warmth. The walls radiated a cold so powerful it chilled her to the core. She crossed her arms over her chest and hugged herself tight.

A fluttering sound made Sam shine her light upward. A bunch of bats flew near the ceiling, dozens of wings beating a cloud of black. They sang a chorus of high-pitched shrieks. One dove toward Anna's head. She covered her hair and ducked. The tip of a wing, soft and fetid, brushed her knuckles. Her hair danced in the draft it created.

They flew up through a hole in the ceiling, and their shrieking subsided, then was gone. Steve offered her a hand, and she stood up, shuddering.

"You want to go back?" Steve asked.

Anna shook her head. They walked on.

The hallway ended in an open door, supported on both sides by marble pillars. A marble slab across the top was inscribed with Greek letters. The two FBI agents walked, guns first, through the door. Anna heard them gasp—then silence. She followed them in.

It was an underground chamber, about the size of a college seminar room. Every inch of wall and ceiling was covered in bones.

Toe and finger bones, the size of macaroni, decorated the walls in elaborate swirling patterns. Femurs made crosses and starbursts. The ceiling was covered in a mosaic of stars, suns, moons, and diamonds, all consisting of thousands of individual vertebrae and ribs.

Anna recalled pictures she'd seen of the Capuchin monks' underground crypts in Sicily, where mosaics were made with thousands of old bones. This looked like that. Except the monks had a tradition of using the remains of fellow monks to create monuments to mortality. Where would frat boys get bones?

"Human?" Anna whispered. There was no reason to whisper, but she couldn't imagine talking any louder.

"Looks like it," Sam whispered back.

"This one definitely is," Steve said. Anna followed his beam of light. A fully intact human skeleton stood strapped to the farthest wall, its feet hovering an inch above the stone floor. It grimaced at them with perfect teeth. A red Beta Psi baseball cap sat jauntily atop its skull.

22

Anna felt dizzy. The musty smell she'd been inhaling took on a more ominous flavor. She fought back a gag.

"Could that be Emily?"

"We'll test," Sam said. "But I doubt it. Even pros can't take a full human body down to clean bones in three days."

"Who then?"

Steve shook his head.

In front of the skeleton was a marble table surrounded by four candlesticks taller than Anna. Massive half-melted black candles topped them.

On the table was a book as big as an unabridged Oxford dictionary. Embossed in gold on the black leather cover was the title, *The Book of Earthly Pleasures*. With gloved hands, Sam opened it. The pages were brittle and yellowed with age. Anna sneezed on the dust.

The first page had large black calligraphy script that said BETA PSI. The fraternity's seal was printed in gold. Sam flipped to the next page. A man's name was written at the top, followed by a series of letters and numbers.

Robert James Vary
1915–1919

Y.J. 9/25/15
S.D'U. 3/12/16
H.V. 10/5/16
G.A. 4/4/17
A.McH. 9/2/17
T.L. 5/3/18
J.W. 10/3/18
M.W. 2/6/19
T.Y. 5/1/19

The skeleton seemed to be watching with its hollow eyes. The next page had four pictures pasted onto it. They were all black-and-white shots of pretty young women with hair in elaborate buns, wearing corseted dresses. Pressed into the book's crease was also a lock of yellow hair bound in faded pink ribbon, and a small piece of lace, cut from a larger garment.

Sam turned to the next page. BRUNO FREITAS, it said across the top, 1916–1920. Below the name was another list of initials and dates. On the next page was a picture, cut from a newspaper, of a beautiful teenage girl in a long, frilly white dress. A caption below the picture said, "Gayle Joseph Makes Her Debut at the Detroit Debutante Ball."

Anna said, "Go back a page." Sam flipped to the list of initials the page before. Anna pointed to the list.

"G.J.," Anna said. "Gayle Joseph."

Sam nodded slowly. "It's a brag book. The initials are the girls. With mementos attached on the next page."

"But what kind of bragging?" Anna said. "Sexual conquests? Or something more violent?"

"You mean, did they kill all these girls?"

Anna nodded.

"I doubt it. Debutantes are so much harder to kill than prostitutes. They're not usually the top choice for serial killers. We'll see."

Sam kept turning the pages, which followed the same pattern. A male name at the top, a list of initials and dates below. The next page was always covered with small mementos: pictures mostly, but also lockets, playbills, snips of fabric. In the 1950s a man named Scott Westerman listed M.M. among the initials. The next page included a glossy picture of Marilyn Monroe and a snippet of platinum hair.

"No way," Steve said.

They kept going, through the '60s, '70s, '80s, '90s. The women's hairstyles changed, the pictures got color, and the mementos became more current: a bar tab from Lucky's, the printout of a text message. But the format was the same. The Beta Psi boy's name, then the initials, then the mementos.

Finally, they came to the pages where the date ranges were current. "Whoa," said Steve when they came to Dylan's page.

Dylan Highsmith
_2011–2015_

_K.G. 11.14.11_
_V.H. 1.5.12_
_G.F. 5.17.12_
_E.C. 9.1.12_
_R.O'T. 9.3.12_
_V.B. 9.5.12_
_M.V. 9.5.12_
_K.L. 9.8.12_
_A.T. 9.12.12_
_T.U. 9.24.12_
_V.W. 9.30.12_
_H.R. 10.4.12_
_O.C. 10.7.12_
_U.M. 10.11.12_
_L.K. 10.18.12_
_S.S. 11.3.12_
_P.R. 12.1.12_
_M.F. 12.8.12_
_N.Q. 1.3.13_
_T.G. 1.14.13_
_K.M. 1.23.13_
_C.W. 1.31.13_
_R.E. 2.2.13_
_V.T. 2.7.13_
_E.D. 2.15.13_
_T.Z. 2.28.13_
_I.R. 3.4.13_
_V.O. 3.15.13_
_U.B. 3.22.13_
_U.R. 4.1.13_
_Y.H. 4.15.13_
_T.E. 4.22.13_
_I.R. 5.1.13_
_M.N. 5.3.13_
_U.O. 5.15.13_

I.P. 5.21.13
R.O'D. 5.25.13
L.L. 6.1.13
R.W. 9.2.13
I.G. 9.3.13
M.B. 9.11.13
K.LR. 9.17.13
J.G. 9.30.13
K.B. 10.31.13
R.T. 12.31.13
D.H. 1.6.14
B.F. 2.5.14
M.H. 2.14.14
J.L. 3.3.14
T.R. 3.15.14
J.G. 4.2.14
P.T. 4.12.14
M.R. 5.1.14
S.McV. 5.2.14
I.S. 5.4.14
Z.M. 6.1.14
E.S. 9.1.14
G.V. 9.2.14
R.M. 9.3.14
K.H. 9.4.14
W.F. 9.5.14
C.R. 9.15.14
T.W. 9.22.14
C.T. 10.15.14
M.V. 11.12.14
I.K. 12.3.14
S.S. 1.12.15
K.J. 2.5.15
J.J. 3.3.15

Anna recognized the handwriting from the notebooks in Dylan's room. These entries had been written by Dylan himself. She skimmed the list, then focused on the fall of 2014. And there it was:

"E.S. 9.1.14." Emily Shapiro, September first. Anna pulled out her phone and took a picture of the page.

"Looks like he really started to get lucky in 2012," Sam said.

"Maybe that's when he perfected his recipe," Anna said. "And he slowed down in the fall of 2014, after Emily's case got some traction. Could've been worried."

"Look at this one, September of 2013," Sam said. "K.LR. Kristen LaRose?"

"Barney's mistress. She gets around."

"Do you think he raped all of them?" Steve said.

"There weren't this many cases filed against him," Sam said. "Not even a fraction."

"Rape is the most underreported crime in America," Anna said. "Over eighty percent of victims never report it."

"Who knows. Some of these might've been consensual."

Sam turned the page. There were several pictures of young women. One picture was of Emily Shapiro, lying in bed next to Dylan, squinting blearily at the camera.

Sam's radio crackled to life. A disembodied voice came through the speaker. "Randazzo, you'd better come up here."

Sam pressed the button on her shoulder and spoke into it. "I'm in the middle of something. Is it important?"

The radio crackled again. "Uh, yeah. There's a guy here, saying we have to stop the search and leave the house."

"Tell him to fuck off. Politely."

"I would," said the radio voice. "Except he's the district attorney. He's got a bunch of state troopers here trying to confiscate our evidence."

Sam cursed a rainbow of obscenities. Then she pressed the button and spoke into the mic. "We're on our way."

23

They jogged back through the dark hallway and up the stone stairs, then climbed out of the coffin into the Crypt. They kept going, out the dynamited door, up the basement steps, and through the handsome foyer. Sam called for all the FBI agents who were searching the house to follow them out the front door and onto the fraternity's wide front porch. Anna took a big breath of the cold outdoor air, incredibly fresh after the bone-lined basement. A big man in a tan suit stood on the porch, facing a stoic FBI tech who was refusing to hand over a box of evidence. A bunch of state troopers in tan uniforms stood on the porch behind the man.

Anna stood next to the FBI tech. She was in charge of legal challenges. She looked at the big man in the tan suit.

"Hello, I'm Anna Curtis, an Assistant U.S. Attorney. May I help you?"

"I want this search stopped," the man said.

"Sir, I'm at a disadvantage, since I don't know who you are or why your wishes should carry any weight."

The man puffed out his chest and pulled out the credential clipped to his belt on a retractable cord. "I'm Bill Xanten, the Tower County district attorney. And this is a lawless travesty."

"Nice to meet you." Anna had read his name in the papers many times and wondered how it was pronounced. Zanten. Good to know. "We have a warrant."

"Let me see it."

She handed him a copy and looked him over as he read. He was a man whose thick waist spoke of meat and potatoes, and whose symmetrical auburn roots spoke of a hair transplant. He wore a gold wedding ring, a gold watch, and a Michigan-shaped American flag lapel pin. His bulbous nose flared with anger as he looked up from the warrant. "I don't know how you got this, but no searches happen in my county unless I'm informed of them. I'm ordering you to stop."

"The warrant is signed by a federal judge," Anna said. "I'm a federal prosecutor, investigating a federal case. With all due respect, there's no signature block for the county DA, and we don't need one. We have jurisdiction, we have a warrant, and we respectfully ask that you step aside."

"You said your name is Curtis, right? You're the girl who assaulted Dylan Highsmith in this very house. Surely you don't think you should be in charge of searching here."

"Mr. Highsmith cannot choose his prosecutor, nor can he choose to get one removed from his case by assaulting her. I have decided to stay on the case despite Dylan Highsmith's unexpected groping. That doesn't change our legal basis for this search."

"You're going to be in charge of this case for approximately two more minutes—until I get you kicked off. I've been the top attorney of this state for the last ten years, and I will be for the next ten. You'll want to be on my good side when I decide whether to prosecute you for assaulting Dylan Highsmith."

"Are you threatening me?"

"Damn straight I am." He turned to his troopers. "Stop this search. Take anything these agents have collected and return it to the house."

"Do not do that." Anna made her voice as loud and authoritative as his. "Mr. Xanten may make whatever legal challenges he'd like—in the future. Right now all he has is hot air. I have a federal search warrant. Any trooper who interferes with this lawful search will be arrested by the FBI and charged with federal obstruction of justice."

The troopers eyed the FBI agents. Standing on opposite sides of the porch, they looked like two sports teams facing off: the locals in tan, the feds in dark blue. Blue outnumbered tan three to one. It didn't change her legal standing, but it helped the practicalities.

Xanten stepped forward till his chest was close to Anna's face. He was six inches taller and probably a hundred fifty pounds heavier. Looking up, she could see the hairs inside his nostrils. His breath smelled of stale coffee and salami. Her instinct was to step back—but she made sure she didn't. She put her hands on her hips and kept herself planted in place.

"Young lady," said Xanten, "you don't know who you're messing with."

She smiled up at his nose hairs. "I think you don't know who *you're* messing with. I grew up in Michigan. I still read the *Detroit Free Press*. I know you were Robert Highsmith's campaign manager the first time he ran for office. In fact, now that I think about it, aren't you godfather to one of his kids? I'd say that's a pretty serious conflict of interest, wouldn't you?"

"I don't know what you mean—"

"Then you'd better look it up," Anna said. "*You* are *exactly* the reason we need federal prosecutors on this case. And right now, you're impeding my search and obstructing justice. As a professional courtesy, we won't arrest and prosecute you—if you leave. Now."

Xanten looked at the twenty-five FBI agents behind her, then at the eight troopers behind him. She could see the calculations whirring through his hair-transplanted head. He would lose a shoot-out. He would also lose any inquiry into the legality of his actions. He'd hoped to bully her into stopping the search. It hadn't worked.

"You're going to regret this, young lady." Xanten turned and herded his troopers down the porch steps. He shot one last furious look back at her. "You have no idea what you just started."

"Thanks for stopping by," Anna said. "Appreciate the assistance."

Xanten slammed into his brown sedan. She waved good-bye, making sure no one could see that her hand was trembling.

VLOG
RECORDED 2.4.15

My whole body is shaking. I'm, like, totally confused.

Dylan is walking around—like he owns the place, same as before. How's this even possible?

I wasn't prepared. If I'd been prepared, maybe it wouldn't've been so, like, shocking.

I was walking a couple dogs, Fenwick and a little white terrier named Fiona. Just having a regular day, you know? Snow was coming down, these big white flakes, and I was thinking how pretty the world looks under fresh white powder. The trees were all glittering like fairy ice sculptures. It was one of those days where you just have to love Michigan and winter.

And I look up, because someone is coming toward me on the walking path, and I go to smile at whoever it is. And it's Dylan.

What the hell? My heart starts pounding.

I thought it was a vision, a mirage in the snow. It's, like, I've worried about him jumping out of the bushes for so long. He's the bogeyman who keeps showing up in my nightmares. Sometimes I see a kid with dark hair and think I need to run. Before it's always been a different boy, right?

So this time, I do a double take, and then I look again. I'm sure it's gonna be someone else. But it's him. Not lurking in a bush, or driving behind tinted windows. Walking through campus, open and notorious. A big grin on his face, like he has every right.

So I'm like, "What are you doing here?"

And he says, "You don't own this campus."

And I'm like, "There's a stay-away order. You can't be here."

He comes right up to me, takes hold of my scarf, and pulls me into him, so his words are fogging my face. And he says, real soft and slow, "I can do whatever I fucking want."

My heart is racing. I'm frozen. Just terrified. It's like my nightmare come to life.

That's when Fenwick bit him. Snarled and lunged and bit him right in the ass. Fiona got in on the action too and started biting his ankles.

Dylan tried to run away and slipped and fell on the ice. A couple kids saw him flailing around in the snow and laughed. I think I might've even laughed too. God, I love those dogs.

I patted them and told them they were good puppies. Fenwick turned to look at me, his big pink tongue flopping out of his big white teeth, and he gave me that amazing dog smile.

Dylan walked off, calling me a "crazy bitch."

I wish I were a crazy bitch. I don't think crazy bitches get as scared as I was.

I'm still, like, shaking. I just can't stop shaking.

Why is he here?

I talked to my friends. Preya heard from her friend Mackenzie, who heard from her cousin Addie, that Dylan's finishing his last semester. He'll graduate with his class this spring. But, I thought, they had to be wrong.

So I . . . well, I called the registrar and pretended to be an HR rep from Smith Barney, checking on his transcript for a job interview. Don't judge, okay? I was flipping out, and I had to know. Anyway, they confirmed it. Dylan is a registered student, expected to graduate with honors this June.

But—how can that be? He was expelled.

He was expelled.

He was EXPELLED.

What is going on?

24

know who killed Emily Shapiro," said the man on the phone.

Anna looked at the caller's info. The number was a 313 area code—here in Michigan—but unfamiliar. She'd answered because any call could be a break in the case. She watched Xanten and his state troopers drive away as she stood on the frat's porch. Sam was telling the other FBI agents to go back in and continue their search.

"Who is this?" Anna said.

"My name is Landon LaRose," said the voice on the phone. "I'm Kristen LaRose's husband."

Anna grabbed Sam's arm and pulled her inside. She led her into an empty den and put the phone on speaker. She needed a witness to this conversation.

"And you say you know who killed Emily Shapiro?"

"Yes."

"Who?"

"Can you come to my house to talk?"

Anna and Sam looked at each other and nodded.

"Yes, sir. Are you available in an hour?"

"Yeah, come on over."

He gave them his address.

Over the next forty-five minutes, Sam sent FBI photographers into the Crypt and the Underground to take pictures. Anna called for a forensic team to collect the bones. She led them down to the tunnels and bone room, where they stared in the same horror she had. They had the grim task of collecting, categorizing, and DNA testing these remains. Anna sent the shimmery scarf from Dylan's room for DNA testing, and the liquor bottles for testing for date-rape drugs. She called the university registrar and requested a list of all the names of students enrolled for the last four years, to compare to the initials in the *Earthly Pleasures* book.

As she ticked off items on her to-do list, her chest tightened with the urgency of getting it all done as quickly as possible. Bill Xanten was a powerful force in Michigan. She'd won the battle today, but Xanten would continue the war, and he'd do whatever he could to protect the Highsmith family. She had to find Emily before he could interfere.

■ ■ ■

After everything was in motion, Anna and Sam left. Steve would wrap up the final part of the search. As Sam drove them to the LaRoses' house, Anna called BlueTube. A young man answered the phone and introduced himself as Chandler Andrews, a senior tech. Anna introduced herself and said, "I'm calling to make sure you received our subpoenas—and to see how quickly we can get the videos."

"Let me see here." Chandler spoke over the click of a keyboard. "I see you're trying to get some video logs that were posted by someone named Emily Shapiro."

"Right."

"Unfortunately, those videos were removed from our site."

"I'd like to find out how, when, and why those videos were removed," Anna said. "And if BlueTube can recover the videos, we are asking for copies of them."

"Let's see." There was a long pause. "It looks like the user herself took the videos down on March 19, 2015. And we don't have any copies saved here at BlueTube."

"That's too bad," Anna said. "Please send me all the paperwork related to the account, as required in the subpoena."

"Will do."

Sam pulled the SUV into the LaRoses' comfortable suburban neighborhood. Anna lowered her phone and looked around. The streets were lined with pretty houses on wide yards, the driveways covered in bikes and toys. It was obviously professors' housing, not students'. They stopped in front of the LaRoses' address. A man stood inside his redbrick colonial, looking out through his storm door. He watched as they parked in the street, got out of the car, and came up the sidewalk. He opened the door.

"I'm Landon LaRose. Come in."

Landon was an attractive man buried somewhere below terrible grooming. When he smiled at them, his teeth were yellow and grainy, as if they hadn't been brushed in a while. His cheeks held a week's worth of mangy stubble. He had a full head of graying sandy hair, but it was matted on one side and sticking straight up on the other. He wore stained jeans and a rumpled button-down shirt that emitted a slightly sour smell, making Anna wonder how many days he'd been wearing them.

Landon led them through a living room, where a girl and a boy, maybe two and three years old, were playing with Legos on the floor. A flurry of toys, dirty socks, and Veggie Booty bags were strewn about them.

Taking Sam and Anna into the adjacent kitchen, Landon gestured for them to sit at a table covered with sticky residue and two bowls of soggy Froot Loops. Anna took the bowls to the sink. Dirty dishes were piled there and on every available space on the counter. She stacked them onto another pile of bowls.

"Your kids?" Anna asked, nodding toward the living room as she sat down.

"Yes. Maddie and Grayson."

"They're adorable," Anna said. They were, but they were as disheveled as their father. The kids both had crusty noses, dirty clothes, and tangled hair falling into their eyes. The boy was wearing a dress. Anna wondered if it was a style choice or just the last remaining clean clothes.

Landon said, "They're having a hard time getting over their mother leaving. But does she care? No. She's an ambitious bitch who loves her career more than her kids."

Anna saw the children look up at the mention of their mother. She got up and closed the door between the kitchen and living room. She lowered her voice so the children couldn't hear.

"Sir, you said you had a tip about who killed Emily Shapiro. Can you tell us what you know?"

He ran a hand through his hair, making it stand up even more. He looked at Sam then Anna. "What you have to understand," he said, "is how perfect our marriage was before."

"Okay."

"We met in grad school. I was her thesis adviser. Kristen was a top student in the English program. At the time, I didn't realize that she wanted me because I held something she was going for. We've been married eight years. I thought we had it all. Beautiful house, beautiful kids. Discussions so much deeper than the average marriage—we'd talk about poetry and beauty and meaning in life."

Anna nodded, hoping this would connect up with Emily's disappearance soon.

"Then she left me. Out of the blue. I was in shock. Until I heard who she was leaving me for. The college president. Of course. She'd been angling to be the dean of English for years. And now that she's with Barney Shapiro, she'll get it. Nothing has ever been able to stop Kristen from getting what she wanted. Until Emily."

"How so?" Anna glanced at Sam and saw the agent was taking notes. Good.

"Emily refused to accept Kristen. There was some dinner at Shapiro's place. They announced they were getting married. And Emily said she'd die before she'd accept Kristen as a stepmother. Shapiro was so upset, he postponed the wedding. You see what was going on? All that was standing in the way of Kristen and everything she ever wanted was this girl."

"So . . ." Anna said.

"So Kristen took her out."

"You're saying your ex-wife, Professor Kristen LaRose, killed Emily Shapiro?"

"Yes. Can't you see? Take a very close look at where Kristen was the night Emily disappeared. When she wants to get something done, she finds a way to do it."

A key part of any investigation, Anna knew, was keeping an open mind. The obvious answer wasn't always the right one. Things happened that were random, unexpected, unbelievable. You couldn't make them up—but they were the truth. Anna once had a case where a woman named Glenda was repeatedly physically abused by her boyfriend. Like many victims of domestic violence, Glenda kept going back to this terrible boyfriend, despite friends and family members who warned that he would eventually kill her. Finally, after a particularly terrible beating, she agreed to leave him. She went to the police, and they put her up in a hotel. The next morning, Glenda was found beaten to death in the hotel room. Everyone assumed the abusive boyfriend had somehow found her. But in fact, Glenda had gone to a bar the night before, met a different bad man, and brought him back to her hotel. They got in a fight, and the new guy beat Glenda to death. The world was a random place. Terrible things could go down in an infinite number of ways. The most obvious one was not always the one that had actually happened.

Anna pictured the scarf on the floor in Dylan's closet. She thought that was more likely to hold a clue to Emily's case than Landon and Kristen's banal domestic drama. Still, she'd have an agent look into where Kristen and Landon were when Emily disappeared.

"Did Kristen ever actually threaten Emily?" Anna asked.

"Not to her face. But she said it would be convenient if Emily were gone."

"When did she say that?"

"The night Emily disappeared."

"Where were you?"

"Here. At my house. She called me."

"Just to tell you that she wanted Emily out of the picture?"

"No. We were talking about the kids' schedule. And she said it was hard to coordinate our kids with Barney's kid."

"Has your wife ever done anything violent before? To Emily or anyone else?"

"She bit my finger."

Anna blinked. "How did that happen?"

"We were having a fight, and I pointed at her to make a point. And she bit it!"

He held out his hand for them to examine. There was, indeed, a small raised scar on his right index finger.

"Did you report this to the police?"

"You're damn straight I did! She spent the night in jail."

Anna glanced at Sam. "Was she convicted?"

"No. I dropped the charges. Because I didn't want to ruin her life."

"Mm-hmm. Did you get some concession in your divorce for dropping the charges?"

"Well, yeah. After I dropped charges, she agreed to give me half of her pension. I absolutely deserved that money."

"Right." Anna looked at the kitchen door, made sure it was still shut, then lowered her voice. "Sir, we had information that during the course of your divorce, you posted some intimate pictures of Kristen to a revenge porn site. Is there any truth to that?"

"Where did you hear that?"

"That's not important. I'm just asking—can you confirm or deny it?"

"Did Kristen tell you that?"

"Sir, I can't reveal my sources during a criminal investigation."

"What if I did post some . . . uh . . . erotic videos of Kristen online. Linked them to her phone number and Facebook account. Hypothetically. Would that be a crime?"

"It could be, depending on the circumstances. I'm not your attorney and I can't give you legal advice."

"I . . . I . . . I'm thinking I don't want to answer questions about revenge porn without a lawyer present."

He might be crazy, but he wasn't stupid. Anna wasn't sure who was more suspicious, him or his ex-wife.

"Let me give you some nonlegal advice," Anna said. "Give your children a bath and a hot meal. Try to enjoy them. They're beautiful. Divorce is a hard time for kids. They need you."

"I didn't call you for parenting advice. What are you going to do about Kristen?"

"We'll look into your tip, sir, along with all the other evidence we're collecting." Anna stood, gave him her card, and told him to call her if he had any more information. "In the meantime," she said, "try to remember that old saying. 'Carrying a grudge is like drinking poison and hoping the other person dies.'"

Law Offices of Kaiser, LeGrand & Dillon
1001 K Street, NW
Washington, DC 20001

January 31, 2015

Lisa Sinrod Brey
Vice President
Tower University
Tower, MI 48021

Re: *Shapiro v. Highsmith, Disciplinary Case No. 14-073*

Dear Ms. Brey,

I write to appeal the sentence of the Disciplinary Committee in the above case. Attached you will find copies of all the paperwork.

While Mr. Highsmith does not dispute the factual determination of the committee (for the purposes of this letter, at least), we believe that the punishment of expulsion is excessive. We ask that you mitigate it.

In support of our request, please consider the following. Dylan Highsmith is in the final semester of his senior year and is due to graduate this May. In fact, Dylan is an honors student, carrying a 3.6 grade point average, and has been on the Dean's List six of his seven semesters. He is also a student leader; he is head of the Greek Council and the pledge master of his fraternity, Beta Psi. In his Greek work, he founded the "Leaders Are Readers" program, which matches college students with elementary-school children with learning disabilities, so that the college students can help tutor the children. As part of that program, he was named a Michigan Young Leader.

Trouble is not in his character. He is a hardworking, compassionate, dedicated young man. He is terribly upset that Ms. Shapiro felt her encounter was not consensual. He believed it was. As you will see from the committee's verdict, no one believes that Dylan forcibly assaulted Ms. Shapiro. What we have, rather, is two intoxicated young people who ended up in bed together, and the shades of gray that result when memories are clouded and intentions blurred by whiskey. Given the entirety of the circumstances, it is a shame to ruin a young man's life because of one alcohol-clouded encounter, which even the complaining witness did not recall with clarity.

And, make no mistake, an expulsion would effectively ruin Dylan Highsmith's life. He is due to graduate this May and has accepted an offer of employment with an investment firm. That offer is contingent on Dylan graduating. If Dylan is expelled, he will have to find a way to finish his education at some other university. He will lose his dream job. He will have a mark on his transcript for the rest of his life.

As you may know, Dylan is a third-generation legacy at Tower University. His father and grandfather graduated from Tower before him. The family has a lot of Tower pride and school spirit and hopes for nothing greater than to have another generation of Highsmith men graduate from Tower.

Of course, some punishment is appropriate. We ask that Dylan be allowed to repay his debt to society through service to the community, specifically, two hundred hours of community service. We would also happily accept a monetary fine, and a written reprimand included in his student file. This would give a consequence that fits the crime, while allowing a well-meaning and hardworking young man to make amends but continue down a positive path in his life.

Thank you for your consideration.

> Very truly yours,
> Justin Dillon, Esq.

25

The Tower County medical examiner's office was a palace of gleaming white. Pristine white walls, clean white tile floors, glinting steel saws hanging from silver hooks. The bones looked yellow in comparison. They were laid out on twenty different stainless steel tables. Each table had a number on it, indicating where in the underground room the bones had been found, corresponding with numbered placards the FBI photographers placed in the room before taking pictures. The bones had been glued flimsily to the walls—the techs had been able to pry them loose in a couple hours. The one intact skeleton lay on its own steel table; the red Beta Psi baseball cap rested next to its skull. Three technicians in white coats walked among the tables, cataloging the bones, taking notes, and beginning their tests.

Jack stood next to Anna, surveying the results of their search warrant. Anna stared at the sprawling field of bones—hundreds, maybe thousands of vertebrae, femurs, tibia, ribs, knuckles—laid out like knickknacks on display at a store. She thought of all the lives they represented. The sight made her sick and furious.

"We have to get Dylan Highsmith," she said.

"Yes," Jack said mildly. "He's not responsible for these remains, though."

"How do you know?"

"For one thing, these bones look old. He's only been in the frat a few years."

"You'd normally wait for the ME to give her findings on bones. What else do you know?"

"The fraternity's national lawyer called me today, after he saw this on the news. He said the underground room used to be an icehouse or root cellar, which was used to store food back in the 1800s. Eventually they moved to refrigeration and the icehouse was abandoned—till the 1920s, when the young men living there then decided to make it into a ritual room. The bones were placed there by Beta Psi members in the '20s through the '80s. Whenever a medical student worked on a cadaver, he was supposed to steal a few bones to add them to the collection. It was sort of an ongoing dare."

"What about the whole skeleton, the one with the cap?"

"A model, stolen from the medical school in the '50s. The lawyer claimed to have several old men, retired doctors, who will admit to stealing these bones decades ago, when they were students."

"Do you believe it?"

"It wouldn't be the first frat to have a stash of illicit bones. The descendants of Geronimo, the Native American chief, sued Yale's Skull and Bones fraternity in 2011. They claimed that Prescott Bush—George W.'s grandfather—dug up Geronimo's remains and hid them in that frat house back in 1918. We'll confirm today's find with DNA and the ME's findings. But if what the Beta Psi lawyer says is true—and I think it probably is—we're still just looking for one missing girl."

"What about *The Book of Earthly Pleasures*?" Anna said.

"According to the lawyer, that is a book of sexual conquests. Consensual ones. Not rapes."

"No, of course not," she said. "They're such upstanding citizens."

If this story was true, the basement was more like a macabre version of boys playing Dungeons and Dragons than evidence of mass murder. Anna had to keep her focus on the one girl they knew was in real, current danger—and the person most likely to have hurt her.

■ ■ ■

Anna borrowed a conference room at the medical examiner's office and pulled out the university's file on Dylan Highsmith that she'd won at the hearing yesterday. She went through the cases again. Three female students had brought disciplinary charges against Dylan before Emily had. None of those cases had ended in Dylan being disciplined.

She checked their initials against Dylan's entries in the *Earthly Pleasure* book. They matched up.

The first case had been brought two years earlier, by a freshman named Ursula Maris. In her statement to the Disciplinary Committee, she said that she went to a party at Beta Psi, met Dylan, and drank a margarita he offered. She blacked out. Her next memory was a flash: waking up in Dylan's bed, with him having sex with her. She blacked out again. When she awoke, she found herself naked in Dylan's bed. She dressed and fled from the house. She didn't report the incident until the following week, when all the physical evidence was gone. Ursula had filed a disciplinary case, then dropped it before a hearing was held.

Anna looked up Ursula's current address and found that she had transferred to Northwestern University in Chicago. Had the incident with Dylan prompted the move? It seemed monumentally unfair that Dylan would get to stay and Ursula would have to transplant her life. Ursula had a cell number listed, and Anna hoped it was still the same. She called it, and was happily surprised when a woman answered on the first ring.

"May I speak to Ursula Maris, please?"

"This is. Who is this?"

"My name is Anna Curtis. I'm a prosecutor investigating a case involving Dylan Highsmith. Do you have a few minutes to talk?"

"Um." The woman paused. "I'm sorry, I . . . don't want to talk to you."

"I know it's a hard subject matter, and I'm really sorry to bother you. But there is a missing girl, and any information that you might be willing to share might help us find her."

"Look, I'm sorry, but I, like, literally cannot talk about this."

"Tell you what," Anna said, "I know it's probably a shock to get this call. How about I give you my number. Think about it. If you change your mind, call me. Any time, night or day."

"I'm not going to change my mind. Good-bye."

Anna set the phone down. There were plenty of reasons a rape survivor might not want to talk to her. It was a hard conversation. Few people wanted to revisit a traumatic experience, especially if it was long ago, and they had gotten over it. But that wasn't the sense Anna got from Ursula. When she said, *I literally cannot talk about it,* Anna hadn't pictured so much a mental block as a legal impediment. She wondered if Ursula had been paid off. Her disciplinary suit had been dropped entirely—what could be more convenient for

Dylan? And if his family had paid Ursula off to keep her quiet, they likely would have included a nondisclosure agreement as part of the settlement.

Anna sent Ursula her phone number and e-mail address. Just in case you change your mind, Anna texted. She wouldn't hold her breath. She turned to the next case in the university file.

The second woman who brought charges against Dylan had transferred to Columbia. Anna called her and had almost the exact same conversation she'd had with Ursula.

She pulled out the final case. The third student was a young woman named Kara Briscoe. Her file had a similar story: a freshman at a frat party, mixed drinks, waking up in Dylan's bed. The difference, for Kara, was that she had pursued her claim all the way through a Disciplinary Committee hearing—where Dylan had been found "not responsible." Anna thought she might have a better chance of getting Kara's story. She was listed as a sophomore at Tower. Anna called her dorm phone number.

"I'm sorry," said the person who answered. "I'm her roommate. Kara isn't here, and she won't be back for a while."

"Oh," said Anna. "Do you know where I can reach her?"

"Um. Not really."

Anna went through the song and dance about being a federal investigator, looking into the disappearance of Emily Shapiro, and how any information would be helpful.

After an uncomfortable silence, the roommate said, "Kara's at New Horizons."

"Do you have the phone number for her there?"

"I'm sorry. I'm not really supposed to give that out. I've already probably said too much." The girl hung up.

26

New Horizons was a private rehabilitation center located on a posh ten-acre campus in the exurbs of Tower County. Sam and Anna drove down a long tree-lined driveway. A white clapboard fence surrounded sweeping snow-covered fields, where weeping willows bordered a stream. The setting sun threw pink light on the undulating white hills. If you had to go somewhere to recover from something, this seemed like the place for it.

Modern white buildings dotted the campus. They pulled up to the Mental Health Center and Residences, a complex of curved white stone and swooping waves of glass. The interior was decorated in soothing neutral tones. A nurse greeted them; they'd called ahead of time and were expected.

"Welcome to New Horizons," said the nurse. "I'm Tamara Welch, Kara's nurse. Before you meet her, I need to brief you. She's doing well today and has been getting better over time. But she's still very sensitive and suffers from serious depression and anxiety, in addition to overcoming an alcohol addiction. Mentally, she's fragile. Please try to steer away from topics that could be alarming or upsetting to her."

"I'm not sure that's possible," Anna said, "given what we have to talk to her about."

The nurse looked at them worriedly. "She really wants to speak to you. But, please, be gentle."

"Of course," Sam said.

The nurse led them to a three-story glass atrium filled with trees, flowers, and a man-made brook. Stone paths were dotted with benches, where people sat reading or talking. Anna could see the snow outside, but inside the atrium was almost tropical. It was beautiful, but the artificiality of it all, the sense of madness barely contained by expensive trappings, felt like a silken straitjacket.

Kara Briscoe sat on a bench, biting her thumbnail and gazing out the windows at the field of snow. She had long, beautiful red hair and fingernails that were ragged and bitten to the nubs. But she smiled brightly at Anna and Sam and stood to shake their hands. The nurse made sure they were all settled, then left them alone with Kara.

"I'm sorry you had to come out here," Kara said, gesturing around her.

"It's pretty," Anna said. "Though I'm sorry you're having troubles."

Kara noticed she was biting her nails. She took her thumb from her mouth and set her hands carefully down on her lap. She wore jeans and a white T-shirt, civilian clothes; the place was designed to feel like a resort rather than a hospital.

"I hear that you're investigating Dylan Highsmith," Kara said. "How can I help?"

Anna took a deep grateful breath. "I don't want to upset you. So please let me know if you need a break or just want to stop."

"Okay."

"It would be helpful if you could tell us what happened between you and Dylan."

"He raped me." Kara smiled bitterly. "There you go. I'll say it again. 'He raped me.' It took me a year of therapy to be able to say that."

"I'm sorry," Anna said.

"You read the university's file?" Kara asked.

Anna nodded.

"Then you know what happened. He spiked my drink, knocked me out. Took me upstairs and had sex with me. Laughed when I confronted him. I brought the case against him through the university disciplinary process—and no one believed me. They found him 'not responsible.' "

"For what it's worth," Anna said, "that verdict was not about you. It was about the university. They want to report zero rapes on campus. It's harder to do that if they find the guy guilty."

Kara ran a hand through her long red hair. "Yeah, I kinda figured that. I wasn't done fighting. I thought if the college didn't believe me, maybe the regular courts would."

"What did you do?" Anna knew there hadn't been a criminal case; it would have shown up on the background check.

"I filed a civil case against him. Sued him and his fraternity for five million dollars."

"Good for you."

"Not so good for me. It was a shitstorm. Excuse my language. The fraternity, apparently, gets all the brothers to sign a code of conduct, which is so stringent no boy could possibly live by it. So then if the frat is sued, the boys are considered in breach of fraternity policy, and the frat throws them overboard. Beta Psi got itself out of the lawsuit. They had a good policy—it was the individual boys who violated it. I could only sue the boys.

"Dylan had the best lawyers in Michigan. He got himself severed from the lawsuit too. The only person left, by the end, was some poor freshman pledge who'd served me the alcohol, which I guess violated Beta Psi policy. His name was Eddie. He was a nice kid, and I didn't have anything against him. His family had to hire a lawyer and defend against my lawsuit. I got a thirty-thousand-dollar settlement from that family. I hear Eddie's family had to remortgage their house to pay for their lawyer and ended up losing it in foreclosure."

She looked around the atrium. "Thirty thousand paid for my first week here."

"I'm so sorry," Anna said. "That sounds like a terrible process. On all counts."

"I feel bad about Eddie. I feel worse about Dylan."

"Did you know Dylan before the assault?"

"I was in a sorority, so I knew of him—he was head of some big Greek event; he seemed really cool. I only met him in person the night he raped me. But I got to know him after that."

"How so?"

"He got me blackballed from Greek life. He knew everyone. Guys taunted me. Girls whispered about me. I've never felt so hated. I tried to stick it out, you know, to make a point. But I felt so alone."

"Being a freshman itself is hard," Anna said. "Away from home for the first time, far from everyone you know and love. And you were put in a terrible situation, right at the beginning."

Kara nodded. "That's when I started drinking. It started as pregaming on weekends, a socially acceptable way to get wasted. It ended with me drinking a fifth of vodka every day, alone in my room."

The sky grew dark, turning the atrium's windows into a wall of mirrors. Anna looked at Kara's sad profile, then her pale face reflected in the glass. "They found me on the bathroom floor, passed out, puke in my hair. They had to pump my stomach. My blood alcohol level was so high, they tell me it's a miracle I didn't die."

Anna put a hand on Kara's arm. Kara turned to her. "What's going on with Dylan now?"

"You've heard of Emily Shapiro?"

"The girl who disappeared."

"He was the last person to see her."

"You think he hurt her?"

"It's possible. He hasn't been charged with anything yet."

Kara brought her thumb back to her mouth and gnawed around her thumbnail. The ragged skin broke open and started bleeding. A few drops of crimson spattered Kara's white T-shirt. Anna offered her a tissue. Kara crumbled it into a ball inside her fist, then continued chewing on the thumbnail.

"Why don't we take a break," Anna said.

"I don't want a break. Why are you here?"

"I'm seeing if we can build a case against Dylan."

"How does what happened to me help you with Emily's case?"

"If he's committed a series of crimes against women, a pattern of assaults on people of one gender, that could be evidence that his actions were committed because of the gender of his victims. Which is a hate crime."

"Of course they were committed because of my gender!" Kara started laughing. "He wasn't drugging the boys."

"Right. It's complicated, under federal law."

"It's always complicated when women are victims. Because the people making the laws are men. It's like the women's bathrooms at football games."

"Sorry, I don't follow."

"There's always a hundred people waiting for the ladies' room at halftime. The men's room you can always walk right into. Because men build the stadiums."

"Ah, got it. I see what you're saying."

"It's 'complicated' because men build the bathrooms," Kara said. She laughed again, a giggly hiccup that she covered with her hand.

"The Highsmiths build the bathrooms." The giggles grew to full-fledged laughter. "Dylan builds the bathrooms!" She rocked backward with the hilarity of it. Residents on other benches looked over. Anna put a hand on Kara's arm and turned to signal for a nurse.

"Kara, we definitely need a break," Anna said.

Kara's laughter grew louder. Between gulps of laughter, she choked out, "Dylan controls the world. You'll see. You'll see!" Her laughs were almost shrieks.

Tamara and two male nurses hurried toward them. The nurses shot Anna an angry look, then helped Kara to her feet and started walking her back toward the lobby. Kara pulled away from them. "No. No! No!" she shouted. "Get your hands off me! No one touch me! Do not touch me!" She tried to run from them. The nurses grabbed her; between the three of them, they managed to keep her from bolting. Tamara pulled a syringe out of her pocket. Kara saw it and panicked. She screamed and thrashed in the nurses' arms. Her red hair whipped their faces as her screams echoed off the glass walls. Tamara plunged a shot into her arm.

As the needle slid into her skin, Kara's scream was so piercing it hurt Anna's eardrums. The young woman stopped thrashing. Her screams stopped abruptly, and her eyes went dull. Her body melted between the nurses. The three nurses got hands under Kara's armpits and half escorted, half carried her away.

Tamara glared back at Anna and Sam. "Please leave."

27

There were dozens of protesters, maybe hundreds, looking like refugees from a war fleeing their homeland. Each carried a mattress. They walked slowly down North Campus Street, their zombielike speed perhaps a way to make a point or perhaps it was just difficult to carry their load. They didn't make a sound. Each mattress carrier had a piece of duct tape over his or her mouth. Heide Herrmann marched in the front, carrying a posterboard sign that said, WE WILL CARRY THIS WEIGHT UNTIL TOWER U PROTECTS RAPE VICTIMS.

The news cameras rolled, their lenses capturing the made-for-TV images.

The mattress carriers walked past the podium where Emily's parents were assembled to give their speech. A crowd stood around the parents, holding candles for the vigil. The mattress carriers silently nodded as they paraded past.

Mr. Shapiro stared at the protesters, then looked down at his feet. The mattress carriers were both supporting his daughter and protesting his university's policies. After his head injury two nights ago, he was probably having trouble standing, much less balancing his complicated work and personal lives. He wore a white bandage on his forehead, a remnant of where Mrs. Shapiro had sliced him with the crystal vase of flowers.

The effects of his concussion would last for several days. The legal effects would too. Mrs. Shapiro, elegant in a gray dress, was the subject of a restraining order mandating that she stay away from her husband—although the judge had made an exception for tonight, so the parents of the missing girl could stand together and issue a joint statement. Beatrice kept her back turned to Kristen, who hovered just off the elevated stage on which the podium stood.

The stage was set up on a concrete circle that surrounded the clock tower. As the Shapiros faced the microphone, they looked at North Campus Street, where Emily had run on the night she disappeared. The street itself had been blocked off for traffic, which allowed the procession of students carrying mattresses. Mrs. Shapiro looked grimly satisfied as she gazed on the procession.

Anna wasn't sure how the mattress carriers knew to come tonight. So far, the news had only reported that a girl was missing—not a girl who'd accused a boy of raping her before going missing. But, Anna supposed, word traveled around campus. The students in Emily and Preya's room had all known about the rape charges. While Anna was prohibited from giving information to the press about an ongoing investigation, it couldn't be long before the mainstream media got hold of that angle. Given the mattress protests, Anna guessed, someone would be telling the assembled reporters about the rape charges before the night was through.

Anna stood respectfully to the side of the podium. She'd organized the press conference and prepared the parents to speak. Anna herself would not make a public statement. The parents' message was a powerful one. Her job now was simply to stand out of the way.

Mrs. Shapiro stepped forward and leaned toward the microphone. Anna knew she was having trouble keeping from crying. She'd been sobbing all the way here, dabbing her eyes with tissues as they walked from the hotel, through campus, and up the three steps to this impromptu stage. Her eyes were pink and her mascara gone. But now she kept her face calm, eyes focused on some point on the other side of the street.

"My daughter, Emily, is one of the sweetest, most caring young women in the world. She loves music, cooking, and dogs," Beatrice said. "She is kind to everyone she meets. She is a wonderful daughter. We love her more than anything. Please, I beg anyone who has any information about what happened to Emily three nights ago, come forward. Please, if you're with her, keep her safe and warm. Know that Emily is a wonderful person and a light in this world. Please help us find Emily. Help us bring her home, where she belongs."

Mrs. Shapiro stepped back and her face collapsed. Her shoulders shook, and she buried her head in her hands. Mr. Shapiro looked at her uncomfortably, then reached into his pocket and pulled out a handkerchief. For a moment, she looked like she was going to refuse it, then she thanked him and used it to wipe her tears.

Mr. Shapiro stepped forward, touched his head wound, and looked around, confused. He blinked toward the microphone and said nothing. The last few days had changed him from a confident president who'd brushed off his daughter's disappearance as a "frolic" to a distraught man paralyzed by the possibility that she was really gone. He turned toward Anna, looking lost. Anna said softly to him, "Just talk to Emily." He nodded and turned back to the microphone.

"Emily," he said. "We love you so much. I pray that we'll see you soon. Anyone who knows anything about where she is, please call the hotline."

The people holding the candles murmured. Someone said "Amen." The mattress carriers kept coming, dozens of them toting their big white mattresses, gazing out above the duct tape over their mouths, silently passing the candlelight vigil.

The assembled press was torn between focusing their cameras on the sobbing parents and the mattress carriers shuffling past. Usually, the grieving parents would be the key shot. But the mattress carriers made such a vivid image.

Modern college students, Anna thought, knew how to work the media far more effectively than did older generations. They'd grown up in a world where going viral was the goal, and they understood like second nature the technology that democratized the chance to do it. They were savvy about how to make their issue become *the* issue. In Anna's day—which was only a decade ago—a student group might do a sit-in. They might have a march. But today's students—fluent in grassroots media like Twitter, Facebook, and Instagram, and steeped in the twenty-four-hour news cycle—were savvier than ever about what would make an impact.

Last month, at MSU, there'd been a "Walk a Mile in Her Shoes" protest, where a bunch of boys bared their hairy legs in shorts and skirts and wore high heels while they walked through town demanding equality for their female peers. That was followed by a "Slut Walk" at U of M, where a bunch of girls—and a few boys—dressed in skimpy clothes and paraded down the street. The girls, in studded leather bras and short shorts, yelled that they had the right to wear whatever they wanted and not be sexually assaulted. A few even went topless, shaking their bare breasts for CNN—which would blur them out—and any nearby cell-phone owners—who would not.

It was a strange sort of feminism, Anna thought, where women used the very bodies they were pronouncing sovereign as a way to titillate the rest of America into listening to them.

She helped the Shapiros down from the stage. She told them they'd done a good job, and that the phones were manned for any tipsters who might call. As well-wishers came up to hug the parents, Anna asked Kristen if they could speak alone for a moment. They walked over to a quiet area with Sam.

"Thanks for your help tonight," Anna said. "If you don't mind, I have just a few more follow-up questions."

"Of course," Kristen said.

"With apologies for asking a personal question. Did you have a relationship with Dylan Highsmith?"

"Mm." Kristen looked to where Barney was standing. She lowered her voice. "Define 'relationship.'"

Sam said, "Did you have sex with him?"

"I don't see how that's relevant."

"We're not here to gossip or start a scandal," Anna said. "But we need to know the truth."

Kristen twisted one of the piercings in her eyebrow. The gesture reminded Anna of an old-timey villain twirling his mustache. "We had a brief fling," Kristen said softly. "Maybe a year and a half ago. He'd been in my Shakespeare class the semester before."

"Was that 'fling' consensual?"

"Yes. Although regrettable. I had been his teacher. I shouldn't have let it happen."

"How long did your sexual relationship with Dylan last?"

"About fifteen minutes."

"Why him?"

Kristen sighed. "I had a very difficult marriage. I turned to many things I probably shouldn't have."

"Is that allowed under school rules? To be with a student?"

"You're very young. One day you'll understand. Rules sometimes fall away in the heat of the moment."

"What I'm asking is: Could you lose your job?"

"It's a gray area. He was no longer my student. There are plenty of male professors who've done far worse and never gotten a reprimand."

"Does Barney know?"

"No. We both lived full lives before we met. We don't need to hash out every detail. Everyone makes mistakes."

"Are there any other mistakes you need to tell us about?" Sam asked.

"My biggest mistake was not taking a restraining order out on Landon. I'm afraid he's not right in the head. Please excuse me. I need to be there for Barney now."

Kristen wended her way back through the crowd and brushed past Beatrice. As Beatrice glared, Kristen looped her arm around Barney's elbow.

28

Anna sat with her laptop in its usual position, balanced on her knees. She had a hard time concentrating on the writing in front of her, though. Between each paragraph, she saw Emily's single shoe, at the bottom of the pit. The red-brown smudge on the back of Dylan's Viper. The silver needle sliding into Kara Briscoe's soft skin.

She took a long sip of pinot noir. It was her second glass. Cooper sat next to her on the couch and held out a bowl of sweet-potato chips. She shook her head. "No thanks." She clicked through to the next case on PACER. She had a paralegal working to identify the girls whose initials were listed in Dylan's brag book. Meanwhile, Anna was looking up every civil case that had been brought against the Beta Psi fraternity in the last twenty years. There were fifty-six.

"Anna, you need a break," Cooper said softly. "Your mind and your body will be better off if they have some time to recover."

"I'm not interested in a break."

"You can't fix everything single-handedly."

"I can't seem to fix *anything*. And today I drove a poor young woman to a breakdown."

Cooper took her computer gently from her hands and set it down on the coffee table.

"Tell me what happened."

She didn't want to tell him what happened today. He might hate her. She wanted to lose herself in the computer and wine. He reached over and took her hands, enveloping hers completely. His palms were big, calloused, and warm. After hours of hearing terrible stories, Cooper's very tangibility was comforting. She gave him a quick summary of her day. He kept asking questions, drawing more and more details from her until she found herself telling him everything—every little detail, and how she felt about it. How it weighed on her. How she feared she wasn't going to find Emily. How Kara's reaction made her wonder if she was doing any good in the world at all. She did her job because she wanted to help people. So what did it mean when she was creating despair?

"You didn't create the despair," Cooper said softly. "But you do have to wade through a lot of it. I'm not surprised some of it rubs off on you."

"I'm not even sure how to do my job anymore. It seems like there are systems—huge powerful systems—that are stacked against getting the right result."

"Like what?"

"The college's response to sex assaults on its campus. The good-old-boys network protecting its own." She gestured toward her laptop. "And these frats. Did you know that men who join fraternities are three hundred percent more likely to rape women than other college boys?"

"Whoa."

"And I'm not convinced their nationals are doing much to stop it. In fact, they seem to encourage kids to go crazy—everyone wants to join Animal House—but they throw the kids under the bus if something goes wrong. They say, 'You served alcohol, that violated our honor code, you're on your own.' The kids' families get hit with huge civil judgments. I don't think parents understand the massive liability they expose themselves to when they send their son to join a fraternity."

"My parents definitely didn't when I pledged."

"You were in a frat?" Anna rocked back. "I didn't know that."

"Yeah. It wasn't like the one you're investigating. I mean, sure, we had plenty of drinking in our basement. But there was community service, leadership roles. I learned a lot, made some good friends. In a big campus, it was a small place to call home. We did a few stupid things, but nothing earth-shattering. Mostly it was good."

"Huh. Why'd you join?"

He shrugged. "I never really thought about it. But, I guess—in our world, there aren't many rites of passage for boys to become men. We don't have gladiatorial contests, right? There's something appealing about being tested and seeing how you measure up."

"They must have *something* going for them. These frats, they have crazy successful alumni who donate fortunes. That's why colleges don't ban them or even really discipline them as much as they should. When colleges try to rein them in, the frats convince their alumni to stop donating."

"Anna." Cooper ran a hand through her hair. "Like I said before, you can't single-handedly fix America's campuses tonight."

"I know." She managed a tired smile. "I'm sorry to rant."

"You're working hard, doing the best you can. So just keep that up. That's all anyone can give. One day, one task at a time. Focus on that. I happen to think that your best is as good as it gets. If you can't find Emily Shapiro, no one can."

Anna sighed and laid her head on Cooper's chest. He wrapped his arms around her and held her for a while. Her eyelids started to drift down. He took her hand and helped her up.

"Come to bed now. You'll figure it out in the morning."

She followed him up the stairs. Cooper wasn't a lawyer or an investigator. He couldn't help her solve this case. But he knew people—he knew her. And he'd always had her back. Always. There was nothing more precious than that.

As she brushed her teeth, Cooper stood behind her, swept her hair to one side, and kissed her neck. It was just a quick kiss, a casual moment of connection between familiar lovers. But she stopped brushing her teeth and concentrated on that feeling, the electric softness of his lips on her skin. When he straightened, she said, "Will you do that again?"

He smiled at her in the mirror. "Anything I can do to help."

He brought his mouth to the side of her neck and kissed her again. She shivered as his tongue played circles on her skin. His hand encircled her breast, tracing the contours. Her nipples hardened, her breaths came quicker, and she knew she wasn't going to sleep any time soon.

She set her toothbrush on the sink, turned, and wrapped her arms around him. They kissed, gently at first, then with rising intensity. After all she'd seen the last few days, she just wanted to lose herself in this. Pure physical pleasure, touch, taste. Something good and easy and true. His hands slipped under her thighs, and she wrapped her legs around him as he lifted her up. He carried her to the bed and laid her on the cover. Their clothes came off quickly; his prosthetic took a moment longer.

She ran her hands across the scars that disfigured the taut muscles of his torso. She was no longer surprised by the wounds that radiated upward from his knee and tapered at his stomach. She did not blanch at the sight of his severed limb, the seam in his leg where the skin simply folded back onto itself. He was beautiful and kind, and she knew without a doubt that he loved her, even if she'd never allowed him to say it.

Anna pulled Cooper on top of her, needing to lose herself in the sweet and simple sensation of skin on skin. "Please," she said. "Now." He slipped inside her, and she drew him tighter still, burying her face in the crook of his neck. He smelled like pine trees; he tasted like Honeycrisp apples. His body brought her intense pleasure; she couldn't get close enough to him. They rocked in deep rhythm with each other. But even as she moaned with the intensity of it, she understood this wasn't just about sex. She was holding tight to the most solid thing in her life.

TUESDAY

29

Anna lay curled into Cooper, blinking into the milky morning light. She could hear Jody puttering around downstairs, speaking in soft singsong to her baby. She sat up, rubbed the sleep from her eyes, took her phone from the nightstand, and started swiping. She had an e-mail from Sam entitled, "Pics from Traffic Cameras." Anna tapped on the five attached images.

All five were photos of Dylan's red Viper driving on city streets the night Emily disappeared. If the Viper wasn't distinctive enough, his license plate was clear. The first picture showed the car on the I-75 highway, southbound. Two silhouettes sat in it, one in the driver's seat, one upright in the passenger seat. The time stamp said 1:34 A.M. The next picture, taken ten minutes later, showed the Viper passing a line of abandoned buildings, their walls covered in graffiti and their windows covered in plywood. Detroit. Anna looked at the location stamp and saw that it was taken on Dequindre Street. Her stomach dropped. Why would a college kid from Tower, fifty miles away, be in downtown Detroit in the early hours of the morning?

The third picture, taken at 2:30 A.M., was different. It was a photo of the Viper from the front, as it idled before a brightly lit glass-enclosed booth. Dylan's face was clearly visible in the front seat, and his best friend, Peter York, was in the passenger seat. The sign on the booth read U.S. IMMIGRATION AND CUSTOMS ENFORCEMENT. Anna recognized the booth. As a younger woman, she'd passed there many times herself, on wild nights out with friends who'd gone that way because the drinking age in Canada was nineteen. This picture was taken at the checkpoint for the tunnel between Detroit and Windsor.

The final two pictures showed Dylan's car driving back toward Tower University at 4:45 A.M. Peter was still in the passenger seat.

A pit in Anna's stomach opened up, feeling deeper than the Pit at

Tower University. There were a few legitimate reasons for Dylan to be heading to Canada the night Emily disappeared. Maybe he went to Windsor to party. It was not uncommon for Michiganders—especially teenagers—to cross the border for a night out. But Dylan and Peter were twenty-one; they didn't need the lowered drinking age that Windsor offered. And the time stamp between his Detroit-bound trip on I-75 and his appearance at the international checkpoint was too long. He'd stopped somewhere for an hour. To dispose of a body?

If you committed a crime, Detroit was a good place to hide the evidence. There were hundreds of abandoned buildings and empty lots. Countless forgotten basements and empty attics. Once home to 1.7 million people, Detroit's population was now under 800,000. The abandoned lots alone would fill the entire city of Paris. The Detroit police, stretched thin and woefully underfunded, had hours-long delays in responding to 911 calls—if they responded at all. A body could lie, undiscovered, for months or years.

Anna could picture it. Dylan and Peter, dragging Emily's blanket-wrapped body from the trunk of the Viper. Carrying the bundle out onto the empty street, where no living soul was around to see them. Walking it into an abandoned skyscraper. Finding an abandoned elevator shaft. Heaving. The silence as her body went down. A muffled thud as she hit the ground.

Anna closed her eyes, trying to shut down the image. She felt Cooper sit up next to her in bed. He put his hand on her arm. "You're shaking," he said. "What's going on?"

She turned to him, trying to find reassurance in his clear blue eyes. But while she found kindness and concern, Cooper couldn't provide the hope she wanted.

"I don't think we're going to find Emily Shapiro alive."

30

A needle in a haystack might be easier to find, Anna thought, *than a corpse in the city of Detroit.* At least a haystack had a finite number of straws. In Detroit, there were countless nooks and crannies, rotting cellars, forgotten buildings, rooms known and rooms unknown. And that was just Detroit. Windsor had to be searched too. She went in to the FBI command center and hammered out the details with Sam, Jack, and the team. They needed police, boats, dogs, cold-water scuba divers, volunteers. Lots of volunteers. The scope of their task was mind-boggling.

But so was Cooper's response. As Anna and Sam pulled up into his driveway three hours later, they had to slow the SUV. His long circular drive was covered in people. The backyard was filled with people. People stood on the porch and spilled into Cooper's house. Anna gaped as she estimated. There had to be over two hundred of them, in jeans and flannel shirts, puffy winter jackets and ski hats, carrying flashlights and shovels, assembled on Cooper's property.

She got out of the car and climbed the steps to his house, saying, "Excuse me," as she moved through the crowd. Cooper came out of the front door, followed by his big white dog. They met on the porch. Sparky sat on Anna's feet and grinned happily as he looked between his owner and her.

"How'd you do this?" Anna asked.

"Everyone wants to help. It's mostly Detroit people, but we even have some students who came in from Tower. I just gave them all a place to meet."

The best search efforts were always those that had volunteers working side by side with the police. Especially in a situation like Emily's where there was so much ground to cover. The more volunteers, the more likely they were to stumble upon a clue, a piece of clothing, the body itself. At Tower University, where Emily had friends, professors, fellow students, there'd been an impressive volunteer turnout. Anna had feared that they couldn't assemble that kind of response in Detroit.

Cooper must have been going full-out since she left this morning, making phone calls, sending e-mails, calling in favors. She knew that he was involved in the community. Living with him the last few months, she'd seen the network of activists, artists, musicians, urban farmers, and religious leaders who came to Cooper for advice or to till a section of his community garden. But this response—and his ability to spark it—shook something inside her.

"Thank you," she said softly.

"Anything I can do," he said, "I will."

They stood an arm's length apart, not touching. Looking up into his kind blue eyes, she felt a connection that was more intimate than anything they'd done in his bedroom.

The sound of a throat clearing made her realize that the crowd had gone quiet as they watched her and Cooper. She turned and saw Jack walking up the porch steps. She was disoriented at the sight of Jack here in Cooper's yard.

"Jack," she said. "I, ah, didn't expect you here."

"I'm coordinating the Detroit search teams."

"I see." She recovered her composure. "Have you met Cooper Bolden?"

"Not yet."

Anna could hear the struggle in Jack's voice, trying to keep it casual and professional. She glanced at Cooper and saw in his face resolve to keep himself polite and helpful as he met his rival. Both were tall and good-looking, both skilled at their chosen work, so different from each other. She'd spent months contemplating what her life would be like with each one. She'd never imagined them meeting each other.

"Cooper," she said, "this is Jack Bailey. Jack, this is Cooper Bolden."

Both men put out their hands in a vigorous male handshake. Both men put on good faces.

"You've assembled quite a team of volunteers," Jack said. "I've never seen anything quite like this. Thank you."

"Glad to be able to help," Cooper said.

Anna realized she wasn't breathing. She exhaled. Jack and Cooper might be rivals, but they were not about to throw down. They were good men who would work with each other to find the missing girl.

A few more police officers climbed the steps, led by Sam. Sam shot Anna a look that said *How you gonna handle this one, sister?*, before huddling into the conversation. They all stood on the porch, hammering out the logistics. After about ten minutes, they had a plan.

Cooper led them through the house. The kitchen table was covered with casserole dishes and Tupperware containers full of food, which some of the volunteers were eating. Cooper had turned his house into a command center not unlike the command center that Sam had established at the FBI's Detroit field office—only with better grub.

Cooper's backyard was a large grassy space, surrounded on three sides by the apple orchard. The skyline of Detroit stood gray and solemn behind the orchard. The trees were bare and the ground was brown. A few sad piles of snow remained in shady areas. Hundreds of people stood in the yard, sipping coffee, huddled in groups talking softly. They quieted as Cooper walked out with the team of investigators.

Cooper stood by his hand-dug fire pit. Jack stood to one side of Cooper, and Anna and Sam stood to the other.

"Thank you for coming here today." Cooper's deep voice carried over the yard. "It means a lot to the family of Emily Shapiro. And it means a lot to me. I appreciate you all giving up your time for this."

"We gotcha covered, Coop," yelled a man.

Cooper nodded. "This is Jack Bailey, the chief homicide prosecutor from D.C., and Sam Randazzo from the FBI. And of course, a lot of you know Anna. They're coordinating the Detroit search teams." He turned to Jack. "You want to take it from here?"

"Thanks." Jack stepped forward and spoke to the volunteers. "We appreciate your help today. It's crucial. Your work may be long and tiring. But please know how important it is." Jack had an air of gravitas, the experience of a man who'd seen all that there was to see and who knew what he was doing. In this crowd of strangers, he held their attention and respect. "We're going to split into a bunch of smaller teams, with each team assigned to a particular area that you can go over in detail. Anything notable should be brought to the attention of me and Agent Randazzo." He gave them a hotline number and e-mail address set up for receiving tips. He laid out the guidelines for the search effort, then stepped aside and let Cooper take the floor again.

"Okay, folks, we'll split into teams of twenty." Cooper starting reading from a clipboard. "First Calvary Baptist Church, you've got the ten square blocks bordered by Woodward, Gratiot, I-75, and the river. Artists Without Borders, you've got the Metropolitan Building, all fifteen floors, rooftop, and basement."

Cooper continued to go through assignments for the volunteers. They were people of all colors and backgrounds, gathered together for the singular cause of finding Emily Shapiro. They would not be paid. They were motivated by the desire to help another human being. In her job, Anna saw so much of the worst things people could do to one another. Seeing the best brought tears to her eyes— the first good tears she'd had in a long time.

Cooper handed out maps to the teams, each with a different section of the city circled in red. Anna felt a sense of pride watching him.

He would lead his own team of teenagers, kids from the local high school who worked on his farm as part of an internship program. Anna would stay and work on the international legalities with Jack. She waved as Cooper and his teams set off.

Within minutes, the yard was quiet. She and Jack were the only people left. It was the first time she'd been alone with him since he'd come to Michigan. She called for Sparky, who trotted after her as she walked back into the house. Jack came with her into the kitchen.

She poured two cups of coffee. They stood facing each other, propped against Cooper's cabinets, sipping.

"He's a good man," Jack said.

"Yes," she said. She didn't want to talk about Cooper with Jack. "Let's see if we can get Canada up and running by this afternoon."

They sat at the kitchen table and started making phone calls. Jack coordinated with the local police to get the Detroit River dredged. DOJ's Office of International Affairs had a Canadian liaison who made the necessary connections with the Windsor authorities. Anna spoke to the consul, getting the final information she needed for an international cooperation agreement. She coordinated with the Canadian police department on the search on their side.

■ ■ ■

By two P.M., all the legal work they could do was done. Jack shut his laptop and looked across the table at Anna. It was so strange sitting with him here in Cooper's house.

"So this is what I'm up against," Jack said, gesturing around the kitchen.

"I wouldn't say you're 'up against' anything," Anna said, feeling defensive. "I didn't come to Michigan looking for something to challenge you with. But you had your own stuff going on. You had to figure things out with Nina. I don't blame you for that. She was your wife, the mother of your child. When she came back to town, you had to see if you could make it work."

"I broke your heart."

"Yeah." Anna sighed. "You did."

"I regret it more than anything else in my life. You know that, right?"

She bit her lip and nodded.

"I want to make it right, sweetheart. Nina was never a threat to us. She's Olivia's mother, that's all. I love you, and only you. There's a beautiful wedding dress hanging in our closet, a diamond ring in my nightstand. There's a little girl who can't wait to be your daughter, and a yellow house waiting for you to make it the happiest place on earth. I want to take you home."

Home. The life he described was the one she'd dreamed of for so long. A daughter she adored, a beautiful house. A husband who was a pillar of the legal profession, and who would gently teach her how to become one too. She'd be one-half of a power couple in one of the most vibrant cities in the world. She'd had a terrible childhood, and part of her had always been afraid that if she didn't work hard enough, if she didn't make all the right choices, she was doomed to repeat it with her own family. Being with Jack was the ultimate proof that she'd made it out.

"You can't want this," Jack said, looking around Cooper's house. "Living in the middle of postindustrial nowhere."

"Hey." She bristled. "This city has a lot going for it. And Cooper is helping it come back."

"With a chicken farm."

"It's an apple orchard. He just happens to have a few chickens. People around here love him; he's a highly respected businessman. Detroit is coming back—and Cooper is at the front of that. And—and—and—I don't want to talk about this with you." She stood. Jack's words stung because they were true. There wasn't a restaurant, store, or even a 7-Eleven for miles. Cooper's house was surrounded by abandoned lots and urban blight. She herself had a hard time imagining living here forever. "I'm going to help the search teams."

Jack stood too. "I'm sorry," he said quietly. "I'll come with you."

■ ■ ■

They drove through the city in silence and parked by Book Tower, a gorgeous thirty-eight-story Renaissance-style skyscraper that was abandoned. Several of its windows were covered in plywood. Jack looked up and whistled.

She pointed down the street. "The FBI building is a couple blocks from here."

Voices came from above and Anna looked up. Cooper stood on the roof of the building, calling orders. She and Jack went inside the shattered foyer. Rotting drywall hung from the walls, and electrical wires hung from the ceiling. Broken chunks of plaster sat in piles on the floor. Anything of value—metal, marble, copper pipes—had been long ago stolen and sold for scrap.

They walked up the graffiti-covered staircase, breathing hard when they came out at the rooftop. Cooper gave her a big smile, which dimmed when he saw Jack emerge from the stairwell. But he waved them over.

"How goes the legal strategy?" Cooper asked.

"It's all locked down," Anna said. "How goes the search?"

"I'll show you."

Cooper led her and Jack over to the edge of the rooftop. She could see the entire city from here. The Detroit River ran to the east, broody and gray. Several police boats moved slowly on the waters, dragging nets. To the west were lower buildings with a few people atop them, walking, pointing flashlights, calling to one another. More people helping with the search. To the north stood several more skyscrapers, standing empty. It was like looking at modern ruins: Angkor Wat or the Library at Ephesus. In the distance, she saw a neat row of trees. Cooper's farm.

Cooper rested his hand on the small of her back as he described the various teams. She saw Jack look at the gesture, and she tensed up. Cooper noticed and pulled his hand away. He swept it across the horizon. "If we don't find anything today, I'll try Central Station tomorrow."

A cell phone rang—Jack's. A picture of Olivia, grinning in pigtails, flashed on his screen. "Excuse me." Jack took a couple steps away to answer the call from his daughter. "Hi, sweetie! How was your day? I'm good. No, you cannot have a Pop-Tart for your snack. Guess who I'm with? That's right. Well, let me see." He lowered the phone and asked Anna, "Can you talk to Olivia?" Anna nodded, and he handed her the phone.

"Hello?"

"Anna!" screeched the little girl.

"Hi, lovey. How are you?"

"I'm good. I miss you."

"I miss you too."

"Guess what I saw today?" Olivia asked.

"What?"

"No, you have to guess."

"Okay. A purple hippo?"

The girl giggled. "No."

"Katy Perry?"

"No, silly. I saw a woolly mammoth."

"That was my next guess," Anna said. "Where did you see a woolly mammoth?"

"We had a field trip to the Natural History Museum."

"That's awesome. Did you see the dinosaur bones?"

"Yes! Guess what else."

"The Hope Diamond?"

"Yes! And?"

"A giant blue whale hanging from the ceiling."

"You know everything."

"No, I just love that museum."

"Me too. I want to go again, with you. When are you coming back?"

"Um, I'm really not sure."

"Anna. It's no fun here without you. We really need you. My dad needs you." Olivia's voice grew serious. "I need you. I love you."

"I love you too. I—I'll see about coming to see you soon. Be good, lovey."

She handed the phone back to Jack, feeling the significance of the gesture. Her tie to Olivia was entirely through Jack. Anna's love for the girl was as pure and true as anything she'd ever felt—but she could only be part of Olivia's life by being with Jack. Without him, Anna was nothing to Olivia. She was just a woman searching an empty skyscraper for a corpse.

She walked to the ledge and gazed out at Detroit. It looked as shattered as she felt.

WEDNESDAY

31

Anna was sitting at Cooper's kitchen table when the case broke. She called the FBI DNA lab right when it opened. "Just checking to see if there are any results." Officially, evidence was processed in a certain order, but unofficially, it was tested faster if a persistent AUSA or agent was calling all the time.

"Hang on a sec," the analyst said. Anna heard a shuffling of paper and the clicking of keys. "Yes, we have a result. The sample taken from the exterior of the Viper's trunk tested positive for human blood. And the DNA matches the control sample. To a one in six-hundred-and-twenty-three-million degree of certainty."

Anna knew what that meant. She said it out loud, just to be sure. "Emily Shapiro's blood was on Dylan Highsmith's car?"

"Yes, ma'am."

She grimaced. "What about the scarf?"

"Let me see, ma'am. Oh, yes, that's a match too. Epithelial cells on the scarf matched DNA from C-1 to a one in one-point-two-billion degree of certainty."

The scarf found in Dylan's room was Emily's. Her skin cells were on it.

"While we're at it, do you have results on the alcohol taken from the fraternity's bar?"

"That's another office." He transferred her. A minute later she was asking another analyst the same question.

"Yes, ma'am. There was one item from your search that tested positive for the presence of Rohypnol. A gallon jug filled with a corn syrup–based red fruit drink."

Anna thanked the analyst and hung up. Her chest buzzed with the excitement of the new leads, and the horror of what they meant. Jody came down the stairs, still in her pajamas, carrying Leigh. As soon as she saw Anna's face, she said, "What's wrong?"

Anna shook her head, as her phone rang again. Cooper's face flashed on her screen. He'd left at seven A.M. to continue his search.

"What's up, Coop?" she answered.

"Anna." His deep voice was shaky. "We found something."

"What's going on?"

She could hear him taking a long, slow breath. Then another. The deep breathing was a technique he used when he was particularly upset. His PTSD had been flaring up less frequently, but he was clearly having an episode right now.

"We found a body," he said.

"Where?"

"Detroit Central Station."

"Is it Emily?"

"It's a Caucasian woman." He took a deep breath. "Not all of her."

"What do you mean? What parts are missing?"

"I—she—Oh God, Anna."

His voice became a hacking cough. Was he throwing up?

"Coop, is anyone there with you?"

No response.

"Cooper!"

Static. He didn't pick up when she called him back.

■ ■ ■

Anna sped through Detroit. She broke several traffic laws, but if she got pulled over, at least she'd have a police escort. As she drove, she called Sam and told her what was going on. "We need Detroit police, the FBI, and a medical examiner. ASAP." Another broken traffic rule, talking on the phone while driving. Sam said she was on it. Anna got to the train station in seven minutes.

The Michigan Central Station was a massive train depot, built in 1913 by the same architects who designed New York's Grand Central. It had all the grand architecture and rococo flourishes of its cousin, but unlike New York's bustling hub, it was vacant, crumbling, and surrounded by acres of nothing. At the time it was built, the Detroit landmark was the tallest rail station in the world, eighteen stories high. It was abandoned in 1988 and now was a striking mixture of glorious historic architecture and modern ruin. Its entrance was modeled after an ancient Roman bathhouse and featured massive arched windows—now shattered and dark—and tall Doric columns—covered in graffiti.

Anna parked at the curb and got out. The street was silent except for the cry of a single seagull drifting through the clouds. "Cooper?" she called. No one answered. She didn't see signs of any other human beings.

Anna walked up to the front doors, moving quickly but on high alert. Anything could be hiding behind those massive Doric columns or shattered marble walls. She wished she were carrying a gun. Cooper always did, because of his army training and the neighborhood where he lived. Jack had long ago tried to persuade her to carry a gun, but she'd resisted, knowing gun owners were more likely to die as a result of the guns they bought than be protected by them. Besides, she knew that the biggest danger to women was not a stranger breaking in through a window but a friend you let in your front door. Still, walking into the giant empty train station, she wished she had something besides her bare hands to protect herself.

One of the heavy front doors was propped open with a cinder block. Beyond the door, the station was dark and unseeable. She could smell mustiness wafting out. She stepped inside.

It took her eyes a moment to adjust to the dark. When they did, she looked around in wonder. It was a cavernous hall, with three-story-tall arched ceilings. Massive pillars stood beneath giant half-moon windows that no longer held any glass. White tile was molded black in patches, and ornate plasterwork was peeling off, exposing brick below. Anything that could be stolen by scrap-metal thieves had been—chandeliers, brass fixtures, balcony railings, the great clock that once hung over the ticket windows. The things that couldn't be taken—marble walls, soaring pillars—were covered in graffiti. A hole in the ceiling allowed a beam of sunlight to fall on the filthy floor. Dust motes danced in the beam. The overall impression was a classical Greek ruin that had met a modern hell.

She still didn't see anyone. "Cooper?" she called. Her voice echoed off the bare walls, resonating through the vast interior. Puddles of dirty water pooled on the floor. The scent of decay—dust, mold, dampness—filled her nostrils. She sneezed, creating an echo of sneezes.

"Hey, Anna! Over here."

She didn't recognize the male voice, but she heard no malice in it, and whoever said it knew her. She followed the sound across the arcade, through a back door, and into an even darker part of the building.

It was completely black except for the beams of two flashlights in a far corner. She realized how alone she was, how remote this place was. How no one would hear if she screamed. She didn't move toward the flashlights. "Who's there?" she called.

"Lamar," said the voice. "And De'Andre."

These were Cooper's interns, sweet local kids who worked on his farm. She walked toward them, slowly because she still couldn't see in the darkness. One of the flashlights came toward her. It tilted upward and lit Lamar's face, which although familiar, looked gargoyle-like with the shadows going up. "Hey, Anna," he said. "Watch your step."

Lamar crooked his elbow and she held on to his forearm. He led her through the rubble-strewn darkness, shining the flashlight on the ground in front of her. She stepped around a big chunk of concrete with rebar sticking out of it. The generally musty smell mixed with a distinctly worse one. Rottenness. As he led her to the figure with the other flashlight, the smell grew stronger. She gagged and covered her nose with her shirt.

"Anna, hey," said De'Andre when she reached him. He had wrapped a bandanna around the lower part of his face, covering his mouth and nose. "Be careful where you step; there's a big hole here."

Lamar turned to her. "You sure you want to see this? Like my mom would say, there are some things you can't unsee."

Her mind flashed to a few of the things she couldn't unsee: a young gang member stabbed to death in a courtroom; a call girl dead on the Capitol steps. She nodded.

Lamar turned and pointed his flashlight to where there should be a wall, but there wasn't. Anna realized it was an elevator shaft, gaping wide-open. He pointed his flashlight down the shaft. She walked carefully to the edge, held firmly to the corner, and looked down.

The elevator shaft went down several stories. At the bottom was a body encased in a pool of black ice. Above the ice, Anna could see a strip of pale white flesh: an arm and a shoulder, the side of a woman's face, and a swirl of long dark hair, all encased in the ice. The rest of the body was hidden below the surface.

The ice itself was thawing and watery in parts. Garbage covered the surface and was also encased in the ice. Beer cans, syringes, dirty socks, used condoms. The corpse's pale arm looked like it was reaching for a bottle of Colt 45.

Anna stepped back from the ledge.

"Let's get you guys out of here," she said quietly.

Lamar let her keep hold of his arm as they carefully wended their way around the rubble, through the terminal, and out onto the front steps. Anna sucked in a lungful of cold outdoor air. A sob bubbled up in her throat, and she choked it back. She turned to the young men. Correction: boys. They were only seventeen years old, seniors in high school. "Are you okay?" she asked.

De'Andre nodded. "That's terrible. But I gotta tell you, the kids at school are gonna wanna hear this story." He gave her a weak grin. She knew he was both telling the truth and using it to cover the fact that he was deeply disturbed by what he'd seen. And if they were all disturbed, how was the army vet with PTSD?

"Where's Cooper?" she asked.

"I don't know," Lamar said. "He left after we showed him the body."

"Okay. You stay here—outside. The FBI, police, and coroner are coming. Tell them where the body is. Don't go back in yourself until they get here. I'm gonna try to find Cooper."

32

"All this can be yours."

No one actually said it. But that was the message, loud and clear.

Wyatt stood on the deck of the yacht, sipping Amstel Light and looking across Lake St. Clair at Grosse Pointe and some of the priciest real estate in Michigan. Lined up on the water was a row of mansions, each architecturally unique, each trying with great success to outdo the other. Three-story walls of windows, saltwater pools with cabanas bigger than most homes, trellises climbing with wisteria, stone walls erected in the 1800s and maintained through the decades by the best architects money could buy. Of course, each house had prominent signs announcing which security system it used.

The Highsmiths' yacht sailed past these lesser mansions. Among impressive houses, the home of Dylan Highsmith was the most impressive of all, a massive Tudor that sported both historic turrets and the finest modern amenities.

Every year, Beta Psi took the pledges on a road trip to Robert Highsmith's house for a luncheon near the end of Hell Week. It was a carrot among sticks. *Hang in there, pledges, and this will be your rich reward.*

On this day, instead of scrubbing beer scum off the basement floor, Wyatt and his pledge buddies got to mingle with Beta Psi alumni, who regaled them with beery stories of their own youthful misadventures. The alumni were the 1 percent of the 1 percent—CEOs, CFOs, lawyers, and execs at the top of the American corporate food chain. The long circular driveway was parked up with their Jags, Cadillacs, and Teslas. Several alums came with a wife or girlfriend who had been nipped, tucked, highlighted, Pilated, and paleo-dieted into a physical state as close to a Barbie doll as humanly possible. Dylan's mother wasn't there. Someone whispered that she spent most of her time at Canyon Ranch. The pledges were not invited to bring dates.

Almost all the pledges wore blue blazers, khakis, and loafers, the uniform of privilege. Wyatt hadn't owned a blue blazer before he pledged Beta Psi. He never mentioned that to anyone else, and he never asked for guidance. He just did his best to observe and replicate the behavior around him. One kid wore bright red pants instead of khakis, but that kid had a trust fund bigger than some countries' GDP. Wyatt would never have the confidence or pedigree to wear bright red pants. At least by now he knew enough to get into the standard uniform. He was never free of the nagging fear that he would get something wrong and expose himself for what he was. An interloper. But he'd learned that if you just looked good and shut up, you could get through 90 percent of all parties.

Like now. The founder of a high-tech company was talking about how he used to piss on the wall of a dormitory that had just been named after him. Wyatt laughed along with everyone else. But he couldn't concentrate.

Wyatt stood next to Dylan and his father and had to work hard not to stare at either one. Robert Highsmith commanded attention because of who he was. Dylan was Wyatt's pledge master. But that wasn't why Wyatt's eyes were constantly drawn to the Highsmith men.

It was the secrets he carried for them. He wanted entrance to this clean riverfront world, away from the dirt and manure of the farm, away from the assembly line where most Holly Grove kids worked after high school if they were lucky. He just had to stick to his plan, which was simple. Keep his mouth shut. What could be easier? It wasn't even like he had to do anything. Stand still, enjoy the ride. Enjoy the cold beer and the feel of the powerful boat purring under his feet. Smile and nod and shut the fuck up. Everything else flowed from that.

So why was it so hard? The secrets sometimes felt like a physical thing, a live creature with teeth and claws burrowing in his chest, trying to find a way out. He wasn't sure he could get through his whole life with it chewing on his heart. Forget his whole life—he wasn't sure he could get through another day without letting it claw its way up his throat and out his mouth.

He took another sip of beer and laughed at a joke he hadn't

heard. He'd hurt no one. He had no responsibility. He did his home-work, cleaned the frat floor, occasionally went home and helped with farm chores. That was enough. If other kids did bad shit, that wasn't his fault or his problem.

The only thing that was his problem was finding his way as a young, unconnected, average white male in an economy that was more and more the terrain of geeks, legacies, and outsourcing. Wyatt wasn't a geek—he wasn't smart enough to write code or devoted enough to stay up all night studying for an exam. He wasn't going back to the farm. That left only one option, as he saw it, which was to throw his lot with the legacies, the kids whose position at the trough had been ensured from the moment they were born. He wasn't one of them, but if he could approximate them closely enough, he could eat at their table.

"What are we gonna do about the bones?" a CEO asked Dylan's father.

The whole boat seemed to shift as the weight of attention turned toward the lieutenant governor. Robert waved a hand nonchalantly. "It'll blow over. Beta Psi'll have a couple weeks of bad press. But it's just hijinks, which happened years ago. Most of those bits and pieces were collected by brothers in the 1920s through '50s. Ancient history. I'm not worried. What I'm really worried about is whether to refurbish this boat. Now *that's* a disaster waiting to happen."

Everyone laughed.

"Do you get out on the water much, sir?" asked a pledge.

"I grew up in a little town downriver. Saw boats going past and knew if I made it out, I'd spend as much time sailing as I could."

That got murmurs of approval, and a palpable feeling of re-lief as they launched into a new subject. Robert talked about how he worked his way up, founding several companies before entering politics. Every rich man had a tale of pulling himself up by the boot-straps, Wyatt thought, even the ones who'd been born in Burberry boots. They seemed to like this story, the American dream of forging a fortune through their bare hands. But Robert's story was a myth. Wyatt had read the Wikipedia page. Robert's father was the down-river scion, and Robert had merely added to his father's already con-siderable fortune. That didn't make as good a creation tale. Robert sold himself as a self-made man.

"Unlike young Dylan here," Robert said, clapping a hand on his son's shoulder so hard it looked like an assault. "Who seems intent on spending the family's fortune faster than I can amass it. And he's shown himself quite adept at that, if nothing else."

It took a moment, but Dylan smiled back and gave a hearty good-old-boy answer: "Everyone's got their talent. I'm glad ours work together so well, Pop."

Father and son laughed, though the smile didn't reach Dylan's eyes.

The yacht docked on a private pier, and the men walked along a winding path up through a long yard and into the house. Inside the big vermilion dining room, they lunched on prime rib. Pity the pledge who asked if there was a vegetarian option. Wyatt didn't need to see the eye rolls to know that pledge wouldn't be receiving an invitation to become a member of Beta Psi.

After six courses and dessert, they had scotch and cigars. Wyatt sipped eighteen-year-old samples of Talisker, Lagavulin, and Laphroaig. They all tasted like smoked moonshine to him: strong, fiery, and barely palatable. But apparently they were quite fine, because the older men murmured their appreciation.

When everyone was good and liquored up, Robert stood at the head of the table and lifted his hands. The crowd quieted.

"I want to thank you for coming this afternoon," Robert said. "This has been a tradition for many years. I was a Beta Psi myself. Being in the brotherhood helped me become who I am today. It taught me about self-reliance. About being a man. It gave me life-long friendships, many friends I see here tonight. And most of all, it was a damn good time."

The men chuckled.

"These days, there's a lot of bad press for fraternities. Like our little cadaver kerfuffle." That got a laugh. "But for each negative story, there are dozens of powerful examples of the very positive side of Greek life. We all know how the lessons of confidence and trust in your brothers sets young men on the path for lifelong success. But it's not just us. It's science."

He read from a sheet of paper: "Eighteen former presidents were in college fraternities. Since 1910 fraternity men have made up 85 percent of U.S. Supreme Court justices, 63 percent of presidential cabinet members, 76 percent of U.S. senators, 85 percent of Fortune 500 executives, and 71 percent of men in 'Who's Who in America.' "

A "Hurrah" came from the crowd, reminiscent of an "Amen" at church.

"And then we have the activities of the current generation," Robert continued. "Several of which were orchestrated by my own son, Dylan. Let's see." He looked at his paper. "The 'Zip Ties and Mai Tais Party' of 2013, where each Beta Psi gentleman was zip-tied to a female guest. The 2014 'Beauty and the Beast' party, where Beta Psis were each encouraged to bring a date and put her up for an award—prettiest, ugliest, hairiest, et cetera—although the girls didn't know that's what they were being rated on. At least not until the end, when the awards were revealed. That was an interesting one to hear from parents about. And of course the 2015 'Save the Ta-Tas Wet T-shirt Contest' with proceeds going to breast cancer research, until breast cancer research refused to take the proceeds because they were so offended by the contest. Way to go, Dylan."

The men at the tables wore expressions between cringes and smirks. Wyatt didn't think it was fair. Sure, some of those ideas had been stupid, but Dylan at least was trying, and a couple of the events had been for a good cause, even if they were kind of immature. But what really struck him was the look on Dylan's face. A thin-lipped grimace. He was trying not to cry.

As much as Wyatt was ashamed of his farm upbringing, much as he wished he had parents who knew how to navigate the mysterious landscape of wealth and power, he had to take a moment to be thankful for his mom and dad, for the simple reason that they were kind. His dad would never purposely embarrass him in front of other people. Craig Bolden loved his sons, and that was that.

Wyatt felt an unexpected rush of sympathy for Dylan. Despite all the Highsmith wealth, Dylan didn't have the one thing that was most precious.

Robert was going on about all the trouble Dylan had gotten into, all the calls Robert had received in the middle of the night, all the things he'd had to "fix" for his son. The amends he'd had to make with the breast cancer organization for the ta-tas party.

Wyatt leaned over and whispered to Dylan. "We all fucking loved those parties."

Dylan turned and looked at him.

"Thanks, bro." Dylan patted Wyatt's knee. He put out his cigar in his scotch and handed the crystal glass to Wyatt. "Take this piss water to the kitchen. And then go to my dad's study. In the bar, there's a bottle of Chivas Regal Royal Salute. Grab that."

Wyatt took the glass of scotch and ashes and wended his way through the house. A team of caterers bustled about the big kitchen. Wyatt set the glass by the sink and slunk out.

He looked around the big foyer. Where was the study? He opened one door and saw an indoor pool. A second door led to a billiard room. He felt like he was in a game of Clue. Finally, he opened a door that led to what could only be a powerful man's study. The room was lined in dark wood and floor-to-ceiling bookshelves filled with leather-bound books chosen for their appearance, not their stories. It smelled of cigar smoke and lemon polish. Pictures of Robert and prominent local figures were placed along the shelves. Robert with Michael Ilitch, the owner of the Red Wings, grinning as they hoisted the Stanley Cup above their heads. Robert and Kid Rock standing onstage at a concert. Robert and Mitt Romney, whose father had been Michigan's governor, sitting on the deck of a yacht.

In the corner was a liquor cart, covered in bottles and a crystal decanter. Wyatt felt like a thief as he looked through the bottles. He kept expecting someone to come in and bust him for snooping. Finally, he found the Chivas and carefully lifted it from the cart. God help him if he dropped this bottle. He'd have to choose between a semester of college and replacing the scotch.

As he walked by the massive antique desk, he stopped to admire a picture of Dylan and his parents standing with George W. in the Oval Office. Dylan was a little kid then, smiling broadly with crooked teeth. Even as an eight-year-old, Dylan had a perfectly tailored blue blazer.

Wyatt straightened to leave, when he noticed some paperwork on the desk. He paused and checked it out, thinking maybe he'd get a stock tip. There was nothing he could use in the S&P, but among correspondence, memos, and a sheet of paper summarizing campaign contributions, was a ticket issued from Delta Airlines to Dylan Highsmith. Round-trip to Caracas, Venezuela. Leaving tomorrow.

Wyatt picked up the ticket and stared at it. He tried to think of a good reason for a college student to go to Venezuela now. Spring break wasn't for another four weeks. The outbound flight was in the middle of a school week.

There was only one reason why Dylan would head to South America now. Things were heating up in his case. The buzz had changed from *if* he would be arrested to *when*. You didn't have to be a lawyer to know that Dylan was in deep shit, legally speaking. He was fleeing the country.

Dylan's father might not love him, he might not even like him, but he wasn't going to let his only son go to jail.

Wyatt's pocket buzzed with an incoming e-mail. Distractedly, he pulled his phone from his pocket. "Step up," the title read. He tapped it open. It was a public service message from Title IX activists, urging bystanders to take action when they saw something wrong going down. He almost laughed. He hadn't done it last time. He didn't see any reason to start now. Wyatt deleted the message. He left the ticket on the desk, picked up the bottle of Chivas, and went out to rejoin the party.

He didn't see Dylan in the dining room. In fact, he didn't see any of the college kids. It was just the old-timers and their wives. Dylan held the Chivas bottle low by his side and slipped back into the foyer. He poked from vacant room to vacant room. Where had everyone gone?

He heard muffled laughter from behind a door. Cautiously, he opened it, and the muffled noise resolved into the cacophony of a party. The door led downstairs to the basement. He went down.

The Highsmith basement was done up as luxuriously as a basement could be. But with the boys gathered in a circle, holding red plastic Solo cups and shouting at something in the middle, it had the same feel as the cement basement of the Beta Psi house. Music pumped from an iPhone docking station. Wyatt shouldered his way into the circle so he could see what was inside. Three exotic dancers were taking one another's clothes off. One stripper was unclasping the other's front-clasp bra with her teeth. A few months ago, Wyatt would've gaped at the show, but by now he accepted it as standard fare.

Wyatt walked over to Dylan and handed him the bottle. "Thanks, dude," Dylan said. He poured a glass for Wyatt. They clinked and drank. "This is a ten-thousand-dollar bottle of scotch," Dylan said. Wyatt almost choked on it. "Don't worry, man. You deserve it. You've done great. Really manned up and showed us you've got the stuff."

Wyatt's chest warmed with the alcohol and Dylan's words. "Thanks, man. You're an awesome pledge master."

"I'm not. But I do my best. It'll all be over soon." Dylan leaned in and said softly, "Two more days, and you'll be a full brother. 'Course it's confidential. I'm not supposed to tell anyone who's in and who's out. So keep it to yourself, Bolden. I know you can keep a secret. That's the quality I like most about you."

Wyatt beamed. Dylan put a hand on Wyatt's back and pushed him gently into the circle. "Your turn," he said with a grin.

A stripper with a small scar on an otherwise beautiful mouth smiled, put her arms around Wyatt's neck, and began grinding against him. The other guys yelled their approval. A second stripper pressed up behind Wyatt and started rubbing his ass. He got hard, fast. It wasn't just the naked bodies dancing against him. Being in the inner circle was a privilege usually reserved for the most important brothers. Wyatt was dizzy with scotch and the fact that he was here. The girls brought over a chair and had him sit. The stripper with the little scar on her mouth unzipped him and pulled his pants and boxers to his ankles. More hoots from the circle of boys. Wyatt was embarrassed and honored and hard as a rock. The dancer turned and danced so her ass was rubbing against him. He put his hands on her hips and let her grind.

The stripper turned toward him and, like a magician, made a condom appear. She slipped it on him, then slipped herself on over it. Her breasts slapped his cheeks as she rode him. The guys' shouts reached a frenzy. Dylan handed him another glass of Chivas. Wyatt drank it between thrusts, laughing and spilling it all over himself. After he came, he looked around the room in a dazed stupor. The guys were cheering; the other strippers were giving lap dances in other corners; Dylan was refilling his glass with Chivas. It was the best time Wyatt had had in college.

The girl smiled at him and stroked his cheek; when she smiled, the scar on her upper lip disappeared. "You liked that, baby?"

"That was awesome," Wyatt breathed. "Thank you."

She kissed him and climbed off.

Dylan walked into the circle and smiled. "My turn."

"Sure, baby," said the girl.

Wyatt zipped himself up just in time to take Dylan's glass. Dylan started dancing with the stripper. Wyatt moved out to the circle, holding both glasses. He watched the action with the other guys. A few clapped him on the back. He was glowing; he could feel it.

Dylan danced with the girl for a minute, then pulled himself out of his pants. He was ready to go. "Sure, baby," she said. She produced a condom, but Dylan shook his head.

"I don't do condoms," he said.

"Well, then, I can't do you," she replied, pouting playfully. "Safe is sexy!"

He put an elbow around her neck and pulled her to the ground. "This is sexy for me."

He climbed on top of her, pulled her G-string to the side, and pushed his way into her. The girl gasped and pushed his chest. "No! Get off me! I said no, not without a condom!"

He clamped a hand on her throat. "Silent is sexy."

"Nn—" Her voice choked off as he pressed down. Her hands fluttered to her neck like little birds, desperately trying to claw his hand off her windpipe. Dylan squeezed her throat harder and pumped away. Her face went pink, then magenta.

Wyatt stood among the other boys, a glass of precious Chivas in each hand. The room quieted. He waited for another boy to say something, to pull Dylan off this girl. He was sure someone would.

The little scar on her beautiful mouth pulsed in a pink line as her face turned purple. The girl's eyes bugged out; the whites were jagged with capillaries. She looked to Wyatt. *Please,* she mouthed. *Please help me.*

Wyatt stood frozen in his spot.

Dylan's hand stayed on her neck; he kept driving into her. The girl stopped struggling. She closed her eyes and was still. The room was quiet as Dylan continued pumping. Wyatt looked around. All the boys in the circle were doing exactly the same thing, looking from Dylan to one another and then back down to Dylan. They shuffled nervously; they elbowed the person next to them. They didn't move to stop it.

The song ended, and the room was completely silent. Dylan grimaced, jerked, and shuddered. His hand relaxed its grip on the girl's neck, and he collapsed on top of her. The girl sucked in a huge breath of air, then started coughing. She coughed and coughed, hacking and wheezing, right into Dylan's ear. Dylan scowled at her, pushed her face to the side, then climbed off. She sat up and held a hand to her throat as she kept wheezing. Her face went from purple back down to magenta and then to pink. Dylan fished in his pocket and threw several hundred-dollar bills at her. They landed on her bare thigh. He walked over to Wyatt and took back his drink.

"Now we're Eskimo brothers," Dylan said. "Same girl in one night. Cheers to that."

He clinked his glass against Wyatt's. They drank the scorching liquid.

The girl with the scar across her beautiful mouth met Wyatt's eyes. He'd never seen such disgust in a woman's face. She turned away and walked to her bag, where she took several long sips of water from a bottle and stood massaging her neck. Then she stashed the hundreds, put on some more lipstick, and turned back to the circle with a determined smile. The other strippers welcomed her back with soothing words and light touches. Someone turned the music louder. The women started dancing with one another again.

"These girls are pros," Peter said approvingly. "They know how to take it."

"Yeah," Dylan said. "Good girls."

The party kept going. Wyatt felt sick. "I gotta take a leak," he said. Dylan pointed up the stairs. Wyatt stumbled up them, out into the foyer, and back into the study. It was still empty.

He collapsed into one of the leather chairs. He'd seen a lot during Hell Week, but this was the worst. Not only what Dylan did—but how Wyatt reacted to it. Was he that much of a pussy? He wouldn't stop a rape? *No*, he thought, *it wasn't a rape, just a dispute over terms. The girl was willing to have sex as long as they used condoms. Afterward, she took the money Dylan gave her and kept dancing. So it was all fine.*

He closed his eyes and shook his head. Dylan could've killed that girl. Wyatt would have stood there watching it happen.

What was he becoming? What kind of man did he want to be? He took a sip of Chivas.

He pulled his phone out and scrolled through his contacts. He stopped at Cooper. He stared at the picture of his brother, smiling in an apple orchard, the metal of his prosthetic leg reflecting the light of the sun. Wyatt took a deep breath, then tapped on his real brother's phone number.

33

Anna stepped out of the shadow of the Central Station and looked for Cooper. She saw his black Harley, parked around the corner, but no sign of him. The station was surrounded by broken concrete and a chain-link fence topped with looping whorls of razor wire. Beyond were empty lots and a swath of patchy grass dotted with a few sad trees. A little sign announced it was Jefferson Park, though it didn't seem like the sort of place that would have kids swinging from monkey bars any time soon.

A solitary figure stood against a tree, head bowed. The rising sun lit the tall silhouette from behind. Anna slipped through a hole in the chain link and walked toward him. Her feet were nearly silent on the grass.

When she got near, she said, "Coop."

He flinched and put his hand to his hip, where his gun was holstered.

"It's me," she said softly. "Anna."

His eyes narrowed and he stared at her for a long moment, as if making sure he was seeing her and not a mirage. He let go of the gun, and his hand dropped to his side.

She stood in front of him. Sweat beaded his forehead. His breath came fast and shallow.

"You okay?" she asked.

"I'm fine," Cooper said. "I'm fine. I'm fine. I'm fine."

She slipped her arms around his waist and held him. His heart thudded rapidly under her cheek.

"I haven't seen a body since Afghanistan. And now I'm flashing to every dead person I've ever seen." He whispered, "There were a lot."

Cooper sank down to crouching and held his head in his hands. She knelt down with him and held him quietly for a long time.

He hadn't had a panic attack in months. She thought that he was doing better, slowly readjusting to civilian life. But partly that was because there hadn't been any triggers recently. By putting himself in charge of a cadaver search, Cooper had put himself directly in a PTSD-provoking situation. For her.

Sirens wailed in the distance, then grew closer. An ambulance pulled up first, which was silly if you thought about it. There was nothing a doctor could do for the girl at the bottom of the elevator shaft. Sam's unmarked sedan came next. Anna saw Sam get out of the car, approach the two young men, and talk to them. Lamar and De'Andre gestured excitedly toward the train station. A police cruiser came wailing up the road. It screeched to a stop in front of the station's entrance. Two cops emerged and slammed their doors shut simultaneously, making a sound like gunshots. Cooper jumped.

A phone buzzed under Anna's hand, from within Cooper's pocket. She expected him to let it go to voice mail, but he took it out and looked at the incoming number. "Wyatt," he said. He never turned down a call from his baby brother.

Cooper stood, took a deep breath, and went through a brief but intense moment of pulling himself together. Shaking a moment before, he pressed send and said calmly, "Hey, Wyatt."

She stepped a few feet away to give him some privacy as he spoke to his brother. Through the chain-link fence, she saw people in front of the train station donning yellow plastic jumpsuits. This was a special FBI team that would descend into the elevator shaft and excavate the body. It was delicate work; they wanted to extricate the corpse while preserving it, so that a medical examiner could be able to make determinations about time and manner of death.

Sam motioned for Anna to come over. Anna and Cooper walked back to the station entrance, while Cooper continued talking to his brother. Anna only heard his end of the conversation. "Can you take a picture and send it to me? Yeah, I think she can keep it confidential. You might want to make yourself scarce, though. No, fuck those guys. You don't need them. Okay, okay. I get it. Just be careful. Okay. Love you."

When they hung up, Anna put a hand on his arm.

"What did Wyatt want?"

Cooper held up his phone and forwarded something Wyatt had texted him.

"He wanted to help."

Before Anna could ask any more questions, Sam asked Cooper to tell her how he and his interns had found the body. She took notes. Then she turned to Anna to discuss logistics. As they were talking, the team in the yellow plastic suits emerged from the station.

They carried a stretcher with a heavy load covered in a black plastic tarp. Anna pictured the vibrant, hopeful college student Emily had been on the last night of her life, her hair curled into ringlets, lips covered in gloss, ready for a happy night out. Anna couldn't quite grasp the difference between the night Emily expected and what had actually happened to her.

"Do we have confirmation on the ID?" Anna asked Sam.

"Too soon to tell by a visual exam. The body is damaged and bloated from the water and whatever happened before it went down the shaft. We'll do DNA."

Anna watched the search team load the body into a white van.

She had a vivid fantasy of going to Dylan's house and shooting him between the eyes. She shook it off. Prosecuting pedophiles, rapists, and abusers, she often had these fantasies. The key was channeling that anger into a meticulous and legally acceptable method of kicking ass.

Anna turned back to Cooper. But he was gone. "Cooper," she called. A few of the officers looked up, but Cooper wasn't among them. "Coop?"

Sam said, "I saw his motorcycle heading away a second ago."

"Oh," Anna said. That was odd, for him to leave without saying good-bye. She hoped he was okay.

She looked at her phone to see what he'd texted her. Her heart started thudding. It was a photo that Wyatt had texted to Cooper, which Cooper had forwarded to her. It was the picture of an airline ticket for Dylan to fly to Venezuela. Tomorrow.

34

D ylan was fleeing the country. Anna had to stop him before he became this generation's Roman Polanski, evading the American justice system forever. Venezuela had no extradition treaty with the United States. Once he got there, Dylan wasn't coming back.

She didn't have as much evidence as she would want, ideally, to make a homicide arrest. The victim's body hadn't yet been identified. But she had enough evidence to squeak by on an assault charge: the video of Dylan running after Emily, her blood on his car, her scarf in his room, her initials in his brag book, the history of their Disciplinary Committee proceedings. Homicide cases could be prosecuted without a body; certainly an arrest for assault could be made. Anna and Sam went back to the FBI command center, huddled over her laptop, and cranked out an arrest warrant and affidavit. The warrant was for the hate crime of assault, not homicide. That gave them less to prove but would allow them to arrest Dylan. When they identified the body, they'd change the charge to homicide.

Anna listed all the evidence that proved Dylan's actions against Emily stemmed from a hatred of women. That included the girls listed in his brag book, the "bitch" he called Emily, and the insults scribbled on the sorority's composite hanging in his room. They attached the paperwork from Tower University listing the other three sex-assault charges brought against Dylan. They raced to the courthouse where Sam swore out the affidavit and Anna filed the papers. Magistrate Judge Schwalbe signed the warrant and his secretary stamped it.

From the courthouse, Sam and Anna drove to Dylan's father's house in Grosse Pointe. In his text, Wyatt said Dylan was there for a Beta Psi alumni luncheon. Anna hoped he still was. As they drove, Anna tried to call Cooper. She got no answer. Where was he? Her discomfort about him driving away from the train station blossomed into full-fledged worry. She called Jody, who hadn't seen him either.

Meanwhile, Sam made phone calls to Steve and other FBI agents. By the time they pulled up to the Highsmiths' sprawling Tudor, the driveway was covered not only in Jags, Cadillacs, and Teslas, but also several unmarked Tauruses, Capris, and vans with federal government plates.

They met Steve on the driveway. He had twenty SWAT agents, who'd already been briefed, and a full operations plan, ready to go. Sam gave him a nod. "You don't mess around, Quisenberry. That's what I like about you."

Steve blushed below his dark stubble.

Anna stood by the Durango while the FBI agents lined up and Sam knocked on the front door. Anna counted under her breath along with Sam. One-one-thousand, two-one-thousand . . .

The door swung open. Behind it stood none other than Lieutenant Governor Robert Highsmith. He wore a blue blazer and held a cigar in one hand and a crystal glass of amber liquor in the other.

"Good afternoon," he said, looking with amusement on the group of twenty FBI agents on his driveway. "What can I do for you?"

"Sir, I'm Agent Samantha Randazzo, FBI. We're here to execute an arrest warrant for your son, Dylan Highsmith. Is he in the home?"

"No, he's not. But I do have several other people here. They are guests, here for a luncheon party. I'd ask that you not disturb them."

"I'm sorry, sir, but we have to ask everyone in your house to step out. And then we have to search your home to make sure Dylan isn't here. Do you know where he is?"

"I do not. And you do not have the legal authority to search my home."

Anna stepped up to the porch as Sam handed Robert the paperwork. "That's a federal arrest warrant, sir, which gives us full authority to search your home incident to arrest."

He shifted the cigar to the same hand as the scotch so he could take the warrant. He skimmed it, then looked up.

"You'll do no such thing." He turned to yell into his home. "Felicia! Bring me those papers from the printer."

A maid hurried over carrying documents. He took the papers and handed them to Anna. They were still warm from the printer. It was an order from a district judge on the Eastern District of Michigan—one level above Magistrate James Schwalbe—overruling the magistrate's order and finding their arrest warrant lacked probable cause.

"Your warrant has been quashed." Robert puffed on his cigar and blew the smoke at Sam and Anna. "You can't come into my home. You can't touch my son."

35

f she weren't so angry, Anna might have been impressed. Arrest warrants were not publicly filed; someone had tipped the Highsmiths off. Then Dylan's lawyer had managed to draft a motion, get it to the courthouse, and have a federal judge sign it—all in the time it took the FBI to put an arrest team together and drive to the Highsmith house.

Anna called Judge Schwalbe's clerk personally to be sure Robert was telling the truth. He was. U.S. District Judge Joseph DeLuca had overruled the magistrate's decision, finding there wasn't enough evidence that Dylan assaulted Emily because of her gender. If there wasn't gender-based animus, there wasn't a federal hate crime. Judge DeLuca quashed the warrant.

Reasonable minds could disagree on how much evidence was sufficient to support a warrant, but Anna was familiar with this particular district judge. She guessed Judge DeLuca had been primarily motivated by the fact that Robert Highsmith was the politician responsible for getting him on the bench.

Whatever the decision was based on, a district judge's order overruled a magistrate's. Only a panel of three judges on the federal court of appeals could overrule Judge DeLuca. There was no way to get a panel assembled today. Tomorrow would be too late.

Sam stopped the Durango at a red light and looked at Anna. "Have they outmaneuvered us?"

Anna stared out the windshield. The Renaissance Center stood ahead of them, dark gray glass against a light gray sky. The skyscrapers were supposed to help Detroit come back in the 1970s but had had little effect. Nevertheless, the city was coming back now. Anna had just seen a *Forbes* article calling Detroit the new Brooklyn—*the* place for hipsters and artists. Detroit was coming back because dedicated, creative people were finding interesting new ways of doing things.

She said, "I have an idea."

■ ■ ■

Anna's paralegal, Nikki Greene, had compiled a list of all the names she'd been able to match to the initials in Dylan's brag book. If Anna could find just one more girl who'd been sexually assaulted by Dylan, it could tip the balance for the warrant. She could show a *pattern* of sexual assaults, and reapply with the additional evidence. This time, she would go through a grand jury and ask them for an indictment. Indictments—the findings of a panel of citizen jurors— had a certain level of gravitas. A judge would be less likely to over- turn a warrant based on a grand jury's indictment. But first she had to get someone to talk.

Nikki had listed phone numbers of the girls she'd found from Beta Psi's *The Book of Earthly Pleasures*. Anna started making calls. The first woman didn't answer. The second, third, fourth, and fifth didn't want to talk. The seventh, a woman named Melinda Bates, reluctantly agreed to have Anna and Sam come talk to her.

Anna hung up and smiled at Sam.

"Let's go to Michigan State."

■ ■ ■

An hour's drive from Tower, MSU was a beautiful land grant univer- sity, hundreds of acres sprawling across East Lansing. Long stretches of parklike campus were bounded by cute shops and restaurants. A seventy-thousand-person stadium held Big Ten football games. It was a larger university than Tower, both in number of students and in sheer geographic space.

Sam and Anna pulled up to Case Hall, a redbrick dormitory. Melinda Bates had transferred from Tower and was getting a B.A. in public policy at the James Madison liberal arts college within MSU. Anna wondered why Melinda had transferred. Was it for the excel- lent education—or to escape the shadow of Dylan Highsmith?

They took the elevator up to the sixth floor and knocked on Melinda's door. It opened a crack, and a light green eye peered out at them. The door closed, a mighty sigh ensued, and the chain slid off. Melinda Bates stood before them, in jeans and a green Spartan T-shirt, looking unhappy but resigned. "I guess you should come in," Melinda said, like a woman inviting an executioner into her house.

"Thanks." Anna introduced herself and Sam. Melinda's place was a neat studio apartment. A small dining table sat under a window that looked out over the basketball stadium. Melinda had light brown hair cut in a cute bob she kept tucking behind her ears. She was whip thin, like someone who was a serious runner or had an eating disorder. Melinda sat at the little table and gestured for them to do the same.

"I don't have a lot of time," Melinda said. "I have class in half an hour."

"We appreciate you seeing us," Anna said. "I wouldn't bother you if it weren't so important. I'm investigating Dylan Highsmith. And I understand that you might know him."

"That was years ago," Melinda said. "Ancient history."

"Do you mind telling us how you knew him?"

Melinda tucked a wisp of hair behind her ear. "I didn't know him well. Just for a night, really."

"What happened?"

"What happens to a lot of girls. I went to his frat party. He plied me with this deadly fruit punch. I passed out; he had sex with me."

"When you say deadly . . ."

"I think there was something in it. I'd hardly had anything to drink. And then I was out. Next thing I know, I'm waking up in his bed naked and sore."

"Did you report that to anyone?"

"I told some friends; he told some friends. Some stuff got posted online."

"What kind of stuff?"

"Someone took a picture of me in Dylan's bed. They tagged me and it showed up in all my feeds. It was my first week as a freshman. I never really got over it, socially." She closed her eyes for a moment, then opened them. "It's how I ended up here. I wanted to get away, have a fresh start. Plus MSU is a better school anyhow. They let me transfer my second semester. Now I'm a junior."

"How are you doing now?"

"I'm older and wiser." She gave them a small smile. "Definitely more careful at parties. My mom is a rock. We thought about going forward with charges, even consulted a lawyer, but it seemed like nothing good would come of it. She got me a counselor instead.

Therapy has been helpful." Melinda glanced at her watch. "I've gotta go soon."

Anna looked into Melinda's clear green eyes. She was credible and was strong. She could handle this. Anna said, "I want to bring a criminal case against Dylan Highsmith—and include the charge that he raped you when you were a freshman."

Melinda looked at Anna for a long moment, then laughed. It wasn't the shrieking hysteria of Kara Briscoe. It was a dry, skeptical laugh.

"Why would I agree to do that?"

"He's still doing it—exactly what he did to you, he's doing to other girls. Someone needs to stop him."

"Good luck with that. It took me years, and now I'm finally over it. I've got no interest in reopening that can of worms."

"I understand what you've been through," Anna said. "And—"

"A criminal trial is public, right?"

"Yes."

"Press might cover it."

"There would probably be coverage. But most major news outlets don't publicize the names of rape survivors."

"Forget major news stations. With bloggers and muckrakers like Drudge, sometimes names do get printed. And it's hard to make a criminal case, isn't it?"

"I'd have to prove the case beyond a reasonable doubt, the highest burden in American law. But that would be my burden, not yours. All you'd have to do is take the stand and tell the truth."

"If you don't prove your case, the world thinks *I'm* a liar." Melinda shook her head. "I'm sorry if he's still doing this to other girls, but I don't see how that's my responsibility. I'm a victim, not his partner in crime."

"That's what makes you particularly powerful, Melinda. You may be the only person who can stop him."

"And he needs to be stopped," Sam said. "He's getting worse. Bolder. We think he's graduated to bigger crimes. Have you heard about Emily Shapiro?"

Melinda slowly tucked her hair behind her ears and stared at them. "Everyone has. You haven't arrested him yet?"

"We can't," Anna said. "Not without you. We need more evidence against him. You might be one of the few people in the world who can make a difference. If you don't come forward now, he'll be free to go after more girls."

"What if he comes after me?"

"That's not something we see often in sex-assault cases—that's more like an organized crime or gang sort of tactic. But if you were threatened, we could put you up in a hotel. You'd get a police escort to and from court. We could even help you move to another apartment if you want."

"If I refuse?"

"I literally cannot make a case without you."

Melinda stared out the window. MSU's campus was more bucolic than Tower's. This felt like a long way from Tower University, and Anna thought of how it must feel for Melinda. Not just in space but in time, how far Melinda had to come to get over what happened to her. To end up here, a successful college student, rather than in a mental hospital with nurses escorting her to her room.

Melinda was silent for a long time. Anna didn't interrupt her contemplation. Sometimes the best argument was letting someone check her conscience. Finally, Melinda answered.

"Okay. I'll do it."

Anna almost fell off her chair, she was so relieved. "Thank you. So much. Um . . . there any chance you can skip your class and come to Detroit now?"

VLOG
RECORDED 2.15.15

They never expelled him.

I'm so angry, I can't stand it.

Aaaghh!

Dammit. I liked that mirror. Now I'll have seven years of bad luck, I guess.

I want to throw my phone across the room too. It's taking all my self-control to talk at it instead.

So this morning, I woke up dead set on figuring it out. Why is Dylan on campus? Did someone forget to tell the registrar about him being expelled? I called Yolanda, our fabulous, ha ha, Title IX coordinator. After half an hour of dancing around it, she finally told me. Dylan appealed the expulsion. His fancy D.C. lawyers must've written some magical fucking brief. Because the committee overturned his sentence. He's still officially "reprimanded," but without being expelled. What does that mean? Nothing, is what.

He gets to walk around campus like it never happened. He gets to graduate. He gets to walk at commencement in a cap and gown; he gets a Tower University diploma to hang on his wall. He gets to continue his regularly scheduled life, just like that. This sucks.

All the names they called me. All those frat boys spitting at me. The girls whispering. The online crap. It was for nothing.

They didn't even let me know, much less ask if I had anything to say about it. I had no clue. I had to find out by seeing him leering at me on campus. I'm, like, shaking all over just remembering it. How can they do that? Didn't they think it mattered to me? That I might, like, have something to say about it? That, if I knew he was coming back, I might try to avoid him, or make sure I'm always walking with a friend, maybe invest in some pepper spray? Or were they worried I'd make noise? Complain. Fight. Refuse to go away quietly, like the good girl I'm supposed to be.

I feel like I've been assaulted all over again.

Only this time, by my own college.

36

Anna stepped into the grand jury room in the federal courthouse. She carried an indictment she'd spent the last hour writing, circulating, and getting approved. Twenty-four grand jurors sat at tables that resembled a college seminar room. They were regular citizens—teachers, moms, a dentist—who'd gotten their summons and were performing their civic duty. There was no defense attorney and no judge. In the grand jury, there was just a prosecutor, her witnesses, and the jurors. The jurors would decide if there was probable cause to believe a crime had been committed, and if so, they would indict the defendant for the crime. The defendant had no right to be present or even to know that the grand jury was assembled to investigate him.

"Hello," Anna said. A few of the jurors glanced up from their newspapers and cell phones. A few didn't. "My name is Anna Curtis, and I'm an Assistant U.S. Attorney from D.C. This is case number 2015-US-1324, *United States versus Dylan Highsmith*."

Now all the jurors looked up from their devices.

The stenographer's fingers flew over the buttons of her machine. Although this proceeding was secret today, one day it might go to trial, and a defense attorney might parse through every line of this transcript, searching for ways that Anna had messed up, in order to try to get the charges dismissed. Anna had read so many of her own transcripts that as she spoke she imagined the words being typed in Courier font.

"Today I will ask you to indict Mr. Highsmith on one count of violating 18 U.S.C. Section 249(a)(2), a hate crime, for assaulting Emily Shapiro on March 24, 2015, because of her gender. In support of this indictment, you will hear from two witnesses today."

The jurors turned to one another and murmured. It was unusual to present just two witnesses and then ask for an indictment on such major charges. Even more unusual was a prosecutor they'd never seen before waltzing in and asking them to indict the son of one of the state's most powerful political lions.

"Our first witness, FBI Agent Samantha Randazzo, will summarize most of the evidence against Mr. Highsmith. You will see video footage of the defendant grabbing and chasing Emily Shapiro the night she disappeared. She has not been seen since then. You'll see traffic-camera photos showing that the defendant took a long drive through Detroit and Windsor that night. You'll hear that the victim's blood was found on the defendant's car, and her scarf in his bedroom. You'll see photos of a secret room below the defendant's fraternity, where Ms. Shapiro's initials were inscribed in a book of sexual conquests. You'll hear that she accused him of drugging and raping her earlier this school year, and that she was planning to publish, or already had published, these accusations online."

All this evidence had been in the warrant that Judge DeLuca had quashed. But Anna would add a little more. The grand jury could make an independent finding of probable cause, considering the additional evidence. If they indicted him, she could get a new warrant for his arrest.

"You will also hear that Dylan Highsmith had a history of drugging and raping young women who visited his fraternity. You may consider this when you decide whether his assault on Ms. Shapiro was based on a hatred of women. My second witness will be Melinda Bates, who is currently a junior at MSU. Ms. Bates will describe how the defendant drugged her when she was a freshman at Tower University, during a fraternity party in 2013. Those drugs rendered Ms. Bates unconscious. While Ms. Bates was incapacitated, the defendant sexually assaulted her."

"Were any tests done to see whether Ms. Bates had date-rape drugs in her system?" asked a gray-haired man. He wore a badge that said FOREPERSON.

"No, sir. You will hear that Ms. Bates did not report the sexual assault to the police when it happened."

The foreperson said, "You're asking us to bring a federal case against a respected young man because a girl says he drugged her three years ago."

"And a wealth of additional evidence," Anna said.

"All of which is circumstantial."

Anna looked around at the arrayed jurors, who comprised a wide range of ages, colors, and sizes. Many were frowning at her.

Statistically, she had to assume that more than half of them had voted for Robert Highsmith in the last election. And Highsmith had been around for a while, kissing babies, doing favors, passing out political pork. Jurors were instructed to recuse themselves if they had a personal relationship with anyone involved in a case, but that rule was hard to enforce. She considered repeating the rule now. But it was unlikely to prompt any recusals and would just alienate the jurors even more.

There was an old saying that a prosecutor could get a grand jury to indict a ham sandwich. But Anna wasn't getting a ham-sandwich vibe. She was getting a sense of palpable hostility. Funny, in D.C. she felt like a midwestern outsider. Here in Michigan, she was the stranger from D.C. coming to indict one of their favored midwestern sons. She wondered if she was a hometown girl anywhere anymore.

"I understand your concerns," Anna said. "Agent Randazzo will tell you that, based on her training and experience, it is not unusual for a sex-assault victim to delay in reporting the assault. Additionally, I'll read to you the jury instruction that says circumstantial evidence is just as valid as direct evidence. And hearsay is admissible in grand jury proceedings."

"We know about the hearsay rule—we've been empaneled four weeks," said the foreperson. "What I'm saying is, I'm not sure I'd vote to indict a man in a case like that."

Anna tried to smile at him. "Sir, I'll just ask that you keep an open mind as you listen to all the evidence, hear these witnesses, and then listen to my closing argument. Then make a fair judgment after you've considered everything."

"Fine," he said. He leaned back in his chair and crossed his arms on his chest. An old lady in the back row pursed her lips like she'd tasted something sour.

They weren't with her. And this was her last chance. Anna's stomach clenched into a hard little ball. "For my first witness," she said, "I call Agent Samantha Randazzo."

37

ylan sat in the first-class seat of the Boeing 747 and frowned at the glass of champagne in his hands. The pretty flight attendant leaned down and smiled at him. "Is there anything else I can get you, sir?"

"How about a real drink?"

She gave him a polite, the-customer-is-always-right smile. "I know, it's so silly how we greet everyone with champagne. What would you like?"

"Scotch, neat," he said magnanimously, forgiving her. "Make it a double."

"Of course."

He leaned his head back against the soft leather seat and watched her ass undulating under her skirt as she went to fetch his drink. He tried not to feel too sorry for himself. But this wasn't how he wanted to be spending the last semester of college. In Venezuela, running from the law.

There wasn't really a choice, though. They'd gotten a warrant to arrest him. His dad had managed to get it quashed, but there was no telling how long that would last. So they'd scrambled to change his ticket to the next flight to Caracas. And here he was. Still drunk from the party at his father's house.

The stewardess smiled as she put the golden drink in front of Dylan. He drained it in a gulp. The airline scotch was piss compared to the stuff in his dad's study. Still, he gestured for another. The flight attendant smiled and took his empty glass. The low-shelf liquor burned a path down his throat.

The engine went from a purr to a hum. The pilot announced that they were on track for an on-time arrival at Caracas International Airport. The aircraft backed away from the gate and taxied to the runway.

His dad had him staying at a four-star all-inclusive resort, at least for the next two weeks. After that he'd have to rent a villa or something. He guessed it could be fun. At least until they got this whole thing dismissed and he could come home.

He'd sit by the pool drinking margaritas. He could hook up with Venezuelan whores and American expats. He'd troll for tourists who'd never see him again, who wouldn't even know if he gave them his real name or not. Maybe he'd start going by Joe. Jimmy. Jim Bob. Whatever.

The plane taxied down the runway. The flight attendant demonstrated how to use the seat cushion as a flotation device. He mouthed, *Where's my scotch?* She winked at him and gestured for another flight attendant, even hotter than she was, to bring him the drink.

Maybe this wouldn't be so bad, actually. In Venezuela, he could do whatever he wanted, *be* whoever he wanted. He could be anonymous. He'd have the sort of freedom he'd never experienced before.

He imagined some of the things he could do. Dangerous, exciting things. He thought of the women he could do these things to. How they would scream. The superhot flight attendant brought him another scotch and he smiled at her.

This could actually be a good thing. He was finally being unleashed.

38

Anna and Sam sped down the streets of Detroit, headed to Tower. Sam drove while Anna clutched the indictment and new arrest warrant. The grand jury had come through and indicted Dylan. Now she just had to get him arrested before Dylan's attorney appealed the new warrant—although she thought it less likely that the district judge would overrule a grand jury's decision. Four government sedans followed behind Sam's Durango. If Dylan wasn't at the frat, they would spread out over campus looking for him.

Anna's phone rang: an unknown caller. Today was not a day to let unknown callers go to voice mail.

"Hello?"

"Hi, Miss Curtis? This is Kenny Carter from the general counsel's office of Delta Airlines."

"Oh, hi, Kenny," she said. They'd spoken earlier today, when she subpoenaed the airline to get a copy of Dylan's ticket to Venezuela. "What's up?"

"Well, you told me to call you if there were any developments. And there has been a new development. A change was made to Dylan Highsmith's ticket. Instead of leaving tomorrow, the ticket was changed for him to leave today."

"Today?" Her heartbeat quickened. "When?"

"Six P.M. from Gate A-36."

She looked at the clock. It read 5:51.

She turned to Sam and grabbed the armrest. She knew how Sam drove. "Turn the car around and head to the airport. Dylan's on a plane."

"Shit," Sam said. She flicked on lights and sirens, yanked the wheel dead left, and careened over the grassy median. The four unmarked cars behind her put on their lights, and followed. Sam got on the highway and sped up to Michigan's 70 mph speed limit, then past it, until they were going 97 mph. Anna held the armrest with her right hand while she pressed the phone to her ear with the left.

"Can you stop the plane from taking off?" she asked Kenny. "I don't think we'll make it there by six."

"Do you have a valid arrest warrant and the FAA paperwork requesting to detain the plane?"

"I have a warrant. I don't have the FAA forms. I wasn't expecting to need to detain a plane tonight."

"Send me the warrant. I'll see if I can pull some strings to just get it delayed. But you'd better hurry. I'm in Atlanta, and I can make some calls, but I don't have a lot of pull in terms of what's going on at Terminal A at Detroit Metro Airport."

"I'll see if I can get someone there as soon as possible," Anna said.

Sam was silent and focused as she raced the car down the highway. The scenery sped by in a blur. Other cars, going 70, seemed to be standing still. While Sam drove, Anna made phone calls. She asked Nikki to send the warrant to Delta and start the FAA forms, although by the time the forms were filled out, they'd probably be moot. It was 5:58. She called a friend named Eric Gallun, who worked at TSA.

"Hey, Gallun, can you send some ICE agents to Gate A-36 right now? We need to pull a guy off a plane." She explained the situation. "And do you know someone at the Detroit airport who can get me and an FBI agent in through security, fast?"

"I can," he said. "I'll meet you at Terminal A."

By the time Sam brought the SUV to a stop in front of Terminal A, at 6:05, Eric was waiting at the doors. They left the car by the curb and ran through the airport, click-clacking down the marble corridors. People in Starbucks craned to watch them run. Eric rushed them through security, and they kept sprinting toward Gate 36. Anna's lungs felt like they were going to burst.

When they reached the gate, at 6:10 P.M., her heart dropped. Several ICE agents stood by the door. But there was no plane. It had already left. They were too late.

She put her hands on her knees, heaving and coughing, and tried to catch her breath. When she finally did, she used it to curse.

She looked up and saw a plane outside taxiing toward them. She straightened and watched as it pulled right up to the jetway for Gate 36. "That's your flight," Eric said.

Anna said, "We owe you a drink."

They showed the ICE agents a picture of Dylan, then walked down the jetway and got on the plane. The flight attendants looked at them with open curiosity.

The first-class passengers sat in cushiony leather recliners, giving them annoyed looks over champagne glasses. Anna saw an older couple, several businessmen, and a Detroit Pistons star. Dylan was not there.

The ICE agents went back through business class and then into coach. They scanned every row, then shook their heads. He wasn't there either. The sinking feeling returned to Anna's stomach.

She spoke to one of the flight attendants working first class. "The handsome young man with the brown hair," she said. "Do you know where he went?"

The flight attendant nodded and pointed to the first-class bathroom. Sam banged on the door. There was no response.

"Dylan Highsmith," Sam called "This is the FBI. We have a warrant for your arrest. Please step out of the bathroom with your hands up."

Silence.

"Can you unlock the door?" Anna asked

The flight attendant nodded and pulled a key out of a bin. She fitted it into the keyhole and fiddled around with it, while Anna imagined what Dylan might be doing. Could he possibly be armed? Had he hurt himself? Anna saw Sam's thumb flick open the strap on her holster.

The flight attendant unlocked the bathroom door and scooted to the side. Sam yanked it open.

Dylan stood, fully clothed, facing the toilet. He looked over his shoulder at them. "Excuse me? I'm pissing!" He reached to flush. Sam grabbed him before he could. She hauled him out of the bathroom and shoved him face-first against the first-class closet. His cheek flattened against the wall. "Dylan Highsmith, you are under arrest. You have the right to remain silent . . ."

As Sam read his rights, Anna glanced into the toilet. A Ziploc bag filled with white pills sat in the blue liquid. Each pill was stamped with ROCHE 2. He'd been taking a stash of Rohypnol to Venezuela.

39

Now that they had Dylan, Cooper was missing. Not really missing, Anna thought as she tried his number again. But she was officially worried. She hadn't been able to reach him since the body had been excavated from the elevator shaft. She tried Jody again.

"It's the weirdest thing," Jody said. "Grady texted me that Cooper's at his house."

"Grady's house? Why?"

"I have no idea."

"Have you ever been there?"

"No. You know me. I've been taking it slow."

Anna called Grady.

"Yeah," Grady said. "Coop's here."

She exhaled. "Is he okay?"

"Uh . . . hard to say. Why don't you come over?"

She followed Google maps to Grady's house, then stared at it in wonder. It was a modern glass palace on the banks of Orchard Lake. Grady was a bartender.

He answered the door, wearing a crisp white polo shirt from which his multitude of tattoos peeked.

"Do you live here alone?" Anna asked.

"Yep," Grady said.

"How?"

"I made some good investments. Come on in; your boyfriend's back here."

Grady led Anna through his airy house, all decorated in white, stone, and metal. It had a gorgeous view of the lake. Anna texted Jody: Your baby's daddy is either a drug dealer or a secret hedge fund manager. As they got nearer the back, Anna heard a thudding sound coming from outside. She followed Grady to the back patio, which had a lovely fire pit and pool. Beyond that, Cooper was chopping at a tree that had fallen in Grady's backyard.

He wore jeans and a Red Wings T-shirt, which was dark around the collar with sweat. He raised an ax above his head and brought it down in a smooth, powerful motion. A piece of wood flew from the downed tree. He did it again, then again.

"What is going on?" Anna asked.

Grady shrugged. "He asked if I had an ax."

Anna called, "Coop!"

He glanced up, squinted into the lights of the house, then kept chopping wood. She walked out, past the pool, through a fence. When she got near, she saw that the ax wasn't moving in the smooth arc it appeared from afar. It was erratic and shaky. So was he. A bottle of Jack Daniel's, almost empty, rested in the grass.

"Cooper Bolden, you stop that right now," she said. "You are drunk."

He stopped midswing and held the ax by his side. She stared at him as he swayed back and forth. She'd lived with him for eight months. He had the occasional beer. She'd never seen him intoxicated. She fought the urge to turn and run back into the house.

"Put that ax down," she said.

He opened his fingers and let it fall to the grass.

She went over and took his hand. It was hot and shaky. "Come on. Let's get you inside."

He nodded obediently and picked up the whiskey bottle as they walked. He took the last swig and staggered with her to the patio, where he sank down into a lawn chair. She tried to get him up, to go inside, but he was unmovable. "I'm too sweaty to go in," he said, spreading his long body out on the long chair. The empty bottle clattered to the flagstones.

She went inside and got several blankets from Grady, then went back out and laid the blankets on top of Cooper. She pulled another lawn chair next to him and climbed in under the covers.

"I've never seen you like this before," Anna said softly. "It—it kind of scares me."

He reached out an unsteady hand and tucked a strand of hair gently behind her ear. His voice was hoarse. "I'd never hurt you."

"I know," she said. "It's just—ever since I was kid, the sight of a really drunk man makes me nervous."

"I'm sorry."

"Was it the body in the elevator shaft?" Anna asked. "Your PTSD?"

"Yeah." Cooper nodded, then shook his head, then closed his eyes. "And the little girl."

"Hm? What little girl?"

"On the phone."

"Olivia?"

"You love her." His words bled together.

"Yes. Very much."

"I can't give you that."

"Believe me," she said, laughing, "I'm not in the market for another potential stepdaughter. It was hard enough to win that one over."

"I can't give you any." His bloodshot blue eyes met hers. "Any kids. At all."

"Why not?"

He waved a hand downward. "When the IED took my leg, it took that too."

She rocked back. "But. But you can—I mean, you can *totally*—in bed."

"Yeah. They say I'm lucky." He gave her a lopsided grin. "I'm glad you enjoy it."

"I really do."

She reached over and brushed a lock of dark hair off his forehead. He kept his eyes on hers as she kept stroking his hair. They lay facing each other without talking for a long time. The night was still and windless.

"I know it's what you want," he said quietly. "I can see it. When you hold Leigh. The way you look at that baby. The way you talk to Olivia. You need to be a mother."

She nodded. Her throat was tight.

"You deserve the sort of life I can't give you. Do you know who can?"

She whispered, "Don't."

"Jack Bailey can."

"Shh."

"That's why I'm breaking up with you."

"You're not breaking up with anyone." She swatted him. "You can't even get out of this lawn chair."

"True." He smiled, then frowned. "But tomorrow I will. And I swear, Anna. It's over. You need to pack your stuff. And get on with your life."

"Shh. We'll talk in the morning."

She lay her head on his chest. He stroked her back softly. Tears streamed sideways down her face. She hoped he couldn't feel his T-shirt growing damp under her cheek. But he did. He reached up and brushed a tear off her cheek.

"I'm so sorry, Coop," she said. "You don't deserve this."

"Nah, I'm lucky. For a little while, I got to be next to you. To me, that's the best place on earth. It's been a gift."

He kissed her forehead. She lay there under the quilts, listening to his heart beat under her ear. Its steadiness was hypnotic. Her tears stopped coming. She was lulled by the warmth of his body and the sound of water lapping on the shore. Her eyelids drifted down, fluttered open, drifted down again. The sky was full of stars.

When she woke up the next morning, he was gone.

THURSDAY

40

The detention decision at Dylan's arraignment should have been a slam dunk. He'd been fleeing to Venezuela at the time he was arrested. What could be a more obvious flight risk?

But Dylan's defense attorney tried to focus the attention away from his client and onto problems with the government's tactics. And he had more to work with than usual.

Anna sat at the prosecution table in the marble-lined courtroom in Detroit's federal courthouse. She wore a black skirt suit and sensible pumps, the uniform of the female prosecutor. She used all her mental willpower to focus on the argument and not her conversation with Cooper the night before. She'd tried calling him twice this morning and had gotten no answer.

Sam sat at her side. Dylan wore an orange jumpsuit and handcuffs, which was a fantastic relief to see. If Sam and Anna hadn't made it to the plane, he might be sitting poolside drinking a piña colada right now, trying to decide which girl's margarita to drug.

The audience was packed with family, friends, journalists, and curious court employees. Dylan's parents sat in the row behind their son, stiff-backed, staring straight ahead, trying to ignore everything around them.

Jack sat in the row behind Anna, in the audience. "It's your case," he'd said. "I'm just here for moral support." He was trying to do what she'd asked—give her more authority, more autonomy as a lawyer. He was taking a backseat so she could run her own case. She tried to smile as she thanked him.

Dylan's lawyer stood next to him. She'd seen his name on briefs and in the *ABA Journal* often enough, but this was the first time Anna had met Justin Dillon in person. He was a slim, handsome man who looked younger than his prominence would suggest. He wore a tailored gray suit and stood pointing a finger at Anna.

"The prosecutor's conduct has been egregious." Justin said it with so much conviction, Anna almost believed it herself. She had to remind herself that *she* was the prosecutor, and she'd done nothing wrong.

"To begin, she kicked the defendant in the groin," Justin said.

Judge Ella Hughes peered at Anna over her reading glasses. She was a pretty woman with strawberry blond hair and a reputation for intelligence. "Is that true, Ms. Curtis?"

Anna stood. "Yes, Your Honor, I did have to use a defensive move when the defendant grabbed me during questioning. Mr. Dillon has already moved to recuse me, and Judge Schwalbe is holding an evidentiary hearing on the matter on Monday."

The judge nodded and sighed. "At this point, I'll credit the prosecutor. A suspect can't get a prosecutor removed from his case by assaulting her. We'll move the evidentiary hearing to my calendar. Anything else, Mr. Dillon?"

"She had a plane detained without the proper FAA paperwork," Justin said. "She accompanied the FBI agent onto the plane to arrest the defendant, making herself a witness to the arrest. And she deliberately made an end run around Judge DeLuca."

Wait till he hears what my sister did with nail polish, Anna thought.

"Ms. Curtis?" said the judge.

"The government's actions in this case have been proper, Your Honor. The airline voluntarily helped us. A prosecutor may of course accompany a police officer, and I did not become a necessary witness—Agent Randazzo is perfectly qualified to testify about everything that happened on the plane. Finally, the grand jury is entitled to make its own finding of probable cause. This grand jury heard even more evidence than was in the complaint and arrest warrant quashed by Judge DeLuca. This indictment is perfectly valid. We're here today for the very simple procedure of arraigning Mr. Highsmith: reading the charges against him, hearing his plea, and making an initial determination about whether he should be held in jail."

"I agree," the judge said. "Defense counsel, please limit yourself to those issues for now. There will be an appropriate forum to discuss allegations of misconduct at a later time, if you choose."

"Oh, I will," Justin said ominously.

Anna sighed. Attacking the prosecutor was often part of the defense strategy, even when there wasn't so much to work with. She tried not to take such allegations personally, although they always felt personal. She saw the reporters scribbling in their notebooks and imagined this afternoon's headline: "Prosecutor Accused of Misconduct."

"The defendant clearly poses a risk of flight," Anna said, trying to get the hearing back on track. "For three reasons. The first is where he was arrested, on a flight bound to Venezuela . . ."

After an hour of argument from both sides, the judge agreed with Anna. Dylan was ordered held. A marshal led Dylan back to the holding cell. It was a satisfying sight. At moments like this, Anna felt like there was nothing in the world more gratifying than being a sex-crimes prosecutor, knowing that her efforts had gotten a predator off the streets.

The crowd started filing out of the courtroom. Anna picked up her phone and looked at what had come in during the hearing. The title of a new message jolted her. She read its contents twice, to be sure.

To: anna.curtis@usdoj.gov
From: leonie.decheusn@fbi.gov
Date: March 30, 2015
Re: Identification of Remains

Per your request, the FBI DNA Laboratory expedited its review of the female remains found in Detroit's Central Station. A DNA profile was determined and compared to the known profile of C-1. The chart below shows the respective alleles at twelve locales. You will note that none of the alleles are a match. We conclude that the person found in the elevator shaft is not the same person as C-1, to a scientific certainty.

The Laboratory then ran the DNA profile of the decedent in the Combined DNA Index System [also known as CODIS]. The decedent's profile matched the known sample of one Kathleen Legendre, a.k.a. Lola Isblissful, to a one in 545,000,000 certainty. Ms. Legendre's DNA was added to CODIS when she was convicted of one count of aggravated assault in 2011. Her NCIC record is attached.

Anna scanned the NCIC criminal history. The girl in the elevator shaft was a homeless felon. Where was Emily Shapiro?

Anna went over to the defense table. "I'd like to set up a meeting to talk to your client."

"No thanks."

"There's still a missing girl. Your client was the last one to see her. We need to know what he knows."

"I'm not letting him talk to you."

"If you sit down with me today, I'll give you early discovery. I'll turn over the grand jury transcripts to you now, instead of months from now, which, as you know, is perfectly within my rights."

She was offering him a good deal, and one that could hurt her. Sam's testimony in the grand jury summed up the entire investigation. Justin could start making allegations of misconduct immediately. He already wanted to turn the entire case into a witch hunt about what Anna had done—and this would give him the basis he needed to try. She was willing to take that risk. Only Dylan knew what had happened to Emily. Only he could give that closure to her family.

"I'll give you an attorney proffer," Justin said.

"Okay," she said. "If we do it now."

VLOG
RECORDED 3.13.15

Dylan poisoned Fenwick. That asshole went to the vet clinic, took the dog for a walk, and fed him rat poison.

Or Peter did it—for Dylan. Or with Dylan. Who knows. They're sick, they're just totally sick.

I went to the clinic today for our regular walk. But when I opened the door to Fenwick's little cubby, he didn't jump up like normal. He was lying in a corner, a pile of yellow fur over ribs going up and down too fast. His eyes were all dull. I went up to him and was like, "Hey, Fennie, what's wrong?" He didn't move, just licked my hand. He didn't give me that happy Fenwick smile.

I'm thinking he's sick, but a walk'll be good for him. So I put the leash on, and he still doesn't get up. I give him a tug and I'm like, "Come on boy, let's go." He gets up real slow like it hurts him to move and comes with me to the front of the clinic. Walking like an old man, hanging his head down, taking forever. And then, right in front of the front desk, he starts shaking all over, and then convulsing, and I look at the guy behind the desk, like, what's going on? Then Fenwick throws up: this big mound of pink meat, right there in the middle of the waiting room.

He's shaking and twitching like crazy. I'm yelling for the vets to come, and someone in a white coat runs out and bundles him away. I try to go with, but they say I can't go back in the vet area. So I'm standing there, shaking almost as much as Fenwick, and I look at the vomit. It's half-digested hot dogs and these little turquoise pellets. I show it to the guy behind the desk. He's one of the student vets, and he's like, "That's rat poison."

I'm going, oh my God, oh my God. Then I'm, like, "Where did Fenwick get rat poison and hot dogs from? Do you keep those in the clinic?" And the guy is like, "No, that's terrible for them, we wouldn't keep it here." So I go, "Did anyone else walk him today?" And he looks in the log—'cause you have to leave an ID when you take a dog out—and it says Peter York walked him this morning.

Peter York. Dylan's best friend. I'm like, "Are you going to arrest him?" And the guy's like, "We're not the dog police." I'm like, "So anyone can walk in here and poison a dog?" And he's like, "We'll take care of this; go home and get some rest; you're hysterical." "You're hysterical" is what men say to women when they don't give a shit and think you shouldn't either.

They pumped Fenwick's stomach, but it wasn't enough. He'd eaten too much poison. So now they have him in surgery, with some vet student doing whatever vet students do. And I'm back here just pacing and pacing and waiting to hear from them. They promised they'd call when he got out. Do you think they'll call? They might forget. I'll call them now. I've already called three times, though.

Oh crap. I really can't handle this. That dog was the one thing in Tower that really loved me. I swear, if Fenwick doesn't make it, I'm going to fucking lose it.

41

They sat in an interview room in the basement of the courthouse, a windowless cubby with a small table and four chairs. Anna and Sam faced Dylan and his lawyer across the table.

In the courtroom, Dylan had managed to look polite and confused for the benefit of the cameras and judge. Back here, he was free to cross his arms over his orange jumpsuit and glare. Anna was happy that was the only thing he was free to do. After their conversation, he would be put on a prison bus and transported back to a central detention facility.

"Mr. Highsmith," Anna said, "we're here for a proffer. Agent Randazzo and I would like to know your side of the story, and your attorney is willing to give it to us."

"But I'll be doing the speaking," Justin said to his client, "as we discussed. Only me. You don't say anything."

Anything that came from the lawyer's mouth during the proffer could not be used against Dylan. But they could use it to find Emily. If Dylan himself said something, it was fair game anywhere.

Dylan nodded. He'd been prepped.

"So," Anna said, "why don't you tell us what happened between Dylan and Emily the night of March 23?"

Justin read from his notes.

"On March 23, my client went to two classes at Tower, the final one of which ended at four P.M. He then returned to the Beta Psi house, which is his residence, and worked on some flyers for his Readers Are Leaders campaign."

Anna managed not to roll her eyes. She didn't want to interrupt. She'd listen to whatever sugarcoated story he'd tell her, and then follow up with questions.

"At around 11:45 P.M., he and some other young men decided to leave the fraternity house and patronize some local bars. Around midnight, they arrived at Lucky's. Ms. Shapiro was apparently just leaving the bar. Dylan said hello to her and they exchanged a few more words." The lawyer looked down at his notes. He was reading them Dylan's story. "Ms. Shapiro was highly intoxicated. My client was concerned about her walking home alone. He offered to walk with her. She refused and began walking away. He followed in order to make sure she was all right. She began running, and he jogged to keep up with her. But she told him to leave her alone. So he turned around and rejoined his friends at the bar."

Justin looked up.

"That's it?" Anna asked. "You're done?"

"That's all that happened."

"We pulled all the video from that night. It shows Dylan chasing Emily down the street. It doesn't show him turning around and walking back to the bar."

"He went back through the neighborhood, which was quieter, and used the bar's back door."

"Do you have people who can attest to that?"

Justin gave her the names of six Beta Psis. She would follow up with them.

"Why was Emily's blood on Dylan's car?" Anna asked.

"He has no idea."

"Why was her scarf in his room?"

"Ah. It fell off when the young lady was stumbling home. Dylan picked it up and tried to give it back to her, but she kept walking. He held on to it thinking he would give it to her at a later time."

"What was Dylan doing in Detroit that night?"

Justin looked uncertain for the first time. He leaned over and whispered to his client. Dylan gestured and whispered loudly. Justin turned to Anna. "Excuse me. I need a moment alone with my client."

Sam and Anna walked out of the room and shut the door. A burly U.S. marshal was sitting outside, keeping guard. Anna offered everyone a mint and checked her phone.

The top headline in the *Detroit Free Press* read: "Frat Used Medical Cadavers to Decorate House." It described how dental records had matched the skeleton in Beta Psi's basement to a person who had donated his body to the medical school. Family members had initiated a class action lawsuit against the fraternity. Anna hoped they got some tremendous settlement; at the same time she was relieved that the bones weren't from a more heinous crime.

She clicked over to the national news. One of the top stories on CNN was: "Rape Protesters Pay Fine with Mattress." She scrolled through the story. Tower's top lawyer sent bills to dozens of students who'd taken mattresses from their dorms to carry in the protest. He fined them $250 each, for destruction of university property, citing a section of the student handbook that said university furniture couldn't be taken out of dorm rooms.

The protesters responded by paying the fine in a single big check made out to Tower University in the amount of $35,250, written on a twin-sized mattress. A group of pretty young women stood on the steps of the administration's headquarters holding up the mattress check. It immediately went viral, as evidenced by the fact that Anna was reading it on CNN.com.

She shook her head. The old men at the university just didn't get it. To the extent that they had held the reins of power for so many years, their power was slipping in this new world. These young women knew how to use images and viral messaging to tell their story. In the end, the best story wins. She wondered what Dylan's was going to be.

Ten minutes after asking for a break, Justin opened the door, and they all sat down again.

Dylan leaned back and laced his hands behind his head, as if he were lounging on the beach he'd almost made it to in Caracas. If he was nervous, he didn't show it. Maybe he was confident his father would get him out. Maybe he was the most arrogant person Anna had ever met. Or maybe some part of him enjoyed this. His lawyer continued as if they hadn't stopped.

"My client and his friend did drive to Detroit that night to visit a house of ill repute."

"A brothel?"

"More of an independent contractor. From Craigslist. A business transaction took place."

"Do you have any paperwork to confirm that?"

"I'm just making a proffer. Confirm whatever you like."

"After the prostitute?"

"He went to Windsor to patronize Caesar's casino. He lost eight hundred dollars there."

"On his credit card?"

"Cash."

Worthless. "Tell me about the bones and *The Book of Earthly Pleasures*."

"The lawyer from Beta Psi will answer any questions you have about that."

"Dylan"—Anna met Dylan's eyes—"a young woman is out there. Let's end her family's uncertainty. Let's let them hug her or put their little girl to rest. You're the only one who can give them that."

Dylan stared at her for a moment. Then he turned and spit on the floor. He wiped his mouth and said, "Fuck you."

Anna stood, opened the door, and signaled to the U.S. marshal outside. He was a huge man, over six feet tall and half as wide, with muscles that stretched his blue U.S. marshals T-shirt. A scar ran across his eye, shutting it halfway. In another life, he would have been a pirate.

"The interview is over," Anna said. "You can take the prisoner back to the holding cell." She gestured to the spit. "And you might want to get some sanitizer for the floor."

The deputy looked at the slimy wad of phlegm on the linoleum. "Who did that?" he growled.

The look on Dylan's face would've been more satisfying if she were any closer to knowing what had happened to Emily.

42

Later that day, Dylan's attorney renewed and amended his motion for Anna to be recused from the case. He added three allegations: first, that she must have given secret grand jury material to her sister; second, that she had prompted her sister to violate Dylan's Fourth Amendment right by entering the fraternity without a warrant; and third, that Anna had left Dylan in the hands of a furious U.S. marshal after their interview. The marshal hadn't actually harmed Dylan, the motion conceded.

The motion itself triggered certain obligations for Anna. Like the first one, she forwarded the motion to the Department of Justice's Office of Professional Responsibility. OPR was in charge of ethics complaints brought against DOJ lawyers. They would conduct an inquiry into her handling of the case. It was intimidating. But all she could do was let OPR officials take care of their job and keep trying to do hers.

The consequences kept rolling in. Jody called Anna, her voice shaking. "My supervisor at the plant called. I've been fired."

"What? Why?" Anna asked. "You've been there for eight years. You have a lot of seniority." When there were layoffs, the newest workers got hit first.

"The head of the plant is in bed with Robert Highsmith. He gets all of us to give money to his campaigns, then bundles the contributions. In return, Highsmith gets him all sorts of favors. I think Highsmith put him up to this." Jody sniffled. "I need the job, Anna. Money's tight as it is. I can't make ends meet if I'm not working."

"Jo, we'll figure something out. I can help with money." She recalled the glass mansion on Orchard Lake. "Also, it seems Grady has some resources."

Jody started crying. "I don't want help, Anna. I've never wanted to be a charity case, and I definitely do not want to rely on Grady. I just want my job."

"Hang in there, Jo," Anna said. "I'm going to figure this out."

Fury burned through Anna's chest. She called Jack. "I want Public Integrity to investigate this."

"Anna, calm down," he said. "We don't have a public corruption case."

"This is bullshit. He's taking this out on my sister."

"She should talk to an employment lawyer. You don't have any evidence Highsmith had anything to do with this."

"Yeah, but—"

"And your sister is just coming back from maternity leave."

"You can't discriminate based on that."

"Let's just see what happens."

"Why are you being so soft on them?"

"I'm being a realist. If you ask Public Integrity to investigate based on your sister's speculation, they won't. And it'll feed into the story line of you being vindictive, and only serve to distract from the murder case. Let's just find Emily Shapiro—and go from there."

By the time they hung up, Anna was even more infuriated. She saw his point. But it was hard to be neutral when her sister was being attacked.

A few minutes later, she got a call from Carla, the chief of the Sex Offense unit in D.C. and her boss. "Anna, hi. I'm sorry to tell you, but a formal complaint has been made against you here in the office."

"There, too, huh? By Dylan Highsmith's lawyer?"

"Of course. We have to investigate. But you know I've got your back. Don't let this worry you."

Carla was a good boss, and Anna trusted that she'd be fair. But all these complaints were nerve-racking. There would be two ethics investigations against Anna: one through DOJ's OPR and one through the DC USAO, which would also eventually be forwarded to OPR. She'd be navigating the alphabet soup of government sanctions for months, if not years. She could lose her license, her job, and the most important thing to a lawyer: her reputation.

"I'm still on the case?"

Carla paused. "For now."

"What do you mean?"

"I'm meeting with the front office later this evening. We're going to talk about whether it's time to put a new AUSA on the case."

"Carla, I've got this."

"I know. We don't think you've done anything wrong. But it's about appearances. And it might be better for you too. This has gotten very personal. You and your family deserve a break."

"I don't want a break. I want to find Emily."

"I know. You've gotten a long way in a short time. Everyone appreciates how far you've taken this. If you have to hand it off to someone else, no one will forget that. So get your files in order. Get a good night's sleep tonight. We'll talk tomorrow."

Anna understood the message. She had one more day left on the case.

43

The knock came right when he expected it. Wyatt opened his dorm room door. Peter York, Brian Mercer, and David Rankin stood there grinning at him. Peter handed him a thick ivory envelope. Inside was creamy ivory cardstock, with the Beta Psi emblem printed in gold.

WYATT THOMAS BOLDEN

* * *

*We are honored to extend to you
this invitation to join the hallowed ranks of
the men of BETA PSI*

"Congratulations," Peter said. "You're a brother."

Brian was carrying a black leather box. They set it on Wyatt's desk and started pulling out the treasures inside. A bottle of Laphroaig. A sweatshirt embroidered with the Beta Psi letters. A key to the fraternity house. Everything Wyatt wanted.

"We're having a party to welcome you and your new brothers tonight," David said. "Greatest party you've ever seen."

Wyatt looked at the guys. He pictured the bar tab signed by President Taft. He felt the solid wood on the yacht mast. He tasted the filet mignon at the Highsmiths' luncheon. Peter held out the key. Wyatt reached out and took it.

As his fingers closed over the cool metal, he couldn't push back the other memories. He tasted the vodka after it ran through Alex's ass crack. He felt the weight of the jug with the red cocktail. He saw the stripper's white scar pulsing against her purple face as Dylan squeezed her throat.

Slowly, Wyatt put the key back in the black box. He packed the scotch back in too. The sweatshirt was the most difficult. He held its soft material and, for just a moment, let his thumb trace the stitching of the letters. He imagined wearing it around campus. The smiles he would get from girls, the respect he would get from guys. He wanted to wear it so much, it was a physical sensation. He put the sweatshirt back in the box.

"I'm sorry," Wyatt said. "I can't accept."

They looked at him like he was insane. Maybe he was.

"You went through all of Hell Week," Peter said. "You got all the shit. For Chrissakes, take the reward."

For some guys, the reward was simple: fun, friendship, parties, status. But for Wyatt, it had become more complicated. It meant keeping Dylan's secrets, over and over. It meant choosing to be the type of person who would keep those secrets. It was the wretched clawed animal trying to dig its way out of his chest, every day for the rest of his life.

"I appreciate the invitation," Wyatt said. "But I have to say no."

Peter stared at him for a long moment. Then he took the box and walked out. As the door slammed shut, the guys were shaking their heads and muttering to one another. Wyatt caught the words *douche bag*.

He sank back down on the couch and sat looking at the thick ivory invitation for a long time.

Then he pulled out his phone and scrolled to the number for Anna Curtis. She answered on the second ring.

"Hi, Anna? It's Wyatt Bolden," he said. "I have to tell you something."

44

A nna and Sam got in the car and drove right over to Wyatt's dorm. They strode into Stringer Hall, jogged up the steps to the third floor, and knocked on Wyatt's door.

He let them in. "Thanks for coming over so fast."

"No problem," Anna replied, as if it were a casual meeting and not the break in the case she'd been obsessively nurturing and hoping for. "Thanks for calling."

They sat on his faded brown couch. The room had the clean, spare look of a place that wasn't used much. Wyatt probably spent most of his time at the frat.

"So, what's up, Wyatt?"

"Listen," he said. "I've seen a lot of bad stuff over the last few months. I want to tell you about it. But I don't want anyone to know that it came from me."

"I can try to keep your name confidential for now. But if the case goes to trial, the defendant has the right to know who gave that evidence."

Wyatt looked out the window. Finally, he looked back at her and nodded.

"I'm not proud of this. But I think that telling you now is better than sitting on it the rest of my life. It's been tearing me up."

"A secret can eat away at you. Coming clean is harder at first, but in the end, it's healthier," Anna said.

"Okay." He took a deep breath. "The night that Dylan and Emily were . . . together, I was in charge of the bar. He had a gallon jug of stuff he called Killer Heart Throb Punch. He had me stash it behind the bar and told me not to let anyone else touch it."

"Did he drink it?"

"No. He only gave it to girls. That night, I saw him pour it for Emily, and then she got really loopy. Stumbling around. Dylan took her upstairs.

"Then, I just thought it was a drunken hookup. It was the first party of the year; I didn't know better. But I saw that same thing go down, over and over. As soon as a girl started drinking it, she, like, collapsed. It wasn't just alcohol. That red drink was spiked. He was drugging girls to have sex with them."

"Do you remember any of the other girls he did this to?"

"I don't know their names. I might recognize one or two if I saw them again."

"Did you see any of the other guys using it?"

"I think maybe some of them knew what was going on. But I didn't see them using it. Just Dylan."

"Did you ever confront him about it?"

Wyatt shook his head.

"Or report this to anyone else?"

"No." He looked at his knees. "I wanted to be a brother."

"We appreciate you coming forward now," Anna said. "That takes guts. Thank you."

"That's not all," Wyatt said. "Things got really messed up a few days ago. Emily published all these videos talking about being raped by Dylan. There was a whole series of them on BlueTube. When Dylan found out, he freaked."

"What did he do?"

"Pulled some strings. A couple of Beta Psi alums work at Blue-Tube, doing tech stuff or something. He got them to take the videos down. I hear Emily was pretty bummed. She hadn't saved them anywhere else, and once BlueTube took them down, she didn't have access to them. I guess they were like her diary of the year."

"How do you know all this?"

"Pledges do chores around the house. I was scrubbing the kitchen floor when Dylan, Peter, and a couple other guys were talking about it. No one really notices you when you're on your hands and knees."

"Wyatt, thank you so much for calling," Anna said. "This is really important, and we'll follow up on it. You should be proud of yourself. You did the right thing."

"For once." He gave her a rueful smile.

When Wyatt smiled, he looked so much like a young version of Cooper. Anna wondered if this was what a son of Cooper's would look like. And then she remembered that Cooper would have no children. She would never have a child with him. The recollection was like a gut punch, stunningly painful.

"Are you going to tell Cooper about this?" Wyatt asked.

"No. But maybe you should. He'd be there for you."

"Yeah. I know."

"By the way," Anna said, "have you heard from him today?"

"No, why?"

"Just wondering. Thanks a lot, Wyatt."

Anna and Sam went down to the car. As they pulled out, Sam said, "To BlueTube?"

"Yeah."

45

BlueTube's headquarters were in the Southfield Town Center, a set of four black-and-gold office towers in the middle of a suburb. Looking out the twenty-fifth-floor conference room window, there were no other buildings to block her view. Anna could see for miles: a crosshatch of streets dotted with little houses, lawns, and trees.

"Thanks for agreeing to meet with us on such short notice," Anna said.

Sam handed her business card across the glass-topped able. "We appreciate your help."

Tara Kennedy, the founder and CEO of BlueTube, took the card and smiled politely. "Please tell me about this 'urgent situation.'"

According to its website, which Anna read on the way over, Blue-Tube had grown from an operation out of the founder's dorm room into a company of ten employees. Tara was young enough to project the company's youthful tech image, but old enough to know what she was doing in business and politics. Anna hadn't looked, but she guessed that at some point, Tara had donated to Robert Highsmith's political coffers.

"We're investigating the disappearance of Emily Shapiro," Anna said. "Maybe you've heard of the case?"

"Heard of it? That's been the lead on the news every day this week. What does it have to do with BlueTube?"

"Apparently, Emily posted several videos to BlueTube over the last year. They've been taken down since then. We sent a subpoena to your company four days ago. According to an employee of yours, Chandler Andrews, Emily took down the videos herself. But we have a witness who says that BlueTube employees removed the videos."

"Are you investigating my company?" Tara asked.

"No," Anna said, "although if there are individuals who lied to us, they might face obstruction of justice charges. But what I'm interested in today is seeing those videos. And finding out as much as I can about the young woman who posted them."

Tara read over the letter and subpoena. Then she picked up the phone and punched in a number. "Chandler, Aubrey, please come to the conference room."

Within seconds, two young men walked into the room. They looked slightly older than the frat boys at Beta Psi, but the jaunty swoop of their hair reminded Anna of the boys she'd seen at the frat house. They sat at the table.

"Gentlemen," said Tara. "I understand that you are alumni of a fraternity called Beta Psi?"

"Um," said Aubrey, glancing nervously at Anna and Sam. "Yeah, we are."

"I've been informed that someone inside BlueTube may have taken down a series of vlog posts to help a young man who is currently a member of that fraternity. Do you know anything about this?"

Chandler bit his lip. "I'm not sure."

"Aubrey?"

"I don't remember," said Aubrey, looking down at his hands.

"Of course, we'll be able to figure out who did," Tara said. "And lying about this would constitute a breach of contract, for which you'd lose your bonus. So let's try that again. Did either of you take down these vlogs?"

Aubrey and Chandler looked at each other. Aubrey looked back down at his hands. Chandler said, "I'm not sure. We do so much here—"

"If you've been doing it so often that you can't recall if you took down these particular videos, that's a problem."

She picked up her phone again. "Security. Please escort Mr. Wattleton and Mr. Andrews to their offices, where they may collect any personal items but may not log onto their computers or take any company property." She set the phone down and looked at the two young men. "You're fired."

"But—but—"

Two security officers walked in and took the young men by their elbows. As they were escorted out of the room, Aubrey started to cry. Anna almost felt sorry for him. Almost.

When Aubrey's sobbing was no longer audible, Tara turned back to Anna. "I'm so sorry for what's gone on. I'll check and see if we can recover the videos. Is there anything else?"

"Thank you," Anna said. "If you could provide the e-mail and IP address that Emily used to set up the account, that would be helpful."

"Absolutely. Excuse me for a moment. Feel free to help yourself to coffee while I step out."

■ ■ ■

Twenty minutes later, Tara returned holding a large manila envelope. "Emily Shapiro uploaded several videos, starting in September of 2014 and going to March of 2015. She had her privacy settings on 'private,' so no one else could view them. On March 19, 2015, she changed the privacy settings to 'public,' essentially publishing her videos for the first time. They were all taken down by BlueTube employees—Chandler and Aubrey—within hours of her posting them. But they're still on the server. I was able to recover them, and I had them burned onto thumb drives for you. The e-mail and IP address are written down. I made a couple copies, one for each of you. I hope that works."

"Thank you so much." Anna swallowed back a lump in her throat.

Tara said, "I have a teenage daughter. I can't imagine what these parents must be going through."

When Sam and Anna got back into the car, they powered up the laptop and immediately slid the thumb drive into it. Emily's happy face appeared on the screen. They started with the vlog entry dated September 1, 2014, and watched them all the way through to one week ago.

VLOG
RECORDED 3.19.15

I feel numb.

Nothing.

No. Maybe what I'm feeling is: I should've known. I have known it, in a sense, my whole life. But in spite of everything, I still somehow hoped that he cared about me more than his college.

Oh God.

Breathe, Emily.

Breathe.

I got the paperwork. They didn't want to give it to me. They said there were privacy interests. I threatened to get Heide Herrmann and her Title IX protesters involved; I threatened to tweet. They finally turned it over.

The decision passed through a bunch of red tape and administrators. They decided expulsion was too harsh. I mean, poor Dylan, right? So they overturned it. He could just do community service. He could come back and finish off his time at Tower, and graduate along with his class. They turned a slap on the wrist into a pat on the back.

And the signature at the bottom of it all?

President Barney Shapiro.

My dad decided to let my rapist go.

I feel like a wrecking ball hit my chest. Maybe I'm having a heart attack. Do eighteen-year-old girls have heart attacks? I haven't been able to get a real breath of air since I read that.

It's funny, because I think the committee only found Dylan responsible in the first place because I'm the president's daughter. And then he overruled them.

He chose his college over me.

I thought it was bad, getting spit at. Threatened. I thought it was bad when Whitney wouldn't talk to me. I thought sitting next to Dylan at the committee hearing was bad.

But this. This is the worst.

I hate everyone. Myself included.

And I just don't care. Fuck Dylan. Fuck my dad. Fuck everyone.

I'm publishing these vlogs. I'm gonna talk to Heide Herrmann and find out what we can do to make sure the world knows this story. I'm gonna write about it in the school paper. I'm gonna call the *New York Times*, and scream it from the rooftops. So Dylan will finally get the justice he deserves. So this will never happen to another girl. So my dad can rot in his own corruption.

46

S he never got to do those things," Sam said. "The *New York Times*. The editorial. Her disappearance was very convenient for Dylan. And her father."

"Or not," Anna said. "A lot of people are paying attention now that she's gone."

"True."

They were still sitting in the car at BlueTube's office building. The sun was setting outside the parking structure. It had taken over an hour to watch all of Emily's videos. As Anna watched, a theory began to take shape.

"Emily said she was going to talk to the Title Nine folks," Anna said. "Maybe we should have another talk with them ourselves."

"Let's do it." Sam started the car.

Fifteen minutes later, they were at the home of Heide Herrmann. She lived in a garden apartment on the scrappy outskirts of Tower. When they knocked, a dog barked at them. After a moment, Heide peeked through the chain, then opened the door.

"Hi! Come on in."

Anna and Sam walked into Heide's apartment, which also served as her activist headquarters. Her walls were covered in corkboard pinned with leaflets, flyers, and charts of different grassroots organizations with which she was coordinating. A big "Yes Means Yes" poster covered the only wall that didn't have corkboard. CNN played silently on the TV. A laptop was set up on her kitchen table.

Heide shooed away a calico cat so Anna and Sam could sit on her couch. "What's going on?" Heide asked. "Do you have news about Emily?"

"Not really," Anna said. "We were hoping to ask you some follow-up questions."

"Sure."

"Did Emily come to you in the weeks before she disappeared?"

"Yeah. She was really frustrated by the university's response to her case. She wanted to know how she could be heard."

"What did you tell her?"

"I said that it's a struggle we've all faced, and we all find our own way. I suggested an editorial in the papers, or a press release. She mentioned a video log she'd kept. I told her if she was courageous enough, she could publicize those."

"Hm," Anna said. She looked at a pamphlet on the wall, announcing the mattress-carrying protest a few nights ago. Heide was listed as the organizer. "That seems pretty tame, from the woman who organized the mattress uprising."

"Ha. Thanks, I guess."

A scratching sound came from behind a closed interior door. "Is that your bedroom?" Anna asked, pointing to the door.

"Um, yeah," Heide said.

"Is someone in there?"

"No, I—what do you mean?"

"I heard some scratching. From inside that room."

Sam stood up and walked to the door.

"Oh," Heide said quickly, standing too. "That's just my dog. He doesn't always like visitors, so—"

Sam put her hand on her gun, turned the knob, and threw the door open. In the bright bedroom stood a big yellow mutt. He walked up to Sam, licked her hand, and then gave her a big doggy smile—just like the doggy smile Emily described in her vlogs.

"Fenwick?" Anna said.

The dog turned to the sound of his name. He trotted over to Anna, sniffed her feet, and let her pet him, smiling at her the whole time. He looked healthy, well nourished, and happy.

"You don't mind if I look around the rest of your place, right?" Sam asked.

Heide's eyes got big, but she shook her head. Sam searched through the closet, under the bed, in the bathroom, anywhere a person could hide. There was no one.

"Um." Heide held a pamphlet and tore little rips across the border. "Am I in trouble for having the dog?"

"Tell me why you think you'd be in trouble," Anna said.

"Okay, well. I don't think he's officially supposed to be out of the vet clinic. But Emily brought him to my house, said he needed a place to stay and be safe. So uh . . . yeah."

"When was that?"

"I guess . . . a few days before she disappeared. Maybe the day before."

Anna's eyes rested on the slim laptop that sat open on Heide's table. It was bright and shiny, without a mark on it. Anna had just had to do a little computer shopping herself, after her own computer was destroyed in Jody's house fire.

"The new MacBook Pro right?" Anna asked.

"Mm-hmm."

"You must've just gotten it. It was released a few weeks ago."

"Yeah, you're up on your tech."

"I just got a new Mac myself. How do you like it?"

"Good. It's got a lot of bells and whistles."

"I know, right?" Anna said. "What was your old computer?"

"A Mac too."

"Brand loyalty. So what'd you do with the old one when you were done?"

Heide paused and bit her lip. "Actually, I lent it to Emily."

"When?"

"I'm not sure. Like, mid-March."

"A few days before she disappeared."

"Right."

"Did she give it back to you?"

"No."

"So you haven't seen your old Mac since you lent it to her."

"I guess that's right."

"Did you report it missing?"

"I'm not gonna report a dead girl for stealing my Mac."

Anna gave her a long look.

"Do you know what happened to Emily, Heide?"

"Honestly, I have no idea." Her eyes opened so wide that the whites above her irises were visible. FBI interrogators said this body language was a sign of stress, and often, that someone was lying.

"Well," Anna said. "I think we might have a lead. All we need is the receipt for your computer."

"Um. I don't know if I can find that."

"No problem." Anna went over to Heide's Mac. "You don't mind, right?" Anna lifted up the computer and looked at the FCC ID number on the back. She pointed it out to Sam, who took a picture of it.

"Thanks, Heide. Please let us know if you have any more information."

Back in the car, Sam said, "You think Heide hurt Emily?"

"'Hurt' is a broad word. I'm not sure what she did. But I'm sure she's hiding something."

47

They set up an impromptu command center down the street at the Tower University police station. Sam called a guy she knew in subpoena compliance at Apple and faxed him the waiver that Emily's parents had signed. As Sam spoke to her friend, Jack arrived. He wended his way through the officers and came over to Anna. "What's going on?" he asked.

She briefed him on what they'd found today.

He said, "You think whoever killed Emily also stole Heide's laptop from her?"

"Maybe," Anna said. "I don't want to speculate too wildly till we know more."

Sam hung up the phone triumphantly. She printed whatever the Apple agent had just e-mailed to her and thumped it on the table. "Heide Herrmann bought two Macs over the last four years: one four years ago and one two weeks ago. Apple was able to use their Find My Mac function to locate the two computers."

The company had sent over two screenshots on maps showing where the computers were running. The newer model was operating from Heide's apartment, as they'd seen. The older one was powered on and operating, too, although at first Anna didn't understand where it was. The bright yellow dot on the map was in the middle of a swath of parklike green on the Tower University campus. No dorms or classrooms were located around it.

"Someone's running the computer from a park?" Anna said. "Like sitting on a bench or something?"

Sam traced a circle around the little yellow dot. "I think that's the university's clock tower."

A commotion made Anna look up from the maps. Dozens of state troopers in tan uniforms were pouring into the university police station. They were led by District Attorney Bill Xanten, who was waving around papers.

"My office is shutting you down," Xanten said.

"The hell you are," Jack replied.

"I have an order from the governor."

"And I have one from the Attorney General of the United States."

"This is a local case," Xanten said, "which local prosecutors have jurisdiction over. I'm ordering you to turn your files over to me and go home. We'll take it from here."

"Have you gone off your meds, Xanten?"

"Turn off that computer," Xanten barked at an FBI agent.

"Now look here." Jack stepped forward and blocked Xanten from coming in any farther. They were both tall, broad men. They stood toe to toe, giving the impression of two boxers about to face off. "Have you heard of the Supremacy Clause?"

As the men argued, Anna slowly backed away, until she was at the edge of the fray. She put a hand on Sam's wrist and tugged her toward the back door. The men's voices were getting louder. They were in full-blown alpha-male confrontation mode. It was a good show. Anna and Sam slipped out the back door without anyone noticing.

"Wanna go check out the clock tower?" Anna said.

"Let's do it," Sam said.

■ ■ ■

The two women pushed out the door, leaving behind the bright lights and loud voices of the police station for a dark and drizzly night. The clock tower was only a few blocks away. Anna and Sam walked.

Pulling her suit jacket tight around her chest, Anna angled her head into the wet air. They strode past a dormitory, where they could hear the sounds of muffled laughter, and the library, where large windows allowed Anna a glimpse of studying students. The drizzle was melting the last patches of dirty snow.

They entered the long stretch of park that surrounded the clock tower and the president's house. The park had to be ten acres wide. The clock tower was the focal point, in the middle.

The park was treed and quiet. The only sound was their footsteps and their breath, coming quickly, as they hurried down the path. Anna scanned the park for any signs of life. The benches were vacant. The trees were bare, their naked branches clawing at the night sky.

The clock tower shone in front of them, lit from below by spotlights. It was a six-story redbrick structure with a sloping slate roof. On each side of the fifth story was a giant clock with roman numerals. Above each clock was a large arched window. At the very top was a bell carillon. The hands on the illuminated round face read 8:47 P.M.

A concrete apron encircled the tower, with benches on the perimeter facing in. Dozens of mattresses were stacked up against the benches. All of them had been inscribed with thick black marker so they looked like giant checks made out to the university in the amount of $250, the price the university had been assessing students who took their mattresses out of their rooms.

The women walked a circle around the tower, checking for anyone hiding in the bushes. There was no one. Anna looked up at the tower. There was no sign of life in the dark windows. A thick wooden door was the only way in. It was solid, hinged with strong metal, and locked.

"Search warrant?" Anna said, hating the time it would take.

"Nah." Sam smiled and pulled from her vest pocket a janitor's key ring loop. Dozens of keys jangled on the ring. "A master set of keys. We still have consent from the university to look anywhere we want, per the original search for Emily."

"You keep a kitchen sink in there too?" Anna nodded toward Sam's vest.

"It's like a mom's purse," Sam said. "Surprising room."

Sam tried key after key, unsuccessfully. Anna wondered if the clock tower was on the set of master keys. Then she heard the satisfying *thunk* of a dead bolt turning. Sam pushed the door open. It creaked on rusty hinges.

The night was dark, but inside the tower was darker still, the complete black that comes only in closets and nightmares. It smelled musty and ancient. Anna froze on the threshold. Every instinct told her not to go in.

Sam pulled out her Maglite and shone it through the open door. The interior was a cement floor surrounded by brick walls covered in moss and streaked with stains. A big stone staircase spiraled up, hugging the walls. Looking up, the stairs created a receding circle, which disappeared into the darkness at the top. Did Anna hear something up there? Soft voices echoing against the walls? She strained against the silence. It might have been her imagination, or the breeze outside.

"Call for backup?" Anna whispered.

Sam shook her head. "Let's do this before Xanten realizes we're gone."

They stepped into the tower. Sam went up the steps first, shining the flashlight in front of them. Anna followed closely behind. The shush of their footsteps echoed off the walls. The darkness closed in behind them, like a tangible thing.

They went up three flights of steps, then paused at a landing with a small leaded window. Anna peered out at the dark park surrounding the tower. It was empty and still. From above, she could see the light shining from the clock.

Now that their footsteps paused, she could hear murmurs coming from above. There were definitely voices. Two men were having a conversation, low and gravelly. She strained to hear what they were talking about. She couldn't make it out.

Sam turned off her flashlight. Anna could hear the slide of metal against leather, the sound of Sam's gun coming out of its holster. "I'm going up," Sam whispered. "You stay here."

"The hell I am," Anna whispered back. She pulled out her cell phone and punched in the numbers 911, but didn't press send. She'd keep her finger poised, ready to press it.

"Turn that off," Sam hissed. "I don't want them to see us coming."

Reluctantly, Anna slipped the phone back in her pocket. They crept quietly up the stairs. Near the top, the voices resolved. Anna could hear the conversation between the two men.

"Red, if you ever get out of here, do me a favor."

"Sure, Andy. Anything."

"There's a big hayfield up near Buxton. You know where Buxton is?"

Anna recognized the men's voices. She'd heard them before, but they were so out of context here, she struggled to place them—police officers? Frat boys? The voices grew louder as they reached the top of the stairs.

"At the base of that wall, you'll find a rock that has no earthly business in a Maine hayfield."

They reached the upper landing and an open door frame, from which a faint light glowed. Sam put her back against the wall, pointed her gun ahead of her, then swung around the corner.

"FBI, police," Samantha shouted. "Let me see your hands."

Anna heard Sam take a big, strangled gasp of air. She'd never heard Sam make a noise quite like that before. Anna strode around the corner.

Sitting against the stone wall, with hands up in the air and a computer on her lap, was Emily Shapiro.

48

They gaped at her. She gaped at them. On Emily's laptop, *The Shawshank Redemption* continued to play. Tim Robbins and Morgan Freeman continued to talk about that hayfield in Maine. The laptop threw gray light on Emily's face, giving her a ghostly glow. Anna blinked hard and looked again. The girl was still there.

"Emily?" said Anna.

"Yes," Emily whispered. She cleared her throat and spoke a little louder. She sounded like a frightened girl who hadn't used her voice in a long time. "You're the FBI?"

"I'm Anna Curtis, a federal prosecutor. This is Samantha Randazzo; she's with the FBI. Is anyone else up here?"

Emily shook her head. The room smelled dank and fetid. Anna remembered going camping one summer, when she hadn't been able to shower for a week. It was that smell, mixed with the scent of soup, mildew, and the faint whiff of human excrement.

"Are you hurt?" Anna asked.

Emily started to cry.

"Stand up," Sam said. "Keep your hands where I can see them."

Emily put the laptop to one side and stood. Her long hair was greasy and pulled into a messy bun. She wore no makeup, but looked clean and well nourished. She wore jeans, a T-shirt, and bunny slippers.

Anna looked around. The large room had four large arched windows, each as tall as Anna, in each of the four walls. She recognized them; they were above the clocks and below the bells.

Moonlight streamed through the glass. A single sleeping bag was laid out on a sleeping roll in one corner. Boxes full of granola bars, canned food, and water bottles were stacked nearby. An overturned milk crate held some books, pens, and magazines. Another held Wet

Ones, deodorant, facial wipes, and other toiletries. Buckets with air-tight lids lined a wall. Had Emily used them as toilets?

"What's going on?" Anna said, although she could pretty well guess.

"No one would take me seriously," Emily said, through tears. "I tried, all year, to get someone to take me seriously."

The world fully rearranged itself in Anna's head. The process was like looking at the sketch of a 3-D box and trying to see it com-ing *at* you when before you saw it angled away.

"You manufactured a confrontation with Dylan," Anna mur-mured. "You made it happen where you knew video cameras would capture it. You knew he was going to Lucky's. And then you came back here and camped out."

Emily nodded.

"You put your blood on his car. Before or after Lucky's?"

"Before." Emily wiped another tear.

"Did Heide know?"

"No, don't blame her. It's, like, we tossed around some ideas, but I came up with this myself. I borrowed her Mac and asked her to watch Fenwick. But I only told her I was doing something big. She didn't know what."

"Weren't you scared to be here all alone?"

"I grew up on this campus. I know every nook and cranny. This used to be my favorite spot. I'd come up here and read and pretend to be Rapunzel and stuff."

"Did you know everyone was looking for you?"

Emily pointed to her computer, plugged into an outlet in the wall. "I could watch the news. It was—you guys were—like, amazing." She smiled shyly at Anna.

"Your parents are beside themselves," Sam said. "They think they lost their only daughter."

Emily scratched her scalp through greasy hair. "My dad only cares about his university. My mom only cares about getting back at my dad."

"Did you see them at the vigil?" Sam asked. "They could barely keep it together."

"Whatever. They give a good impression of caring. But let me tell you, they only started caring after I was dead."

"I don't think you understand what you did. Hundreds of volunteers have been looking for you. Police, prosecutors, dogs, divers, federal agents."

"It's kind of cool, right?" Emily said. "If you think about it—seriously, just stop and think about it for a second—they got what they were fighting for. Even if they didn't totally know how they were doing it. Everyone's talking about campus rape. How to protect our girls. It's what I wanted to start."

"You were pretty damn effective," Sam said. She pulled her radio to her mouth. "Backup needed at the university clock tower. We have located Emily Shapiro. Repeat: we have located Emily Shapiro."

"But what was your end game?" Anna said. "You couldn't stay hidden forever."

Moonlight from the big arched window behind Emily lit her hair like a halo. *Everyone was going to hate her,* Anna thought. *Dead, she'd been canonized. Alive, she'd be demonized.*

"I just wanted justice," Emily said, "and I got it. I'm not worried about afterward."

Emily turned, pushed open the big window behind her, and stepped through it.

49

Emily moved fast, a young woman in the prime of her physical life who knew exactly what she was doing. She just pushed the window, swung it out into the cold night air, and stepped onto the ledge.

"Stop playing games and come back in here," Sam said. She reached for her gun.

"Or what? You'll shoot me?" Emily laughed. "Go for it."

She pressed her back against the tower and inched farther along the concrete ledge, away from the window. The breeze ruffled her hair, blowing wisps back from her face. She gazed out over the campus.

Anna stepped toward her. "Emily."

"Don't come near me," Emily said. She lifted a foot from the ledge and dangled it out in front of her. Anna's stomach somersaulted. The concrete apron below would be a deadly place to land. Anna recalled a case she'd had two years ago, where a woman had been pushed off a three-story balcony of the U.S. Capitol. When her head hit the ground, her skull had shattered. This was higher. Anna swallowed back a wave of nausea. She could not come this far, finally finding Emily—a live, whole girl—only to watch her kill herself.

"Emily," Anna said, staying perfectly still. "This isn't the answer."

Emily put her foot back, so both feet were on the ledge. She turned to look at Anna.

"I'll bet you came from a really nice family, didn't you?" Emily said.
Anna shook her head. "What?"

"I'll bet your mom loved you, and you knew it. I'll bet your dad checked your homework every night. So of course this wouldn't seem like the answer. But to someone like me—who only gets love and protection when I'm dead—well, this seems pretty logical, right? I'm not trying to be, like, melodramatic here. I'm just saying. What's the point?"

"The point is, dead girls can't tell their stories," Anna said. "You have a story to tell."

"Don't you get it? I told my story. I told it over and over. To the Disciplinary Committee. To my dad. On BlueTube. It didn't matter. Only dying did."

"People will listen to you now," Anna said. "That's for sure."

"You didn't answer my question about your family."

"Okay." Anna slowly stepped toward the window. Emily shook her head and Anna stopped moving. "Okay. I'll tell you about my family. My mom was beautiful and kind and had a weakness for my dad. He used to beat her up."

Emily was listening, so Anna kept talking. She wasn't sure that the story of her childhood was going to inspire anyone to live. She wasn't trained in talking down someone contemplating suicide. But she remembered hearing somewhere that you just got them talking. The longer they talked, the better the chances of a good outcome. Anna hated talking about her family. But she would, if it kept Emily from taking that last step. She let the words flow out of her.

"He kept apologizing. And she kept forgiving him. Saying he'd do better, he'd change. He was never kinder to her than right after a beating. And she wanted to believe the best in him. She wanted to believe that he could change, for her, and that she could help him. So she kept taking him back. And things would be okay for a while. Until they weren't, and he'd beat her up again."

"He sounds even worse than my dad," Emily said. "And that's a high bar. How'd you get over it?"

"I'm not sure I ever really did," Anna said slowly. "I think I spent a lot of my life looking for the dad I never had."

She thought of all the bad-boy boyfriends she had in high school and college. At some point, she'd realized that if she kept dating the worst guy in any room, she was going to end up just like her mom. Getting engaged to Jack had been the final proof that she was not destined to relive her mother's life.

"So how'd you end up here?" Emily asked softly.

Anna glanced back into the dark room. Sam was gone. Anna was alone talking to Emily.

"I'm in the same place you are," Anna said. "You and I are standing in exactly the same place."

"No. We're worlds apart. You got over it."

"Mm," Anna said. "'Got over it' is not how I would describe myself. Every day, I muddle through. I try to do the best I can with what I've got."

"The thing is," Emily said, "this is the best I've got."

"No. You're so much more than this."

"Stop. Not you too. I'm so sick of being a good girl. These ridiculous expectations. Be sweet, be polite. Play well with others. Don't complain. Laugh at 'boys being boys.' Don't ruin anyone's life, even if they ruined yours. Go along, be easy, be nice. Always, always, be nice. God, we're so trained up, from the moment we can talk. Make everyone else happy. Smile and laugh and fucking take it."

Sirens wailed. Anna could see blue and red lights flashing in the distance.

"Come on down," Anna said softly. "Come back. We'll fight this together. I've been looking for you for so long. I feel like I know you—but I don't, not really. I want to get to know the real Emily Shapiro. I want to help you. I'll fight for you. With you."

"You already did. But you can't get me what I want."

"What do you want, Emily?"

"I want to go viral."

She was smiling at Anna as she jumped off the ledge.

50

ater, the news stations would play the video over and over, at actual speed and then again in slow motion, in loop after loop, repeating on local channels, on national outlets, on YouTube and BlueTube and Vine. Emily standing on the ledge of the clock tower, bending her knees and springing up ever so slightly before going down. The lights meant to illuminate the tower lit Emily's fall spectacularly. Her long brown hair escaped from its band and flowed around her head. Her arms wafted to her sides like wings. In slow motion, she floated toward the ground, her hair swirling around her like she was underwater. At real speed, she just stepped and fell. It took less than two seconds for her to go from the top of the tower to the concrete below.

A few local reporters had gotten there just in time to catch Emily jumping. They'd heard Sam's calls for backup on their police scanners. They arrived moments before the police did, just in time for their camera operators to jump out of the vans, race to the tower, and point their cameras at the girl on the ledge.

The anchors narrated what the video cameras had captured. "Emily Shapiro, the girl who has been missing for a week at Tower University, suspected of being kidnapped and murdered, was found alive," said NBC Local 4 anchor Carmen Harlan, "only to throw herself off Tower's five-story clock tower before firefighters could arrive."

They showed the video again, in slow motion: the flowing five-story fall, Emily's long hair billowing in the wind. And the landing, the most telegenic part of all.

She landed on Sam.

Not squarely on her. Emily's ankle caught Sam's shoulder, knocking the FBI agent down to the sidewalk. Sam's head hit the cement, hard. The stations played that over and over too. Sam's skull knocking the cement. A grimace of pain, before her eyes shut. A gash on her temple and a pool of blood. Emily herself fell into the heap of mattresses that Sam had been dragging under the window.

"Emily Shapiro is in the hospital, with serious injuries," said Fox 2 anchor Huel Perkins.

"A mattress, or even a stack of them, is not sufficient to break a five-story fall," said 7 Action News anchor Stephen Clark, "although Emily Shapiro's exact injuries are not being disclosed by the hospital at this point."

"Her parents have not returned calls from this station," said Harlan.

"We've received word that the FBI agent who saved her life may have sacrificed her own," Perkins said. "Agent Samantha Randazzo was rushed to the hospital with life-threatening injuries."

They played a video of EMTs carrying Sam away, her dark curly hair spilling over the side of the stretcher. Sam was pale and motionless. They loaded her body onto an ambulance and sped off into the night.

"Neither the hospital nor the FBI has any comment at this time," said Clark. "According to FBI sources, the agency will not issue a statement about a fallen agent until her family has been notified. We'll keep you posted with any breaking news. Stay tuned."

FRIDAY

51

Anna woke up disoriented and sore. She was curled in a scratched pleather chair she'd never seen before. The bright, unfamiliar room smelled of bleach and metal. She slowly unfurled herself and looked around. The walls were mint green; a curtain hanging from the ceiling separated two beds. One was empty. Sam lay in the other. Her eyes were closed. A bag of saline dripped clear liquid into an IV tube going into Sam's arm. Anna finally recognized where she was. She'd spent the night in this hospital room by Sam's side.

Anna pulled the chair next to Sam's bed and held her hand, which was cool and dry. Sam wasn't the touchy-feely type. Anna never would've dared hold her hand if she were conscious. The fact that she wasn't slapping Anna's hand away was frightening.

Anna sat there for a long time. The sun rose outside, shining into Anna's eyes until it got so high she couldn't see it anymore. Medical personnel bustled in and out of the room, checking Sam's monitors, replacing saline bags, giving her shots through the IV. Sam didn't move. The monitors beeped and whirred, the fluorescent lights hummed and flickered, footsteps in the hall clicked and clacked. The noises were driving Anna crazy.

Anna picked up the remote control and turned on the TV mounted on the wall.

Barney Shapiro was holding a press conference on the lawn of Beaumont Hospital—which was where Anna was. She might be able to see them if she went to the window. She was too exhausted to check. His ex-wife, Beatrice, stood next to him, solemn and quiet. He spoke somberly into a microphone.

"First, Beatrice and I would like to extend our heartfelt thanks to all those who came together to try to find our daughter. We have been overwhelmed by the generosity of friends and strangers. Thank you for caring, for your time, for your efforts. They were not for nothing. They helped Beatrice and me get through a very rough time. Thank you.

"As you may know, my daughter was found safe and alive yesterday. We are unbelievably grateful and relieved. We're still working with authorities and witnesses to discover what led to her disappearance. We are happy to announce that Emily is doing well. She suffered only a broken ankle from her fall, which is a miracle. We will be reaching out to counselors to get the help Emily and we need."

"I hope they know some good counselors," Anna murmured. "I hope they put 'em on retainer."

Barney gripped the podium and pursed his lips in the universal signal of a man who is in deep, deep shit. "I am also announcing that I am stepping down as president of Tower University, effective today. Obviously, this is a time when my family needs me. Resigning will allow me to spend the time necessary to help heal with my daughter. As of tomorrow, a committee will be formed to search for a new president. But in the interim, I'm pleased to announce that Dr. Susan Blum will be named acting president of the university. She brings to bear the knowledge, wisdom, and skills that this university so badly needs."

"And the ovaries," Sam whispered.

"Yeah," Anna said. "Sam! You're up! How are you doing?"

"I can't believe she broke my fucking shoulder."

"It's your head we're all worried about."

"Eh. I've got a thick skull. When can I get out of here?"

"Soon, I hope," Anna said. She pressed the call button.

On the screen, Barney stepped aside and let Dr. Blum take the podium. He and Beatrice left the stage and walked together toward a waiting car. Kristen LaRose was nowhere in sight.

Dr. Blum spoke into the microphone, "I'm honored and humbled to take this role. I hope to keep steering the Tower University ship in the profitable direction that President Shapiro so skillfully did. At the same time, I hope to focus on issues of gender equality here on the campus, making sure sex-abuse survivors are heard and recognized. We will be hiring a new Title Nine coordinator and a team of consultants . . ."

"About time," Sam said. She started to sit up.

"Hey, wait," Anna said. "Stay in bed. I called for a nurse."

"I don't need a nurse. Where are my clothes?"

"I'm not telling you where your clothes are. Lie down."

Sam pushed the bedsheets away, swung her legs over the side of the bed—then closed her eyes and swayed. Anna caught her before she fell to the floor. She held Sam's shoulders and gently laid her back down on the pillow.

"You stubborn mule," Anna murmured. "Cut that out."

Sam nodded and didn't try to get up again. A nurse finally came in. "Oh, look who's up!" she said cheerfully. "You'll have a lot of people happy to see you."

The nurse took notes in Sam's chart and spoke to her. "We were worried about you for a while there. But we gave you a CAT scan, and everything inside is looking good. No internal bleeding. Just a good old-fashioned concussion, which is like a bruise on the brain."

"Will it affect how I think?"

"You might get headaches. Let us know if you have nausea or vomiting. But you were lucky. I'd say the most you'll suffer is some mood effects—like being more prickly, grumpier for a bit."

"Even more than usual?" Sam said.

The nurse smiled at her. "You also broke your shoulder. It'll need time and rest to heal. You won't be able to do gymnastics."

"Never my thing," Sam said. "Is Emily in this hospital?"

"I can't answer questions about other patients."

"I'm the FBI agent on this case. Her parents signed a medical waiver."

"I gave it to the front desk," Anna said.

"Ah, right. Ms. Shapiro is right down the hall."

"Is she okay?"

"For the most part," the nurse said. "You did a wonderful thing."

Sam met Anna's eyes. "If you hadn't kept her talking, I never could've gotten those mattresses there in time."

"I'm a lawyer. Talking is pretty much all I've got."

"Can we go see her?" Sam said to the nurse.

"You need to rest," Anna said.

"A little outing will be good for her," said the nurse. "You can push her in a wheelchair."

The nurse helped get Sam into the wheelchair. Anna pushed her down the hall. Emily Shapiro's room was guarded by two police officers, who were supposed to keep strangers away and the patient in. When the officers saw Sam and Anna, they let them through. Inside, the room was full of balloons, stuffed animals, and flowers—but only one person.

Emily sat in her bed, her left leg in a cast. She was staring out the window, watching her parents walk away from the press conference.

"Can we come in?" Anna said.

Emily turned toward them. She looked nervous, but nodded. Anna pushed Sam to Emily's bed and sat in a chair next to it. Close up and in the light of day, Anna noticed details about Emily she hadn't the night before. Her skin was unnaturally pale, probably from having been out of the sunlight for a week. There were bluish circles under her eyes.

"Am I, like, under arrest?"

"No," Anna said. "You're not under arrest. We just wanted to check on you and say hi."

"Hi." Emily looked at Sam. "I'm sorry I hurt you last night. I didn't want that to happen."

"I know," Sam said. "But it's not great that you wanted to hurt yourself either."

Emily sighed. "I'm not sure I was in my right mind."

"We have resources that can help you get there," Anna said. "Advocates. Counselors. Will you let us hook you up with them?"

"I will. At least I'll try, for all the other girls who are watching me now." She gestured to the TV.

"And for yourself," Anna said.

"That's what my mom says. My parents were sitting here when I woke up. It was the first time I've seen them together, not fighting, since they broke up. My dad—I've never seen him cry before."

"He was worried sick."

"I was . . . surprised . . . to see that."

"They love you," Anna said. "Even if they are sometimes wrapped up in their own lives."

"I guess so," Emily said. She looked at Sam's badge. "So you guys aren't going to arrest me. Who is?"

"You will face some repercussions for misleading the police,"

Sam said. "But now's not the time for that." Anna didn't even want to think about the civil suit that Dylan's family could bring.

"I'll be picking up trash on the side of the road, wearing an orange vest."

"Maybe you can help clean up all the mattresses," Sam said with a smile.

Emily smiled back.

Her parents walked into the room. Anna stood, not certain what kind of reception they'd get. Emily's mother rushed over and pulled Anna into a big hug. Then she leaned down to Sam and did the same. "Thank you," Beatrice said. "You saved my baby."

Barney reached out and shook both of their hands. "We are very grateful for all your work."

"Where's Kristen?" Emily asked.

"We . . . er, she broke up with me. After she learned I'm stepping down."

Beatrice couldn't suppress a smile, but she quickly straightened it out. "We'll all just concentrate on Emily for a while," she said.

"That sounds like a good plan," Anna said. She turned to Emily. "I'll visit again. I really would like to get to know the real Emily."

Emily smiled. "I'd like that."

52

As Anna pushed Sam down the corridor, they saw a tall, dark-haired man waiting in the hallway outside her door.

"It's your partner." Anna leaned down to Sam and whispered, "When are you two gonna hook up?"

"I dunno." Sam looked back at her with a grin. "There's not that much to do in a hospital. Maybe this afternoon."

Steve hurried toward them, holding a shiny red box. Anna stopped the wheelchair. Steve knelt down on a knee, dropped the box, and put his hands on Sam's arms. "God, Randazzo, it's good to see you. Don't scare me like that again, okay?"

Sam nodded and rested her forehead against his. He wrapped his arms around her. They held each other for a long time. Anna quietly backed away.

As she walked away, she heard Sam saying, "Are those chocolate-covered strawberries?"

"Of course," said Steve.

Before Anna got to the elevator, her phone rang. It was Dylan Highsmith's lawyer. Anna stepped into an empty hallway and answered.

"Ms. Curtis," he said. "I take it that my client is no longer under suspicion of murder."

"That's right."

"I'd like you to drop all charges against him now."

"That's not going to happen. He still drugged and raped several young women, and I have a boatload of evidence of his hatred of women generally. Not only am I asking that he stay in jail pending his trial against Melinda Bates, I'm going to recommend adding more counts to the indictment, as we find every young woman he ever did this to. We already have four more. And he was smuggling Rohypnol into Venezuela."

He paused. "Would you consider a plea deal?"

"Only one that would include jail time for your client. Seven years. Plus registration as a sex offender. All the victims will have to be found and notified and given a chance to weigh in on this and speak at his sentencing."

"See if you can work that out. I'll see about this end."

She wanted to ask for her sister's job back too. But that would taint everything else. If Jody wanted to fight that fight, Anna would find a good civil lawyer. And maybe it wouldn't be so bad if Jody gave up her job. Maybe it would push her in the direction she should've gone eight years ago. College. Jody had been talking about it since her visit to the Beta Psi house. *Also,* Anna thought, *if Jody had the inclination, she'd make a damn fine detective. Being yanked off the assembly line might be a good thing for her.*

Anna said good-bye to Dylan's lawyer and hung up. There was going to be years of litigation, criminal and civil, for Emily, Dylan, and their families. Anna wouldn't be involved. The important thing for her was that she'd found everyone with a pulse and a heartbeat. She was ready to get off the case while she was still ahead. She took the elevator down to the first floor, walked through the lobby, and went outside.

Spring had finally reached Michigan. The dirty piles of snow had melted into the earth. Crocuses poked their lavender heads from the ground.

When she looked up, she almost bumped into Jack, who was coming from the parking lot with a bouquet of yellow tulips. He pulled her into a hug.

"Sweetheart," he said. His lips brushed her temple. "You did it. You found her."

"I'm so relieved, Jack."

She stepped back, out of his embrace.

"How's Sam?" he asked.

"Giving the nurses a hard time."

"Glad to hear she's back to herself."

"You, um, might want to give her some privacy for a bit. Steve is up there with her."

"Nice. When are those two going to hook up, anyhow?"

"He did bring her chocolate-covered strawberries."

A couple came out of the hospital's automatic doors. The woman held a newborn infant in her arms, as the man pushed her in a wheelchair. The man beamed as he brought them to a car at the curb.

"Congratulations," Anna said.

The new parents thanked her. The baby peered at Anna with amazed eyes. Anna watched them bundle the infant into a car seat and drive away.

"I'm so sorry I wasn't there," Jack said. "I'm sorry you had to do that by yourself. While I was arguing with that outrageous Xanten guy."

"It's okay," Anna said. "I do okay on my own. And that's actually something I needed to learn. I've been so reliant on you—for advice, for a role model, for steering me in the right direction."

"We'll have to be sure you have more cases without me."

"That's not what I mean. Oh God. I don't know how to say this. I love you, Jack. Part of me always will. And I love your life. I'm so honored that you would invite me into it. But I have to see what I can do on my own."

"Are you breaking up with me?" A sad smile played on his lips. "Again?"

"You'll always be a part of who I am. But I need a peer, not a boss. Not a fathewr figure."

"I'm not trying to be a father to you. Not by a long shot."

"I know."

"This never would've happened if Nina hadn't come back."

"Maybe. But maybe that just saved us some grief in the long run."

He shook his head and looked up at the sky. He blinked back what might have been a tear. She swallowed through a lump in her throat and waited for him to compose himself. Finally, he took a deep breath and brought his gaze back to hers. She knew him well enough to know that he wanted to say more, but that he would accept her decision with the best grace he could.

"Will you stay here?" he asked. "Go back to D.C.?"

"I have no idea. I need to take a deep breath and figure out my life." For the first time, she'd try following her heart instead of her head.

He pulled her into a hug. "Good luck, Anna."

He walked toward the hospital and disappeared inside the sliding glass doors. Her perfect life disappeared with him.

She watched it go and felt no regret.

53

Anna walked through Cooper's house, calling his name. He didn't answer. The house was quiet and cold. "Cooper!" she called. She looked in the den. It was empty. She peered into the kitchen. Nothing. There was not a light on in the entire house.

A rhythmic thumping came from the backyard. She followed the sound to a window. Cooper was outside chopping wood. He put a piece of a log on a big stump, raised the ax above his head, and brought it down in a perfect arc. The log split into two neat halves. He threw the halves into a pile. He did it again, then again. His muscles were covered in a sheen of sweat. The pile of fresh-cut firewood towered next to him; it was bigger than his equipment shed. He'd been at this for hours, maybe days.

Anna took a blanket from the couch and went out the back door. Cooper looked up from his work and lowered the ax. He wiped his face with a bandanna. She walked over and kissed him lightly on the mouth. He tasted like apples; there was no more whiskey on his breath.

"I'm staying," she said. "There's nothing you can do to get rid of me. So don't even try."

She walked to the orchard and spread the blanket under an apple tree. She lay down on it, put her hands under her head, and waited. Above, the branches formed a lacy latticework. A few pink buds were starting to push their way out. She smelled grass and apples and the earthy scent of spring.

For a while, she heard nothing but birds calling to one another and a siren pealing in the distance. A few rows over, a chicken pecked at the dirt. Then came the sound of Cooper's asymmetrical footsteps in the grass. He lowered himself down, so they were lying side by side. His shoulder brushed hers. She took a deep breath, deeper than she had in a while.

"In my job," Anna said, "I see a lot of kids. Great kids who don't have a family or anyone to love them. A couple times a week, I wish I could take one of them home with me."

"I'm guessing prosecutors can't adopt their witnesses."

"No. But. What I'm saying is: there are lots of ways to become a mother. Or a father."

He reached for her hand at the same time she reached for his. His calloused palm felt warm and safe.

"I'm so glad you came," he said. "I was running out of trees."

She laughed and squeezed his hand. She didn't want to think about tomorrow or yesterday. She didn't want to analyze or annotate or figure anything out. She just wanted to be here, now, her fingers interlaced with Cooper's, breathing this soft spring air. "You were right," she said. "This is the best place on earth." They lay on the blanket, looking up through the apple trees at the clouds drifting across a bright blue sky.

ACKNOWLEDGMENTS

Many thanks to real FBI Agent Steve Quisenberry for his constant generosity and expertise on all things FBI. Thanks to Glenn Kirschner for sharing his incredible stories and knowledge. A big thank-you to the real Justin Dillon, my former AUSA colleague and now a national expert in defending college sex-assault cases, for giving me the defense perspective.

Thanks to the talented writers in my critique group, Rebecca Coleman, Alma Katsu, and Kathleen McCleary, who helped shape this story from start to finish. Thanks to Kathy's daughter, Grace Benninghoff, for her insights into modern college life and language. Thanks to my wonderful friend Lynn Haaland for inspiration and hilarious stories about growing up on a college campus, and to Jessica Mikuliak for her wise and gentle honesty. Thanks to Boyd Morrison, who saved Fenwick's life, and to Boyd's wife, Randi, who periodically saves mine.

As always, I owe a debt of gratitude to a team of amazing women: my agent, Amy Berkower; my publicist, Shida Carr; my publisher, Susan Moldow; and my editor, Lauren Spiegel, who has expertly guided Anna through five books. I am grateful to Genevieve Gagne-Hawes, whose advice greatly improved this novel and encouraged this writer. Thanks to the entire team at Touchstone and Simon & Schuster; I feel very fortunate to have worked with all of you in developing this series over the last six years.

A world of thanks goes to my family, especially my husband, Mike, my first and most important reader, and my two little boys, who make everything worthwhile. Boos, I love watching you become the kind, funny, thoughtful boys you are. I love that you're enthusiastic readers and writers too. I promise you'll be allowed to read this book when you turn eighteen. Meanwhile, never forget that your mama loves you more than anything.

THE LAST
GOOD GIRL

...

FOR DISCUSSION

1. Although Emily is missing from the first pages of the novel, we hear her voice through a series of vlogs she recorded for one of her classes. Why did the author choose to insert Emily's voice so directly into the narrative? How do the chapters told in Emily's point of view impact your understanding of her character and your ideas about the reasons behind her disappearance?

2. Were you shocked by how Emily is treated—by her fellow students, parents, and campus authorities—after she reports her rape? How do you think universities could change their handling of rape and sexual assault cases to make the process less traumatic for victims? How does the way Emily is treated impact her friendships and her personality?

3. In what ways does Anna herself confront sexism throughout the course of her investigation of Emily's disappearance? How does Anna handle herself when faced with these situations? Have you ever found yourself in a position where you had to deal with sexism on the job, and, if so, what did you do about it?

4. As she watches students protesting sexual assault on campus by marching down the street carrying their mattresses, Anna is impressed by

how savvy Tower University students are in their use of social media to publicize their message and further their agenda. What are some real-world examples of activists taking advantage of new forms of media to advance their causes? How has the art of protest changed since the sit-ins of the '60s and '70s?

5. How does the city of Detroit become a character in the novel? Compare the scenes set in Detroit with the scenes set in the tony mansions of Grosse Pointe. How do both settings prove crucial to the story and to Anna unraveling the mystery of Emily's disappearance?

6. The hazing that the pledges undergo in their efforts to become members of Beta Psi is degrading and is described as dangerous. Were you surprised by the lengths the young men went to in order to join the fraternity? What would you do if faced with similar demands to join a group or organization? Why are the pledges so willing to put themselves through horrifying acts to join the frat? Is it for future connections in the world of business, for the feeling of being a part of something exclusive, or something more?

7. Compare and contrast Cooper Bolden and his younger brother, Wyatt. How does Wyatt change over the course of the novel, and how does Cooper contribute to the decisions that he ends up making in regards to the fraternity?

8. What dangers does Jody risk by going undercover at the frat without notifying Anna in advance? Why is Jody willing to go through such danger to help her sister? Have you ever done anything dangerous or risky to help a loved one?

9. In a lighter subplot of the novel, Anna finds herself in the middle of a love triangle with her former fiancé, Jack, and her new love interest, Cooper. What are the benefits of a life with Jack, and what are the benefits of a life with Cooper? Do you agree with the decision that Anna makes at the end of the novel? What do you think the future holds for her current relationship, and also for her relationship with the man she did not choose? How does Anna's choice impact her growing desire to be a mother in the future?

10. Were you surprised by where Anna and Sam find Emily by the end of the novel? Why did Emily do what she did? Do you think her actions are justified after all she has been through?

11. What do you think the future holds for Anna? Will she stay in Michigan; return to Washington, D.C.; or end up somewhere else entirely?

Now that you've written five novels featuring Anna Curtis, what do you know about her that you didn't know when you began? How has her character surprised you?

She surprised me when she fell in love with Jack in the first book. I didn't intend for that to happen. I'm a pretty detailed outliner—at the outset, I know how my stories are going to play out—but all of a sudden there was all this unexpected sexual tension crackling between these two characters. I think, actually, I fell for Jack first, and Anna followed shortly thereafter. I've been trying to break them up ever since!

On a more serious note, it's been satisfying to watch her grow. She started off so green and naive in *Law of Attraction*. Since then, she's become a formidable legal adversary. She's stumbled and fallen, been hurt and disappointed, but mined those experiences for wisdom and strength. I've put her through quite a lot the last few years, and was happy to find that she was up for it.

How has your writing process evolved since your first novel? Do you find that anything has gotten easier after five books?

Nothing is easier. But at least now I understand that the hard parts are part of the process. At some point during the writing of each of my books, I said to myself, *This is impossible. It will never happen. I'll never get it done.* And then, of course, it got done. So now when I get to the this-is-impossible stage, I understand it's not actually impossible. That feeling is just part of the process.

Your books always involve very current, ripped-from-the-headlines plots. How do you choose your next topic? Were you already thinking of writing about the issue of campus rape before the University of Virginia article in *Rolling Stone* came out?

Yes, I was writing *The Last Good Girl* before that horrible article came out. The *Rolling Stone* article has done more to set back American sex-crimes prosecutions than much I can think of in recent history. People naturally tend to doubt sex-assault victims. They think rape survivors are more likely to lie than, say, victims of a mugging—which is totally untrue. Sex assaults are fabricated at exactly the same rate as any other crime. But that badly researched article reinforced the unwarranted skepticism toward sex-assault survivors, which advocates have been fighting for decades. Sigh.

As for how I choose my topics: I always have a bunch of ideas perco-
lating, because, unfortunately, there's always some bad man doing some
bad thing. (Sorry, it's almost always a bad *man* in my line of work.) There's
plenty of "inspiration" to mull. When it's time to pull the trigger on a book
idea, I talk to my editor, my agent, my husband, and a few trusted friends
about these ideas, spinning out how they'd work. After several conversa-
tions, I start to get excited about one in particular, and that's the one I
write.

**How would you advise universities to improve their sexual-assault report-
ing procedures? Do you think there is a solution, or is this a problem that
won't go away as higher institutions strive to keep their reported rapes at
zero to appeal to potential students and donors?**

A few of my sex-crime prosecutor friends and I have actually talked about
forming an organization to try to help colleges figure out how to improve
their policies. It's a complicated issue, trying to balance the safety of victims
with the rights of suspects. I think we're heading in the right direction—
federal DOJ oversight of campuses has made it a lot harder for colleges to
ignore rapes. But we've got a long way to go.

The legal process has to be fair, transparent, and consistent. But solu-
tions outside the legal box could have as much of an impact. Some suggest
dry campuses—since so many assaults are facilitated by alcohol—while
others suggest lowering the drinking age, so that students wouldn't come
to college with no drinking experience and go overboard or binge drink. I'd
love to have a study comparing those two models!

Right now, all Greek parties are held in fraternities, not sororities. It's a
throwback rule, totally sexist, and I think it contributes to sexual assaults.
I believe holding parties in sororities would change the dynamics, making
it much harder for predator boys to use their home turf to prey on vulner-
able victims.

**Do you keep up with your friends from the world of federal sex-crimes
prosecuting? Do they ever give you ideas for your novels?**

The friends I made at the USAO are some of my best friends in the world,
and will be, I expect, for my entire life. Our relationship is a little bit like
that among war vets. We went through the trenches together; experienced
something difficult, crazy, harrowing, rewarding; saw each other through
tough times, heartbreak, and victories. There are few legal jobs like that.

And, yeah, I shamelessly pick their brains for story ideas. Folks have been very generous in sharing the best and worst of what's happened to them in any given week. And most everyone wants to have a character named after them. ☺

Which is more stressful: prosecuting a high level sex-crimes case in front of a judge and jury, or turning in your manuscript on time to your editor?

Ha! Maybe if my editor were cruel and sadistic, I'd be more stressed out, but I've been lucky that Lauren Spiegel, the woman who's edited all five of my books, is terrific. Kind, smart, savvy, funny, a pleasure to work with. Turning in a manuscript is undoubtedly stressful—you know that the whole world can read it and judge you. They say publishing a book is like walking down the street in your underwear. But for pure adrenaline and stress, there's nothing like prosecuting a sexual predator. I think that's why I started writing, actually. It was my way of processing everything, of handling that stress.

What do you like to read and watch when you aren't writing about the intense world of sex-crimes prosecutors?

Crime novels and courtroom dramas, of course! Although now there's an element of "doing my homework" when I read and watch these. It's hard to just enjoy the story; now I'm thinking, *Ooh, I should have done that!* Or, *Hm, I could've done that better.* Or, the worst: *Damn, I'll never be able to do it that well.* I'm always picking at the seams, peeking beneath the fabric, analyzing the construction. I love literary fiction, too, though the same problems apply. For true relaxation, I watch *The Bachelor*. Whoa, wait. I can't believe I just admitted that. I take it back. I'm . . . um . . . I'm pleading the Fifth.

ENHANCE YOUR BOOK CLUB

1. Read another Anna Curtis novel and discuss how Anna has changed over the years. How has her approach to prosecuting cases changed as she's gotten older and more confident in her role?
2. Visit www.rainn.org to learn how you can volunteer to support rape and sexual abuse victims, advocate for public policy changes, and help raise money to support victims' rights.
3. Watch the documentary *The Hunting Ground*, which is about campus sexual assault. What themes are similar to those in the book?